PHYLLIS EISENSTEIN

The Crystal
Palace

Grafton
An Imprint of HarperCollins*Publishers*

Grafton
An Imprint of HarperCollins*Publishers*
77–85 Fulham Palace Road,
Hammersmith, London W6 8JB

Published by Grafton 1992
9 8 7 6 5 4 3 2 1

First published in Great Britain by
HarperCollins*Publishers* 1991

From *The Crystal Palace* by Phyllis Eisenstein
Copyright © Phyllis Eisenstein 1988
Published by arrangement with NAL
Penguin Inc., New York, New York

The Author asserts the moral right to
be identified as the author of this work

ISBN 0 586 20729 5

Set in Times

Printed in Great Britain by
HarperCollinsManufacturing Glasgow

For Martha and Hank Beck

Chapter 1

Time had been kind to Castle Spinweb. A dense coat of ivy had covered the cracks in its pale stone walls, and all around it the forest had regrown, thick and tall. Only a scattering of charred stumps, half hidden by mossy undergrowth, hinted that a wild sorcerous battle had once raged here. Now, morning glories bloomed again along the parapets, birds nested among their twining stems, and insects of all kinds sheltered beneath their leaves.

Beneath one particular leaf, on this bright summer day, a large yellow caterpillar was spinning itself a cocoon. It worked quickly, steadily, back and forth, circling its plump body with thread after thread until only its blunt head was exposed, then only its mouth. Then, with a final convulsive effort, it pursed that last opening shut, and the cocoon lay still, glistening whitely in the morning sunlight.

A few moments passed, the space of three or four human heartbeats, no more, and then the silken envelope began to writhe. As if the seasons had run their course and come to summer once more, the cocoon split apart and its occupant emerged, transformed. The head was small now, with tapering antennae, the body was sleek, and the many stubby caterpillar legs had been replaced by six long, delicate ones. With these new legs, the creature took a few wobbly steps and clung, upside down, to a morning glory stem. Then it unfurled its yellow wings, each as large as a man's hand, and flexed them slowly.

There were nectar-bearing flowers all around, on the walls and in the garden enclosed by those walls, but the butterfly ignored them. Instead, it launched itself upwards, broad wings flapping more like a bird's than an insect's.

7

High above the treetops it flew, swiftly, purposefully, over rivers and lakes and rolling meadows, over grain fields and villages, walled towns and mighty castles, and at none of these did it stop, at none did it even dip downwards. Only when it reached a line of mountains far beyond Spinweb's horizon did it slow its flight.

Among these peaks, the butterfly swooped and circled, skimming over streams and water-worn gullies, sweeping past overhangs where landslides had recently exposed the soil, venturing into the dark mouths of caves. At last its preternatural senses detected the telltale signs of gold, and it lighted in a crab-apple tree whose roots seemed to penetrate the deposit.

The tree was in full bloom. The butterfly selected a flower and sampled its nectar, seeking some trace of the special flavour of gold. Finding none, it examined the petals, the calyx, the stem. Delicately, it walked the branch that bore the flower, peering into other blossoms, tasting, smelling. It even scraped at the bark with the tip of one slender leg. Nothing. It flitted to the ground then, to inspect the herbs and mosses that grew at the base of the tree, even the mushrooms that clung to the partially exposed roots, but there was not the faintest hint of gold in any of them. The nearby undergrowth was equally barren, and finally the butterfly soared skywards to search elsewhere.

Three days it stayed in the mountains, questing in the sunlit hours, sleeping amid leafy branches at night. It found more gold, but none in any plant. On the morning of the fourth day, it gave up its search and flew back to its birthplace.

The garden at the heart of Spinweb was home to many a butterfly. Open to the sky, it was filled with flowers, especially with sweet-scented roses. On this day, as on thousands of others, the mistress of the place sat upon a sun-warmed bench in the midst of her roses. Dressed all in blue feathers, she hummed a soft tune as she embroidered on a piece of bleached linen.

The yellow butterfly alighted on the bench beside her.

'Ah,' she said, smiling at the bright insect, 'I was beginning to wonder when you'd be coming back.'

The butterfly flexed its wings once, twice, and then they began to shrivel as if they had been made of wax and held too near a flame. The contours of the sleek body changed, four of the legs became stubbier, and the other two shrank into the torso even as the antennae shrank into the head. Abruptly, instead of a butterfly, a naked mannikin sat on the stone bench. A few heartbeats later, Cray Ormoru had grown back to his normal size.

For a moment, he stretched his arms up to the sky, letting the heat of the summer sun wash through him and ease the stiffness that the insect form had left in his muscles. Then he made a small gesture with one hand, and his clothes fluttered down from the high window of his bedchamber and scurried across the garden to him like so many puppies eager to greet their master. The woman helped him dress, and as she laced up his shirt, he kissed her forehead and grinned, saying, 'You were right about my being hungry, Mother. I'm ravenous.'

Delivev Ormoru laughed softly. 'Yes, I've never found nectar very filling, myself. But there's a cold roast fowl and fresh bread waiting for you in the kitchen.'

Linking arms, they strolled into the shaded coolness of Spinweb's corridors. They looked much alike, mother and son – both tall and fair, both young and vigorous. Only her eyes betrayed the extra centuries Delivev had seen.

In the kitchen, a creature made of cloth, with trews for legs and gloves for hands, served Cray his meal. As he tore into the fowl, Delivev seated herself on the edge of the table. She said, 'Did you find what you were looking for?'

He shook his head. 'Just ordinary greenery. Not a single plant with gold in its structure.'

She pursed her lips a moment. 'Perhaps . . . the deposits you located were too small? Or not close enough to the surface?'

'I wish that were true.'

'Well . . .' She lifted her shoulders in a slight shrug. 'Then you've created something new in the world.'

He sighed. 'I would rather have found a natural model to give me some guidance. Still, I think I understand what's wrong now. I always assumed that at worst gold would be an innocuous addition. Now I think that the gold itself is stunting my poor tree's growth.'

Delivev stroked a stray lock back from his forehead. 'It isn't so very stunted.'

'I wanted it to be taller.'

'It's tall enough. I wouldn't care for it to shade too much of the garden.'

He smiled up at her, a wry smile. 'Mother, you are too satisfied with things as they are. You have no ambition.'

She laughed. 'My ambitions have all been fulfilled.' Playfully, she tweaked a tuft of his close-cropped beard. 'As you well know.'

Cray finished the last of the fowl, then wiped his hands on the cloth servant's empty sleeve. 'Come,' he said, pushing away from the table, 'now that I've a full belly and can think clearly again, let's see how my little beauty is doing today.'

The tree grew in a corner of the garden. It was not a tree whose identity was easy to discern; rather, it was a composite of many different kinds of trees, fused together while still in seed by the power of Cray's sorcery. It was not tall or many-boughed or densely leafed, yet it would have stood out in any forest. It fed, as all trees did, on the nourishment of the soil, but to that soil Cray had added ensorcelled gold, which the tree had taken into itself. And so its bark was shot with flecks that sparkled in the sunshine; its leaves, whose upper surfaces were glossy green

10

and broad as a sycamore's, shone a rich, translucent red when held up to light, with veins like golden wire; and its flowers resembled daffodils, but grown huge, the petals delicately edged with gilt.

The leaves rustled softly as Cray pulled one trumpet-shaped blossom close to his face and breathed of its perfume. Compared to the other flowers of the garden, the scent was faint, but he found it sweet. For him, it was the best part of the tree.

He had learned the sorcery of woven things from his mother, learned of spiders and caterpillars, of nesting birds, of twining snakes, of thread and cloth. And then he had moved beyond that knowledge, to perceive the structure of living things, to recognize that they, too, were patterned, but on some level deeper than the surface, deeper than the human eye could see. Life itself was woven of a multitude of twisting strands, of interlocking pieces, as surely as a tapestry, as surely as a suit of chain mail. Feeling this principle in his very being, Cray was able to use it to make living things grow and change, to make a thick forest out of ashes, to make a new kind of tree blossom in Delivev's garden.

Glancing sidelong at his mother, Cray smiled. The sorcerer to whom he had once been apprenticed, Rezhyk the demon master, had scorned Delivev's powers. He had thought his own metallurgical skills superior to anything governing mere cloth and spiders. But if he had known where weaving could lead, he would never have been so arrogant.

Yet metallurgical sorcery had its strengths, not the least of them demon mastery. The smelting of power into a handful of rings could give a sorcerer absolute control over as many demon slaves. He could command them to fetch whatever he desired, to build any edifice, to destroy any person or thing, and through them he had access to the vast knowledge that lay in the demon worlds of Fire, Ice,

11

Air, and Water. Cray knew that sort of magic, but though he had cast hundreds of rings in his years of sorcery, he had done so only to give eternal freedom to their demons. He wanted no demon slaves. The raw metal itself was what he wished to command.

As in the tree which, just now, was the centre of his life.

He sighed as he looked at it. It seemed such a poor, feeble thing, with its spindly boughs and sparse foliage. Yet, Cray thought, if sparkle pleased the eye, if an individual leaf or blossom could compensate in some part for the flaws of the whole, then the tree was not a complete failure. Gently, as if it were a small animal that could respond to his affection, he caressed the flower that he held, and the branch that bore it. Then he let them bob away, and he sighed again.

'It's so lovely,' said his mother.

He shrugged. 'I'm glad it pleases you. I wish it pleased me more.'

She slipped an arm about his shoulders. 'Have patience, my son. This is a new kind of magic for you, and you can't expect perfection all at once. I'd hate to tell you what my first tapestries looked like. There can be other trees, as many trees as you wish, as much practice as you need.'

He shook his head. 'I'm not finished with this one, yet.'

She looked up at the tree, its top scarcely half again as high as her own head. 'What more is there to do? It won't grow any larger.'

'No. But it can bloom.'

Delivev looked at him quizzically, then waved a hand at the tree, as if to say that it had bloomed already.

'You'll see,' he told her. And he would speak of the matter no further.

They were dining in the garden at sunset, two beeswax candles lighting the meal, when a flame appeared in the

12

sky above them. A ball of yellow fire the size of a horse, it swooped down to settle beside their table, banishing dusk from the garden but shedding no heat. In a moment, it had begun to elongate and to pinch in at the middle, and then its glow faded as it transformed into a tall young man with dark hair and ruddy cheeks. He was Gildrum, a fire demon set eternally free by Cray Ormoru. Over one shoulder he carried a sack almost as large as himself.

Gildrum threw his burden down and, smiling, opened his arms to Delivev. They embraced, two ageless people who had lived together ten years already and could look forward to centuries yet; they embraced like young lovers in the first flush of devotion. Cray smiled to see it, for he loved them both.

When he loosed Delivev at last, the demon gave Cray a hug, and then he opened the mouth of the sack. For all its bulk, it had not been a heavy load – it was sheep's wool, cleaned and carded, ready for spinning.

'She struck a hard bargain, your shepherdess,' Gildrum said to Delivev. 'I had to promise that the coverlet for her bed would be worked with silk embroidery.'

'No matter. I have plenty of silk.' Stooping, she picked at the surface of the fluffy, cream-coloured mass, testing the fibres between her fingers. 'She knows the value of her harvest.'

Gildrum laid a hand on her head and stroked the brown hair that was as soft as the downy feathers of her dress. 'My dear, she knows you *must* have it, and she dares to set the price accordingly. She's completely lost her fear of you.'

She looked up at him. 'And of you?'

'Oh, yes. She was as friendly as if I'd been her lord's tax gatherer come to give her payments back. It seems you've made her rich; since last year, her two-room hut has become a mere annexe to a much grander house, and she has acquired two servants as well. She doesn't even shear her own sheep any more.'

13

Delivev stood up slowly. 'All that from a few embroidered hangings? I'm flattered that my work should be worth so much at market!'

Gildrum laughed. 'The hangings decorate her new home. It's the wool that brings her wealth – her wonderful wool that's fine enough for sorcerers. It's in demand and therefore carries a high price even for ordinary mortals. And plenty of herdsmen have paid even better for the use of her rams as breeding stock.' He circled her waist with one arm. 'She made a good bargain with you.'

She leaned against him, her head tilted to his shoulder. 'Let her be rich. As long as she sells me wool.'

He kissed her forehead. 'My dearest Delivev, how many other sorcerers would say something like that? Most of them would just take all her wool and leave her poverty.' He kissed her nose. 'But then, you are a most unusual sorcerer, in every way.'

Cray picked up the load of wool, slung it over his shoulder. 'I'll put this away for you, Mother.'

'If you like,' she replied, but her eyes were all for Gildrum.

Her workroom was a tower chamber. There, her spinning wheel and looms stood, and a multitude of half-completed projects awaited her pleasure – tapestries, fabrics, hoop after hoop of embroidery, crewel, needlepoint. And everywhere were skeins and spools of every sort of fibre, coarse and fine, dull and shiny, and every colour of the rainbow. Cray dropped his bundle beside the loom that held a silk brocade, a rich maroon and black fabric worked with golden threads. It was for a dressing gown, he knew, a gift for Gildrum. The demon needed no clothing, of course; it could manufacture garments from its own substance. But Delivev took pleasure in creating such things, and in seeing them used. She had already made Cray a similar gown, and he wore it sometimes to please her, though it was really too magnificent for his own

14

taste. She had made him many gifts over the years. And though he had given in return gold and wood given form by his own hands, still he felt it had never been enough.

He had meant the tree as another gift. From a window of the tower chamber, he could see it, candlelight glimmering faintly on its gold-flecked trunk. He leaned in the window for a time, looking down, frowning. At last, the candles guttered.

Patience, he told himself. *Patience*.

When he returned to the garden, it was empty and silent; Delivev and Gildrum had retired for the night. By starlight alone, Cray made his way to the tree. He could barely see it, but that did not matter. He knew every twig, every leaf; he had touched it a thousand times, guiding its growth with the warmth of his flesh and the words of his spells. He reached out for the branch he had chosen, the flower he had caressed. The blossom was gone; he knew it must lie shrivelled somewhere near his feet. In its place was a new bud, as small and hard as a pearl. He whispered to it. 'My beauty,' he called it, and it warmed beneath his touch. He could feel the force of life within it, stronger than in any other flower of the garden. He smiled in the darkness.

Patience, he thought.

Some days later, he was in his workshop weighing odds and ends of gold when a small spider scuttled across the windowsill and leaped to his arm. It was a brown mite speckled with white, one of the web chamber spiders, and it never came to Cray unless some communication was waiting for him there. With all of his family at home, that communication could only be from one person. Leaving the gold on the scales, Cray hurried off to receive it.

The web chamber was bright with morning sunshine, the thick spiderweb draperies that festooned its walls shining translucently like the finest human-woven silk. Cray seated himself on the velvet-covered bed at the centre of the room, then waved one hand toward the nearest web. It began to turn opaque, a soft grey sheen spreading over its surface, and upon that sheen a human face took shape: a man's face, as young and unlined as Cray's own and, because of their friendship, as certain to stay so for many ordinary lifetimes.

Smiling, Feldar Sepwin said, 'Good morrow. I hope the day is as bright and beautiful at Spinweb as it is here.' Behind him, as if to belie his words, there was no day at all, just the torchlit limestone interior of the cave he shared with the Seer Helaine.

Cray studied his friend's smile a moment. There was some news behind it – he knew that by the dimples in those beardless cheeks and by the animation in those eyes of two different colours. With a smile of his own, he said, 'How are you, Feldar?'

'Excellent. Never better. But I need some spiders.'

Cray leaned back on his elbows. 'I thought I left you a dozen the last time I was there. Did you forget to feed them?'

Sepwin shook his head. 'I don't mean the kind that spin these webs. Special ones, to spin a special web of my design.'

'*Your* design?' Cray chuckled softly. 'Feldar, what do you know of spider magic?'

'More today than a week ago, I think.' His expression became more serious. 'Three days ago I was walking in the forest not far from here. And upon this one tree, spun among its branches, there was a spider's web, just an ordinary one, but quite large. It was early morning, with dew everywhere, on every leaf, every flower, and droplets of dew outlined the web. And even though it was so early, the sky was clear and the sun was bright already, and the light made those dewdrops glitter like faceted diamonds. And as I stood there, admiring the beauty of the web, the notion came to me that there was something special here.

16

Something very special.' An unfocused look had come into his eyes, as if instead of seeing Cray within the magical web in his cave, he was seeing that other web in the forest again. 'I stood there . . . quite a long while. Directing my skills toward it. I knew it would answer them somehow. All it needed was . . . myself, standing just so, thinking just so . . .' He blinked and shook his head, and he was looking at Cray once more. 'It was a mirror, Cray, and it showed me myself.'

'A mirror?'

'Yes. The angle of the light, the shape of the web, and myself standing in just the proper position made it a mirror. But not like a mirror of polished metal. No. By the chance configuration of branches, by the chance selection of anchor points by that spider, the web had the shape of a shallow cup with its mouth toward me. The image of myself hung in the empty air within it, and vanished if I took one step to left or right. And that image was not of Feldar Sepwin standing in the forest and gawking but of Feldar the Seer sitting by the pool in this cave, his hand trailing in the water. I saw . . . what can I call it? My essence. No, more than that. My heart's desire.'

Cray said, 'Yourself at home, doing what you usually do, is your heart's desire?'

'Yes, exactly.'

'And . . . what do you want these special spiders to do for you?'

'To spin another such web in my cave.'

Cray frowned, puzzled. 'But since you know your heart's desire, what future purpose could such a mirror serve?'

'It would show *anyone* his heart's desire, Cray – anyone who stood in the proper place and looked when the dew was fresh. I thought that here in the cave I could spray a fine mist of water on it whenever I wanted to use it. I've made a form for the web, with the anchor points marked, as you can see . . .' He lifted a kind of openwork basket into view. It was as wide as his outstretched arms and made of thin wooden hoops joined by struts into a shape that was not conical, not hemispherical, but somewhere in between. White pigment marked nearly a hundred places upon the wood. As Cray looked at the thing more closely, he realized that the hoops were actually one continuous spiral deformed by the struts.

'I see,' he said. 'But I don't understand why anyone would be interested in looking into this mirror. Or at any rate, in travelling any great distance to do so. I mean . . . don't most people already know their hearts' desires?'

Sepwin smiled slightly. '*I* didn't know. When you met me, I thought all I wanted from life was a full belly and a warm bed. But I really wanted *this*, and I didn't even know it existed.'

Cray shook his head. 'How could you have wanted it if you didn't know it existed?'

'The heart knows, Cray. Fifteen years ago, if I could have looked into the mirror, I would have seen what I saw in the forest.. I have no doubt about that.'

'But would you have understood what you saw?'

'Ah.' His smile broadened. 'Only a Seer could have told me what it meant. And that is why a Seer should own such a mirror.' He lowered the wooden form. 'They come to me to find out who they are, where they should go, whom they should love, whom they should kill. They come as you came to the lady Helaine, to be told what to do with their lives. Heart's desire is part of that, isn't it? They'll come to see the mirror.'

'But what of the pool?' said Cray. 'Can't you see enough in that to satisfy your visitors?'

Sepwin shrugged. 'The image in the mirror will be visible to their own eyes; it won't be just a pool of black water.' He glanced down at the wooden form. 'More than that, I feel I *must* make the mirror. It lies within my power to produce something marvellous. Why should I not do so?'

He looked up. 'If you were in my place, would you shy away from it?'

Cray thought of the gold-nourished tree and had to say no. 'How many spiders do you need, Feldar?'

'Half a dozen, perhaps, to make the work go quickly. It may take some time to create just the proper web, but I'll know when it's right. You'll have to be here, of course, to guide them until they have it. For the rest, I've already rigged a small bellows to spray the fine mist of water.'

Cray rolled to his side to consider the problem. Spiders he had in plenty, trainable to any kind of spinning. But the artisan in him rebelled at the need to remake the web every time it was damaged and to spray water on it for every use. Sepwin was not Delivev, who needed the purity of spidersilk in her webs. Ultimately, there was nothing of spider sorcery to this mirror; there was just shape and sparkle and the play of light in the viewer's eye.

'Feldar,' Cray said, 'what if we replace the water on the web with some silvery metal? Finely dispersed metal droplets polished to the brightness of sunlit water. It seems to me that would do as well.'

'Metal?'

'I can promise you it would never tarnish, and it would be so much more permanent.' He looked up at the high ceiling as he pondered the project. 'Yes, I think we might be able to make you a fine mirror of metal.'

Sepwin's voice was doubtful. 'I don't know if it will work as metal.'

Cray propped himself up on an elbow. 'If it doesn't, we'll try again with spidersilk and water. But I think it *will* work. Now, you'll have to come to me, Feldar; I can't work metal properly in your cave. I'll ask Gildrum to fetch you.' He sat up. 'I'll have everything ready by the time you arrive.'

'What – today?'

'Why not? The sooner started, the sooner finished.'

'But you must have your own work to do –'

'Nothing that can't wait.'

Sepwin hesitated just a moment. 'You're sure you couldn't do it here?'

'You already know the answer to that, Feldar.'

Sepwin sighed. 'All right, I'll be waiting for Gildrum.'

By the time Gildrum returned, a light lunch had been laid in the garden, and Cray was waiting beside it. The demon settled near him as a ball of flame, and from that incandescence Sepwin emerged, clutching his wooden contrivance; only then did Gildrum coalesce into his human shape.

Sepwin staggered as he took a step toward Cray. 'I think I shall never become accustomed to flying,' he said, reaching out with his free hand to clasp Cray's arm, half in greeting and half to steady himself. 'Give me a horse any time.'

Cray pulled a chair out for him. 'You know it's too long a trip on horseback, Feldar. Even with a magical horse.'

Gently, Sepwin set the wooden form on the table. Then he closed his eyes. 'I know you enjoy flying, Cray, but my stomach does not. I think I would like to lie down for a little while.'

'I'll carry you upstairs,' said Gildrum.

'No thank you, good Gildrum, no thank you. Cray, if you'll just give me your arm, I think I can stumble inside . . .'

'No need,' said Cray. 'I can string you a hammock in a moment.'

'No, no hammock, please. Perhaps I'll just stretch out under that tree . . .' He gestured toward the gold-nourished one. Cray helped him, and by the time they reached its shade, several cushions had tumbled from a tower window and hurried to make a bed there. Sepwin sank down upon them with a sigh. 'Oh, steady earth,' he murmured. 'You know I was not meant to fly.'

Cray knelt beside his friend. 'You'll be all right.'

Sepwin moaned. 'Next time I *will* take a horse, and never mind the extra time. *I'm* not in such a rush.' He closed his eyes. 'Is your sorcery so dull these days that any change draws you like an ant to honey?'

Cray rocked back on his heels. 'Well, I'll admit that freeing demons is not the fascinating occupation it once was. And though I do have other projects to keep me busy, none is so intriguing as your mirror.'

Feldar opened one eye, the blue one. He gripped Cray's arm above the elbow. 'There is something wrong, my friend. I feel it in you now. I thought I felt it even when I spoke to you in the web. What is it?'

'I don't know what you mean, Feldar. Nothing is wrong.'

Sepwin opened the other eye and focused them both on Cray. 'You don't know your own mind. You amass knowledge, but it doesn't please you. You feel a lack.'

Cray covered Sepwin's hand with his own, trying to soothe the stiffness he felt there. 'Do you speak as a friend, or as a Seer?'

'Both. I see it in your face, and I see it in your heart. The mirror is for you, Cray. You must look into it and find your heart's desire.'

Cray shook his head. 'Not I. I know what I want – to hone my skills and be the best sorcerer that I can. If I do feel some lack, it is that so much knowledge still remains beyond me.'

'No. Something else. Something more important than sorcery.'

Cray's hand tightened on Sepwin's. 'Where is your pool, Seer? Where is the source of your power that you can see so deep inside me? We have no water here for you to run your fingers through.'

'I don't need it to read you, Cray. I know you almost as I know myself, and as I am content, I know that you are not, no matter what you say.'

21

Cray looked up at the tree, whose dappled shade spread over them. Then he shrugged. 'Perhaps you are right, Feldar.' He reached out to snap a leaf off the lowest bough. 'You see this? I made it, this thing of green and gold. I practise a new form of sorcery here, and with every attempt, I find some small improvement in myself.' He tossed the leaf aside. 'No, I am not content, my dear friend. But I do find some pleasure in expanding my knowledge. And that, I think, is as much of my heart's desire as I will ever have. Come, look here.'

As Sepwin eased into a sitting position, Cray stood to pull a branch close and show him the new growth upon it. From the size of a pearl, the bud had developed till it was as large as a man's fist. It had the form of a tightly closed daffodil, petals squashed snugly into the bell of the trumpet. What showed above its calyx was burnished gold.

'Will you call Mother?' Cray said to Gildrum. 'Today is as good as any for what I wish to show.'

Gildrum smiled, and then his human shape melted into fire and soared up to Delivev's tower workroom. In a few moments he returned to the garden, human once more, with her on his arm.

'Good morning, Feldar,' she said. 'It's good to see you again.' And to Cray: 'You wished to show me something, my son?'

He touched the unopened blossom. 'This is for you, Mother, if it turns out as I hope.' With his two hands spread, he traced an invisible sphere about the bloom, concentrating all his power, all his knowledge in that small space. Between his palms, the petals twitched once, twice, as if some creature were trapped within them, trying to escape. Then, they unfurled with a sound like the thinnest metal foil crinkling, and the flower showed itself to be a daffodil of polished yellow gold, a delicate, ruff-encircled trumpet as large as a wine goblet.

'Oh, how lovely,' said Delivev. 'See how it shines in

the sunlight. Will it close at night, Cray, like the other flowers?'

'Yes, for it is just as alive as they are.'

'Ah, but look at the others,' said Gildrum. 'Look at all the blossoms around it.'

As the golden flower had opened, holding all their attention, the nearest gilt-edged blooms had closed, and now, withered, they were dropping off the tree.

'It's stolen all their life force,' said the demon.

Cray raised a hand to his forehead, then rubbed his eyes as if they were crusty from sleep. 'And some of mine as well,' he murmured. 'This new sorcery is wearing.'

His mother caught his arm. 'Are you all right? The flower is beautiful, but we need no golden flowers at the cost of your health.'

'No, no,' he said. 'I just feel . . . as if I had run too far.' He smiled tiredly. 'To give dead metal life is no light task.'

Sepwin was kneeling beneath the tree, a dozen withered blossoms in his hands. 'To steal life in one place and bestow it in another – is that not the ultimate desire of every sorcerer? To say what shall live and what shall die?'

'That was hardly my purpose,' said Cray. He let his mother help him to the stone bench, and he sat down heavily. Gildrum poured him a cup of wine.

'Sorcerers are no better than kings,' said Sepwin, letting the withered flowers fall, one by one, from his fingers. 'No better than the thousand petty princes I have seen in my years with the lady Helaine. Eternally, they search for power.' He looked up at Cray. 'You, too, my friend.'

Cray drank his wine at a draught and then held the golden goblet up. 'I made this,' he said. 'And I wish to make more beautiful things. What better use for sorcery? Better than enslaving thinking creatures; better than making the mortal countryside cringe in fear at the mention of my name.'

Sepwin stood up slowly. 'I know what I see when I look at you, Cray. I know what I feel in your flesh.' He came away from the tree and sat on the stone bench beside his friend. 'Look at me and tell me what this golden flower means to you. Tell me you are not going the way of power for its own sake, the way of Rezhyk.'

'Oh, Feldar,' Delivev whispered. 'How can you make such a comparison? He's harmed no one. The power he seeks is not evil.'

'I do not speak of evil. I speak of his heart and his future. The search for power is endless. It consumes the seeker and never satisfies him.'

Cray met Sepwin's mismatched eyes. 'Let it be so, then. At least it will fill up the hundred mortal lives of my span. Or would you suggest I change to some other line of employment?'

Sepwin's gaze was level, unblinking. 'I say only that you need the mirror, my friend. Others may use it, but now I know we will be making it for you.'

Cray pursed his lips and looked to his tree, where the gold blossom glinted in the midday sun. 'If you're so sure I'm on the path to self-centred power, aren't you afraid of what I'll see in it?'

'No.' He caught Cray's arm, his grip firm. 'What you see in the mirror will open your eyes to your true self.'

'You think I don't know myself?'

Sepwin smiled, but it was a wintry smile, quite at odds with the warm summer breeze that played about the garden. 'The mirror will tell you the truth. But perhaps you're the one afraid.'

Cray looked at him squarely. 'Not I.'

Sepwin's smile broadened. 'I didn't think so.' Then he turned to Gildrum and Delivev and said, 'Please excuse us. We have work to do.'

To help them, Cray called on three demons – Berith of Ice,

a very young ice demon with the form of a small snowball; Elrelet of Air, a cloud no larger than a man, white and puffy as bleached wool; and Gildrum, the ball of flame. When all were ready, Cray hung the wooden frame on a wall of his workshop and directed his spiders to weave a dense sheet of silk upon it. Sepwin inspected this web closely, calling for a score of corrections before declaring himself satisfied. Then he and Cray retreated behind a ceramic baffle while Berith spread itself behind the frame, chilling it and the web until clouds of condensation began to form around them. At that, Gildrum took Cray's ingot of silvery metal into its incandescent body. A moment passed, and then, with a powerful blast of superheated air, Gildrum spewed out a white-hot mist of metal. Like fog, the tiny particles saturated the space all about the web till silk, wall, and floor were plastered with a thin layer of metal. The condensation vanished, replaced by heat shimmer. Yet quickly as it came, the heat was gone, neutralized by the ice demon; a few heartbeats later, the metal limning of the web was cool enough for human hands to touch. The wooden form had not even been tinged by char.

Berith withdrew.

Cray examined the new surface. It was fine-grained, as if covered with dull grey dust. Cray nodded to the ice demon. 'You have done well, friend Berith, and I thank you for your aid. We have no further need of you.'

Berith shot out of the window and vanished in the afternoon sky.

'Now Elrelet,' Cray said, turning to the cloud that floated near Gildrum's flame, 'your gentlest touch.'

The air demon scooped up the mound of fine rouge that waited on Cray's workbench and leaped to the metal-coated web, its body shrinking and rounding till it exactly filled the concave bowl. Then that fluffy whiteness began to boil like a pot of beans over a high flame, and when

25

at last it withdrew, the metal surface was left glittering brightly, as if a million tiny silver beads had been packed together upon the wooden form.

'Very useful to have all these demons at your service,' Sepwin observed. 'As good as having a fistful of rings.'

Cray shook his head. 'I can't count on any but Gildrum and Elrelet.' He glanced at them affectionately. 'For the rest – it amuses them to help a sorcerer now and then, knowing that they needn't obey if they don't want to.'

Sepwin placed himself before the mirror, and slowly he moved his head back and forth, left and right, up and down. And suddenly he froze, knees bent slightly. 'There! There it is! You were right, Cray – the mirror *can* be made of metal!'

Cray stepped close to look over his friend's shoulder. 'I don't see anything. Just glitter.'

'You have to be in exactly the right spot. Bring the chalk and the staff.'

Cray outlined Sepwin's footprints on the floor and marked the level of his eyes on the staff.

'Now you try it,' said Sepwin.

Cray stepped into the footprints, but no matter how he adjusted his head, no matter how he squinted, he saw nothing in the mirror but glitter. 'Perhaps it only works for you.'

'I can't believe that.'

'Or perhaps one has to be a Seer.'

'No. That doesn't *feel* true.' He motioned to Gildrum. 'You try.'

Gildrum coalesced into human form and stood in Cray's place. Immediately, he smiled. 'I see something indeed.'

'What?' asked Sepwin.

'The lady Delivev, of course. Your mirror seems to work well enough for demons, friend Feldar.'

'Elrelet – will you be next?'

The cloud compacted itself to the size of a human fist

26

and floated to the staff to hover beside the chalk mark. 'My eyes are not as human eyes,' it said, 'but I do see the image of my home in Air, which is surely my own heart's desire. What a clever thing this mirror is.'

Sepwin turned to Cray. 'Now, will you ask your mother to come?'

Cray fetched her, she looked, and – like Gildrum – she smiled. 'Congratulations. Your labours have been rewarded.' She glanced at the fire demon, and her smile deepened. 'Though I didn't need your mirror to tell me my heart's desire.' She held her hand out to him, and he came forward to kiss it.

'Look again, Cray,' said Sepwin. 'If it works for your mother, it will surely work for you.'

He looked again, and again he saw nothing but the sparkle of a million silver beads. 'Perhaps my heart's desire is too abstract to make a picture. After all, how would the mirror show . . . knowledge?'

Sepwin let the staff tilt against his shoulder. 'I think there would be some way, if knowledge were truly your heart's desire. Perhaps you'd see this room, and yourself at work.'

Cray stood silent a long moment, and then he turned away from the mirror, saying softly, 'Perhaps I have no heart's desire.'

Sepwin laid a hand on his shoulder. 'I don't believe that. The mirror is for you. I'm not wrong about it.' He pulled gently at Cray's arm. 'Look once more.'

Cray shook his head. 'Twice is enough.'

'Please.'

'There's no purpose in it, Feldar.'

'*Please.*'

He shrugged Sepwin's hand away. 'This mirror is a fragile thing. We don't want it damaged on your journey home. I'll find something sturdy to pack it in.' And he strode from the room.

Sepwin looked at the mirror unhappily. 'I'm not wrong. I know what I felt when I touched him.' He gripped the staff with white-knuckled hands. 'Why won't it show him something?'

Delivev and Gildrum came to him then, and each put an arm around him. 'You are so worried about him,' Delivev said softly. 'Yet he is young. There is time for anything he might wish to do. Must he have a heart's desire so soon in life?'

'Everyone has a heart's desire,' Sepwin murmured.

'I think not,' said Gildrum. 'I think that some mortals simply live from day to day, doing whatever comes to hand and never looking to any real goal.'

Sepwin looked into the demon's eyes. 'Those are just the ones who don't know what they want. The very ones who will come to look in the mirror.' He turned to Delivev. 'You'll see – someday the mirror will speak to him.'

She stroked back his lank hair. 'I know you only mean him well, Feldar, but don't badger him about this. I think that . . . it disturbs him that the mirror has nothing for him. It may be best to put the matter aside for now. Come, it's almost time for supper.' She glanced at the air demon. 'Elrelet, will you stay?'

'Thank you,' it said. 'I appreciate an invitation from such a fine cook.'

Supper was somewhat strained, for neither Cray nor Sepwin would speak much, though Delivev and the demons were able to chat amiably enough. Afterwards they all sat in the garden over wine until Sepwin decided it was time to pack up the mirror.

'I'll carry you and it home, if you like,' offered Elrelet, 'as a small repayment to my lady for the excellent supper.'

'Thank you,' said Sepwin. 'Flight would be safest for the mirror. But for myself, I'd really prefer a horse.'

'That's a simple matter. My old master gave me a horse's form so he could roam the world in disguise. As a talking and untiring horse, I am at your service.'

Sepwin shook his head. 'I wouldn't want to keep you in the human realm so long. The journey is a long one.'

Elrelet chuckled softly. 'I don't mind the human realm, as long as I'm visiting it of my own free will.' For the meal, the demon had assumed a vaguely man-like shape, with torso and limbs of puffy white and a blob of a head with a large mouth but no eyes, nose or ears. Now it settled to the ground, all four limbs straight beneath it, the torso arching. The insubstantial looking cloud solidified, smoothed out, became sleek and graceful. The horse that had been Elrelet tossed its white-maned head, and a pale leather saddle took form from the powerful muscles of its back.

Sepwin stood and bowed awkwardly to Delivev. 'Perhaps you'll give me some provisions for the trip, my lady . . ?'

Her smile was puzzled. 'You're not going this very moment, are you, Feldar?'

He glanced sidelong at Cray. 'I don't know. Perhaps you're all weary of me . . . and my foibles.'

Demon and human alike, they turned to Cray at that, waiting for him to pass judgement on his friend. For just a moment, his lips made a thin, exasperated line; then he shook his head and rose to clap Sepwin on the back. 'Of course you'll stay. Do you think I brought you all this way to have you leave in less than a day?'

Sepwin hesitated, looking into Cray's face, and then his mouth curved into a slow smile. 'It does seem an inefficient use of time.'

'Of course it is. Elrelet can take you home a week hence as easily as now. There's a game of chance I've been wanting to try with you, one I observed in the webs some time ago, very popular in the south, and I was wondering if your powers as a Seer might have some effect on the outcome . . .'

Sepwin stayed the week, and in that time he did not speak of the mirror again.

The fame of the Mirror of Heart's Desire spread far during the next few years. Kings and commoners came to look into it. The young, the old, the wandering, the people wanting to be told what to do with their lives, where to go, who to serve – all the folk who did not know their own minds came to the mirror. In it they saw objects, places, people, or they saw themselves in strange surroundings, doing unfamiliar things. And the Seers stood by, Sepwin and the lady Helaine, to tell them, if they asked, what those visions meant.

But though he visited the Seers' cave often in those years, and though he passed the velvet drapery that hid the mirror a dozen dozen times, Cray did not look, no matter how obliquely Sepwin suggested it.

Chapter 2

Atop the only remaining tower of a ruined castle, a gaunt, pale-bearded man raised his arms in conjuration. He was Everand, who had lived three mortal lifetimes already and called himself a sorcerer. His clothes were rags, his fingernails and the creases of his skin were dark with grime, his eyes were reddened with lack of sleep, but he smiled. He savoured the moment as if it were fine wine, and then he could not keep from shouting, 'Now! Now!' as exultation rose strong within him, and power. And with a wild gesture, he flung both at the clear evening sky.

From the horizon, scattered wisps of cloud, flushed pink by the setting sun, came like starlings to a cherry tree. From every direction they sped, meeting above the crumbled walls of the castle in a wild cyclone, darkening as they gathered and piling up, up, into a towering thunderhead. Roiling, billowing like smoke from some vast conflagration, the cloud expanded upwards until its summit began to flatten and spread as against some invisible barrier. Only then did the first bolt of lightning lash earthward, illuminating Everand and his lonely citadel with a ghastly whiteness.

The castle stood in the heart of a great and trackless forest. Once, it had been many-spired, its lofty walls and turrets built of demon-quarried marble. Once, solid and polished smooth and ever-renewed, it had been the proud residence of a powerful sorcerer. But with his death the castle, too, had died, its towers collapsing, roofs caving in, walls crumbling. Now, where stone still stood on stone, weeds grew from the cracked mortar, and even trees had taken root.

Everand called the ruin his home; he had no other. His poor shelter of wood and broken stone, patched together with his own hands against the base of the standing tower, betrayed his weakness as a sorcerer. Though he could command clouds, though he could strike men dead from afar, though he could turn the forest night into day with a nod of his head, he could not build himself a proper dwelling. For three mortal lifetimes he had studied sorcery, and still there were many things other sorcerers accomplished easily that remained beyond him. Too many.

In the castle's open courtyard, upon the bare ground where the lightning danced and crackled, lay a circlet of copper-gold alloy as big around as a man's arm. Bolt after bolt of lightning played about it, making its ruddy, polished surface gleam sun-bright; Everand could feel the force of each stroke in the fine-drawn copper wires wound about his wrists and arms, in the copper-gold ring on the first finger of his right hand. And with each stroke he looked for flames to gush abruptly from the circlet, flames that would roar and thrash and finally subside into some bizarre, misshapen creature that would yield him its name and do his bidding forever. A fire demon. The first of many fire demons. Everand's fingers curled and worked against each other with his eagerness.

Brilliant in the lightning's glare, the arm ring lay empty on the steaming earth.

Empty.

Thunder seemed to echo in his ears long after darkness had settled upon the castle, long after he had allowed the cloud to shred apart like rotting cloth and reveal the icy stars. He stood in the dark for a time, the after-image of the armlet glowing in his mind's eye. Step by step, he called the details of the conjuration from his memory, searching for some flaw. But no; everything had been perfect – the weighing and mixing and smelting of the alloy, the words, the gestures, everything precisely as

32

Regneniel had taught him. Yet the procedure had yielded nothing.

Rage grew thick and hot within him. He snapped his fingers to bring a dazzling blue-white spark into being on the nearest wall and, by its glare, stalked down the tower stairs. In the courtyard, he picked up the copper-gold armlet and turned it slowly in his hands. It had not changed; its inner surface was blank where he desired a demon's name to be inscribed. He gripped it hard, and its edges pressed painfully into the flesh of his palm, his fingers. For a moment, he focused all his rage on that piece of metal; he wanted to slam it against a wall, to trample it under his feet, to hurl it into the furnace and melt it down to a formless lump, as if any of those actions could somehow force it to obey him and produce a demon. He gripped the circlet so hard that his hands shook. At last, very softly, he said, 'Regneniel, come here.'

The creature that answered his summons was taller than a man and grotesquely storklike. It walked on two spindly, multijointed legs, and its apple-sized body sprouted three tiny arms as well as a snaky neck that blended into a long-beaked head. It had no eyes or ears, no feathers or fur or scales, just a smooth unbroken skin as polished and gleaming as milk glass. Sinking to the ground at Everand's feet, it said, 'My lord, what is your will?'

Everand tore his left hand from the armlet and raised it as a fist. The third finger bore a silver band set with a large, faceted diamond, and that gem caught the glare of the blue-white spark and shattered it into a thousand colours. Playing across the unearthly creature's skin, these fragments of light shivered with the tremor of the hand.

'By this ring I command you, ice demon,' said Everand, and now his voice, too, shook with his anger, though it was very low. 'Have you lied to me, my slave? Have you given me false instruction in any particular?'

The beak tilted upward, as if the eyeless head were

watching him. The voice was human as his own, but level and emotionless. 'My lord, I have done everything you required.'

'Think before you speak again, creature! Think of the prison I could send you to, of the dark solitude that would close you in for the rest of your slavery. Think of that, and tell me again if you have obeyed me to the letter!'

'My lord,' said the demon, 'your conjuration was correct in every detail. I swear this on the ring that binds me to you.'

'Then where is my fire demon?' He raised the armlet as if to strike his slave. As so often before, though Regneniel bent low to the ground, Everand saw defiance in that posture rather than submission. The demon despised him, he knew it. 'Speak!'

'My lord,' said Regneniel, 'there are none to be had.'

'What? What do you mean?'

'No more than that, my lord. At this moment, there are no fire demons obliged to answer your summons.'

'What – every one claimed by some other sorcerer? Am I to believe that?'

'Many are indeed claimed,' said Regneniel.

'And the unclaimed?'

'They are all beyond your reach.'

He did strike the creature then, anger overpowering him, and the copper-gold armlet rang against that glassy surface as against bare metal. 'Why are they beyond my reach?' he shouted. 'Is it you, you cursed monster? Don't you know how to conjure them?' He struck again, harder, and this time he felt the armlet go cold and the cold rush up his arm as if he had plunged it into icy water to the shoulder. The sensation merely fuelled his rage, turning from ice to fire inside his heart. 'I am a sorcerer, and I will be a greater one! You shall not stand in my way!'

'My lord, I am not to blame,' whispered the demon.

'Are you saying that it's *my* fault? Do you dare to say that, slave?'

'My lord – '

'Monster, beware – you walk close to the brink!'

The beak sank to the ground, almost touching his feet. 'My lord, you misunderstand me. Forces outside the two of us prevent your conjuration from being successful.'

Everand glowered at the creature, the pressure of his rage a beating pain in his throat, at his temples, inside his ears. The demon's voice was so calm, so quiet that he wanted to smash it into a million milky shards. Cursing, he turned away, and then he tossed the copper-gold circlet from him as if it were a piece of rotten meat.

Slowly, he regained control of himself. Losing his temper at the demon was pointless, he knew that. He could not punish it – he needed its services too much. He had no other slaves. He hugged his icy arm to his chest and massaged away the chill. When he turned back to the demon at last, he was the image of cool restraint, though his throat was hot and raw.

'What forces do you speak of, my slave?' he said quietly.

Regneniel's beak barely moved with its words. 'There is a sorcerer, my lord, who gives eternal freedom to masterless demons. He has been doing this for some years now, and as long as he continues, there will be no reservoir of potential slaves.'

Everand stroked his pale beard with the hand that bore the diamond. 'None at all? Fire, ice, water, and air – none?'

'None, my lord.'

'And Regneniel, my slave, did you know this before you began to teach me how to conjure them?'

The demon hesitated for just a moment. Then it whispered, 'Yes, my lord.'

'So, all the while you were teaching me this useless knowledge, you were mocking me behind my back.'

'My lord, you bade me teach you how to conjure a fire demon, and I obeyed.'

Everand drew a ragged breath and kept his voice from rising into a shout again. 'Yes, you did obey me. And you taught me more than you think, my icy slave. I promise you, this lesson shall not be forgotten. Now – tell me if there is any way I can acquire a fire demon, or any sort of demon, in the future.'

'It will not be easy, my lord.'

'So I suspect. Still.'

Regneniel arched its neck, swanlike, raising its head to the level of Everand's knees. 'This sorcerer knows when demons are loosed by their master's deaths, and also when new ones are born. He is always ready, it seems, with rings to conjure them and set them free. You could not be quick enough to snatch them from him, my lord, not even with my help. Therefore, if you wish another slave, you must prevent him from practising his art.'

Everand stared down at the beak that poised, motionless, before him. 'Prevent? You mean . . . kill him?'

'That would be the surest way.'

Everand looked up to the jagged battlements of his citadel, to the ruined towers and the crumbled walls. He shook his head. 'In a contest with another sorcerer, *I'd* be the one more likely to die.' He lowered his gaze to the demon once more. 'Tell me, slave – why has no other demon-conjurer killed him already? Surely his work does harm to all of them. Or is he so very powerful that they dare not try?'

'My lord, they cannot touch him. They don't know who he is.'

Everand's eyebrows showed his disbelief. 'How is that possible? They have only to ask their slaves for his name.'

'My lord, his identity is the great secret of the demon worlds. Those he has freed never reveal it to those still enslaved. All I know of him is that he exists, and he is a man.'

'No more than that?'

The beaked head wagged in a very human fashion. 'No, my lord.'

Everand's lips tightened for a moment. 'Not easy,' he whispered. 'Not easy.' His hands curled into fists at his sides. 'Hear me, my icy slave. This is my command – that if ever you should encounter the slightest hint of his identity, you will inform me immediately. I hope that is clear, Regneniel.'

'Quite clear, my lord. I am not the first demon to be given those instructions.'

'No, I wouldn't think so.' He looked down to the bare ground of the courtyard. Here, and for a narrow space about the castle walls, Regneniel had frozen the earth with its icy breath, frozen grass and shrubs and trees, frozen even unsprouted seeds to death. Regneniel was a destroyer; its breath on the walls would make stone fracture and mortar crumble until even the wretched ruins that now stood fell to dust. The only structure such a demon could build would be of ice, a frigid dwelling whose master would be forced to live in furs summer and winter alike. Everand needed fire demons to make him a proper castle, to fulfil all his deepest desires. He glanced sidelong at the spark that had bloomed to his bidding. With a nod, he snuffed it and stood in the darkness, a greater darkness growing in his heart. Three lifetimes of study had yielded so little! He raised his eyes to the castle's single standing tower, its outline barely visible against the starry sky. He lifted a hand toward it, and pale St Elmo's fire leaped from its crenellations, slid down to the lower battlements, and flickered across the ruined walls till the whole perimeter of the citadel was crowned with shimmering light.

'They laugh at my sorcery,' he said in a low, tight voice. 'They call it . . . pitiful.' He looked down at the demon, a pale ghost at his feet. 'You are all I have, Regneniel. Now between us we must find another way to gain power.'

The demon lowered its head to the ground. 'I don't know what to tell you, my lord,' it murmured. 'I am only an ice demon.'

Everand rubbed the diamond with the palm of his ringless hand. 'All the knowledge of the human realm, and more, can be found in the demon worlds. You and I shall pick over that knowledge, and we shall find a way, Regneniel. They shall eat their laughter, my icy slave; they shall choke on it. And *he* . . .' His voice dropped to a harsh whisper. 'This secret, nameless sorcerer. For what he has done to me . . . he shall die. Somehow. Someday.'

At his feet, Regneniel said, 'You command me, my lord, and I obey.'

By nature, Cray was as curious as he was stubborn. As long as Sepwin seemed to want him to look into the Mirror of Heart's Desire, so long he ignored it; but once his friend could pass the velvet drapery without glancing at it meaningfully, Cray's interest began to revive. He found the mirror invading his dreams, where once again he saw the metal fog settling on the web-covered wooden frame, the air demon polishing that curving surface, and the glitter that resulted, the empty glitter. In his deepest slumber, the mirror seemed to call to him, and often he awoke then, to toss fitfully and wonder if he should answer.

In eight years, hundreds of men and women had looked into the mirror. Nearly all of them had seen *something*. Why, Cray thought, should he be one of the few denied a vision? What quality did he lack that the mirror withheld its boon?

Eight years.

It was long enough.

On his next visit to the cave, he waited until Sepwin and the lady Helaine were busy preparing a meal, and on the pretext of fetching flowers for the table, he slipped away from them.

The mirror chamber was large and high-ceilinged, and the black velvet curtain appeared to lie flush against its farther wall. Only when the drapery was drawn aside did the alcove that lay behind become visible, a shallow space where the Mirror of Heart's Desire hung between two empty brass sconces. Cray took a pair of torches from the room's entrance and set them in the sconces, and their light made the mirror glitter as in his dreams.

In the curtain, at about the height of Cray's eyes, was a slit as wide as his hand and two fingers high. That was the precise place from which supplicants always looked at the mirror, from which they saw – what? Cray let the curtain drop between himself and that glittering surface, and he looked, wondering.

For a moment, the torches dazzled his eyes. Then he focused on the mirror, and saw the image, clear and sharp as a reflection in a still pond. But it was not a reflection. No.

Mirror of Heart's Desire, he thought, *what have you given me?*

The still and silent likeness of a six-year-old child.

Chapter 3

When he tore his eyes away from the mirror at last, he found Sepwin standing beside him, a silent question on his face. Cray nodded slowly. 'I saw something.' And then he shook his head. 'But it seems a very peculiar heart's desire.'

Sepwin frowned. 'Perhaps if you could describe it to me . . . ?'

'It was a child.' He turned back to the slit, and the image had not changed. 'A little girl, perhaps six years old, rather pretty, though her face is dirty. Dark hair, very large eyes. Plainly dressed. A peasant child, I'd guess.'

'Keep looking,' said Sepwin, touching the back of Cray's neck with the flat of one hand. 'Fill your mind with her image.'

'What are you doing?'

'Trying to feel her through you, to locate her.'

'There's no need for that.'

'Of course there is. You must go to her.'

Cray turned to stare at his friend. 'Go to her? Why?'

'She's in the mirror; isn't that a good enough reason?'

'Feldar, don't talk nonsense. She's just a child, a baby.'

'Even so. If you go to her, you will surely find out why the mirror shows her to you. Now look again so that I can help you.'

Cray's lips made a firm line. 'It's nonsense, Feldar.'

'Humour me, my dear friend. Can it hurt you?'

With a grunt, Cray turned back to the child.

After a time, Sepwin set his other hand on top of Cray's head. 'Look at the background. Tell me what you see there.'

40

Cray squinted. 'I'd say it was a very cloudy sky, except that there's an object hung on it. So it must be just a poorly whitewashed wall.'

'What sort of object?'

'A lozenge-shaped plaque.'

'A coat of arms!' Sepwin cried eagerly. 'She might be a servant in some great house!'

'I've never seen a coat of arms like this before. It seems to be of glass inlaid with copper ribbons. The field is quartered, and the quarters are all faintly blue in colour, alternating darker and lighter, with no two quite the same. The bands repeat the lozenge shape concentrically five times.'

'Some great houses have been known to set their arms in stained glass,' said Sepwin, 'but I don't recognize this pattern.'

'Nor do I.'

'Can you see anything else? Is there a carpet under her feet? Any special decorations about her clothing?'

Cray shook his head. 'There's just a plainly dressed child and a plaque. Nothing more.'

'Look closely, Cray. Oh, if only I could see her myself!'

Cray studied the image for a long moment, and then he said, 'There is one more thing, though I don't know how it could help you. She's holding some sort of stuffed animal half behind her back, but it's so grey and shapeless that I can't tell what kind it might be.' He looked to Sepwin. 'Well?'

Slowly, the Seer lowered his hands. 'I can't feel her at all.' He sighed heavily. 'She might as well be nowhere.'

Cray reached out to grasp his arm. 'If one of your skill can't find her . . . perhaps she *is* nowhere. First the mirror was blank, and now . . . perhaps it's playing a joke on me.'

'No. The mirror tells only the truth.'

'But not enough of it.'

Sepwin's shoulders slumped. 'No. Not in this case.'

Cray clapped him on the back. 'No matter, Feldar,' he said firmly. 'What could I possibly say to a six-year-old child? And what could she say to me? No, it doesn't matter at all.' And he turned his friend away from the Mirror of Heart's Desire.

That night, over dinner, Sepwin asked the lady Helaine to look into her dark pool for Cray, but she refused. 'For all my age, Feldar, for all these white hairs, I cannot read Cray half as well as you can. If you could not find her, I shall not be able to. But I will tell you this –' She touched his wrist lightly. 'I can read you very well, my dear, and I know that you will be involved in the quest for this child.'

'Quest?' exclaimed Cray. 'There isn't going to be any quest.'

'Yes, there will be. But not until the time is right.'

'And when will that be?' demanded Sepwin.

'You will know.'

'I? Not Cray?'

'I said I could not read *him*.' She stroked his forearm with her delicate pale fingers. 'You must be careful, Feldar. There will be danger.'

He shot Cray a quick glance. 'We've been through danger together before. I'm not worried.'

'What will this danger be, lady?' asked Cray. 'Where will it come from?'

The Seer shook her head sadly. 'Do not ask too much of me, Cray Ormoru. I see and feel a few things, but most of the future is murky to me. It depends too much on decisions not yet made, on paths not yet followed. The past is so much clearer.'

'And yet you say there will be a quest.'

'I see one.'

Cray folded his arms across his chest. 'And what if I say there will be no quest, that I have no interest in finding a person I don't know and have no reason to know?'

She touched his arm in a soothing gesture. '*You* make your future, Cray. No matter what I say, you can wrench your life away from it. You can turn my truth to a lie.'

'Very well,' he said. 'I'll remember that.'

Sepwin looked at him long and hard but said nothing. They finished dinner in silence.

Cray spent the next few years expanding his powers over living, growing things. He learned to combine not just gold but silver, copper, and other metals with the substance of plants, and to make those plants mature into whatever forms he wished, with or without metal. Eventually he was able to grow himself a castle.

It was a huge place, much larger than Spinweb. Instead of stone, its walls were thick tree trunks crowded so close together that no gaps were visible between them. Their branches began high above the ground, rising stout and square like crenellations, with leaves clustered only at their tops, shading the battlements from the summer sun. At the angles of the walls, the trees rose taller, forming turrets, and on their inner sides great staircases grew, with deep window slits at frequent intervals. The buildings of the courtyard were also made of trees, and inside them chairs, tables, and even beds grew from their wooden floors. Wherever cushions were needed, dense-leafed branches offered themselves, and where a hard, smooth surface free of bark was required, the trees obliged.

Though the castle was comfortable enough, Cray did not choose to live there. He visited often and kept an army of ensorcelled shrubs there as servants, commanding them to uproot themselves and walk whenever he wished something cooked or cleaned. But usually he was only there to make changes, to cause an extra chair to grow, a wall hanging of twisting woods to take form, a partition to expand or wither away. The place was just a toy to him; it was too large and lonely to live in.

He often talked about it to Sepwin, talked about his most recent changes, and the ideas he had for more. The castle had replaced the tree as the centre of his life, and if Sepwin sighed when he said that, if Sepwin glanced sidelong at the velvet curtain every time they passed it, Cray pretended not to notice. They didn't speak of the mirror these days, nor of the enigmatic image of the child.

Yet Cray thought of them sometimes, especially when he woke in the darkest part of the night and lay in his bed, listening to the stillness. At those times, he could not keep himself from thinking of them.

One afternoon, he found himself alone by the Seers' dark pool. In the kitchen, Sepwin was cleaning the breakfast dishes, and outside, the lady Helaine was watching for the arrival of her next supplicant; neither of them needed him. The cave was very quiet, as quiet as the darkest part of the night. For a time Cray trailed his fingers in the water, watching the ripples break up the reflection of his face. Here was an ordinary mirror, he thought, offering no enigmas, just uncluttered reality. Only for a Seer could it be more, not for him. He wiped his hand on his tunic and rose, stretching, thinking he would join Sepwin and dry a dish or two. But his path took him past the chamber of the mirror, and he could not help seeing the velvet curtain through its doorway. He paused then, alone, staring at that curtain. He paused, and at last he took up a pair of torches to hang beside the mirror, and he looked.

The image had changed.

The child had grown. She was taller, slimmer, less babyish, and her hair that had been a short, dark tangle now fell past her shoulders in two smooth braids. Her face was clean, and her dress was of finer stuff. Only the grey and shapeless toy clutched in her hand had not changed. Behind her, the lozenge was gone, leaving the wall featureless and cloudy white.

'Feldar!' he shouted.

Sepwin came at a run, wiping his hands on his apron. 'Is something wrong?' Then he saw that Cray was at the curtain.

'She's different,' Cray told him. 'Older.'

'Well, she *would* be, after five years.'

Cray frowned at the image. 'Who is she, Feldar? And where?'

'Ah,' murmured Sepwin. 'So it isn't nonsense any more.' But when he laid his hands on Cray's head, he found no more answers than before.

'This is so strange,' Cray said. 'I feel almost as though I'm looking at some ancient tapestry, seeing a scene that was real sometime, for someone, but not for me. Feldar, I don't understand why the mirror is showing me this person from nowhere!'

Sepwin studied his friend's profile for a time, and then he said, 'I think you don't understand because you don't wish to.' And he left Cray looking, still looking, into the mirror.

Every year after that, Cray went to the mirror at least once. In a series of still and silent portraits, he watched the child grow, watched her face and limbs lose their baby fat and become slender, even angular, watched her carry the same stuffed animal year after year. And all through that time Sepwin could not feel a hint of where she might be, nor could Cray guess, from any background in the vision. She seemed to live in a place filled with light, yet it was neither sunlight nor torchlight but some whiter radiance, almost blue-white. And when that cloudy wall was not behind her, then there was no background at all, just pale, featureless haze.

'She must serve a sorcerer,' Cray said one time. 'Only a sorcerer's walls could hide her from you so completely.'

Sepwin shook his head. 'My bond with you is too strong for that. I would know at least where those walls lay. But

45

I have been thinking . . .' He hesitated. 'Perhaps . . . she is a demon.'

Cray looked at him sharply.

'Demons are beyond me,' Sepwin said. 'A Seer can only deal with things of the human realm.'

'But . . . a child, a growing child?'

Sepwin shrugged. 'Who can say what whim a sorcerer might have, to give his demon a slightly older human form each year, as if it were growing up before his eyes. I've heard of stranger things.'

'Well, if she is a demon, and with such an unusual form, then Gildrum might know of her.'

But he did not, and when he asked among his fellow demons, he found none who had ever heard of such a creature.

When the girl was in her late teens, the stuffed animal finally vanished, and with it, at least in Cray's eyes, went the last vestiges of her childhood. Now she was tall and slim, with an almost regal carriage. Her eyes were large and dark, her skin as pale as milk, her hair a shining cascade all about her shoulders. From a pretty child, she had metamorphosed into a beautiful young woman. Her clothing, too, had transformed with her, into the finest velvet. No one would mistake her for a servant these days; she would have to be the daughter of the house, perhaps of a very great house.

And now, upon her breast, dangling from a thin gold chain and rimmed by a silvery band, was a faceted pendant of purest white sapphire.

'I've never seen a gem so large,' Cray said to Sepwin. 'It makes a handsome piece of jewellery. And possibly . . . more than that.'

'More?'

'A hoop of precious metal set with a gem is a ring, Feldar, even if it isn't worn on the hand.' He turned an exultant smile on his friend. 'A ring might command a demon, and if it does, then Gildrum can find it. And its wearer.'

With the skilled eye of one who had cast hundreds of rings and set nearly as many stones upon them, he scrutinized the pendant. He estimated its weight, drew its shape, enumerated its facets, pinpointed its colour. And by the time he was finished, Gildrum, who had been his mentor in ring-making, knew the stone and its setting as well as he did.

'Whether it does command a demon or not, I can't say,' Gildrum told him. 'But this gem was cut and polished and set in metal, and some demon will know what happened to it, even if it is only a piece of jewellery. Even if it lies inside a sorcerer's home, some demon will know that it was delivered there.' And he turned to flame and soared into the sky for his search.

Gildrum was gone for days. Cray could have returned home for that time, returned to the studies that had been so much of his life. But all the restlessness, all the impatience, all the desire for accomplishment that he had ever felt seemed focused on that image in the mirror, and he could not tear himself away from it. He looked at it again and again, as if afraid that now he had some way to find her, the girl would vanish. He discovered that her image changed each afternoon, the old one dissolving into nothingness and a new one taking shape, a fresh instant in time. He watched her, day by day, as she moved about against those incomprehensible backgrounds, in that unearthly radiance. Once, she held a large book in her hands, but squint as he might, he could not make out the title. And once, just once, she seemed to be gazing directly out at him, as if she could somehow see him spying on her. Every time he looked at her in that pose, he shivered; she was staring at him and yet she was not, she was a total stranger and yet she was not, the mirror had bound the two of them together and yet they had never met.

When Gildrum returned, Cray and Sepwin and the lady Helaine were sitting together by the pool, drinking white wine.

'I would have come sooner,' the demon said, striding toward them in his human form, 'but I thought it best to stop at home and let your mother know I was back.'

Cray scrambled to his feet. 'What news?'

With a smile, Gildrum accepted a cup of wine from the lady Helaine and raised it to Cray. 'Success.' He drained the wine at a draught. 'I know where your white sapphire and its owner are.'

'Where?'

'Ah . . . well, that is not so easy to explain.' Gildrum set his cup down on the rim of the pool. 'You know, we demons do most of our travelling by way of the demon realm itself, and so we learn little of human geography. I may be an exception to that, thanks to your mother; still, this place where the young woman lives – I can't really tell you in what direction it lies, and how far, not in terms of a horseback journey. But it can be reached through the demon realm.'

'Very well,' said Cray. 'Will you take me there now?'

'I told your mother you would say that.'

Sepwin sprang to his feet. 'I'm ready.'

Cray shook his head sharply. 'No, Feldar, you're not coming along.'

'But this is the quest that the lady Helaine predicted!'

Cray gripped his friend's arm. 'Just so. And I will not expose you to its dangers. No, no arguments. This is my quest and my decision.'

Sepwin looked to the lady Helaine beseechingly, but she said nothing. Then to Cray he said, 'You'll come back here afterward? You'll tell me everything?'

'Of course.' Cray smiled and let him go. 'Shall we be on our way, Gildrum?'

'As you wish,' said the demon and, turning to flame, it scooped Cray up.

Out in the bright sunshine, they soared into the sky, and somewhere above the treetops they crossed over from the human to the demon realm. Though Cray closed his eyes tightly against the intolerable glare of the world of Fire, he could see it still, red against his eyelids. Gildrum had been born in Fire, and like all demons it could only traverse from the demon realm to the human one through portals in its native world.

When the redness dimmed, Cray opened his eyes, knowing he was within the smoky barrier between Fire and Air.

'Elrelet is to meet us at the boundary of Air and Ice,' said Gildrum, 'with a co-operative ice demon, if such exists.'

'Why do we need so many demons? Can't you just take me to her yourself through a portal in Fire?'

'I could, but the part of her home that lies in the human realm is too well guarded by sorcery for visitors to come even within shouting distance. The other part, however, lies embedded in Ice, and with a knowledgeable ice demon for a guide, we can travel to its very walls.'

'Embedded in Ice? I've never heard of such a thing.'

'Nor had I, until now.'

The smoke was beginning to thin, and in a moment they had emerged into the untrammelled blue of the world of Air, a place without ground, without landmarks visible to any human eye, even without sun, though it was suffused with light. Only the flow of wind past his exposed skin showed Cray how swiftly his demon steed travelled through this emptiness – the flow of wind and the rapid fading of the smoky limits of Fire behind them.

Like the other boundaries between the demon worlds, the one between Air and Ice seemed infinite in extent, up, down, right, left. At first, far off, it appeared as just the slightest cloudiness in the vast blue of Air, but soon it loomed ahead like an enormous wall, faintly white, like water with a few drops of milk stirred in. And within this whiteness were a few greyish streaks, like colossal strands of spiderweb – huge fractures in the body of Ice, flaws in that single gigantic crystal. Cray and Gildrum were still far from the immense flat surface when he began to shiver from the chill that drifted toward him from it.

Gildrum, noting the shiver, warmed Cray with its flame.

Against the enormous expanse of Ice, Elrelet became visible as the merest puff of cloud. It extruded an arm to wave at the travellers, and they joined it.

'You've had some luck, I hope,' said Gildrum.

'I think so. At least, I have a tentative offer.'

'How tentative?'

'Middling,' said Elrelet. 'Cray freed this one eleven years ago, and it still seems to have a little gratitude left. As much as any of them have. Sometimes I have the impression that ice demons think they're doing Cray a favour by letting him free them.'

'They're just proud,' said Cray.

Elrelet made a rude noise. 'I can think of a better word for it.'

'And it can probably think of a lot of words for you,' said Gildrum. 'Now no more of this talk while we're so close to Ice. And come, take Cray. He'll be more comfortable for the journey with you.'

Cray felt only the briefest gust of frigid air as Gildrum withdrew and Elrelet enveloped him in its pale, cloudy substance. For a moment, he saw as through a grey veil, all his body encased in cloud no thicker than a finger's width. And then the substance became transparent, as if Elrelet had vanished, though Cray knew from its warmth that the demon still clothed him.

The three of them moved closer to the boundary of Ice, close enough to touch it. A light dusting of snow covered it, white particles drifting away at random, filling the air with a fine, glittering mist. Cray waved his demon-gloved hand above the area nearest him, clearing it and setting the mist awhirl with eddies. His nose almost touching the surface, cushioned only by the layer of Elrelet that surrounded him, he peered into the depths of Ice. The light from Air seemed to penetrate far, revealing a solid, transparent world marred only by its fractures and an occasional cloudy patch caused by trapped air bubbles.

'Our guide,' said Elrelet, and a puff of cloud materialized beside Cray's eyes to become a stubby, pointing finger.

Deep in the transparency before him, parallel to – no, *within* – one of the fractures, Cray saw motion. A slim, whitish object pressed toward him, forcing the fracture open just enough to let it pass. It was a slender cone, not unlike one of the heavy icicles that depended from Spinweb's parapets in winter, and its surface was frosted with a thousand tiny scales, like pinhead snowflakes. Cray pushed himself to one side as the fracture opened to Air like a mouth and the creature emerged. As it floated free of Ice, and the fracture closed behind it, the demon's slender form expanded like a bird fluffing its feathers. Multiple icicles fanned outward from its cone shape like a spray of fronds, expanding, unfolding, growing branches, spines, spicules until the demon was a multiplex form like a hundred giant snowflakes clustered together, a star made of openwork lace. It rotated slowly, and Gildrum's nearby flamelight flashed from its delicate structure, casting scintillations in every direction.

'Greetings, O ice demon,' said Cray. 'I am Cray Ormoru. I believe we have met before.'

'We have,' said the demon, and it floated closer to Cray, circling him slowly. 'I am Leemin. I understand you require my help.'

'It was I who asked for it,' said Elrelet. Though Elrelet

51

was invisible to human eyes, demon senses perceived it easily. 'Now I ask again: will you give us safe passage to the mortal's dwelling?'

'All of you?'

'Yes.'

'Even that one?' One of its spicules elongated for a moment, like a spear feinting in Gildrum's direction.

'Yes,' said Elrelet.

'I warn you that a thousand of my kind will come to push you all out if it dares to melt any of our Ice!'

'It shall not, I promise you. It will keep its flame small and cold. But we have need of its light for Cray Ormoru's eyes. Will you guide us?'

The ice demon was silent for some time, floating around and around Cray. Finally, it said, 'I suppose you think I should, mortal. I suppose you think I owe you favours.'

'My gift was freely given,' Cray replied. 'You owe me nothing. Still, I do need your help.'

'I have never understood mortals,' said the ice demon. 'I have never understood why you set me free.'

Cray smiled. 'If I were a slave, I would want to be free. There is no more to it than that.'

'No more than that,' echoed the demon. 'No, I do not understand at all. But I have benefited, even without understanding.' It halted its circling and floated motionless between Cray and the surface of its home. 'Few mortals have ever entered Ice. Fewer have emerged. It is not a place for mortals.'

'Yet the young woman I seek is there.'

'I know. Half in one realm and half in the other. A most peculiar situation.'

'Will you take us to her?' asked Elrelet. 'We mean no harm to Ice. If there were some other way, believe me, we would prefer not to travel through Ice at all.'

'There are no entries to her dwelling in Ice, you know,' said Leemin. 'Not unless she wishes to open one.'

52

'We hope she will,' said Elrelet, 'when she sees Cray Ormoru.'

'Ah. That might be interesting to watch. To see if she does let him in. I've only ever seen one other mortal with her.'

'Will you take us there, O Leemin?'

It hesitated one more moment, and then its spicules began to fold in on each other. 'Very well. But that fire creature must remain small and cold!' A sleek cone once more, the demon nudged the surface of Ice with its point, reopening the fracture. 'Stay close behind me,' it said, and it slid into Ice. There, its base expanded, forcing the fracture open enough to accommodate Cray.

Elrelet carried him in after the ice demon, and Gildrum followed closely, as small as the flame of a torch, and cooler. As they moved forward, the tunnel gradually narrowed behind them, and within moments Cray could no longer see the clear blue of Air at its mouth; it had no mouth. Yet the radiance of Air still enveloped them, showing fractures like broad grey ribbons running into infinity and scattered cloudy areas like patches of haze, but above all showing the enormous transparency of the place. Cray began to feel like a fly in amber, and for one fleeting moment, before he could resolutely put it out of his head, he knew the fear that if his demon guide so chose, he would be that fly indeed, trapped frozen, crushed, stranded forever in the vast transparency of Ice. He shivered.

'Are you cold?' whispered Elrelet.

'No,' said Cray. 'Just . . . overwhelmed.'

Elrelet snorted, and Cray felt it like a puff of breath against his cheek. 'I suppose it's pretty enough. But I'd sooner live in any of the other worlds. At least in them a creature can move without feeling closed in on all sides.'

Ahead, the fracture split in two, and they took the fork that bent sharply. Sometime after that, they made another abrupt turn, and then another. By then, there was not a trace of Air's radiance left around them, and they moved instead in the broad pool of Gildrum's glow.

'Why so jagged a route?' asked Cray. 'I see no barriers to our passage except Ice itself; why not open a path straight through to our destination?'

'Every flaw makes Ice less transparent,' said Gildrum, 'and since the demons value that transparency, they try to avoid creating new ones. I presume this path is the shortest that our guide could find.'

'It is,' Leemin said flatly.

A long while later, though Cray could not judge precisely how long because there was no sun, no moon, no stars to gauge by, they came to a halt.

'Are we there?' he asked. Looking all around, he saw no change in the substance about him, certainly nothing like a human habitation.

'We shall have to go back a bit,' said Leemin. 'This path will take us near the home of the Old One, and I see now that I was wrong to think it was not in residence. Stay still a moment.'

'The Old One?' said Cray.

'The oldest of all the ice demons. It has returned from the human realm since I was here last, and when it is at home, we younger demons never disturb it.' As Leemin spoke, its cone shape altered, hollowing out and opening up until the cone had become the thin outer shell of a cylinder. The cylinder then slid so that Cray and his two demon friends passed through its centre. When Leemin had completely exchanged relative places with them, its nose slimmed back to a point and its hollowness closed up. A stubby cone once more, it began to move back in the direction from which it had come; its companions had no choice but to follow.

After perhaps a dozen more turns – Cray had lost count of them by that time and certainly no longer knew one direction from another – the ice demon halted again. 'There,' it said, and became a hollow cylinder once more so that they could look out along the fracture they travelled in.

At first, Cray saw nothing new, but as he stared into the distance, and as Gildrum's glow gradually dimmed till all around him Ice was dark and sombre as a winter evening, he began to make out a faint luminosity far, far away. It had no shape to his eyes, no solidity; it was only a pale radiance, no brighter than the new moon in the old moon's arms.

'Surely we can go nearer than this,' Gildrum said, flaring into torchlight.

'As near as you wish,' Leemin replied, and closing into its cone shape, it moved on.

The fracture they travelled branched and branched again, and almost imperceptibly, the light that bathed them began to change, to cool in hue, as Gildrum's sunny incandescence was diluted by another, bluer radiance. The fracture branched once more, and as a new flaw carried them almost at a right angle to the last, Cray could see their goal to one side of Leemin, could see clearly now that the patch of luminosity that had appeared so faint before was actually a source of light as bright as day.

It hardly looked like any sort of dwelling. Though tall and broad as any sorcerer's castle, it was not made of stone or brick or wood, and it had no battlements, no turrets, no gates. Rather, it was a cluster of gigantic crystals, more like some natural excrescence of Ice than any planned structure, and the walls that bounded it were wide, smooth planes as beautifully transparent as the purest glass. Through those walls, Cray could see open interior spaces and walls behind walls until the depths of the whole were lost in a maze of facets. And from the entire edifice flowed a radiance that was neither sunlight nor moonlight nor flamelight, but something more akin to the blue-white of lightning.

'This is where she lives?' gasped Cray.

'Yes,' said Leemin. 'I have seen her enter often after she has walked about in Ice.'

'She's a demon master, then,' said Elrelet, 'with at least one slave to open the way for her.'

'She needs no slaves for that,' said Leemin. 'She does it herself.'

Elrelet's sharply indrawn breath whistled past Cray's ear. 'Is this possible?'

'I have seen it.'

'How long has she been here?' asked Gildrum.

'When I first saw her, she was a child.'

'And this huge . . . building?'

'It appeared shortly before that. But it was much smaller then; it has grown considerably since.'

Cray leaned against the side of the tunnel, staring into that marvellous structure. Amid its tangle of interior facets, he could see no furniture anywhere, no carpets, no hangings, no ornaments of any kind, just empty spaces. There was no trace of any human pattern, no sense of where a mortal might sleep or sit or eat a meal. He wondered what kind of person could live in such a place.

'Can we approach more closely?' he asked.

In answer, the ice demon moved onward a short distance and then nudged open a fracture that pointed directly at the strange building. This path brought the travellers all the way to its walls, terminating abruptly against one of those broad, transparent planes. There, Leemin became hollow once more so that Cray could peer inside.

'I don't see anyone,' Cray said.

'She rarely comes to these outer rooms,' replied Leemin, 'and neither your senses nor mine can penetrate farther.'

'On the contrary, I can see quite deeply into the place.'

'No, you only think you can. The interior we view from here is mostly illusion; the inner surfaces that seem transparent walls are really mirrors. If you look carefully, you can see your own faint reflection in them.'

'So I can. Well.' Thoughtfully, Cray eyed the glassy surface before him. 'Even if we can't see in, I imagine she can see out if she cares to, so we must attract her attention somehow. But there are no windows to shout through, and no gates to hammer at.' He rapped on the wall experimentally, but his demon-gloved hand made only a small sound, as if there were no hollowness beyond.

'Perhaps this will help,' said Gildrum, and from the depths of its flame it produced a silver bell no larger than a daffodil.

Cray took its tiny handle between two fingers. 'This won't make much of a sound,' he said.

'You'll be surprised.'

Cray shook the bell sharply, and its peal was high and sweet and piercing – so piercing that he could almost feel his bones vibrating in sympathy. Even after he stilled his hand, the sound echoed on; in fact, it built with every passing moment, multiplying upon itself, acquiring harmonics, till it was a veritable chorus of bells. On every side, Cray heard them, loud and pervasive. He clutched the silver bell around its cup, held fast to its pea-sized tongue, but he could feel the metal vibrating anyway.

'What's happening?' he said, and though he spoke loudly, he could scarcely hear his own voice.

'Ice itself is ringing,' said Gildrum. 'She can't help but hear it.'

'Fire demons!' cried Leemin. 'You would burn down a whole forest for a few sticks of charcoal! You make this terrible noise just to attract some mortal's attention, and you don't care that you disturb countless demons! Countless!'

'The sound will die away soon,' said Gildrum, and

indeed, the echoes were already beginning to fade. 'Still, I do apologize. I didn't realize the bell would be quite so loud.'

'Didn't realize,' muttered Leemin. 'I warn you – don't ring it again! I won't be responsible for anything other demons may do in their anger!'

'There won't be any need to ring it again,' said Gildrum, a tongue of its flame taking the bell from Cray's hands. 'We've caught someone's attention inside.'

The far wall of the room they had been peering into had suddenly vanished, revealing the chamber beyond. This was as large and empty as the outer room except for one thing – in its midst, looking small and fragile against the immensity of the place, stood the young woman. She hesitated just a moment, and then she began to walk toward Cray and his demons.

Cray watched silently as she came all the way to the wall and looked out through its transparency at his face. Her gaze was level, without surprise, without distaste, without welcome. She was an arm's length away, and he almost felt as though he were seeing her in the mirror again. His eyes met hers, and a shiver went through him.

'Hello,' he said, not knowing if she could hear him, if his voice could carry through the material that separated them. He raised his demon-gloved hands to the clear smooth outer surface of her residence, pressing against it gently as Elrelet kept him from floating away backwards. 'My name is Cray Ormoru, and I've come a very long way to make your acquaintance.'

And then the transparent wall turned to air beneath his hands, and he pitched forward into that strange and wonderful building.

Chapter 4

She had stepped aside and allowed him to fall at her feet. And he had indeed *fallen*; though he was still within the demon world of Ice, or so he thought, he had weight once more. And though Elrelet no longer wrapped him, for he had struck the crystalline floor with his bare hands, with his unprotected knees, he felt no chill; the floor and the air around him were pleasantly warm. He glanced over one shoulder and saw, beyond the transparent wall, his three demon companions. He waved to them to show he was unharmed, and then he rose to his feet and faced the woman.

She was as tall as he, dressed all in white velvet, and at her throat was the white sapphire pendant. She looked him up and down, looked especially at his hands, and then she circled him with a slow step as he stood very still. At last she said, 'Are you a sorcerer?' Her voice was low-pitched and soft, yet commanding, the voice of one accustomed to obedience.

He smiled and made a small bow. 'I am. Cray Ormoru of Castle Spinweb at your service, my lady.' He gestured toward the demons beyond the wall. 'And these are my companions, Gildrum of Fire, Elrelet of Air, and Leemin of this world. May they enter, too?'

She glanced at them for just a moment, then returned her gaze to him. 'No,' she said. 'Do you live in Ice?'

'No, my lady. Spinweb lies in the human realm.'

'But you use Ice for your travels.'

'This is the first time I've ever done so.'

She tilted her head a bit, as if to see him from a fresh angle. 'Ice can be a dangerous place for those not accustomed to it.'

'So I surmised. But I was willing to face that danger in order to meet you.'

A faint frown creased her pale brow. 'And how do you know of me, Cray Ormoru of Spinweb? I know nothing of you.'

He smiled again. 'My lady, I know nearly nothing of you, too, and yet, in a way, I know you well. You could say, in fact, that you and I are old, old friends, though our acquaintance has been somewhat one-sided till now. I think I have a tale that will divert you; could we, perhaps, sit down while I tell it?'

She looked at him with that faint frown still clouding her face, looked at him with eyes that were as dark and cool as a winter night, and at last she said, 'Very well.' Raising one hand to the level of her waist, she spread the fingers horizontally, palm downward. Immediately, a section of the floor rose up in a block behind her, smooth and silent, and then shards of the block broke free to thrust farther, till the whole had become a massive crystalline throne with broad armrests and a high back. She sat down on it, her spine very straight, her arms draped gracefully upon the rests. After a moment, she lifted one hand slightly to point to Cray's left, and only then did he realize that a second seat had risen there as silently as the first.

He sat. And then, looking at her as she waited for him to speak, he had to laugh softly. 'I can scarcely believe that I'm finally seeing you, the real you, after all these years.'

Her eyes narrowed. 'The real me.'

'Yes.' He leaned back in his chair. 'You see, some time ago, I was involved in the creation of a marvellous magical device.' In some detail, he told her of the making of the mirror, of its popularity with ordinary mortals, of its initial emptiness for him and its ultimate revelation of herself as child, youth, adult. He spoke of the frustration of being unable to find her and the triumph of identifying the gem at her throat. 'Once I knew where you lived, I couldn't stay away. I had only known you still and silent, as in a painted portrait. I had to see you move, to hear your voice. I couldn't let the mirror keep showing me a stranger for ever.'

She lifted one hand from the armrest of her chair, a languid gesture that ended at her mouth; she stroked her lower lip with one finger. 'And now that you have found me?'

He grinned. 'We will start where two strangers should, of course. I've given you my name. Perhaps now you'll tell me yours?'

She inclined her head slightly. 'I am Aliza.'

'And the name of this place?' He waved a hand to encompass the building.

'Must it have a name?'

'Most sorcerers name their homes.'

'Why?'

'Well . . .' He shrugged. 'To identify them. And to identify their inhabitants. When I introduce myself, I say I am Cray Ormoru of Spinweb, and so people know a great deal about me without my having to say more.'

'Do they?' She stroked her lower lip again. 'I have this information and it tells me nothing about you. As well call yourself X from Castle X for all it means to me.'

'Many would recognize those names,' he said. 'Spinweb and its mistress, my mother, enjoy a certain fame in the human realm.'

'Oh? As what?'

'As a place and a person of power. My mother is Delivev Ormoru, known as the Weaver. Perhaps you have heard of her tapestries. Sorcerers vie with each other to purchase them, and even kings have been known to gird up their courage and inquire about them.'

Aliza shook her head. 'Her name and work are not

known to me. But then, I pay very little attention to the human realm.'

Cray glanced about the chamber, at the bare crystalline surfaces on every side. 'This place could benefit by a few tapestries.' He envisioned one of his mother's prizes hanging nearby – perhaps a landscape of soft browns and greens, with an azure sky above, the whole lit by its own internal golden light, a sharp contrast to the bluish radiance that suffused the room. There was no sunshine in Aliza's residence; that was obvious from her pale complexion. He could bring it to her, in yarns of all sunny colours. 'I could arrange very prompt delivery.'

One of her dark eyebrows rose a trifle. 'And what would I be required to give your mother as payment for a few of these much-sought-after tapestries?'

'Nothing,' said Cray. 'They would be my gift to you.'

'You are very free with gifts to a stranger.'

'I hope we will not remain strangers.'

She gazed at him without speaking for a long moment, her cool eyes searching his face, as if she could find answers to her questions without having to ask them. At last she said, 'You believe that I am your heart's desire?'

He hesitated, then sighed softly. 'To be perfectly honest, I don't know. Feldar says the mirror never lies. Yet we've only just met. I thought . . . perhaps . . . we could be friends and let the rest go for now.'

'I have no friends,' she said.

'None?'

She shook her head. 'I have no time for friends. My life is filled up by my studies.'

He gestured toward the pendant at her throat. 'But you seem to have at least one demon.'

'A demon is a slave, not a friend.'

He shrugged. 'I suppose the two could be considered mutually exclusive. Yet a demon can be as good a friend as any mortal.'

She fingered the pendant delicately. 'I don't understand that.' Then she glanced past Cray, toward the wall where Gildrum, Elrelet, and Leemin waited. 'You consider those your friends?'

He decided to let the question of Leemin's status go for now. 'I do.'

She looked to Cray once more, to his hands, to the open collar of his shirt. 'You wear no rings that I can see, no gems. How do you command them?'

'I don't. When they help me, they do so of their own free will, for friendship's sake, not because of any sorcerous compulsion.' He leaned an elbow on the arm of his chair and rested his chin on his upraised fist. 'But you must have one friend at least – Leemin told me another mortal has been seen with you from time to time.'

'My grandfather,' said Aliza. 'I am his apprentice, and he comes here once a year to evaluate my progress.'

'Once a year? That leaves a large number of days to be accounted for. What of your parents? Do you visit them?'

'My parents died when I was a child.'

'And your other relatives . . . ?'

'I have none.'

'Ah.' Cray eased back in his crystalline seat. 'Well, many sorcerers are solitary, friendless creatures, living alone in their isolated castles. Living alone, truly, in spite of all the rings their hands can hold. I've met a number of them in my life, and it has always seemed to me that such an existence is a sad one. You're very young to be sad, my lady Aliza.'

She frowned. 'I don't know what you mean. I'm quite content the way I am. I don't wish any disturbances.'

'Yes, they often say that sort of thing. And by the time they're a century or two old, they have forgotten how to deal with other people. Sorcery has consumed them and they are no longer entirely . . . human. How unfortunate it would be if that happened to you.'

'It hardly seems unfortunate to me. I have no desire to deal with other mortals.'

Cray studied her pale, beautiful face. He saw innocence there, an innocent certainty, sheltered here in Ice, away from all outside influences. He asked her, 'Is sorcery, then . . . everything to you?'

'Yes. Of course.'

'And this is what your grandfather has taught you.'

'He had no need to teach it to me. It was obvious.'

'Was it?' Cray nodded slowly. 'I suppose it must have been, from every word he said, every gesture he made. He is trapped already in that way of life, dried up, with all capacity for human feeling lost. He has apprenticed you only because it is proper for a sorcerer to apprentice his own flesh and blood, not because he loves you and wants the best for you. It probably pains him to visit you even once a year.'

'Let it pain him then,' Aliza said coolly, 'as long as his teaching continues. I care nothing for his motives. He is a powerful sorcerer and has chosen to apprentice me, and that is all that matters.'

Cray said, 'How long has it been, Aliza, since you spoke to another human being?'

'My grandfather was here – '

'Aside from him.'

She hesitated. 'I don't recall.'

'A year? Two years?'

'Longer than that.' She looked away from him, down, long lashes veiling her eyes. 'I was five when my grandfather brought me here, and I have been here ever since. I have spoken with no other mortal but him in that time.'

'Not since you were a child?' Cray said, wonder in his voice.

'There was no need for it. My demon fed and clothed me and taught the lessons my grandfather set, and he came once a year to see how well I was doing.' She lifted her eyes to his once more, and there was defiance in them. 'Other mortals would simply have intruded on my studies.'

Softly, he said, 'As I am doing now?'

Her lips made a thin line. 'Yes, as you are doing now.' She stood abruptly. 'I don't have to justify my life to you, Cray Ormoru. And I don't have to speak to you any more.'

He gazed up at her. 'What sort of demon is it, my lady Aliza?'

Her hand went to the sapphire. 'Ice.'

He nodded. 'A good match for the life you lead. The demons of Ice thrive on solitude. They hate disturbances. But a human being is not an ice demon.' He stood, too, and as there was barely an arm's length between them, he reached out to touch her arm. Before his outstretched fingers could make contact with the velvet of her sleeve, though, a barrier sprang up between the two of them, as crystalline and transparent as the walls, the chairs, but thin as vellum. His knuckles banged against it, and he pulled his hand back in surprise. 'Are you afraid to be touched by human flesh, my lady?'

She stared at him, unblinking. 'I am afraid of nothing. I am mistress of this palace, and everything in it obeys my will. Everything.'

Cray inclined his head. 'I will obey, then, too. I would not cause you distress. But hear me, lady, and believe me. I have been a sorcerer longer than you have been alive, and I know the value of friendship. I think you need a friend.'

'I think not.'

'And I think that once you have experienced friendship, you will come to cherish it.'

'And *I* think that you had best go home and ask your mirror for another heart's desire.'

'I'm sorry if I have offended you.'

'You have not offended me,' she said. 'I simply have no

more time to spare for a visitor. As a sorcerer, you know how much study still lies ahead of me. I wish to return to it now.' She pointed past Cray's shoulder. 'You can leave at the same place where you entered. Your friends are still waiting for you there.'

'I had hoped to leave a friend behind, here.'

'I have no need of friends,' she said firmly.

He sighed. 'As you will, my lady.'

'Good-bye.'

The wall was only a few paces away. Facing it, Cray reached out to that transparent surface and, for a moment, it was hard beneath his hands; then it melted away, and he felt the cold breath of Ice on his body. He shivered and took a step, and then, straddling the boundary between Aliza's home and Ice itself, he turned and smiled one last time at her. And as he smiled, he felt himself pushed away, outward, by something hard and transparent and irresistible – the wall, resolidifying itself. He was still watching her, still smiling, when she glided out of the room and the mirrored wall sprang up behind her.

Elrelet enveloped him with warmth. 'What happened?' it whispered.

Cray let himself float in the midst of Leemin's hollow cylinder. 'It didn't go well.'

'We couldn't hear,' said Gildrum, 'but we thought the look on her face betrayed some . . . lack of enthusiasm for you.'

'Something like that,' said Cray. He folded his arms across his chest, feeling cold in spite of the demon, a deep, penetrating cold. 'It's been a strange experience, my friends. My friends.' He shook his head. 'Feldar criticized me once for seeking power for its own sake, for having nothing else in my life, and I scoffed at him. Now I see precisely that in Aliza, and it chills me more than Ice itself. What a terrible fate she's condemned herself to. And she doesn't even know that it's terrible. She doesn't have anything to compare it with.'

'Is it really so terrible,' said Gildrum, 'if she doesn't realize that it is?'

'She's hardly more than a child, Gildrum. Power is still a game to her, the novelty pulling her attention away from all else. But someday she'll be Rezhyk's age. You knew him. You were with him in the years when he cut himself off from every human influence, the years when his search for power became a mania. Was he sane, Gildrum?'

'I think not.'

'Was he happy?'

'Hardly.'

'And you were fire, Gildrum. Aliza's demon is ice.'

'Her only demon?'

'So she implied.'

'A poor choice for one who desires power.'

'A cold choice for one's only companion,' said Cray. 'Of course I mustn't forget her grandfather, who comes by once a year to say hello. Once a year! What wonderful company he must be! How much he must care for her! Oh, Gildrum, she is so terribly alone; what can she know of friendship, of warmth, of cheer?'

'Of love,' said Gildrum.

'Least of all of love.'

Gildrum sighed a very human sigh. 'Cray, she is a child of the sorcerous breed. Sorcerers are not known for their warmth.'

'My mother is warm.'

'As I've said before, your mother is an unusual lady.'

'*I* am warm.'

'Of course. You are Delivev's son.'

Cray's hands curled into fists. 'There must be something I can do to help her. She can't be lost so young.'

'And so beautiful,' Gildrum added softly. 'Seeing her, I began to understand why you had to come on the quest.

It's a shame that such beauty should remain alone and unappreciated. Certainly it can't be much appreciated by an ice demon.'

'Human beauty is meaningless to us,' said Leemin. 'And if you weren't so human yourself, fire demon, it would be equally meaningless to you.'

'It's a cold beauty, Gildrum,' said Cray. 'I think she would have pleased me more if she had been plain and smiling.' He dropped his arms to his sides. 'I would like to make her smile.'

'How?' asked Gildrum.

'I don't know. But the mirror gave her to me, and I don't intend to let her go this easily.'

'I can't say that I really liked her, Feldar,' Cray said, yawning. He had arrived tired, wanting only to lie down on the Seer's guest bed and sleep, but Sepwin had insisted upon the promised full report. 'She wasn't a very likeable person.'

'It was an awkward situation,' Sepwin said. 'You shouldn't have told her about the mirror. I mean, you were a stranger pouring out some wild tale about her being your true love. What was she supposed to do, throw herself at you?'

'I didn't mention anything about true love.'

'Heart's desire, then – is there any difference? You should have said that you were just passing through Ice when you saw her palace, and you just had to take a closer look. You might have got a little hospitality then.'

Cray leaned back in his chair and let his legs sprawl. 'I told the truth because I didn't want to have to worry about being consistent. Once you start lying, you're hedged all around by those lies.'

'You could have told her the truth later on. Now she'll be wary of you. Women don't like importunate suitors.'

'I don't see myself as an importunate suitor, Feldar. I told her I just wanted to be her friend.'

Sepwin snorted. 'You think *that's* why she threw you out?'

'I think she threw me out because it was easier than trying to traffic further with another human being.'

'Especially one saying things she didn't want to hear.'

Cray closed his eyes wearily. 'I suppose I may have been a little harsh. I suppose I may even have insulted her. But I had to say what I did, Feldar. I had to try to shake some sense into her.'

Sepwin leaned forward. 'What will you do now?'

Cray yawned again. 'Go to sleep.'

'You know what I mean!'

Cray grinned around another yawn. 'And in the morning I'll go home. Don't push so hard, Feldar. One would think this were your heart's desire rather than mine.'

Sepwin slumped back in his chair with a sigh. 'I wish you would let me help you.'

'You've already helped me enough, Feldar. Let me do the rest myself. Whatever it might be.'

'If you need me . . .'

'I know; you'll always be ready. That's what friends are for. If only I could convince Aliza of that.'

The next morning Gildrum, who had gone back to Spinweb after dropping him at the Seer's cave, came to fetch Cray home. Over breakfast, Cray told his mother all that had transpired in the crystal palace. She listened without comment, her eyes on the fruit that she pared for both of them. Only when he was quite finished did she look up at his face.

'I had hoped,' she said, 'that when you fell in love it would be with someone as kindhearted and loving as yourself. I really hadn't expected it to be one of the sorcerous race.'

He shook his head. 'I haven't fallen in love, Mother. It wasn't love that I felt when I looked at her, either in the mirror or face-to-face.'

'What was it, then?'

Elbows on the table, Cray interlaced his fingers and rested his chin on them. 'There was a certain . . . fascination, I'll admit that. For her looks, and then because of her very coolness. But it wasn't until I tried to touch her, Mother, not until that instant, that I understood that my feeling toward her was . . . pity. She is so lost, Mother; I think I must have known it early on, looking at her in the mirror. She held to that stuffed animal for so long. It was all she had. And now she seems to have nothing but that all-consuming desire for power.' His fingers tightened on each other. 'He has done this to her, the grandfather. He has doomed her to the coldest, most unfeeling life of all.'

Delivev's gaze was compassionate. 'And it pains you to think of her so.'

'Yes.'

She smiled softly. 'Don't you think that this could be a kind of love, my son?'

He let his clasped hands fall to the table, and he stared down at them. 'If it is, then it is the same love I would feel toward a fox caught in a trap or a fawn that has lost its mother.' He raised his eyes to her face. 'Don't you see, Mother, the mirror has shown her to me because I can help her. That is my heart's desire – not Aliza herself but her freedom from this trap that her grandfather has set.'

Delivev touched his hands with one of her own. 'From what you tell me, though, she doesn't even know she's in a trap. Like so many sorcerers, she has welcomed this . . . doom.'

'Then I must open her eyes,' said Cray. 'Will you help me?'

'Of course,' said his mother, 'but how?'

He caught her hand between his. 'Weave for me.'

Normally, Delivev preferred to create her tapestries in the ordinary fashion, weaving the threads with her own delicate fingers to a sketchy pattern laid out on a large square of canvas beneath her loom. She liked the feel of wool in her hands, liked the firm resistance of the treadles under her feet, liked to watch the smooth and steady increments of design growing before her. She rarely rushed a work to completion, for the activity itself was what pleased her most, not the finished product. As with her other crafts, she moved at her own leisurely pace, and even so she produced a great many beautiful things each year, more than enough to barter for every other luxury she could desire.

For this tapestry, however, she used sorcery. Cray wanted it quickly, and he also wanted it to be a duplicate of the tapestry that hung in his bedchamber, a sunny scene of the forest margin, with deer drinking at a brook. With such a detailed pattern to follow, Delivev could sit back and direct the new tapestry to weave itself while she worked on some other project. At her gesture, the white warp thread began to reel off its spool and string the loom. At another gesture, a dozen bobbins wound themselves with varicoloured yarn from as many skeins and skittered to take their places beneath the warp, each ready to add its share of weft. As the weaving commenced, Delivev took up a fresh piece of linen marked for embroidery, a cloth destined for a king's table, or perhaps just for her own, depending on her mood. Occasionally, as she worked her silken design, she looked up to examine the progress of the tapestry, to ascertain that it was going well and had no need of her interference.

The tapestry was finished long before the cloth.

Cray helped her pull it from the loom as the two raw

ends were knotting themselves. 'Beautiful,' he said, smiling at the glossy greens, the sun-drenched ochres and golds, the silver-limned sparkle of the brook. 'Perfectly beautiful.'

Delivev began to roll it from the upper end. 'As perfectly beautiful as the original.'

'It's my favourite,' said Cray. 'It will always be beautiful to me, no matter how many copies you make.'

'I hope she likes it. It doesn't strike me as the sort of thing an inhabitant of Ice would want, though. I wonder if you wouldn't please her more with something familiar, an ice demon perhaps. They're very pretty in their star-like form.'

'And she can see one any time she likes. I prefer the idea of contrast.' He helped her tie the bundle securely with three broad ribbons. 'Is Gildrum ready?'

'Gildrum and Elrelet both. They're in the kitchen. I'll call them.' But she hesitated a moment and, looking into her son's face, raised one hand to his cheek. 'Good luck,' she said, and she kissed him softly at the corner of his mouth. 'Very good luck.'

Leemin was waiting for them once more at the boundary of Air and Ice. 'You are a most persistent creature, Cray Ormoru,' it said. 'You admit that the woman told you to go away, and yet you wish to return.'

'She didn't really want me to go away,' Cray said. Elrelet had already enveloped him, and the tapestry floated an arm's length away from him, under Gildrum's care. 'I was making her uncomfortable, and she had no other way to deal with that discomfort.'

'And now you go to make her uncomfortable again.'

'I hope not. You told Elrelet you were willing to guide us again.'

'Yes,' said Leemin. 'I am a trifle curious to know if she will let you in once more.'

'As I am. Lead on then.'

The fracture opened for them as before, and they entered. And this time the journey was shorter, for the Old One was gone and they could take the route that passed its residence. Soon they saw the light from Aliza's home spilling into Ice all about them, and then they reached her walls.

'Shall we ring the bell again?' asked Elrelet.

'I didn't bring it along,' said Gildrum, 'in deference to our guide.'

'Then how shall we attract her attention?' wondered the air demon.

'I was thinking that Leemin could form me a hammer of its own substance,' said Cray, 'and that I could pound on this wall hard enough with that to be heard inside.'

'Very well,' said Leemin, and immediately an icicle erupted from its cylindrical body almost at Cray's feet and grew quickly into a long-handled sledgehammer as transparent as the finest glass. It broke free of the demon's flesh and floated to Cray's hands.

'I didn't expect anything so formidable,' he said, 'but it will do.' Bracing himself with widespread legs and taking a short grip on the handle, he tapped experimentally at the wall before him. The sound of the blow was an unimpressive clack, as if he had tossed a pebble at one of Spinweb's stone ramparts. There was none of the hollowness he had expected. He tapped again, a little harder, then much harder, and the results were only marginally louder. Then he waited. But the room beyond the wall remained empty.

Elrelet said, 'The sound doesn't seem to carry very far. We would have been much better off with the bell.'

'No bells!' cried Leemin.

'Yes, yes, we know,' said the air demon. 'Still, here we are, stymied. Gildrum, don't you think you could find a bell that could be heard inside this building without driving our icy friend into a frenzy?'

73

'I don't know,' said Gildrum. 'I hesitate to try another one. Perhaps . . . we should just leave the tapestry here with a letter saying you'll be back later and asking her to provide you some way to signal your arrival. A special door knocker or some such. Leemin could open this fracture a bit wider and we could spread the tapestry out against the wall so that it would be pinned there when we withdrew. She'd be certain to see it next time she came to this chamber.'

'Whenever that might be,' said Cray. He shook his head. 'No, I'd rather give it to her personally. Now.'

'But how?'

'Well, I can only think of one other thing to try.' He took a deep breath, and in his battle voice, he shouted her name: *'Aliza!'* It was a high-pitched, piercing cry, almost musical in quality, its timbre quite unlike his ordinary speaking voice. He had learned to use the battle voice during his training for knighthood, the training he had given up for sorcery; it was the voice that a commander needed to be heard by his warriors above the din of steel on steel, of screaming men and screaming horses. Not every man could manage it. Now, after so many years of the sorcerous arts, most of Cray's old knights' skills had faded, but he still had the voice. He used it a second time. *'Aliza!'*

Leemin broke the long silence that followed. 'She might have heard that. I never knew a human voice could be so . . . penetrating.'

'If she did hear,' said Elrelet, 'she isn't making any sign. I say bash away with the hammer again; batter a hole in this wall and go on inside. I'll help you.'

'I don't think it's possible,' said Gildrum. 'She may be only an apprentice, but the spell on this wall seems strong enough to keep out any demon. And any demon hammer.'

'Then let's go back to the human realm and fetch something made of steel.'

Cray laid his demon-gloved hands flat against the glassy wall. The chamber beyond seemed terribly empty, and quite unfamiliar in its barrenness, even though he knew he had walked about within it. The chairs that Aliza had summoned for the two of them were gone, the floor where they had sprung up clear and seamless, the far wall faintly reflecting Cray's own face.

'Her demon, at least, ought to know someone is out here calling her name,' Cray muttered.

'Perhaps she's away from home,' offered Leemin.

'I don't think she's away very often. Travel would interfere with her studies.' He made fists of his hands and pounded on the transparency of the wall, but softly, in frustration rather than any attempt to make a noise. 'Aliza,' he whispered. 'Hear me.'

After a long moment, he sighed heavily. 'You know, I thought . . . she might be watching for me. Just in case I came back.'

'But she threw you out,' said Leemin.

'Even so. I was a novelty; I thought that when she had a chance to reflect, after I had gone, that she would realize my novelty hadn't worn off yet. Or so I flattered myself.' He turned and caught at the bundle that was the tapestry, tugged at the ribbon fastenings. 'Now Gildrum's plan seems best to me.' He stripped the bindings away and began to unroll the bulky load. 'Help me spread this out, Gildrum?'

The demon assumed his human guise and grasped the side opposite Cray. Between them, they plastered the tapestry against Aliza's wall. But as Leemin was expanding the fracture to accommodate its corners, Gildrum reached out to tug at Cray's arm.

'There she is,' he said. He was looking through the gap between the straight edge of the tapestry and Leemin's curve.

Cray peered through the gap on his side and saw her. She

75

stood where the mirrored barrier had been, and she gazed directly at the tunnel in Ice. As she slowly walked closer, he realized that her eyes were focused on the tapestry rather than on either of the human faces beside it. She halted very near it, nearer than the two crystalline chairs had been to each other, and she looked from one part of it to another and back again. Only when she had examined it with the greatest attention did her gaze slide past its edge and fasten on Cray's face. Standing there, she seemed to scrutinize his smile as closely as she had his mother's handiwork.

A small circle of the wall, a space not much larger than his hand, opened before him. Through that, he could hear her voice, though it sounded thin and distant.

'You called my name,' she said.

'I brought you a gift, as I said I would.'

She glanced at the tapestry again, her eyes shuttling back and forth across it. 'There was no need.'

'I'm sure you'll recall that I thought there was. Do you like it?'

She considered the question for a long moment, then answered, 'It is very well executed.'

'I think it is very beautiful. My mother hopes you'll like it. She made it especially for you.'

Aliza frowned a trifle. 'She doesn't even know me.'

'I told her about you. I told her that you were beautiful and that you should be surrounded by beauty.'

She studied the tapestry yet again. 'The colours are very interesting,' she said at last.

'Take it,' said Cray. 'It's yours.'

She shook her head. 'You don't owe me any gifts.'

'One cannot *owe* a gift. It must be given freely or else it's not a gift but a payment.'

'But what shall I do with it?'

'Hang it on a wall, of course. Your home is so large, it must have plenty of walls.' He slipped four fingers through the circular hole and gripped its rim; he felt

Elrelet's substance peel away from those fingers like rind from a fruit, exposing them to the chill breath of Ice as it passed through the aperture. 'I'd be glad to help you find an appropriate place for it.'

'Ah,' she said. 'You want to come in.'

'I wouldn't be here if I didn't want to come in and talk to you again. Perhaps I could help you with your studies. After all, I've been a sorcerer myself for quite a few years.'

She stared at him. 'You would help me with my studies? Of your own free will?'

He nodded. 'Why not?'

'You would reveal the nature of your skills to me?'

'Again, why not?'

'Aren't you afraid I might use them against you?'

'No more than I'm afraid you'll use your own skills against me,' he said. 'I'm a reasonably likeable fellow, and I generally try to live in such a way that I don't incur the anger of other people. I certainly have no desire to incur yours.' He brought his other hand up to join the first at the gap in the wall; it was a supplicating gesture. 'Won't you let me see the interior of your magnificent palace? Won't you let me try to divert you for just a short time? You can always throw me out if you find me boring.'

For a moment, she looked at the tapestry once more, then turned her gaze back on him, cool and remote. 'I understand from my demon that you have journeyed here from the boundary of Ice with Air.'

'That is true, my lady.'

'It is a long way.'

'That, too, is true.'

'What will you do if I turn you away right now?'

'Come back another time, with another gift. The length of the journey means nothing to me, my lady. I would travel twice as far to see you.'

'Why are you so persistent?' she said, and there was wonder in her voice rather than annoyance.

He felt a pang of pity for her wonder, for her innocence, for her ignorance. 'The sorcerous breed is a lonely one, my lady Aliza,' he said softly. 'Even I, who have more friends than most, have need of every new friend I can find. I think if you knew what friendship was like, you would not scorn it so.'

'Friendship,' she said, and Cray thought he heard more than a touch of scorn in her cool inflections. 'You come here as a friend, and yet this visit would keep me from my studies.'

Cray smiled sadly. 'A few brief hours, perhaps. In the long run, will such a little time really make any difference to your skills? I think you exaggerate its effect, Aliza, because you are . . . afraid.'

Her shoulders straightened fractionally. 'I am afraid of nothing.'

'You are afraid of me and of what I represent.'

'And what do you represent?'

'The outside. Everything that does not lie within the compass of this crystal palace of yours. The human realm and everything in it.' He felt Gildrum's hand, hidden from Aliza by the tapestry, touch his shoulder, and he knew that it was meant as a warning, but he ignored it. He had no other path to follow; he had opened this one and could not turn back. 'But you are human, Aliza. You are not made of Ice. You must believe me when I tell you that the human realm is worth knowing, worth being a part of.'

She pursed her lips. 'And letting you . . . be my friend . . . would be a way of knowing the human realm, would it?'

'It would be a start.' His smile broadened. 'And look – you don't even have to leave your home to do it; I've come to you.'

'I am not afraid of you.'

'I wish that were true, because then you would let me in and we could sit together and talk comfortably over a glass of wine instead of like this, as if one of us were a prisoner and the other come to pass messages through the bars. Which one of us would you say is the prisoner, Aliza?'

'If I let you in,' she said, 'you would be the prisoner. Your demon friends would never be able to get you out unless I wished it.'

'I trust you,' he said.

'If I really became tired of you, I could seal you up in one of these rooms and leave you there. You would starve to death. Then you wouldn't bother me any longer.'

'Well . . . I do have some sorcery of my own that does not depend on demons. I suspect that it might get me out if absolutely necessary. But I would hope that I might never need it.'

She stood silent, her eyes focused first on him and then on the tapestry, back and forth, back and forth, as if she were weighing one against the other. Her cool expression was tinged with wariness. She backed up one step and then another. 'Very well,' she said at last. 'A glass of wine.'

The transparent wall melted away under his hands and, caught unprepared once again, he pitched forward to the hard floor of the chamber, Elrelet peeling from his flesh like wet clothing. The tapestry collapsed with him, tangling him in its suddenly heavy folds. By the time he climbed to his feet, the wall was solid again, his three companions sealed away on the other side.

'I see you brought a mortal friend along this time,' Aliza said, gesturing toward the demons. 'I hope you had no intention of asking me to let *him* in as well.'

Cray glanced back to the wall. 'That's Gildrum,' he told her. 'You saw him before as a ball of light.'

'A demon? With a human form?'

'Gildrum has a number of human forms. And animal ones.'

'Indeed?' said Aliza. 'And how is that possible?'

Cray grinned. 'I see I most certainly have something to teach you, my lady. You didn't know that a demon master may give his slaves whatever forms he can make with his own two hands?'

'How do you mean . . . *make*?'

'I mean carve or chip or mould. Clay is used most commonly, but snow or ice or even stone will do. I gather you've never tried it.'

'My demon has not yet taught me this art,' she said. 'And I can't recall that I've ever needed it.'

Cray shrugged. 'It can be useful, especially in dealing with ordinary mortals. They have less fear of a familiar form. Of course, if one wishes to inspire fear in them, that is not an advantage.' He looked into her cool dark eyes. 'Do you wish to inspire fear, my lady?'

'I do not concern myself with ordinary mortals,' she replied. 'Let them fear me or not, as long as they leave me alone.' She turned from him then and strode briskly toward the inner chamber. 'Come, Cray Ormoru. You asked for a glass of wine and conversation, and I can think of a dozen places in my palace more comfortable for both than here.' She paused and glanced back at him. 'Unless you would prefer to stay where your friends can see you.'

Cray bent over the tapestry and began to roll it. 'If you'll wait a moment till I gather this up, I'll follow wherever you wish.' He tied the ribbons securely and hoisted the unwieldy bundle to one shoulder.

'You needn't carry it,' said Aliza. She made a small gesture toward the floor, and a section near her feet rose up as a slender pillar, sprouted two glassy arms, broke free of the floor with two glassy legs, and marched stiffly to Cray, holding its arms out for his burden.

'This floor is very versatile,' Cray murmured, giving the tapestry over to the creature.

'This is my home,' said Aliza. 'It obeys my will. Perhaps you would be wise to remember that.'

'Oh, I shall. I shall.'

The crystalline creature followed behind them as they moved farther into the palace.

At first glance, the inner chamber seemed much like the one Cray already knew. It had a level floor, and it was walled by a multitude of planes that rose at varying angles to that floor and to each other. Some of these walls soared upwards smoothly, joining a vaulting, faceted ceiling high above Cray's head; others, especially those that slanted sharply outwards at their bases, were cut off by more vertical planes, some of them more than once, and so reached the ceiling in a series of short, angled spans. Light emanated from every horizontal surface, filling the room with the same blue-tinged radiance that spilled out into Ice.

In this chamber, however, there was no mirror-bred illusion of crystalline depths beyond those walls. There was, instead, the reality. Behind Cray, Ice was still visible, and before him, Aliza's palace spread out in all its glinting, gem-like splendour. He felt as though he were walking through the heart of a diamond. Plane upon plane was visible ahead, uncountable facets creating a maze-like space that stretched up, down, right, left. In the kaleidoscope of angles, he saw walls that bent so obliquely they could as easily have been called slanted floors, ceilings that could have been tilted walls, floors that were ceilings for rooms below his feet, and ceilings that were floors for rooms above his head. And here and there were stairways, clear as finest glass, embedded among the facets. On the far side of the chamber was such a stairway, cut into an uptilting section of floor, climbing to a gap where a wall should have been. Aliza mounted these steps, Cray close behind her, and they entered another chamber. This one had four stairways, each leading up or down to another room; Aliza chose the nearest, a right turn.

As they walked, and as his eyes became accustomed to perceiving the boundaries of a room by the reflections in its crystalline walls, Cray noted that the rooms were becoming steadily smaller. The outer one, where he had entered the palace, was larger than any in Spinweb, the size of a king's audience chamber. The one inside that had been perceptibly smaller, though still grand enough for any royal banquet. The next, however, was on a lesser scale, the next still more so, and the one beyond that could have served as Cray's own workroom. It was this room that was the first he found to be furnished.

The furnishings were sparse and betrayed the fact that this palace had only one occupant. In the very centre of the room, in the very centre of a thick grey carpet, stood a low ebony table broader than a man's reach, its polished surface reflecting the light overhead. Beyond the table stood a well-padded couch upholstered in grey silk brocade and long enough to lie down upon. Beside the couch stood a waist-high ebony cabinet. The rest of the room was empty.

'Sit down,' Aliza said, indicating the end of the couch farthest from the cabinet. While Cray settled himself there, she opened the cabinet's double doors and brought out a tall crystal decanter half full of a deep, translucent red fluid. There was a goblet behind it, just one, but she stooped, and a second goblet, identical to the first, thrust up from the floor and into her hand. She set both of them on the table and filled them from the decanter.

Cray took the nearer goblet. The wine was light, pleasantly tart, and refreshing. As he sipped it, he surveyed the bare, faceted walls all around him. 'This room would be a fine place for the tapestry,' he said. The crystalline servant had stopped at the doorway and now stood there motionless, the tapestry upon its outstretched arms. 'The colours would relieve the severity of grey and black.'

'Very well,' said Aliza.

'I'll help you hang it, if you like.'

'No need.' She waved, and a second crystalline automaton sprouted from the floor. Between them, the two creatures unrolled the tapestry and held it up against a vertical section of wall. 'Higher,' said Aliza, and the creatures' arms and legs elongated until they could raise the tapestry higher than a man could reach. 'Yes, there.' A row of transparent hooks thrust out from the wall then, each hook catching one of the loops at the top edge of the tapestry, supporting it. When the automata released their burden, it hung straight and close against the crystalline wall.

Cray had to admit, though not aloud, that it looked a trifle peculiar, a multicoloured blotch upon the clarity of Aliza's palace. Yet, off in a slightly different direction, the one opposite the entrance they had used to this room, there were many blotches, most of them dark; he supposed them to be furnishings, though their exact nature was impossible to make out because of distance and intervening walls. He guessed that the area in which they were most concentrated was the heart of the palace, Aliza's bedchamber, her kitchen, her workroom. She had not chosen to take a stranger there.

He smiled at her. 'I hope you will think of me every time you look at this tapestry.'

'I don't believe I shall be able to avoid that,' she said.

'Do you spend a lot of time in this room?'

'Some. When I feel like drinking a little wine and thinking. The table is useful for spreading out a great many things and looking at them all at once. The couch is comfortable.'

'That it is.' He leaned back against the end of the couch and hooked his free arm over it. 'And as fine a piece of furniture as I've ever seen. Was it perhaps made by one of the artisans in Covrin Town? The style seems something like theirs.'

'I wouldn't know,' said Aliza. 'Whenever I need furniture, my demon brings it.'

'Your demon has been lax, then, judging from all those empty rooms I saw.'

She sipped from her goblet. 'There's little point in furnishing those rooms. I never use them.'

'Oh? Then why did you have them built? I know you did – Leemin told me the palace was much smaller when you were a child.'

Aliza inclined her head slightly. 'Leemin was quite correct. In fact, when I first came to live here, the entire palace consisted of just one small room. But that room was the seed crystal of the building. Before a year had passed, a second chamber had budded off from it, and after that a new one was completed every few months, each larger than the last. Only lately, since the rooms have become so very large, has the rate of growth slowed. But the nature of the place itself is to be ever growing. I have no control over it. Not yet, anyway.'

'But how did it begin?' Cray wondered.

'My demon constructed that first room from the substance of Ice and set the spell.'

'The same demon that serves you with food and clothing and furniture? That teaches you sorcery?'

'The same.'

'You have only the one, then.'

'I need no more.'

'It must be a very powerful creature.'

She shrugged a shoulder. 'It has enough power for my purposes. I value its knowledge more than its power.'

Cray held his glass up, turned it in his fingers. 'Yes, you prefer to manipulate the world around you directly rather than depend upon a demon to do it for you.'

She nodded.

'That's a preference I share,' he said.

'Oh? I thought your demon friends did your bidding.'

'No. Occasionally they give me a little help, but my sorcery does not require them.'

She crossed one leg over the other and balanced her goblet on the upraised knee. 'And what kind of sorcery is it that you practise, Cray Ormoru?'

'Various kinds, my lady. I learned from more than one master, and I've also devised a certain amount on my own. I work with metals, but I also work with living things. I have made golden flowers grow on a tree and trees grow where I wished. And I have a degree of power over cloths and yarns as well. For instance, I could make that tapestry unweave itself and reweave in some fresh pattern – though I fear I haven't the talent to create one as pleasant as that. Or I could make this carpet fall apart, or crawl about the room, or stand up and bow. Perhaps you would be interested in a small demonstration of what can be done with just a simple shirt . . . ?' He plucked at his own collar while gazing at her inquiringly.

'Go ahead,' she said.

Setting his goblet on the table, he stripped off the shirt and tossed it to the centre of that broad ebony expanse, where it lay in a limp heap. With the slightest movement of one finger, he made the shirt rise on its sleeves as on a pair of legs and walk toward Aliza. In front of her, it bent at newly defined knees and knelt, the body of the shirt leaning forwards like a human torso, in a deep bow. Then it stood once more.

'I can animate an entire suit of clothes this way, and with buskins on the feet and a hood or a scarf where the head should be, no one would be able to tell, at a glance, that it was not a human being.'

Aliza reached out to touch the creature, to wrap her fingers about one of those hollow limbs and squeeze.

85

Instead of crushing in her grip, the sleeve stood as solid as if an invisible arm were filling it. 'So these are the kinds of servants you have in Spinweb,' she said.

Cray nodded.

'Yet . . . you seem to know a great deal about demons. If your sorcery does not require them, how did you happen to meet the ones you call your friends?'

The shirt walked back to Cray and collapsed into a pile that looked as though it had never been animate. He slipped it back on. 'I was apprenticed to a demon master once, and Gildrum belonged to him. Working together for a number of years, we became very close. He was just like another human being, and warmer than some I had known. Through him, I met Elrelet and Leemin.'

'Then Gildrum is a slave,' said Aliza. 'Doesn't that make your friendship somewhat . . . difficult? I mean, what if you and the demon were doing something together and its master called it? It would have to go, perhaps leaving you in an uncomfortable situation, or even a dangerous one.'

'Gildrum's old master is dead,' said Cray, 'and he is free.'

'*He.*'

'Yes, I think of Gildrum as *he*. He wears a human form most of the time these days. In fact, he lives at Spinweb that way.'

'Lives at Spinweb?'

'Yes. My mother and I consider him part of our family.'

'Oh,' said Aliza. She fingered her wine goblet thoughtfully. 'And the other two? Are they free as well?'

'Yes.'

'But they could be enslaved at any time, any or all of the three. Perhaps even while you are here in Ice. How would you get home if all three were snatched away from you? It seems a precarious sort of relationship to me, this friendship with demons.'

Cray grinned at her. 'Are you planning on a bit of ring

making while I'm here? I thought you didn't need any more demons.'

'Not I. But one can never tell what other sorcerers may be doing.'

He picked up his goblet and drank from it, then eyed her over the rim. 'Perhaps you're thinking of telling your grandfather their names so that he can try to claim them.'

She shook her head. 'Why should I do that? He has plenty of demons, and plenty of power to conjure as many more as he likes. He needs no help from me. But I was thinking of the foolishness of depending upon creatures that could be taken away and even used against you by some enemy. That would be an ironic reversal, would it not – your friends forced to harm you?'

'It would if it were possible,' he said. 'But in this case it is not. Neither Gildrum nor Elrelet nor Leemin can ever be enslaved again. I have seen to it.'

'Ah . . . you are more cautious than I thought.'

Cray emptied his goblet, then set it down. 'I don't call it caution. But if you like, you can view it that way.'

'How do you view it?'

He looked at her speculatively. He could not tell her the whole truth; no mortal stranger could be trusted with that. But he thought he could offer her a small piece of it. 'While Gildrum was still a slave,' he told her, 'he met my mother and fell in love with her, and she with him. He wanted to be with her, of course, but as you so rightly pointed out, a slave has no control over his own life. And Gildrum's master kept him very busy. But after that master died, Gildrum was able to go to her, and I didn't want him to be taken away ever again. So I set him free.'

'For which he owes you a great deal.'

'He owes me nothing,' Cray said firmly. 'He has made my mother very happy.'

'And the other two?' asked Aliza.

87

'I didn't wish to see my friends forced to do a master's bidding. Would you wish to be a slave?'

Her lips curved in a cool smile, the first smile he had seen upon her face. 'I have been an apprentice,' she said. 'Is that so very different?'

He laughed, more at seeing her smile than at her words. 'That depends on what sort of apprenticeship it is. Mine with the demon master was indeed little better than slavery in some respects. I did quite a lot of scrubbing and cleaning for him.'

'And you had to study your lessons or face his anger. You couldn't stop to follow your own fancies.'

'Well, I could have, but he probably would have thrown me out.'

'For the time you were his apprentice, your life belonged to him,' said Aliza, her expression serious once more, as if the smile had never touched it. 'He taught you sorcery. He could as easily have taught you to conjure up your own death as to summon a demon. How would you have known the difference? You were in his power completely.'

'Yes,' Cray admitted. 'But only for a handful of years. Apprenticeship does end. Slavery can go on for centuries.'

'A demon's life is far longer than that.'

'Yet demons feel the passage of time just as we do.'

Aliza gazed down into her goblet, where only a swallow or two of wine remained. For a moment she appeared to be contemplating that clear red fluid, and then she said, 'Have you known many demons?'

'My master had quite a number of them.'

'Of all four kinds?'

'No, just fire demons. But through Gildrum I have met some of the others as well.'

'You think you understand them?'

'In a small way, yes. They are not really so different from mortals.'

She raised her eyes to his, her cool, dark eyes. 'I know only one demon. It serves me swiftly and without complaint. It instructs me in sorcery and answers my questions. But it has no desires, no fears, no . . . individuality. It is not a *person*. It is as inhuman as the crystalline creatures that hung your tapestry. I cannot conceive of a demon that is any more than that. Are the demons of Fire and Air and Water so different from those of Ice?'

'They vary,' said Cray, 'both individually and from one kind to another. The demons of Fire tend to be the most sensitive, or at least they show their feelings more than the others. Air demons are more lighthearted, gregarious, and talkative. Water demons are solemn and serious, almost pompous. And ice demons – well, you described yours as inhuman, and I suppose that is close enough. They are aloof, cold, and solitary. And in some ways they hate slavery more than all the others – because it is such an intrusion on their privacy.'

'My demon does not appear to be capable of hatred. It has no more emotion than this goblet.' She held it up.

Cray shrugged. 'It's a cold sort of hatred, my lady, but hatred nonetheless. Ice demons do not display their emotions. But they like freedom as well as the others do. Leemin was certainly willing to accept my offer of it.'

'Leemin is only one demon.'

'I've heard the same from more than one of them.' He leaned toward her. 'Can you really imagine that they accept slavery willingly? Why, a demon slave doesn't even receive the benefits that a human slave would. A demon has no need for food or shelter or clothing or protection from wild animals. A demon receives absolutely nothing of value in return for its services. Unless you consider the absence of punishment by its master to be some sort of gain.' He shook his head. 'I wouldn't want to *be* either kind of slave, and so I can't keep either kind. I wouldn't be able to sleep at night, knowing I held thinking, feeling creatures prisoner. And so I practise a variety of sorcery that does not call for them.'

She shifted her posture on the couch, as if all her muscles had become stiff through long sitting. She drained her goblet and set it on the table. 'More wine?' she said.

'Yes, thank you. It's very good.' He watched her fill both vessels. 'Where does it come from?'

'A place called Maretia.'

'I don't recognize the name. Where does it lie?'

'I wouldn't know. My demon fetches the wine.'

'Ah. Of course.' He raised his goblet to his lips. Over its rim, he could see that she was studying him as he drank – studying him as if he were some strange and wonderful creature, not simply another mortal. Cray could not remember ever studying another human being so intently. Perhaps he would do the same, he thought, if he had seen only one other – and that one infrequently – since he was five years old.

Finally, she said, 'How can you compare demons to yourself, Cray Ormoru? You are as unlike my demon as I can imagine.'

He smiled at her. 'Their concerns are, generally, not the same as ours. But that doesn't mean I can't feel for them. Perhaps because I've known Gildrum so well, demons don't seem strange and inexplicable to me. No more so than other human beings, at any rate. Some of *them*, in fact, seem somewhat more strange and inexplicable.'

Her eyes narrowed. 'Are you perhaps speaking of me?'

'No, my lady, no. I don't think you're inexplicable. I think you have lived so long with an ice demon as your only companion that you have come to resemble it somewhat. That doesn't seem strange at all.'

'I? An ice demon?'

'I meant no insult in the comparison, my lady. I simply meant that you are cool-tempered and aloof and you wish to be left alone. You wish freedom from all encumbrances.'

She lowered her gaze. 'My demon has never asked for freedom.'

'They rarely ask,' said Cray. 'They know what the answer would be.' He held his goblet up and contemplated the translucent colour of the contents. 'How would you get wine, after all, without a demon?'

'I could compel mortals to bring it to me.'

'Another kind of slavery.'

She looked up at him defiantly. 'And how would you propose I do it?'

He sipped his wine before answering, savoured it. Maretia, he thought – he would have to remember that name. 'You could barter for it, as my mother barters for things she cannot make. A goblet like this . . .' He turned it in his hands. 'A goblet like this, so finely crafted, so clear and perfect, would be worth a great deal at any king's castle. Or didn't you realize that?'

'No,' she said. 'I didn't.'

'With your powers, you could make any number of beautiful things and trade them for everything you need. A demon would be quite superfluous.'

She frowned. 'But I need the demon anyway. It is my tutor.'

'Your apprenticeship will end someday. Perhaps you might think of letting it go then.'

'Letting it go?' She clutched at the pendant. 'I've had it for such a short time.'

Puzzled, Cray said, 'Surely you don't consider the greater part of your life to be such a short time.'

She shook her head. 'It belonged to my grandfather until last year. He commanded it. He dictated exactly what it would teach me, what it would feed me, how it would clothe me. I could ask, but he was the one that decided whether I would receive or not. But a year ago he gave it to me, and now I am the demon master. But a year *is* a short time.'

'I was a demon master for far less than that,' said Cray.

'I am not you,' she said in a clear, strong voice. 'And my demon is not your Gildrum. Perhaps *he* did care about his freedom. Perhaps, for the sake of your friendship, you did set him free. But my demon and I are not friends; we are master and slave. And as long as it remains useful to me, we shall remain so.'

Yes, he thought. *You are very like an ice demon. Cooltempered and aloof and quite self-centred.*

He inclined his head. 'I would not presume, my lady, to dictate how you should use your powers. The demon is indeed yours, for as long as you wish. Such is the meaning of that gem.'

She let it go abruptly, as if it were hot. 'I worked long and hard at my studies to win this prize. I value it.'

'I'm sure you do.' Cray's eyes focused on the pendant. The narrow silvery band about the gem would be inscribed on its inner surface with the demon's name. White gold, he thought; white gold for an ice demon. 'It is unusual for one sorcerer to give a demon to another. Even parent to child or master to apprentice. Knowing that, I would have guessed your demon to be of little value, young, weak . . . except that it built this palace.' His gaze swept the crystalline walls, the light-drenched ceiling, and he wondered how many rooms lay beyond them, wondered if Aliza even knew, or if she had stopped counting long since. 'Ice demons are not generally valued for their constructive talents. They can make ice and pile blocks of it into any structure a sorcerer might want, but in the human realm, a palace of ice would be a poor dwelling at best. It would have to be maintained through the warm weather, which would surely keep more than one ice demon too busy for any other work. And all year

92

round it would be unpleasantly cold, forcing its master to walk about muffled up in furs; he wouldn't dare light any but the smallest fire, or else his own walls would drip on him.' Cray waved to encompass the room and the entire building. 'Yet here in Ice you seem to have found solutions to all these problems. The walls are solid and dry, and yet the air is comfortably warm. How is that managed?'

Aliza lifted her goblet. 'Is this made of ice?'

Cray considered his own. It was cool to the touch, but not too cool, and smooth as fine glass. 'No. If it were ice, the heat of my hand would start melting it.'

'But it is,' said Aliza. 'It and the whole of this palace are made of the substance of Ice itself, but purified and transformed, just as the ice demons themselves are. You could never melt an ice demon with the heat of your hand, or even with a charcoal fire.'

Cray turned the goblet slowly. 'But how could frozen water become something like this?'

'The world of Ice is far more complex than mere frozen water. It contains many substances, and they can be drawn out individually at need, by one who knows the proper methods.'

'And you know the proper methods?'

She inclined her head. 'I am studying them, among other things. Someday, I shall be able to direct the growth of this building rather than merely watch it grow at its own random whim. I shall be able to obtain any materials I wish directly from Ice itself rather than from the substance of my palace. I shall be able to construct anything I like in Ice, even to reorganize its very structure.'

'Those are high goals indeed,' said Cray.

'Not too high for me.'

'You will be able to manipulate Ice as an ice demon could.'

'Better,' said Aliza.

Cray wondered if she understood where she aimed. She said she needed only one demon slave, yet if she gained so much power over Ice itself, she would have effective command of all of them. Their entire world would be her hostage. And no sorcery of his could set them free. The only way to do that would be . . . to kill her.

He found himself frowning mightily, and he drank a deep draught of his wine to hide the expression from her. When he lowered the goblet at last, he had fixed a smile on his face, and though it felt unreal to him, he thought she would probably not be able to perceive that. 'All of this from one demon,' he murmured.

'The proper sort of demon,' she said. 'An old and experienced one, a powerful one. Not weak at all, you see.'

'I see.'

'It tells me I have much talent for this kind of study.'

'And, of course, all the perseverance necessary.'

'Of course.'

'I think . . . I would like to meet this demon,' Cray said, 'if you have no objection.'

She raised an eyebrow inquiringly. 'Do you want to become its friend?'

'I don't think that being on good terms with such a powerful creature would be a bad thing . . . but no – I am merely curious to meet your only companion. Perhaps then I will understand you better.'

'You could understand me as well – whatever that may mean – from meeting one of my crystalline servants as from meeting my demon,' she said.

Cray shrugged. 'Still, if you don't mind . . .'

She pursed her lips and looked down into her goblet. 'You call it my companion, but it is not. It's more like a piece of furniture than anything you could carry on a conversation with. It tells me my lessons and it answers questions, but it's really quite boring. I've had a stuffed animal that was less boring, believe me.'

'A small grey one, wasn't it?' said Cray.

She looked up at him sharply. 'How did you know?'

'I saw it in the mirror. I thought . . . I might even see it here.'

Her brow wrinkled slightly. 'It's with my toys, of course. My childhood toys. I'm a bit old for stuffed animals, don't you think?'

He felt his stiff smile soften as he watched that small frown play across her face. All at once he realized that she was very young, not so much in years as in experience. At her age he had already travelled far, he had known triumph and disappointment, he had even killed a man. But Aliza had been locked in Ice nearly all her life, and her dignity was affronted by the suggestion that she might still be carrying a stuffed animal about with her. Whatever she might wish to become, she was still really only a child. A child whose future was not a certainty, not at all.

He said, 'I see nothing wrong with a stuffed animal as a pet. It would be clean and undemanding. You ought to have a pet of some sort, for your softer side. You are surrounded by so much that is hard, that needs to be compensated for. Your grandfather should have given you a pet.'

'What – a cat, or a caged bird?'

'Something of the sort.'

She shook her head. 'I have no time to care for a pet.'

'I had a pony,' Cray said. 'And, of course, my mother kept spiders and snakes and birds. They were all good companions for a growing child. But a stuffed animal is a better companion than none at all. And as I still keep my living pets in Spinweb, so I would not have been surprised or dismayed to see that you still had your kind.' He hesitated just an instant before adding, 'Was it your grandfather that told you such things were not suitable for an adult?'

Aliza sighed faintly and then nodded. 'Often. As I grew

older, I would hide it whenever he visited, but he always knew that I still carried it. The demon told him, of course. Eventually, though, I was able to give it up. It was a part of my childhood, after all, and one *must* give up childhood sometime. He was pleased by that. He respected me more afterwards.'

'He would rather see you with an ice demon, wouldn't he?'

'He would rather see me stand on my own two feet than lean on the imaginary support of a stuffed animal.'

'He has forgotten, I suppose, that he must have had a stuffed animal of his own, once. And parents, too, probably till he was older than five.'

'On the contrary,' said Aliza. 'He was apprenticed young, and he grew strong from it. And he wants the same strength for me.'

Cray finished his wine at one swallow and held his goblet out to her. 'If you fill this again, you'll have emptied the decanter and will have to call for another. Your demon could bring one, unless you insist on keeping it away from me.'

She poured another serving of wine for him, and it did very nearly empty the decanter. 'Why should I keep it away from you?' she said.

'Because you're afraid that I *will* make a friend of it. You've seen three of my demon friends, one of them ice, and you think that perhaps somehow I could win its loyalty.'

'Nonsense. I command it, and it must obey.'

'But you suspect that some small part of its devotion might turn to me, and you don't want to chance that.'

'What difference would that make? It would still be my slave.'

'Then don't be afraid to let me meet it.'

'You'll be disappointed,' she said.

'I am no stranger to disappointment.'

She leaned back against her end of the couch. 'Very well. You shall have your wish.' Her voice rose slightly in pitch. 'Come, Regneniel!'

The creature that answered this summons arrived so silently that Cray was not aware of its presence until it was passing behind him on its way to Aliza's side. He saw it then, out of the corner of his eye. An awkward, spindly-looking thing, it walked on two thin legs, and the snaky neck that sprouted from its tiny body swayed with its steps like a fern in a summer breeze. A beaked head at the end of that neck and diminutive arms at equal intervals about the body completed its anatomy. It was very ugly, Cray decided, in spite of the singular beauty of its actual substance, which looked like gleaming milk glass.

'Well, here it is,' Aliza said, gesturing toward the demon.

'Greetings . . . Regneniel,' said Cray.

The demon made no reply.

'It does speak?' Cray said to Aliza.

'Yes, but not frivolously. If you wish to hear its voice, ask it a question.'

To the demon, Cray said, 'Is your form one a previous master gave you, and if so, were you ever given others?'

The demon still made no reply.

'This is not a very successful conversation,' Cray said.

Aliza turned to the demon. 'Regneniel, answer his questions unless I bid you keep silent.'

In a deep and resonant masculine voice, the demon said, 'As you wish, my lady. O mortal, this is my true earthly form, that I was forced to take when I was first conjured. I also have two forms given me by a previous master.'

Aliza said, 'What, demon? Why have you never told me this?'

'You never asked, my lady.'

'Well, I ask you now – show me these other two forms.'

'As you wish,' replied the demon.

'Wait!' exclaimed Cray, and his voice was so urgent that Aliza raised her hand and bade her demon pause.

'What is it?' she asked.

'Before it changes,' said Cray, 'let Regneniel tell us if either of these forms is too large to be contained by this room.'

Aliza regarded him with a puzzled expression. 'I thought you said that a demon's forms were made by the hands of its master. Surely such would not be so very large, and this is no small room.'

'Small enough,' Cray said. 'I have seen demons take far larger forms. I once saw a demon that had the semblance of a full-grown tree. In attaining that size it would have burst through this ceiling, not to mention what its branches would have done to these walls, or its roots to this floor.'

'My walls cannot be harmed by any tree,' said Aliza. 'Nor by any demon. They are impervious to spell or power.'

'That may be so,' said Cray, 'but Regneniel made them. I could not guess what effect its force would have upon them.'

'It obeys me. I would not allow it to harm them!'

'As I said, my lady, I could not guess what effect its force, its inadvertently applied force, would have upon them. Or upon the room's furniture and occupants. You may be quite safe as commander of the demon, but I . . . I am as fragile as gossamer.'

Aliza pursed her lips and turned to the demon. 'Are these forms too large for this room?'

'No, my lady.'

Cray asked, 'How much larger than a human being is the larger of these two forms?'

The creature hesitated, as if calculating. 'In volume, approximately four times larger,' it said.

Aliza glanced at Cray. 'You see, you worried unnecessarily.'

He shrugged his shoulders. 'But you did not worry at all, my lady. Of the two attitudes, I believe that mine was the more realistic.'

Her cool, dark eyes gazed at him for a long moment, and then she said, 'Yes, you are quite correct. I must not allow my ignorance to trip me up. You do have some value, Cray Ormoru.'

He smiled. 'I like to think so.'

She directed her attention to the demon once again. 'Stand over there.' She pointed to the far side of the ebony table. When the creature had obeyed, she said, 'Proceed with the demonstration of your larger form.'

'As you wish.' Immediately, its body began to alter in both size and contour. The torso grew swiftly, elongating to the height of a man and more, pulling the legs to one end and the snaky neck to the other. The neck itself shortened and thickened, the head became rounder and opened a pair of pale, staring eyes. The three arms lengthened and sprouted dense rafts of white feathers, transforming into a tail and two broad wings. The demon was now a bird, though like no other bird Cray had ever seen. It flexed its wings, and the sudden draught generated by those powerful pinions whipped Cray's and Aliza's hair back from their faces and even caused the near-empty wine decanter to slide a short distance across the polished surface of the table.

'Who gave you this form?' asked Aliza.

'My first master,' the demon replied. 'Folroy of Midwood.'

'What was it used for?'

'For travel in the human realm. My master would ride upon my back.'

'Very well. Show us the other form.'

The huge white bird folded its wings and, like a snow sculpture caught in the spring sun, only faster, so much faster, it lost its clearly defined shape and shrank, shrank, into a dirty, lumpy mound no bigger than a mastiff. And then it shrank further, darkening in colour until at last it was the size of a mouse. It sprouted a tail and fine whiskers and blinked bright, beady eyes. It *was* a mouse. It sat up on its hind legs and tucked its paws under its chin. But when it spoke, it had the voice of the demon, the voice of the bird, deep and resonant and entirely at odds with the tiny fragile semblance it wore.

'This is my other form,' it said. 'Now you have seen them all.'

'Who gave you this one?' asked Aliza.

'The same.'

'And what was it used for?'

'Spying on other mortals.'

Cray laughed softly. 'Vermin do have their uses, surely. But tell me, Aliza – is this Folroy your grandfather?'

'No. Do you recognize the name?'

He shook his head. 'But that means your grandfather gave the demon no new forms.'

'It means he had no need of them,' said Aliza. 'His other demons probably had all the forms he required.'

'But this demon is yours now. And surely you'll want more than a bird and a mouse. That's a slim selection if ever I saw one.'

'I have no skill at sculpture,' she said. She gazed at him speculatively. 'Could you . . . perhaps . . . do the work for me?'

'Ah, my lady, I fear that's not possible. I can give you guidance, and I will, gladly, but the demon is yours and so the sculpture must be executed by your hands.'

She dismissed that notion with a wave of her hand. 'It's a matter of curiosity only. Should I need a bird or a mouse, I know I have them. Beyond that . . . I can't even imagine needing either of those.'

'To travel. To spy.'

'Neither interests me. This is my whole world, this palace and Ice, and they are enough.'

'And yet,' said Cray, 'your palace exists in the human realm as well. Have you no curiosity about *it*?'

'No. My interest in the human realm is limited to the few things Regneniel fetches from it. Wine, for example. Regneniel, fill this decanter up with Maretian wine.' She held it out toward the mouse on the far side of the table.

Within a few heartbeats the demon had grown back into its angular earthly form. It wrapped one of its tiny arms about the decanter, and with this burden, larger than its own body, it marched off through a doorway directly opposite the one by which Cray and Aliza had entered the room. Cray watched it through the transparent walls until it merged with the blotches that lay in that direction.

'Must it go far for the wine?' Cray asked.

'Not far,' she replied, 'for a demon.'

'Perhaps you should keep more wine in your palace.'

She smiled slightly, only the second smile Cray had seen on her lips, and he thought it sweetened her face considerably. She said, 'I thought what I had would last a bit longer than it has.'

He lifted his goblet to her and drank. 'A good wine deserves to be consumed.'

'I would never deny that.' She sipped from her own goblet, which had scarcely emptied at all since its second filling.

Cray shifted his position on the couch and found that his shirt was sticking to his back. He pulled it away from the skin, then loosened the ties of his collar. 'The warmth in this room seems so much at odds with its icy appearance. You have no hearth, and no fire demons, yet there is no chill. If anything, the place is too warm.'

'That is the wine,' she said.

He smiled into his goblet. 'Perhaps so. Still, I was

comfortable before I drank any wine, and we are entirely surrounded by Ice.'

'No, we are surrounded equally by Ice and the human realm, and in the human realm it is summer. That summer heats these rooms.'

'And when the human realm has winter?'

'Then I do keep hearths, wherever I need them.'

'It must be very cosy here in winter,' Cray murmured. 'To curl up on this couch before the fire, with the flames glimmering off the walls and the light so much ruddier, the firelight washing out this harsh white glow.' He stifled a yawn behind his hand. 'I don't see how you can sleep with all this light around you.'

'I don't find this light harsh,' said Aliza, 'but if I wish I can extinguish it.'

Cray stifled another yawn. 'You can have day or night, whichever you please.'

'Yes.'

'Without regard to what may reign in the human realm outside your home.'

'I told you, I pay very little attention to the human realm. Why should I be regimented by the sun?'

'Why, indeed?' said Cray. Not only did he feel warm, he felt heavy as well, and sluggish. 'You sleep when you wish, you rise when you wish. An excellent existence.' He yawned again, and this time he could not keep his mouth from stretching wide behind his hand. 'I, however, am tied to the sun, and though I don't know how much time has passed since I rose this morning, I suspect it is a great deal.' He tried to blink the film from his eyes, but failed. 'Forgive me.'

'It's the wine,' said Aliza. 'I should have warned you not to drink so much.'

'Good wine.' Looking down into his goblet, he saw that it was empty. 'I must remember where it comes from.' He lowered the vessel to his lap, where it tipped over, but as it was already empty, nothing spilled from it. He closed his eyes for just a moment, and found that opening them was very difficult. He managed it, but not for long. The last thing he saw before they closed again was Regneniel the demon, come back with a full decanter of translucent red liquid. He wanted to say that he'd had enough, not to fill his goblet again, but his mouth was too tired to form the words.

Chapter 5

Cray woke to total darkness; not a shred of light, not a candle flame, not a single star, showed anywhere about him. He lay on something well-padded and narrow, with an upright section close against his left elbow and an edge beyond his right. He sat up slowly, clutching at the taut fabric beneath him, feeling dizzy and disoriented. He swung his legs cautiously over the edge of his bed, and his shins barked against some unyielding object before reaching the floor. He felt for the object with both hands, found it low and broad and smooth-topped. He squinted into the darkness, trying to see what he touched, trying.

Then, so slowly that at first he did not realize what was happening, a faint light began to fill up the space around him. Faint, bluish, but becoming brighter with every passing heartbeat, it played an eerie sunrise to the world of his senses. The room came into focus for him, the ebony table under his hands, the grey brocade couch upon which he sat, the crystalline walls on every side, not transparent now but rather so many perfect mirrors, reflecting his image back at him from a hundred angles, except where his mother's tapestry covered one panel. He stood up and looked all around and found himself alone with all his images. And nowhere was there any doorway, only mirrors and stairways leading up or down to mirrored walls.

He stepped away from the couch, and on every side his reflection moved with him, a kaleidoscope of reflections that made him dizzy just to watch.

'Aliza!' he shouted. The sound of his voice seemed to echo back at him from all those images.

He went to the place where he remembered a door, where he remembered the demon had passed. It was a mirror now. He raised a hand and knocked on it tentatively. The sound of his knock had no hollowness, as if the space behind the wall were filled solid.

'Aliza!' he shouted.

There was no answer.

He looked back toward the couch, toward the table. At her end, the decanter stood, filled to the brim with red Maretian wine; a goblet was beside it. Cray did not want any more wine. His throat was dry and fuzzy, and his tongue felt thick. He knocked on the mirror again, much harder this time, hard enough to break ordinary glass. But this was not ordinary glass; this was the substance of Ice itself, and he was locked inside it.

'Aliza!'

He put his hands on his hips and surveyed the room with a careful eye. There were things he could do to this room to free himself from it, but none of them would leave it in very good condition. None of them would ingratiate him with its lady. And perhaps, he thought, none of them would work. He had never tried escaping from another sorcerer's spell.

As he stood there weighing his options, all the walls around him abruptly became transparent once more, and a deep resonant voice as close as his elbow said, 'Follow me, O mortal.'

Startled, Cray twisted about to see Regneniel standing where a mirror had been and now a doorway was again. Without waiting for him to say anything, the demon turned and walked off. Cray hurried after.

'Where are we going, Regneniel?' he asked, after they had passed through three empty rooms, each somewhat smaller than the last.

'To the bathing chamber,' it replied, and almost as soon as it had uttered the words, it guided Cray up a steep flight of steps and into a room no larger than his own modest bedroom in Spinweb.

It was a bathing chamber such as any prince might envy, with fixtures for every purpose. Here was a shallow marble basin, delicately veined in grey and pink, suitable for washing the face and hands. Beside it was a deeper basin, still marble, just large enough for an entire human body. Farther along stood a bronze tub with lions' paws holding it up off the floor, a tub broad and deep enough to drown in. Beyond that was a crystalline shower stall with a finely perforated bronze nozzle hanging at head height; the stall had only three walls, but Cray knew that Aliza could put up a fourth at will. And everywhere that water was needed were taps of gold, some wrought in the shapes of wild beasts, some as plain and utilitarian as bulls' horns, every one with a handle set upon it to turn the flow of water on and off. Even the shower had its pair of taps, joined by a bronze tube to the nozzle. From all of these taps copper pipes ran, hugging the walls, connecting each to one of two large crystalline tanks set on high pedestals at the far end of the room. Beneath one tank, in a copper pan, the embers of a charcoal fire glowed. Cray tested the nearest tap that drew from that tank and found the water quite hot. The other, of course, was cold. He cupped his hands beneath its flow and drank deep.

When his thirst was quenched, Cray surveyed basins and tub and shower. 'A broad choice of bathing styles,' he observed. 'But how do you dispose of the used water?'

'I freeze it and discard it in the human realm,' answered Regneniel.

'And you bring fresh in the same manner? Frozen?'

'Correct.'

Cray strolled the length of the room, to the rather plain wooden frame that crouched like a skeletal armchair over its milky crystalline container. 'And the contents of the

106

chamber pot,' he said. 'They, too, are frozen and discarded in the same way?'

'Yes.'

Cray nodded. 'Very well, Regneniel, I will use the various appurtenances of this room, and my thanks to your lady for them. But I would like to do so in privacy. That is, with the walls and floor and ceiling opaque. You can accomplish that, can't you?'

'As you wish, O mortal,' said the demon, and the boundaries of the room became mirrors.

'And would you, after you've gone out, please close the room up with a door? I'll knock on it when I'm ready to come out.'

'As you wish, O mortal.'

'Go now,' said Cray, waving a hand.

It backed out of the room, and the doorway by which they had entered became a mirror.

Cray used the lion-footed tub, reclining in it while he watched the level of water sink in both crystalline tanks and rise about him, up to the level of his chest, the base of his throat, his chin. The heat of it felt good, soaking away the last traces of sleep. At Spinweb, the tub was small and shallow, filled from their well with buckets carried by cloth servants rather than by pipes, filled with the cold clear water of the earth beneath the castle. But no fires were needed to heat it, not since Gildrum had come to live there; the demon had merely to plunge his arm into the water to make it as hot as anyone could wish.

Cray sat bolt upright at the thought of Gildrum. Were he and Elrelet and Leemin still waiting outside the walls? He was sure that two of them, at least, must be – they would never desert him. What did they think had happened to him? How long had he slept?

He washed quickly with Aliza's sandalwood-scented soap, and he dried himself on a towel that hung behind

107

the tub and threw on his clothes. He pounded on the mirrored door.

Regneniel opened it.

'My friends outside the palace,' Cray said. 'I must go to them and tell them I'm all right.'

'I have already done so,' came Aliza's voice. 'I told them you would be staying another day, to come back tomorrow.' She stepped into view from behind one of the mirrored walls. She wore pale lavender velvet now, and Cray judged that her change of clothing meant that she, too, had slept. 'They seemed reluctant to leave,' she said. 'Perhaps they didn't believe me. But they went at last, out of my sight at any rate.'

Cray exhaled a deep breath. 'Thank you. They were probably beginning to worry. I should have thought of them sooner.'

'You must be hungry. I know I am. Come into the dining hall and have something to eat with me.'

He bowed. 'I thank you for your kind hospitality. And I apologize for imposing on you so very much last night. Or whenever it was that I fell asleep. The wine was stronger than I guessed, or perhaps my stomach was emptier.'

'I've done the same. When you started on the third glass, I should have known what to expect. You slept very soundly.' She turned and led him in a new direction, away from the room that contained the tapestry, deeper into the heart of the palace. Regneniel followed along behind them.

Their route to the dining hall took them up a flight of steps and through a bedchamber that was obviously Aliza's own. The bed was of ordinary size, without curtains, the green plush coverlet thrown back, the pillows still marked by her head. Opposite it was a large open wardrobe where a number of gowns of various fabrics and colours hung; velvet seemed to be her preference, but Cray noticed a few of silk and at least one of linen. They were all

108

very plain, without a touch of embroidery or lace. The room, too, was plain, almost stark, with only the bed and the wardrobe and a small grey rug as furnishings. The transparent walls, as usual, were innocent of any decoration. He recognized those walls now, those same crystalline walls that surrounded him as he moved from room to room. They were the background he had seen in the Mirror of Heart's Desire, the background he had been unable to identify. He smiled to think that, once, he had not been able to imagine a sheet of glass as tall as a man; how could he ever have foreseen that someday he would walk through a palace made entirely of crystal?

The dining hall lay down a shallow ramp from the bed-chamber, and though it was large enough to seat a duke and three dozen retainers in comfort, it was furnished, of course, only for one. The table itself was impressive in both size and construction – a double armspan wide and more than twenty paces long, it was made of a single oaken plank, the very heart of a great tree, thick and finely finished, supported by half a dozen trestles. Halfway down one side of the table was a single chair, also oaken, with wide, curving arms and cushioned seat. Before the chair was a place-setting, napkin and plate and tumbler of water, and beside that a tray of fruit, a bowl of hard cooked eggs, and a loaf of white bread, all waiting for one person to sit there and breakfast.

'Regneniel,' said Aliza, 'fetch the chair from my study and then set a place for Cray Ormoru.' As the demon hurried past them toward a doorway at the opposite end of the hall, she turned to Cray and said, 'I think you'll be more comfortable in a chair you can move back and forth.'

'As long as it has a cushion,' he replied. 'I remember that crystal chair as a bit too firm for any long-term comfort.'

She smiled just a trifle. 'Yes, it was, wasn't it?'

He smiled back at her. 'I presume you don't use crystal chairs very often.'

'There is much fine furniture in the human realm. Why should I not avail myself of it?'

'Why not, indeed.' Stepping close to the table, he ran one hand across its smoothly polished surface. He wondered how many artisans had worked to achieve that soft, warm gloss, how many hours, how many weeks they had laboured with sand and rouge and oil. 'This is truly a beautiful piece,' he said. 'I have seen its like only in very great houses. Such things are costly, in mortal terms.'

'I wouldn't know about that. My grandfather had Regneniel bring it when I asked him for a table to suit this room.' At that moment the demon entered with the chair. 'Put it opposite mine,' she told the creature.

As Cray and Aliza seated themselves, the demon opened the doors of a large wooden cabinet that stood against the wall nearest Cray's place. Inside, neatly arranged on the many shelves, he could see all manner of elegant crockery and table utensils, from serving platters and carving knives to saltcellars and cream pitchers. The demon selected a napkin, plate, and tumbler from this collection and set them before Cray. The napkin was linen of a fine weave, almost too delicate to be used at table; the dish was hard-fired ceramic, painted and edged with enough gold to suit a king; the tumbler was thick and solid in the hand, and difficult to knock over with an errant elbow.

Cray held the tumbler up. 'Your work?' he asked Aliza.

She nodded.

'I like a vessel that defies the clumsy,' he said.

She smiled again, a little more broadly this time. 'Are you often clumsy?'

'As seldom as possible. But still, I tried to keep a good hard grip on last night's goblet.'

'It wouldn't have broken, you know.'

'I suspected as much. But I was thinking more of the wine spilling, to tell the truth.' He looked closely at his

110

plate. The design was not only richly executed but showed considerable skill as well. 'You seem to have quite a few of these. From your grandfather again?'

'Yes. Everything I have, that I don't make myself, comes from him.'

'He is rich, then, as well as powerful.'

Aliza took a pear from the tray of fruit, cut it in half with the bread knife, and bit into one half. 'Power can provide riches, if one so desires,' she said.

Regneniel had gone out and come back with a carafe of water; it filled Cray's glass and set the carafe down. Then, at Aliza's sharp gesture, it left the room by the nearest door.

She began to peel herself an egg. 'Aren't you hungry?'

'Me? Why, yes, somewhat. I was just looking at my plate. It seems such a shame to put something on it and hide the decoration.'

'Yes, I suppose it's pretty enough. Would you perhaps like the other half of this pear? It's a little too much for me.'

He took it and found it tart enough to remind him of Maretian wine. That memory made his head spin a bit, with just the barest trace of a headache, and in trying to push those sensations away, he realized that he was very hungry indeed. He finished the pear and cut himself a slice of bread; it was warm, shot through with currants, and delicious.

'Your grandfather also provides your food?' Cray asked.

Aliza nodded. 'Regneniel fetches it every few days.'

'He seems to look after you reasonably well, at least so far as creature comforts are concerned.'

She shrugged. 'I am his apprentice, after all. When he made me that, he took on the responsibility of making sure I stayed alive and healthy as well as of teaching me sorcery.' She nibbled delicately at a thin slice of bread. 'Everything I have, everything I am, I owe to him. It is my only debt, and one I doubt I shall ever be able fully to repay.'

'Do you think he expects any repayment?'

'I have never thought otherwise. He has expended a great deal of effort on my education. Of course, I have sent him little gifts over the years, gewgaws of crystal that I've made, some of them more useful than others. He must have quite a display of them by now, ranging all the way from my first pitiful efforts to some rather elegant pieces that I've done lately. But my grandfather is a rich and powerful sorcerer, and he needs no crystal bric-à-brac from me, I know. They don't represent any true sort of repayment. But someday, when I am as powerful as he, I will give him real value for all he has done for me.'

Cray picked over the seeds from his pear core, rolling them meditatively between his fingers. 'And yet,' he said softly, 'what *has* he done for you? He has assigned one of his army of demons, one which by your own admission he will not miss, to be your tutor. He sends a little food, a few pieces of furniture. And once a year, a very small allocation of time, surely, he comes by to check on your progress. In terms of his own life, he has really given you very little.' He looked at her across the table. 'As far as I can see, he hasn't given you anything at all of *himself*.'

Her eyes were puzzled, her cool, dark eyes. 'I don't understand what you mean. I am his apprentice; he is giving me his knowledge.'

'At one remove,' Cray said. 'From what you've told me, you might as well be Regneniel's apprentice as your grandfather's. The knowledge comes by way of the demon. The master seems to have little at all to do with it.'

'He sets my lessons.'

'But does not administer them. Most sorcerers do. Most sorcerers have their apprentices living with them, under their eyes at all times. This apprenticeship at long

112

distance is a very strange situation. It hardly impinges on the master at all.'

'His time is valuable,' said Aliza. 'I would not wish to impose upon it. And how could I live with him and still have direct access to Ice and to the transformed substance of Ice which I manipulate? His is an ordinary castle, a demon master's castle. Our goals conflict. Our powers would conflict. No, I *must* be at a distance from him.'

Cray took another pear, but he did not bite into it. He said, 'Must you be at a distance emotionally as well as physically?'

Aliza said nothing, only looked at him uncertainly, as if she had not quite understood the question.

'Do you love your grandfather?' Cray asked.

Aliza pursed her lips, frowning. 'Love,' she said. She looked down at her plate, and with one forefinger she flicked at the breadcrumbs and bits of shell scattered upon it. 'I suppose I may have loved him when I was a child. But now I respect him. That's a more appropriate attitude for an adult.'

'You could love him as well, if he were worth loving.'

'You think he's not.'

'I think he doesn't love you,' said Cray, 'and therefore is not worthy of your love. And that's a shame, considering that he is all the family you have.'

She shook her head. 'It doesn't matter. I have no time to waste on love.' She raised her eyes to his, and, as once before, he saw defiance in them, and much pride. 'A sorcerer must be strong and independent. He must not lean on anyone or anything.'

Slowly, he eased back in his chair. 'You think love is a weakness?'

'I think that I would never be completely free of my grandfather if I did love him. And one must be free someday. You said as much yourself.'

113

'Yes, I did. But I've never thought of love as being a set of chains.'

'It ties people together, doesn't it?'

Cray smiled. 'But they wish to be tied.'

She lifted one shoulder in a shrug. 'I don't.'

Elbows on the arms of his chair, Cray folded his hands together beneath his chin and studied her as she peeled another egg. 'I suspect that if you had grown up loving and being loved,' he said, 'your attitude might be a bit different. Losing your parents so early has had a considerable effect on you.'

'I don't remember them very well,' she said. 'It was a long time ago.'

'They were sorcerers?'

'Yes.'

'What happened to them?'

'They died in a sorcerous accident. They were both apprenticed to my grandfather at the time, working together, and apparently they made some sort of mistake. He told me he never did determine exactly how it happened.' She took a bite of the egg and chewed slowly, washing it down with a swallow of water. 'I learned something from that, Cray Ormoru. I learned to follow instructions very carefully. I learned not to allow myself to be distracted.'

'It must have been very hard on you,' Cray said, 'losing them so young.'

'As I said, it was a long time ago.'

'I wonder how well a man like your grandfather could have comforted you. Or was he different back then?'

She dropped the uneaten remains of her egg onto her plate and pushed it aside. 'You're asking me about a time that is almost like someone else's life to me. Before I came to this place, before Regneniel took over my care. I was very young, after all. I only remember it as if it were a dream. My mother, my father – they're like phantoms.

114

I don't even think about those times any more. They no longer have anything to do with what I am and what I wish to become.'

Cray rubbed his chin against his interlaced fingers. 'Don't you wonder, sometimes, what you've missed? What your life would have been like if your parents had lived?'

'I can guess some of it. For one thing, I'd almost surely be apprenticed to one of them. And I'd probably be living with them in an ordinary castle, practising whatever sorcery they practised. Demons, I assume. But they're dead, and my grandfather made my decisions for me instead. And he decided that I would learn a special kind of sorcery. I know how rare it is, I know that there are no other sorcerers capable of walking in Ice by themselves. I know that I will be the first to manipulate the very substance of Ice. An accident of sorcery has accomplished this for me; I had no control over it, but I am willing to use its fruits. I accept reality and do not yearn for anything that might have been. How foolish that would be!'

Cray sighed. 'Foolish, perhaps, but a common mortal foolishness.'

'I have no desire to be a fool,' said Aliza, 'or a common mortal.'

He studied her face, so pale and composed, the eyes so steady, so self-assured. This was what loneliness accomplished, he thought – it wrapped you up so thoroughly in yourself that only your goals became important, and all else was mere foolishness. What would she do, he wondered, when the entire world of Ice lay in her grasp and there was no more to learn? Or would there always be something more for her, always another goal beyond the one attained?

He said, 'And so you believe you are happy with this reality that you accept so completely?'

'Happy. It's not a word I would use to describe myself,'

she said. 'When I was a child I was happy, playing mind-lessly with my toys. Now I would rather say that I am satisfied. My life is filled with interesting pursuits, and I am content with them. Can you say as much?'

He shrugged. 'I suppose not. I have my pursuits, but if I were truly content with them, I would never have come looking for a new friend.'

'Perhaps you should find some new kind of sorcery, then, to refresh your enthusiasm for it.'

He lowered his hands to the table, his palms flat against the smoothly polished oaken surface. His sensitive fingers could perceive the direction of the grain, though it had been buffed to a satiny finish. 'I have practised many kinds of sorcery in my life, my lady. I could have made this table myself, by sorcery – caused the tree to fell itself and peel its own bark away and split off a perfect plank from its very heart; caused cloths to rub it smooth with all the proper abrasives; caused saplings to grow precisely into the forms of these trestle-legs. It would have been a simple thing, the work of a day or two, perhaps. A great many things come simply to a sorcerer of my strength – food, clothing, comforts. I could learn more, of course. I *do* learn more, constantly. But . . .' He frowned, trying for the first time to put into words the feelings that had haunted him for so many years. The impatience. The restlessness. The accomplishment that never turned out to be quite so satisfying, quite so desirable as he had hoped. The gold-shot tree. The golden blossom. The castle of living wood. 'I learn constantly,' he said, 'but not because I have any need to learn more, not because it gives me any real pleasure. But simply because . . . I can think of nothing else to do with my time.' He shook his head. 'I suppose that must set me apart from other sorcerers.'

Aliza gazed at him with puzzlement in her eyes. 'Are you saying that you are *bored* with sorcery?'

He smiled wryly. 'I am bored with the notion that sorcery is its own reward. You spoke of leaving your toys behind with your childhood. Yet what is sorcery but one more toy?'

'Sorcery is power,' said Aliza.

'Power is a toy, isn't it? Mortal princes play with it frequently, striving against each other like children at king-of-the-mountain.'

'But you must have enough power to protect yourself from your enemies.'

He looked at her sadly. 'Have you so very many enemies already?'

'I?' She seemed surprised at the question. 'None that I know of. But one must be prepared.'

'You expect to acquire some in the future?'

Lowering her gaze to the fruit tray, she fingered the stem of an apple, then twisted it between her thumb and forefinger. 'I don't expect it, but I don't rule out the possibility. My grandfather has told me that the more powerful I become, the more other sorcerers will fear me. Under such an impetus as fear, anything could happen.'

'Your very powerful grandfather – he has many enemies?' She nodded.

'What an ironic situation it would be,' said Cray. 'Ten or twenty or a hundred years from now, when you have a host of enemies and not a single friend.'

She looked up at him sharply. 'I'll have my grandfather.'

'Will you? Or will you have become so powerful that he, too, will be an enemy? Such things have happened in sorcerous families before. And in ordinary mortal ones, too, for that matter. After all, you and he are not *friends* now.'

Her mouth became a thin, hard line. 'And who is to say that a *friend* could not also become an enemy?'

'It could happen,' Cray admitted, 'but not, I think, if

there were good faith on both sides.' He smiled at her. 'My closest friend and I have had many a disagreement, but we are still friends.'

Her eyes narrowed. 'You've been a sorcerer for some time. Have you no enemies?'

He waved airily. 'I lead a quiet life. I bother no one. If I do have any enemies just now, they have not made themselves known to me. Perhaps, by sorcerous standards, I don't really have so very much power. I can't move mountains or toss lightning about or drown the countryside with salt water. To make a tree grow, to cause a piece of cloth to walk about – these are such small things. Who could be afraid of them?'

'Don't you have any desire to learn those other skills?'

He laughed softly, shaking his head. 'You don't understand, do you? You don't understand how one could have no real interest in such vast powers.'

'No, I confess, I don't.'

Cray stroked the tabletop with three fingers, back and forth, back and forth. 'Perhaps we should just say . . . that not everyone needs to be a king.' He watched his fingers work upon the smooth wooden surface. 'I almost wasn't a sorcerer at all,' he said. 'I was almost an ordinary mortal. As a boy, I wanted to be a knight. Just a common knight, with a sword and a shield and a suit of armour. I wanted to go about the countryside righting wrongs and punishing evildoers. That was what I dreamed of.' He shrugged. 'A child's dream. But I followed it for a time. I was even a squire, briefly. But I gave up the dream because sorcery was more appropriate to my goals. It seems so very long ago.' He sighed, and then he looked up at her. 'I needed sorcery very much for a relatively short period of time, to vanquish an enemy. Yes, I did have an enemy once. Just the one. And I killed him. And after that I couldn't go back to being a knight. I was a sorcerer. My mind was . . . different. A sorcerer's mind. But I've never forgotten what it was like to be something else. To be *someone* else. More sorcerers should try it. It would give them a fresh perspective on life.' He leaned forward and reached out to her, barely touching her wrist with two fingers of his right hand. 'You should go out, Aliza. You should go out into the human realm and see what you've missed by being locked into this palace all your life.'

She looked down at his hand, and he realized abruptly that he was touching her, flesh to flesh, and she had raised no barrier between them to prevent it. It was the most tenuous of contacts, but it was real. He made no attempt to move his hand, and she made no attempt to move hers.

'I am not locked in,' she said quietly. 'I can go out whenever I like. I choose not to.'

'The lock is of your own devisement, my lady, but it is there, nonetheless.'

She pursed her lips, her eyes still focused on his fingers. 'What is so wonderful about this human realm?'

'Nothing. Nothing at all. But it is reality. You were the one who said you accepted reality. Yet you don't, you truly don't.'

Her chin went up a little, and her eyes lifted, but not to his, not so far. 'I remember visiting a mortal town once, with my mother,' she said. 'There were horses and dogs everywhere. And people, so many people. They stared at us; they knew we were sorcerers. And a one-legged beggar came up to us and tried to touch my hair. My mother gave him a piece of silver, I remember. He was very dirty, dressed in rags, barely dressed, and there were running sores all over his body.' Now she did meet Cray's eyes. 'There's your reality.'

'I never said reality was all pleasant. But it is instructive.'

She shook her head. 'No, I have no desire to experience more of it. I have my own reality here. That is enough.'

'There are other things besides beggars out there,' Cray

said. 'There are great houses, handsome men and beautiful ladies, fields of grain and flowers of every colour and shape. Rivers and lakes and the ocean. Mountains and valleys. You miss so much being in here – much more than other sorcerers. They, at least, can look out of their castle windows and see sky and earth and greenery.'

She raised one eyebrow. 'You think I can't see any of that, do you?'

He glanced about the room, and all he saw through the transparent walls was other rooms surrounding it, room upon room. 'Not from here.'

She stood up abruptly, knocking her chair back, so that it teetered on two legs and she had to catch it by one arm to keep it from falling over. 'Of course not from here,' she said. 'Here we are in the heart of Ice. But you've only seen a small fraction of my palace. You think I never see the sky? You think I have no windows? How wrong you are, Cray Ormoru. Come along with me and I'll show you what I can see from my palace!'

He had to hurry to follow her, so swiftly did she stride from the room, never looking back once to see if he were behind her. She led him through the bedchamber and then, with a sharp turn and a short climb of steps, into a room in which two parallel rows of shelves flanked a broad desk. Scattered upon the shelves, standing upright or lying on their sides, were many oversized volumes. Some were even open, though Cray passed them too quickly to judge their contents, except that they were handwritten. Several more books were piled on the desk, with quills and inkpots close beside them, and vessels of sand for blotting the wet ink. The absence of a chair at the desk, as well as the chamber's proximity to the dining hall, indicated that it was Aliza's study. She did not pause there.

Down a flight of steps at the far end of the study, through a doorway, and down a second stairway much steeper than the first she led Cray. Now they were in a sitting room, by far the smallest chamber he had yet seen, small enough to be called snug. A sumptuous divan occupied its centre, an armless velvet lounge with one upcurling end, closely surrounded by low tables and cabinets, with only a tiny empty space at one side giving access to its well-upholstered seat. The tables and cabinets were of various kinds of woods, light and dark, but the divan, like the other couch, like the rugs, was a pale grey. Aliza strode through the door beyond it.

The next chamber, just one step up, was the most unusual he had yet seen. Unlike all the others, its boundaries were not transparent but rather suffused with a creamy cloudiness, as if they were made of water into which milk had been stirred. The room was tiny, scarcely six paces across, and seemed to be a storage area rather than any true living space. On one side of the narrow aisle that joined its two doors was a row of crystalline bins as cloudy as the walls, their contents only faintly visible through their translucent sides. Opposite these, crammed shoulder to shoulder in the limited space, were a wooden table and chair suitable for a child half Cray's height and a bed of comparable dimensions. The bed was made up with linens and a pillow. Behind it, just peeking out at one end, Cray thought he could glimpse the forequarters of a rocking horse. He had no chance to look closer, though, for Aliza hurried on.

They climbed next the steepest stairway Cray had yet encountered in the palace, and it, too, was cloudy, enclosed on all sides by cloudy crystalline walls, so that it was more like a tunnel than a stairway. Cray felt as though he were walking through mist held magically at bay. At the top of the staircase was more mist – and then he realized, as Aliza reached it, that the top was barred by a mirror.

When he had joined her on the last step, Aliza swept her hand in an arc across the mirrored surface, and the solid wall drained away like water streaming from oiled wood.

Abruptly, the light all about them changed, the blue-white radiance of Aliza's palace swamped by a golden light. Dazzled, Cray rocked back on his heels, barely keeping his balance, barely avoiding a fall down that long, steep flight of stairs. He felt as though he had just emerged from a cave, just left subterranean autumn for the summer of the outer world. Even the air that flowed about him through the new-made doorway smelled different from the rest of the palace, smelled hot and close. He shaded his eyes against the glare and, blinking, tried to see something in the space before him.

'Come along,' said Aliza, and she stepped forward.

Trailing after her, Cray found himself in an empty room much like any other in the palace – crystalline walls on all sides, separating it from other rooms, layers and layers of other rooms on all sides, all empty. The cloudy-walled staircase had vanished as soon as he crossed its threshold, and along with it the storage room and the furnished portions of the palace – all had gone from his sight just as his own human realm did every time he and Gildrum used a demon portal to enter Fire. He knew there was such a portal somewhere behind that threshold, behind the mirror that Aliza had already re-created behind his back, that double-sided mirror that now gave him his own face instead of a view down those cloudy crystalline stairs. He was in Ice no longer, in the demon realm no longer, for beyond the numberless facets that surrounded him, beyond all the intervening transparent layers, far above his head, the summer sun shone bright and hot in a clear blue sky.

'The human realm,' he said.

'Yes,' said Aliza. 'This is the part of my palace that lies there. Come. We have some distance to go yet.'

They crossed the room, which was not very large, and entered another by way of the usual sort of stairway. That, Cray thought, and everything else about this part of the palace, save the light and the heat, were just the same as before.

'It's very warm here,' he said, wiping sweat from his forehead with the back of one hand.

'This is my source of heat,' she replied. 'The sun's own heat, collected in these rooms and flowing through all the walls of the palace. Even in deepest winter it keeps away the worst of Ice's chill.'

'No doubt. But you and I will be roasted pheasants fairly soon if we have to stay in it.'

'I've opened a wall in one of the outer rooms, and there will be a cool enough breeze waiting for us there. Walk a little faster and you'll reach it all the sooner.' To set the example, she stepped up her own pace.

The distance to the outer rooms of this portion of the palace was not so great as that in Ice, or perhaps it merely seemed so to Cray because they were moving fast. Even before they reached their goal, however, he began to notice the landscape beyond the building, distorted though it was by intervening crystal. He could see that great mountains rose in the distance, their flanks cloaked in greenery. Closer, the land appeared to be some sort of low, sun-bleached savannah.

He felt the breeze as they entered the next to the last room, and it was refreshing indeed. It puffed through the doorway at the far end of the room, spreading like a cool spring into a sun-warmed pond. The final room was cooler yet, almost too cool. There, Cray shivered as his sweat-drenched clothing began to dry on his body.

Aliza, in her velvet gown, was not sweating at all. He wondered, looking at her, if her power over Ice included the ability to bring a pocket of its chill with her into the human realm.

In the outermost room a huge expanse of the outermost wall, a giant window with its transparent sill at waist height and its upper edge beyond any human reach, stood open to the elements. Wind gushed through it intermittently, now buffeting Cray and Aliza fiercely, now leaving them to walk in stillness. As they approached this window, Cray realized that they were far above the ground, higher than the topmost tower of Spinweb, higher than any building he had ever seen, sorcerous or not. From this vantage, he could see a landscape spread out before him that was unlike any he had ever encountered before. In every direction, in a circle about the palace that must have been an hour's walk in extent, the earth was bare and dry and white. And flat. Flat as the surface of a pond on a quiet day. Beyond that was the greenery he had already noticed, and an unbroken line of mountains so rough and craggy that he could hardly believe anyone could cross them without demon assistance.

'I have seen clearings around sorcerers' castles,' he said, leaning on the windowsill, 'but never any that were quite so . . . thorough.'

'It's sand,' said Aliza. 'Coarse-grained quartz sand so heavily spell-laden that no wind can blow it away. Nothing living can cross it, not mortal or demon. No one can set foot on it. No one can fly in the air above it. Not unless I give permission.'

'That's a strong spell, my lady.'

'I used a stronger one to raise those mountains.'

Cray stared out at the jagged peaks so distant, their summits glistening whitely, as if snow-covered even in the mild season. 'You raised them?' he said, his voice tinged with wonder.

'It was a simple task, really. They were two lines of hills already, I merely bade them grow a bit and completely enclose this valley. All they needed was time. The human realm is easy enough to manipulate in such ways. It has so many crystalline properties. What are mountains, after all, but giant crystals?'

Cray shook his head. 'I've never thought of them in that way.'

Aliza turned her back on the vista that stretched out before them and leaned against the waist-high sill. 'So now you see that I do know about the sun and the sky and even green growing things. I'm even aware that leaves change colour in the autumn, just as your tapestry shows. Though I must admit that those trees out there are not nearly as colourful as the ones your mother portrayed.'

'The view has a certain magnificence,' Cray said slowly, 'because of the mountains. But, otherwise, it's . . . rather barren, don't you think? I mean, nothing but sand, sand, for such a long way. Do you never yearn to see something else outside these walls – shrubs or wild flowers, or even grass?'

'No. They couldn't grow on the sand, of course, but I have no interest in them anyway.'

He gazed at her sidelong. 'You don't spend much time here, I suppose.'

'Not much.'

'Have you ever crossed those sands?'

She shook her head.

'Not even to raise the mountains?'

'It wasn't necessary.'

'You've never climbed them, then? Never flown over them?'

'Why should I?'

'To look down on the other side.'

'I know what's there. Trees. Rocks. Rivers. And mortals. None of which have any importance in my life. I can't seem to convince you of that, can I?'

Cray shrugged. 'You've convinced me that you don't *want* them to have any importance in your life. Here you've created two barriers between yourself and them, where one would have served. The magical sand keeps all living things away from these walls, yet you felt some need

125

to raise those mountains as well. Not to keep anyone out, I think, but to keep yourself *in*. To isolate yourself in this valley, so that you don't even have to *see* the human realm stretching out to the horizon. This isn't the human realm at all, Aliza. This whole valley has been so changed by your hand that it might as well be part of Ice.'

'It is as close to the human realm as I wish to be,' she said. 'And if my palace could be totally within Ice, that would not displease me.'

He shook his head slowly. 'I've never heard of a sorcerer that didn't have *some* interest in the human realm. If only for what it could yield him.'

'What? Gold, silks, and furs? Power over other mortals?'

He nodded. 'Suchlike things.'

She gathered a handful of her velvet skirt in one fist. 'You see this, Cray Ormoru? My grandfather gave me this. I would be as happy in plain linsey-woolsey as in velvet. I don't care what I wear, and I don't care for ornaments without use.' She held the white sapphire out toward him, the golden chain pulled taut. 'I wouldn't wear this except that it serves me. Everything I have serves me, and I have no desire for more . . . objects. Let others have the human realm. I want only a bit of food and my studies.'

He stretched an arm out toward the mountains, but meaning to encompass all that lay beyond. 'Is not the human realm worth studying? You and I were born of it, after all, and your grandfather, too.'

'And other sorcerers have studied it thoroughly, I'm sure. I have chosen to study that which other sorcerers have not. It will serve me as I wish to be served.'

'You never chose,' said Cray. 'Your grandfather chose.'

She shrugged. 'At the beginning, yes. But the more I study Ice, the more I think it was a good choice. I could give it up, you know. I could always *choose* to give it up. I control the demon now. I could choose to require it to teach me some other form of sorcery. Something more ordinary. But I do not wish to be *ordinary*.' She looked out across the white sand and waved a hand at that vista, a short, sharp, contemptuous gesture. 'This is nothing,' she said. 'Less than nothing. Look!' She extended both arms, fingers splayed stiffly. Out in the whiteness, sand began to fountain upwards as if some buried giant were exhaling his deep and powerful breath. Sparkling motes danced in the sunlight, falling, splashing against the ground and being caught up once again to rise on high. Gradually the fountain solidified, its central shaft taking on the form of an obelisk, fewer and fewer grains falling from that column until it stood solid and gleaming, its four sides crisp and smooth and flawless.

'There,' said Aliza, dropping her arms. 'That is what I can make of the human realm. And I could form a hundred more of them, with walls between, and roofs and turrets – a castle fit for any king, filled with crystalline furniture, and crystal servants to do my bidding. It would be easy, the work of a few afternoons, no more. My grandfather tells me there are sorcerers who have studied all their long lives to do just that, and count themselves skilled and fortunate to accomplish it. They have not grown up in Ice, as I have. They are not part of a realm that *is* crystalline in its very nature, a nature I have absorbed so thoroughly that their long-studied skills are like child's play to me. But Ice itself, Cray Ormoru! Ice is not a simple place like the human realm. Ice resists me, as it resists its own demons. They and I are to Ice as an ordinary mortal is to *his* realm. We must labour hard to bend it to our bidding. And yet, we are capable of such labour, the ice demons and I. Only because I was not born there, because I am not *completely* of Ice, has it come so slowly to me. But by that same token, by my very otherness, I have the potential to manipulate ice more effectively than the demons who are *of* it. I have a stronger will than they, more perseverance, more desire.

Regneniel says that if I were a demon, I would be one of the greatest of them. I have spent my life becoming so, and I am not about to give it up for the paltry rewards of the human realm!'

Cray had backed off a step at the vehemence of her speech, and now he gripped the windowsill hard with both hands. Her words and her manner made him afraid, not for himself, but for her. She was still a child, he felt it in his heart, but those were not a child's words, and that was not a child's vehemence. They were the words and the vehemence of an old and jaded sorcerer, one who had lived long and never acquired enough power to satisfy himself.

He must have told himself it was for her own good, he thought, looking at the implacable expression on her pale and beautiful face. *And there was no mother or father for him to answer to. Only an innocent child.*

Aliza would have power indeed – power that no other sorcerer had ever had, because no sorcerous parent had ever been willing to give a child up so completely to sorcery. Cool they were, those of the sorcerous breed, but they usually had some affection for their children.

He shivered, though his clothing was dry now and the air that gushed in through the window no longer seemed so cool.

'You call the rewards of the human realm paltry,' he said to Aliza. 'Yet what do you really know of them? Do you remember flowers? Do you remember the sparkle of sunlight on a brook? Do you remember grassy pastures smooth as the finest carpets and a thousand times larger? Do you remember laughing people?' He held his hands out toward her, though he did not try to touch her. 'Come with me and travel beyond the mountains to see what you can have at no cost to yourself, no expenditure of gold or power.'

She looked at him long and hard. 'The cost would be

in time,' she said, 'and I have none to spare for such a journey.'

'The time would be well spent, I know, my lady. Think again of your answer.'

She turned away from him, away from the window, to gaze back into the depths of her palace. 'I do remember these things,' she said. 'And I do not value them as you seem to. And you cannot make me value them. We are too different, Cray Ormoru, you and I. You may doubt that, but I do not.'

'Your grandfather lives in the human realm,' said Cray. 'You think he rejects it?'

'I am not my grandfather.'

'Perhaps the reason he visits you so seldom is that he doesn't like Ice. He prefers the human realm. Can he be wrong, Aliza?'

'He may be correct for himself. Come now – haven't you had enough of this bright light for now?'

'I am accustomed to it. I walk in it often. I like it.' He took a step toward her. 'Perhaps if you went out, once, in that naked sunlight, if you commanded Regneniel to fly you to the highest of all those peaks and you looked down to the other side, perhaps you *would* change your mind. Does the prospect of possibly changing your mind frighten you, Aliza? Are you afraid that all your carefully made decisions might no longer seem so right if you went out beyond the mountains?'

She did not look back at him, but she straightened where she stood. 'I am not afraid, Cray Ormoru. You seem often to see fear where there is none. It's a very strange quirk of your mind. You are the one, I think, that wants to go out beyond those mountains. You are the one who wants to travel in the human realm, and you think, somehow, that everyone must feel the same.'

'I have travelled much in the human realm,' he said, 'and I know how interesting it can be.'

Now she gazed at him over one shoulder. 'If you wish to see what lies beyond the mountains, I shall command Regneniel to take you there.'

'Regneniel could take us both.'

'No. You shall go, and you shall satisfy your curiosity.'

He heard the wariness in his own voice. 'Are you throwing me out, my lady?'

She frowned slightly. 'You don't wish to go?'

'I thought . . . from what you told my friends, that you were willing to let me stay until tomorrow. It isn't tomorrow yet, surely.'

She hesitated, and when she spoke there was a hint of a smile about her lips. 'You don't wish to see all those wonderful sights you spoke of so glowingly and then come back and tell me how much I've missed?'

He felt himself relax and answer her faint smile with one of his own. 'As long as you allow me to come back.'

'I told your friends to return tomorrow, and I intend to deliver you to them in Ice at that time. Unless you choose to find your way home now, through the human realm.'

He glanced out of the window once more. 'I would like to explore a bit of it, yes, just for my curiosity's sake. But I would also like to come back here and spend the evening with you. We could look at the stars together from this room.'

'The stars,' murmured Aliza. 'You find them interesting.'

'Yes. Not only are they beautiful, but they are among the few things that no sorcerer can control.'

'Yes, that must be a source of great frustration to many of them.'

Cray laughed. 'Of what use would it be for a sorcerer to control the stars?'

'Of what use is anything?' said Aliza. 'Save that some person desires it. I see no use in watching the stars, but apparently you do.'

'I look at the stars for the same reason I look at a fine tapestry – for the pleasure it gives my heart. And you know that pleasure, too, or you wouldn't have accepted my gift of a tapestry. Come and look at the world with me, Aliza. It will give you even more pleasure.'

'No. Go yourself if you like, but you shall not drag me along. Regneniel!'

The demon came swiftly – they could see its approach from several rooms away, see that though its form was wingless, it flew, its long legs held out stiffly behind, beaked head stretched out in front. When it reached them, it lighted on the floor without a sound, as delicately as if it had been made of thistledown.

'Regneniel,' said Aliza, 'you shall take Cray Ormoru out to those mountains and wherever beyond them he may wish to go. You shall look after him and keep him from harm, and you shall return here with him in time for supper.' She looked to Cray. 'I trust that will suit you well enough?'

'Very well,' said Cray. 'I am grateful indeed for the loan of your only demon.'

'Think of it as payment for the tapestry.'

'I need no such payment. I told you that.'

'Then as my gift to you. Does that suit you better?'

He made a little bow to her. 'It suits me excellently, my lady.'

To the demon she said, 'Use your bird form for this journey. I wish to see it fly.'

In a moment Regneniel was the great white bird, its wings folded close against its body, its head cocked to one side, one large pale eye staring at the two mortals. It squatted, belly to the floor, and two rows of feathers just behind its head fanned upwards to form the pommel and cantle of a saddle. Cray mounted, and long white feathers closed over his thighs and legs to hold him securely in his seat. Then the bird stood once more and walked toward the window with a curious, bob-bing gait.

'Are you ready?' asked the demon's deep, resonant voice.

'Yes,' said Cray.

With a spring of powerful leg muscles, the bird launched itself through the window, clearing the sill easily and only opening its wings when it was outside, in mid-air. Two beats of those powerful pinions lifted it high into the sunny sky, and when Cray looked back, Aliza's palace was far below and behind the demon's splayed tailfeathers. He could no longer see Aliza, nor even the window, from this height. Sunlight flashed from the walls of the palace as from the facets of a jewel. The palace *was* a jewel, set down upon the white sand and ringed all around by the mountains, as if it were lying on the bottom of a vast, shallow bowl.

Buffeted by the wind of his demon steed's flight, Cray clung fast to his feather saddle, bending low over Regneniel's head. Far beneath him, the sand rushed by, and then, quite suddenly, it was gone, replaced by dark earth and the greenery that grew on the flanks of the mountains. From his new vantage, Cray could see that this greenery consisted almost entirely of trees whose like he had never seen before. They were twisted grotesquely, as if constantly windracked, though he could see from the stillness of their leaves that, for the moment at least, there was no wind among them. Their tops were flattened, the boughs grown up only so far and then turning down-ward, many reaching the ground, where they branched and spread like ground-hugging vines.

The demon bird began to wheel upwards to cross the mountains, and Cray saw that what he had taken for snow capping those peaks was in reality exposed crystal upon which no growing things had taken root. The myriad jagged shards flashed and sparkled as he passed.

The far side of the mountains seemed familiar and unfamiliar all at once. Familiar because the land was low and rolling and cloaked by the soft greens of intermittent forest, a soothing contrast to the angular, near-colourless world he had come from. But unfamiliar because he recognized not a single tree of all the multitude that passed below him. Where were the oaks, the maples, the walnuts? Instead, he saw trees with thick, branchless boles tapering gradually to a tufted summit, trees that seemed to have no trunks at all but rather roots that grew straight up into their crowns like bundles of staves, trees with leaves like waving pennons, trees with leaves as fine as human hair. He felt as though he flew through some other world than his own, a world that resembled the one he knew only if he squinted hard and allowed just the colour green to penetrate his lashes. And then, swooping low over a large clearing, the demon flushed a number of animals, and Cray stared down at them in astonishment. The largest ones looked a little like deer, with four legs and antlers, but their bodies were too stocky, their necks too elongated. Some of the others might have been large rabbits but for their red-gold colour and lack of visible ears. One creature might have passed for a wild cat, though it was completely tailless and had ears much like those the almost-rabbits lacked. Cray wondered if they would all seem even more peculiar if he were at ground level rather than gliding above them; animals, after all, did not tend to look up at the sky and show their faces to observers there.

Then he saw the town.

It hugged the high bank of a narrow river perhaps half a day's horseback ride from the foot of the mountains, and it commanded a magnificent view of them. The water of the river ran a deep reddish hue, derived, Cray presumed, from deposits of red clay that must lie farther upstream. The town itself was red, made of bricks that probably came from that same deposit – the houses all red brick, the streets paved with red cobbles, even the town wall that same mellow shade. The wall was, of course, no barrier to the demon bird, which flew high over it and, at Cray's command, circled the town in a shallow, ever-descending spiral.

There were real birds roosting on the red tile rooftops – birds of every colour Cray could imagine, and some he had only seen before in flowers, not plumage. Birds. But no human beings.

The streets of the town were empty. There was not a horse, a dog, a rat to be seen. Not a child playing, not a woman hanging laundry, not a man wheeling a barrow.

As Regneniel spiralled lower, Cray began to see the signs of abandonment – the broken roof tiles, the gaping shutters, the doors ajar, the walls cracked and crumbled by years of rain and wind and hot summer sun. Everywhere, plants had taken over where mortals would have cut them back, on those roofs, in those cracks, even on the very doorsteps of the houses. Cray bade the demon land in the town square, where a low platform must once have been a gathering place for bearers of news and for barter. Now it was deserted. Cray walked slowly about the perimeter of the square, calling at windows, knocking at doors, even entering a few buildings. Everywhere he found the same – not a stick of furniture, not a pot hanging on a hook by a fireplace, not a rag, just echoing emptiness. And everywhere, the dust of years lay thick on the floors, showing him his own footsteps and nothing more.

'Do you know what happened here?' Cray asked the demon bird.

'Yes.'

He waited for the rest of the answer, then realized he would get none without further prompting. Some demons, he thought, were just too literal-minded. 'Tell me about it,' he said.

'When the hills began to grow into mountains, the people left.'

'Ah. Well, I suppose I can understand that. It must have been a rather frightening time. Were there earthquakes?'

'None discernible to mortals.'

'How long did the whole process take?'

'Which – the mountains growing or the people leaving?' Cray shrugged. 'Both.'

'The mountains completed growth to their present height in approximately eight months. The last mortal left this town some four months before that, though the bulk of the population had gone even earlier; the last few remained behind to harvest the crops that had been planted the previous spring.'

'Brave souls,' remarked Cray, 'to stand fast in the face of all that sorcery.' After one last look around the square, he mounted Regneniel and bade it fly on. As they rose into the air, Cray could see the fields in which those crops must have stood, their boundaries obliterated now, encroached upon by thousands of strange plants. Only the small size of the trees that grew in certain broad areas betrayed the fact that not very many years ago they had been cleared and planted with food for human beings.

The demon bird flew westward, and below, the intermittent forest gave way to grassland cut regularly by sluggish, tree-lined rivers. Each river was a different colour, and now Cray could no longer attribute those colours to clay deposits, for he knew of no clays that were aquamarine, citrine yellow, garnet red. Rather, he could see, when he commanded Regneniel to swoop low, that the beds of these rivers were thick with coarse gemstone sand that sparkled through the clarity of the water. Garnet, aquamarine, citrine, and a dozen other gemstones were here for the choosing, one kind to a river, probably washed downstream from deposits in distant mountains. He knew of one river near Spinweb that bore occasional jewels in its gravels, but never any where the jewels *were* the gravels.

There were occasional animals on the grasslands, most of them too small to see clearly from the air, brown-furred and fast-moving, catching Cray's eye only in the instant that they streaked for cover. Farther on, though, he began to see small groups of what, from a distance, appeared to be sheep. Certainly they were domesticated animals, for each group of fifty or sixty was accompanied by a human being with a heavy wooden staff. The creatures had fat bodies covered with thick grey wool, and they grazed slowly, heads down. But as Cray came closer, he saw that they were not sheep, could never be sheep, for their legs were long and slender, and their heads were at the ends of long, curving, heavily furred necks.

Cray could not help wondering if that was the wool Aliza's carpets were made from, and how it compared to the wool that his mother used for her tapestries. One could not really judge its quality from such a distance, but still . . . he liked the look of it, thick and falling in great loose folds from the animals. The grass looked rich enough to support a high level of quality. And Aliza's carpets were very fine, though of monotonous colour.

Not far ahead, he could see the walls and rooftops of another town and, about it, the cultivated fields that marked it as inhabited.

'What a shame you haven't a horse's form,' he said to Regneniel, 'for then I would ride you into yonder town and offer a bit of silver for some of the wool we've just seen. They must have it for sale so near the source.' Absently, he patted the demon bird's head, as if it had been a true animal steed. 'Have you any suggestions as to how I might enter that town as an ordinary mortal rather than a sorcerer?'

'I can fly you into the centre of it, if you wish.'

'Nothing of the kind! I *don't* wish to frighten the towns-folk. I merely wish to buy a little wool.'

'They will give a sorcerer all the wool he might require.'

'I'm willing to pay,' said Cray. He felt the pouch at his belt, reassuring himself that there were indeed a few coins inside. 'I prefer to pay. And an ordinary mortal can learn considerably more about a town than a sorcerer can. It's hard to talk to people when they are cringing before you. And the point of this journey is for me to learn, after all.'

'As you wish,' said the demon. 'There is a large grove of trees not far from the town. I could set you in it, and you could walk from there as an ordinary mortal traveller.'

'Is this a deserted grove?'

'At this moment it is.'

'Very well, take me there.'

The town stood on the near bank of a river with the deep purple colour of finest amethyst. Close by were only a few isolated trees, but farther downstream, where the river widened, they grew more thickly, especially on the far bank, until at last they formed a sizeable grove. As the demon bird wheeled toward this grove, Cray gauged its distance from the town. Demons' notions of distance in the human realm could be misleading, for they flew so much more easily than a human being could walk, but in this case the grove really was not far from the town. They dipped among the trees, and leafy branches raked Regneniel's wings and Cray's arms as they glided to a feather-soft landing.

Cray dismounted and, surveying the nearest trees, selected one whose pennon-shaped leaves seemed tough enough for his purpose. With a word and a gesture he directed the largest of these leaves to pluck themselves from their branches and fall at his feet, there to shred themselves into narrow strips and weave into a coarse fabric. When the fabric was finished, it shaped itself into a knapsack, complete with cords for tying around a waist and across a chest. Cray packed the knapsack with other leaves to make it seem like a traveller's burden, and then he strapped it on.

'You will wait here until I return,' he told the demon.

'My lady Aliza told me to look after you,' said the demon. 'How can I do that if I cannot follow you?'

Cray shook his head. 'You can't come along. You're too obviously something sorcerous.'

The bird cocked its head to one side and regarded him with a pale eye. 'A mouse is small enough to fit inside that pack.'

'Very well,' said Cray. 'But you must remain silent and still unless I call for you.'

The bird hesitated. 'I must use my own judgement on that, Cray Ormoru. My lady's commands must supersede yours.'

'I understand that. Still, *you* must understand that I have travelled much among ordinary mortals, without any demon help, and I know how to deal with them. I will know better than you if I need your assistance. You will not be doing me any favour if you reveal yourself without my permission.'

'You might not be in any position to give permission,' said the demon. 'You might be bound and gagged. You might be wounded, or even killed, before you realized what was happening.'

Cray crossed his arms over his chest, gripping the cords of the knapsack. 'You have a very low opinion of mortals, it seems.' At his nod, a sapling a few paces away shed its branches and bark with a violent shake and, snapping its trunk off cleanly a few hand spans above the ground, became a stout staff that fell into Cray's outstretched hand. 'But I have my dagger and now this weapon, as you can see, and I assure you that I know how to use them. I doubt, though, that as a peaceful traveller I'll be in any real danger. I saw no signs of war about the town, no sentries on the walls, no men-at-arms along the road that leads to it. Is there perhaps something else, some other danger here that you know about and I don't?'

'It is an ordinary town, like many another,' said the demon. 'I know of no danger in it save the mortals themselves. Mortals are very unpredictable creatures.'

Cray could not help smiling. 'That I know already. Very well, be a mouse, Regneniel, but try hard to stay inside my pack unless I call for you or you know that I am not able to do so.'

When the demon had shrunk sufficiently, Cray stooped to let it scamper up his arm and dive into his knapsack. Then he headed for the river.

The flow was shallow here, broken by many rocks, and Cray could cross by hopping from one to the next, scarcely wetting his feet. Through the clear, slow-moving water, he could see the thick layer of amethyst sand on the bottom, most of it as fine as any sand he had ever seen, but with a scattering of coarser gravel, and some stones even bigger. And one of the rocks he stepped on was an amethyst boulder, or at least half amethyst wedded to a greyer granite, the boulder worn velvet-smooth and cloudy by water. Before he finished his crossing, Cray stooped to pick an egg-sized purple stone from the riverbed; it was rounded but with a recently broken end, the sharp edges and one plane not yet gentled by wear. Pulling a leaf from his pack, he wrapped the stone well and slipped it into the pouch at his belt.

On the other side of the river, fields of half-grown grain pressed close to the water, leaving only a narrow path of hard-packed yellow earth on the bank. Farther on, the land began to rise and the riverbed to narrow and deepen till, at the town wall, the water was more than two man heights below the bank, and fast-flowing.

The wall was of yellowish brick thick with flecks that

glistened in the sunlight – amethyst crystals, Cray guessed, turned yellow by kiln firing. The town gate stood open, its doors of massive logs lashed together pushed to either side. Inside, he could see people moving about their daytime tasks, men with bundles on their backs, women with baskets on their arms, dirty children trailing after them with striped and spotted dogs trotting at their heels. The path he followed became the main street of the town, broadening after it passed through the gate, and twisting and turning among the close-packed houses until it reached the open space that lay at the heart of the town. Here, Cray found almost nothing offered for sale – it was late in the day for marketing – but he did find a knot of gossiping people whom he approached to ask where he might purchase some wool. They looked him up and down, but without any fear, and when, in answer to their queries, he had gestured vaguely upriver to the supposed source of his travels, they directed him to a house down a side street. He thanked them, and they smiled at him, and they stared curiously as he walked away.

The house they sent him to had a door and a window open to the warm weather. As he neared it, he began to hear the faint familiar hum of a spinning wheel. He looked in the window and saw a woman of middle years, plump and rosy-cheeked, spinning grey wool into fine and even grey thread. Several full bobbins stood on a rack beside her, and the one on the wheel itself was filling steadily as he watched.

'Good morrow!' he called to her, and when she looked up, he smiled his friendliest smile. 'I'm told that I can purchase a bit of wool here.'

She looked at him with an open mouth, and then she rose and dusted her hands on her apron and hurried to the window. As had the gossipers, she looked him up and down, took in the knapsack and his plain clothing. Then she answered his smile with a small one of her own. 'Yes, we have wool here. What would you want to purchase it *with*?'

'I have a little silver,' said Cray.

'Silver? We don't see much of that around here.'

'Will you accept it?'

Her expression was doubtful. 'How much wool would you want?'

'Only as much as I can carry comfortably. But if the person I wish to show it to finds its quality suitable, I'll be back for more.'

Her expression took on a tinge of indignation. 'Our wool is very fine here, suitable for anything you might wish.'

'Then you will sell me some?'

'Yes. Yes, of course. Come in and we'll see how much you require.'

Inside, he found that the room containing the spinning wheel also served as bedroom and kitchen, with a double bed at one end and a hearth, table, and cooking implements at the other. Beside the wheel stood a bin containing some of the same loose grey wool that was being spun.

The woman went to the rack of full bobbins and took down three; they filled the crook of her arm. 'Will this be enough?'

Cray shook his head. 'No, I want the unspun wool, not the finished yarn.'

'Just the wool?'

'Yes. The lady prefers to spin it herself.'

'Very well.' She looked down at the bin, but there was only a small amount left there, no more than a double handful. Then she went to a door at the back of the room, near the bed, and opened it. Through the doorway, Cray could see bin upon bin of grey wool, washed and combed and carded, ready for spinning, and a whole wall full of bobbins already filled and waiting for weaving. The woman bent over the nearest bin and scooped out an overflowing armload to bring back to Cray.

'Perhaps this will suit you?' she said.

'Yes. Very much so.' He felt of the wool, rubbing it between his fingers. It was definitely not sheep's wool in either appearance or texture, but it seemed to make a soft yet sturdy cloth, judging from the clothing of the townspeople. He pulled a silver piece from his pouch and held it out to the woman.

She stared at the coin for a moment before taking it, and when she did take it, she went to the window and peered at it carefully. Then she tasted it. 'Is this a king's likeness on this coin?'

'I don't know,' he said, though he did know; he had even met the king. But a land where the rivers ran with gemstones was far, far from that lord's domain, and Cray preferred not to try to explain how he had come by the coin. 'I picked it up in my travels upriver. It looks old, doesn't it?'

The woman shrugged, turning it over and over in her hands. 'It is thin,' she said.

'Will it be enough?'

The woman smiled and then she laughed. 'This is more silver than I've seen in many a year. I don't know what I'll do with it. Perhaps hang it on a thong about my neck. I haven't much use for silver. But it is a pretty thing, isn't it?'

It was a simple silver coin, kept bright by passage from hand to hand since it was minted. Cray had several more just like it in his pouch.

'We don't use silver among ourselves,' said the woman. 'You must be from a city, where everything is bought with coins.'

'I've visited a few larger towns than this in my travels through the years,' Cray admitted.

'Take the wool, then. I've spun many a bobbin of yarn in my day, and I deserve a bit of jewellery for my efforts. Here, I've an old apron I can wrap it up in for you. You

142

can tie it to your pack and leave your hands free for leaning on that great staff you carry.' She took the apron down from its peg by the hearth and wrapped it about the wool, crushing the package down as small as possible. Then she bound it with yarn from one of her bobbins.

As she was finishing the tying, a man came to the street door of her house and called a greeting.

'Come in,' she said over her shoulder.

He was a tall man with a hard stride, his heavy boots pounding loudly on the wooden floor. He had a short beard, grizzled and grey, and a face sunburned by outdoor labour. His expression was wary, the first wary face Cray had seen in the town. Instead of addressing the woman, who obviously knew him, he spoke to Cray: 'So you're the traveller, are you?'

Cray bowed to him. 'Good morrow.'

'I'm the mayor of this town,' said the man. 'Rinveer is my name, and it is my business to know what goes on here.' He eyed the bundle that the woman had made. 'I see you'll be taking some of our wool with you on your journey.'

'It seems to be very fine wool,' said Cray.

Rinveer reached out to feel of a small tuft that protruded from the wrapping. 'Yes, this is quite fine. I am surprised that Rominda has given you some of our highest-quality wool. We have so little of it. This was a bad year, unfortunately, and we haven't much that is of such excellence. A bad year. A number of our animals sickened and did not produce as they should have; a few even died. A bad year indeed.'

Cray murmured sympathetically. 'Well, perhaps next year will be better.'

The mayor shook his head. 'Pasturage becomes worse every year. It isn't what it was when I was a boy, I can tell you. The animals don't fatten up the way they used to, and the wool shows it, too. No, I don't expect next year to be much better. If you want more wool of this quality in the future, you'd best go somewhere else, where the weather and the fodder are better.'

Cray gazed at the man thoughtfully, remembering the animals he had seen from the air, their fat bodies, their wool hanging almost down to the ground. Both pasturage and animals looked more than adequate to him. And then there was all that wool in the back room of this very cottage, surely the most recent shearing, and though he had not examined it closely, he thought it probably belied the mayor's words. Why, he wondered, was the man lying to him when the woman had seemed willing enough to give him as much wool as he could carry?

'What a shame,' said Cray, 'for truly I have seen little wool of this quality in my travels. I think that once she has examined it, my lady might well be interested in obtaining more.'

'And who would your lady be, sir?' asked the mayor.

Cray decided to offer the truth rather than invent a tale that might trip him up later. 'She is Delivev Ormoru of Castle Spinweb. Perhaps you've heard of her?'

Rinveer shook his head. 'Is this Spinweb far from here?'

'Very far,' said Cray. 'I couldn't begin to tell you how far I have travelled to come to this place.'

The mayor stared at him, a puzzled expression on his face. 'You travel far looking for wool?'

Cray smiled. 'No. I travel far for my own pleasure, to see new sights and meet new people. But if I happen to notice something interesting along the way, I stop to look more closely. In this case, since my lady is partial to spinning and weaving, and I encountered this wool, I thought to take some home to her. If she likes it well enough, she'll reward me, I can tell you, and she'll send for more, either by myself or some other servant.'

'She is a wealthy lady?'

'Comfortably so.'

Cray could see the conflicting attitudes at war on the man's face – doubt, hope, suspicion, greed. He *wanted* to say yes, come back; Cray sensed that strongly. But something kept him from it.

'She would pay in silver,' said Cray. 'Or, if you wish, in some form of barter. She is a tapestry maker of considerable renown, and her silk embroidery is excellent. Some arrangement could be made, I'm sure.'

The woman, who had stood silent while the men talked at cross purposes, now fingered Cray's sleeve. 'This wool,' she said. 'It is not like ours.'

'Oh?' said the mayor, and he bent close to Cray, peering at the fabric of his collar. 'No, it is not. Where did you get it?'

'My lady acquired it,' said Cray, standing very still while they examined the cloth. 'I receive all my clothing from her, of course.'

Rinveer looked up into Cray's face. 'I've never seen wool quite like this.'

'Its source is far from here. My lady trades widely for her fibres. She is a very particular person.'

The man rocked back on his heels. 'Then perhaps . . . perhaps you have not been sent here by Lord Olerat?'

'I don't know any such person,' said Cray.

'And you haven't come from Castle Vale?'

'I come from Spinweb and nowhere else, sir.'

'And you aren't one of Lord Olerat's tax gatherers?'

Cray looked at the very serious expression on his face and then broke into a soft chuckle. 'Ah, I see. You think I'm here to spy on your harvest in order to collect heavy taxes. No, no, not at all, good sir. Believe me, I am a traveller, and I have no connection whatever with your taxes and your lord. I was merely suggesting an honest exchange of goods. Your taxes are your own concern, not mine.'

Rinveer smiled tentatively. 'Then . . . perhaps we can make an exchange of some sort. Next year. Not this year, no. The wool *is* poor this year. But next year . . . perhaps.'

Cray decided to let the matter go at that. If next year's wool actually turned out to be finer than this year's, he guessed his mother would be quite pleased. In the time between now and then, Mayor Rinveer would have an opportunity to send his own spies to the castle of Lord Olerat and determine that the traveller who had taken away a sample of this year's wool was not a tax gatherer.

'Then next year,' Cray said, 'I will attempt to return, or, failing that, to send another servant from Spinweb, in the hopes that your harvest will be bountiful and of high quality. And perhaps my lady Delivev will offer an exchange that will benefit both you and her.' He tucked the packet of wool under one arm and then bowed to the mayor and to the woman Rominda. 'Now I must be on my way, for while the sun stands above the horizon, I travel.'

As he turned toward the door, Rinveer plucked at his sleeve. 'A moment only,' the man said when Cray looked back at him. 'We have told you our names, but what is yours?'

'Cray.'

'Ah. Well, perhaps we shall see you again next year, Cray of Spinweb.'

Cray smiled and passed through the doorway and started down the street. He had gone no more than a dozen paces, though, when he heard the woman's voice.

'Master Cray!'

He halted and half turned. 'Yes?'

She and the mayor were standing in the doorway. She glanced at the mayor before speaking again. 'Don't you want to tie that bundle to your pack? I could help you do it.'

He shook his head. 'I can carry it like this for now, thank you. Fare you well, good lady.' He went on, smiling to himself, sure that she had called him at the mayor's command, just to find out if he answered to the name he had given. He wondered if Lord Olerat laid such a heavy burden on these people that they feared to expose the quality of their wool to him, or if they were simply too greedy to pay him his due.

Rather than go back to the square, Cray took a meandering route to the wall and then followed that to the gate. In this way he was able to explore a large part of the town and to observe a number of artisans at work – the smith, the wheelwright, the potter, the tinker. He saw much that was familiar among these men; at one time or another, he had himself attempted most of the work he saw them engaged in, though for sorcerous, rather than ordinary purposes. With the smith, especially, he felt a kinship, and he stopped there for the longest time, to watch molten metal being poured into a mould. The smith, sweating and grimy, seemed hardly to notice him.

The sun was riding low in the western sky when Cray left the town at last, retracing his steps upriver toward the grove of trees. He was perhaps halfway there when Regneniel spoke, its deep voice emanating from the pack, but so softly that no one three paces away could have heard it.

'Five men are following you.'

Cray whirled to face them, his staff held out in both hands, held awkwardly because of the bundle under his arm. The men were spread out upon the path a dozen paces behind him, and they carried shorter staves than he, cudgels, really, and one of them had a drawn dagger. That was the mayor.

'What is this?' cried Cray, backing up warily.

'Your mistake, Cray of Spinweb, or whoever you really are,' said the mayor, 'was to go back the way you came.

Toward Castle Vale. You think no one saw you enter our town?' He was advancing steadily, in front of the others.

'The day is waning,' said Cray. 'I dawdled in your town too long, watching the smith, and now I've decided that yonder grove would be a fine place to spend the night. Better than lying out in the open downriver.'

The mayor halted, but only until the rest of the men caught up with him. Then they all came on. 'Try a better tale than that, O traveller.'

'It is the truth,' Cray said mildly.

'Oh, yes. As true as the one about travelling the world for the pleasure of it, with nothing more than a pack on your back. As true as the one about your mistress in a faraway castle, that none of us has ever heard of. Either you lie smoothly or you are mad. Either way, we shall do what we must this day.'

Cray continued to back off. 'I have done you no harm, and I mean to do you none. Leave me now, and I will forget this happened.'

'You will do us no harm,' said the mayor, and he lunged for Cray.

Years had passed since Cray had done any hand-to-hand fighting, but though the skills he had learned as a youth had faded, they were not entirely gone. Letting the bundle of wool drop away, he brought the lower end of his staff up and rammed it into Rinveer's belly. Then he slammed its upper end into the side of the next man's head. And then he leaped away from the fray and sprinted into the field of half-grown grain that lay beside the path, the three remaining men close at his heels.

'Let me fly you away from here!' came Regneniel's voice.

'No!' shouted Cray as he tore through the parallel rows of waist-high grain. All about him, the stalks began to wave wildly, as if the mild summer breeze had changed in a moment to storm, though the sky was clear and cloudless.

Between him and his pursuers, they stiffened suddenly, no longer mere plant stems that bent before a man's sweeping arms; now they were strong as steel rods. They whipped against the townsmen's legs, tearing at their trews, tripping them up and sending them sprawling between the rows. And when the fallen men tried to rise, the grain stalks bent over them like cage bars, trapping them firmly against the ground. Cray could hear the men crying out behind him, first in confusion and then in fear.

He came to a halt some distance from them and turned. The men themselves, lying pinned to the ground, were not visible, but their positions were clearly marked by the gaps in that sea of standing grain. Cray walked toward them slowly, stopping beside the nearest. He was thoroughly trapped, even his cudgel overlaid with crisscrossed stalks. Even so, he was struggling frantically, babbling in terror.

Cray kicked him in the shoulder, not very hard, but hard enough to get his attention. 'Be quiet!' he said.

The man seemed to swallow his words and half choke on them. He rolled his eyes to look at Cray; the stalks would not allow him to raise his head. 'Who are you?' he gasped. 'What have you done to us?'

Cray looked toward the path, where the two injured men were just staggering to their feet. One held his head, the other could not stand up straight. Cray caused the row of grain nearest them to become a rigid fence, its uprights too close together for them to pass. But they were making no attempt to do so.

The other two men, only a few paces from Cray, were quieting now, waiting, helpless, for their fate.

Cray bent to pull the cudgel from the nearest man; the stalks about it relaxed to release it, and so did the man's fingers. Cray hefted it in one hand, leaning on his own staff with the other. 'So this is how you treat an innocent traveller,' he said. He tossed the cudgel away and kicked the man again, a bit harder this time. 'I could kill you,

you know. I would be perfectly justified in killing you.'
He made the stalks that held the man tighten suddenly,
and the man gasped but did not cry out. Cray knew he
could barely breathe and, after a long moment, allowed
the stalks to loosen once more. 'Do you know what I am?'
he said harshly.

The townsman was panting. 'My lord,' he whispered.

'Louder,' said Cray. 'Loud enough for the others to
hear.'

'My lord!' wailed the man.

'I am a sorcerer,' said Cray. 'I came to you in peace and
friendship, offering good silver for your wares. And what
did I receive for my troubles?' Once again he kicked the
man, and when he had done that he felt better, the bulk
of his anger vented. 'You are fortunate indeed that I don't
much care for killing. Some sorcerers would not hesitate
to wipe out the lot of you. But you – you'll only have a
few bruises to show for your evil intentions.'

'Thank you, my lord, thank you,' the man babbled.

'Quiet,' said Cray. 'You'll tell all the rest of the town, I
know, what happened to you here. And you'll remember,
won't you, that Cray Ormoru of Spinweb is *not* a tax
gatherer.'

'Yes, my lord, I swear it. I swear it.'

'And none of you will ever lie to me again, or to anyone
from Castle Spinweb, about the quality of your wool.'

'It shall be as you say, my lord. Always.'

Cray dropped his staff and gestured for his bundle
of wool to come bouncing through the grain to him.
Then he shrugged off his knapsack and drew Regneniel
from it. 'Become a bird, O demon,' he said, and he
tossed the mouse a few paces off. In moments, his
feathered steed was ready for flight, and he mounted,
and together they leaped into the sky. As they soared
upwards, Cray released the spell that made the grain
stalks strong as steel, and when he looked back and

down he could see the men on their feet, staring after him as he flew away.

He sighed. *Poor fools*, he thought. They had got more than they reckoned for on this day. Yet he had no feeling of triumph at the outcome. Rather, he wished they had not forced him to reveal himself, for he knew now that they would live in fear of him, always wondering if he might not change his mind someday and return for stronger vengeance. Now they would watch the skies, and every white bird would seem a signal of danger. *Poor fools*. He shook his head. 'You were certainly right about these mortals, Regneniel. They were unpredictable indeed.' He scanned the horizon but saw nothing between it and himself save fields and pastures and the winding amethyst river. 'Do you know this Lord Olerat's Castle Vale, Regneniel?'

'There is a castle some distance up the river,' replied the demon. 'There is none closer. But I do not know its name.'

'Let us fly there. I am curious to see it.'

'As you wish.'

High above the river, they cut a straight path across its lazily looping course. The land rolled below them, a human being or an animal visible now and then, even a peasant hut close by the river, and later a whole cluster of them, a village. They were just passing over the village when Cray caught his first glimpse of the castle on the northern horizon. The sun was low to his left, an orange ball floating above the gentle hills, and the castle was a jagged silhouette against the deepening blue ahead. As they approached it, Cray realized it was as large as any mortal castle he had ever seen, its walls enclosing enough space to contain an entire town such as he had explored this day. It commanded the summit of a hill that, though low, was the loftiest in sight, and it sprawled from that summit down to the very base of the hill, its many-towered walls ringing that base like a crown. Such a castle had to be the seat of a powerful lord, and Cray wondered how the townspeople could have had the courage to defy him. Then, turning to look back the way they had come, he realized that the town lay far beyond the horizon, perhaps farther than a man on horseback could travel in half a month. By the standards he knew, that placed it on the periphery of even the most powerful lord's domain. He shook his head wryly. Riding a demon, he had begun to think of distance as a demon did, and any two places he could visit in a single day seemed close together.

The river deepened as it passed the castle, cutting a gorge that made that side unapproachable by ordinary mortals. In the red light of the lowering sun, the fast-flowing water sparkled, its purple colour drowned in the ruddy light. And the castle itself sparkled, catching the sunset on dozens of crystalline windows set high in its towers. With so many different kinds of crystal plentiful hereabouts, Cray mused, it was only natural that a power-ful – and therefore wealthy – lord would have very large pieces placed in his windows to keep out the weather while letting in the sunlight. Cray smiled at that, and he fingered his pouch, where the egg-sized amethyst nestled; perhaps he would bring some of that large crystal home someday, to make a window or two for Spinweb.

High above the castle they soared, circling its towers, its courtyards, marking its perimeter in the sky. Below, soldiers on the walls seemed toy figures, their pikes like knitting needles, their torches like firefly-glow. The sun sank below the western horizon, and the whole castle was outlined with torches, like a pattern of luminous beads upon the hill.

'We can stay no longer,' said Regneniel. 'My lady com-manded me to bring you back for supper, and we have only enough time for the return trip.'

'Very well,' said Cray. 'I won't play the traveller here today. Another day, perhaps.'

The great bird wheeled and started southward at high speed, and Cray clung close to its feathered back in the deepening dark. There was no moon to light the way, but a demon needed none, needed not even the stars to show its course, for it had senses other than human ones to guide it. On Cray's right, the last faint glow of the sun faded away, and above him the stars brightened till they were white and crisp and cold in the black sky. Below, the ground was invisible. Cray flew, somewhere in the middle of nothingness, with only the unimaginably distant stars overhead to show that there was a world outside his wind-buffeted self.

And then he shivered, and not just because the wind that whipped his flesh was chill with the loss of the sun. He shivered because, looking up at that vast array of pinpoint lights, he recognized not a single one. He had watched the sky ten thousand nights from Spinweb's walls, and he knew the patterns of the stars as he knew the flowers in his mother's garden. But not these patterns, not these stars. Where was the Wain, the Hunter, the Lion? He could not even find the Northern Star, which should have stood high over his shoulder, about which all the rest swung.

Crystalline mountains. Rivers running with gemstone sand. Strange plants and animals. And now the sky itself transformed.

I am very far from home, he thought. *Very far*. And a piercing sense of loneliness assailed him, there in the unknown sky, a loneliness such as he had never known before.

He was glad when the demon bird swooped down toward their destination, toward the palace that glowed like a living jewel with its own internal radiance, glad to see those transparent walls draw near, and gladder still to see Aliza herself waiting by the open window, her pale face tilted up to watch him descend. Here at least was some refuge from the loneliness, a familiar place, a familiar voice, familiar cool dark eyes. He and his steed slipped smoothly past her and lighted with the gentlest of thumps on the crystalline floor.

Chapter 6

'You've been gone a long time,' Aliza said as Cray dismounted from his great white demon steed. As soon as his feet touched the floor, the bird began to dwindle, and in a moment it had regained the awkward, angular shape in which it normally served its mistress.

Cray bowed to her. 'Forgive me for causing you worry, my lady. But Regneniel assured me we would be back in time for supper.'

'Yes, yes, you are,' Aliza said quickly. 'I wasn't worried. I knew Regneniel would look after you. But . . . I thought you would tire of the human realm a bit more quickly.'

'It's a most interesting place,' he said, smiling at her. 'You should try exploring it sometime.'

Her lips quirked, as if she were suppressing a smile in answer to his. 'Precisely what I expected you to say.' She gestured toward the bundle under his arm. 'I see you brought something back with you.'

'A packet of wool for my mother. There's something of an adventure connected with it, if you'd like to hear.'

'Something *interesting* that happened to you in the human realm?'

'I think so.'

'Why don't you tell me about it while we sup?' She pointed past him, and when he turned to look in that direction, he saw that the far end of the huge room now had a bit of furniture in it – a crystalline table set with a cold supper for two, flanked by a pair of familiar wooden chairs. 'I thought we could sit over there,' said Aliza, 'out of the wind but still in full view of those stars you spoke of earlier.'

'The stars. Ah, yes.' He fell in step beside her as she

walked toward the table. 'I suppose you don't look at them very often.'

'Not very often.'

As they reached the table, the luminosity above and below them began to fade. At the same time, the table itself began to glow softly, radiating as much as a dozen candles, an eerie sort of illumination that left the plates as pools of shadow and the wine in crystalline goblets like hemispherical chunks of stained glass. The transparent walls of the palace seemed to vanish in the darkness, leaving the table and two human beings suspended in air, with only the star-strewn sky as their roof.

'If you really want to look at them,' Aliza said, 'there's no use in having so much light to drown them out.'

He did not even have to lift his eyes to see them. But he was not looking at them now. He was looking at Aliza's face; lit from below, it had hollows he had not noticed before, and her dark eyes seemed deep set in the shadows above her cheekbones. He raised his glass. 'To you, my lady Aliza, and to the marvellous worlds in which you live.'

She stared at him, her expression puzzled. 'What's that you're doing?'

'Making a toast, of course.'

'What is a toast?'

He had to laugh. 'I have more to tell you than I thought. Much more.' He sipped from his goblet. 'Ah, Maretian. I see Regneniel did fetch more.'

'Yes. Yes it did.' Her eyes strayed from his face and focused on something beyond his shoulder. She waved sharply, and when Cray turned to look in that direction, he saw the faint light of the table glinting from Regneniel's retreating form.

'Where does your demon go when you dismiss it?' he asked. 'Out to Ice or to some hidey-hole here in the palace?'

Aliza shrugged. 'Does it matter? It comes when I call; that's the only important thing. Now . . . you were going to tell me what a toast was.'

Over the years, the ruined castle had gradually been rebuilt, though by human rather than demon workers. It had not regained its former grandeur in the process; its towers were stubby now and far less numerous, its courtyard-facing rooms were walled as much by wood as by stone, its keep rose only two storeys, and those shallower than once they were. But the loose debris was gone, most of the chambers had roofs, and if some of the stairways were still crumbled, why, they led nowhere important anyway.

One addition had been made to the structure, never planned by its former master: copper. Every layer of new mortar had copper strands embedded in it, every window opening was rimmed with copper ribbon, every doorway, every crenellation of the battlements was outlined in copper. If the stone could all suddenly become invisible, the shape of the castle would remain in ruddy copper lines.

A few of the workers that had laboured on the castle still lived in it, or their children, or their brothers, their sisters. They came from the nearest village, ten days' journey away; they came to serve the sorcerer Everand in exchange for his protection of their village. In exchange for his promise not to kill them all with a wave of his hand. They stayed in simply furnished quarters to one side of the courtyard; they had made all of the furnishings themselves. Everand lived in the keep, at the heart of the castle, and save for a few crystalline gewgaws, the furnishings of his quarters were no better than theirs.

To the keep came Regneniel. Its journey, which would have taken a month on horseback, required only moments by way of Ice.

Everand was sitting at his worktable, drawing copper

wire. When he saw the demon at his window, he put the tongs aside and stood up. 'What news?'

The demon bowed low before him. 'The visitor wished to explore some of the human realm near her palace, and she commanded me to fly with him while she remained behind. Shortly after full dark we returned, and now the two of them are supping together.'

'Supping together,' muttered Everand. Then he struck the table so hard with one fist that all the apparatus upon it jumped. 'I won't have it!' he shouted. 'What right does this Cray Ormoru have to interrupt her studies?' He pointed a finger at the demon. 'If he does *not* leave tomorrow morning, you will remind her, gently but firmly, that she has work to attend to. My yearly examination is coming up, and I expect a certain amount of progress from her, and every moment that she wastes with this, this *visitor* is a moment that would otherwise have helped her to achieve the level of competence that I expect!' He clutched the edge of the table with white-knuckled fingers. 'She'll tire of him, of course. It's just the novelty of another mortal. At least she didn't go off exploring with him! She knows her purpose. But this Cray Ormoru and his stupid mirror! I thought she was safe from all outside influences.' He clasped his hands behind his back and, turning away from the demon, paced out the length of the room once, twice. Then he stopped at the far end of the table and picked up a length of copper rod as big around as his wrist. He rolled it between his palms. 'Perhaps I'm making too much of this. Perhaps it's really nothing at all. A day or two – what difference will they make in the long run? One visitor, one curious young man . . . Very well; I remember being young and curious. And attracted by a pretty girl. But he'll tire of her. She's cold as an ice demon, cold as you are, Regneniel. He'll tire of her.' He waved one hand at the demon. 'Go back now, I have work to do.'

*   *   *

'I don't understand why you're so reluctant to use your power in front of ordinary mortals,' Aliza said, sipping from her second goblet of wine. 'You could have avoided all that unpleasantness if you had done a few tricks at the very beginning. Then they would never have suspected you of being a tax gatherer.'

Cray nodded. 'You're quite right. They would have bowed and scraped and cringed before the great sorcerer. They would have given me anything I wanted, out of fear. But I don't much care for inspiring fear. I suppose I'm just not comfortable being a master. Which makes me a rather unusual sort of sorcerer, doesn't it?'

Aliza shrugged. 'Power and mastery – are they not the same thing?'

'Not necessarily. One can use power to help others rather than to dominate them. If I had completed my training as a knight, I would have had a certain amount of power – not just skill, but authority as well – and I would have been expected to use it in the service of my lord, in promoting his justice and defending his honour.' He looked into his goblet, into the deep red of its contents. 'Of course, I didn't delude myself on that score. I knew there were nobles as greedy and selfish as any sorcerer, who used their knights to oppress common folk and to make war for unjust gain. I had seen much of the world in my mother's webs, and I had few illusions. Still, I felt that if I searched long enough I could find an honest lord to serve, a decent and just master whose purposes would never shame me. I think I found such a one in my travels; I trained for a winter at his castle. Perhaps I would have joined his household permanently if sorcery had not called me back. Perhaps.' He looked up at her. 'You see, I had no objections at all to serving rather than commanding. It just turned out not to suit my purposes.' He took a swallow of wine. 'Those were good days, in my youth. I didn't appreciate them enough at the time.'

'I can't imagine living as an ordinary mortal,' Aliza said.

'Few sorcerers can, I think.'

'Without any power at all. Having to scrape at the earth for food, or barter things made by my own hands.' She frowned. 'I remember, on our way to that town I told you of, with my mother, we passed fields of grain, and people were working there, bent over. The men had their shirts off, and they were sweating. It was a warm day, but *I* wasn't sweating, and I remember thinking how hard they must be working to sweat like that.'

'Oh, yes,' said Cray, 'sorcery has its advantages – there is no doubt about that.'

'What was it like,' she wondered, 'training to be a knight?'

'Sweaty.' He smiled at her. 'Have you ever seen a knight?'

'Yes. Once. Out there.' She pointed to the darkness that lay beyond the transparent wall. 'It was a long time ago. I hadn't raised the mountains yet, and there was still forest all around the palace, no sand at all.' She glanced sidelong at Cray. 'Yes, hard as that may be to believe, there was forest here at one time, so close that if I opened a window I could put my hand out and touch the leaves on the trees.' She gazed out into the night again. 'The palace was much smaller then, but its uppermost rooms were already above the treetops. He must have seen them from the hills. Regneniel called my attention to him; even then, I didn't spend much time in this part of the palace. When I saw him he was crashing through the trees on his horse, hacking at the downhanging branches, as if he were angry with them – there wasn't any path, of course. He came right up to the wall and he stared at it for a long time, and then he rode all the way round the building, apparently looking for an entrance. When he didn't find one, he began to bang on the wall with his lance. It made a terrible racket. Terrible. He spent most of the day doing that, on one wall after another, and then he built a fire right outside and stayed awake the whole night, staring, just staring. In the morning he tried the lance again, but eventually he got tired of that and went away. I was glad to see him go, too. Aside from the noise, I thought he might do some damage to my walls.' She looked back at Cray. 'That was before I realized how strong they were. Or perhaps I should say, that was *when* I realized how strong they were.'

'How did you know he was a knight if you'd never seen one before?'

'I didn't at the time. He was just a very large man on a very large horse, and he carried a lance and a shield and wore a suit of steel plate. Later my grandfather told me what such people were called.' Her eyes slid downwards from Cray's face to his arms and shoulders. 'I suppose you have to be very strong to wear all that steel. Somehow you don't quite look like you could manage it.'

He chuckled softly. 'It was a long time ago, my lady. And I never did get to wearing plate. Just chain. That was heavy enough, believe me. I told you it was sweaty work to be a knight.' He cupped his goblet in his two hands – his second goblet of wine, but he had hardly touched it. He wanted to stay awake this evening. 'But tell me: you watched him for so long, didn't he ever try to communicate with you? To shout, or perhaps to write messages in the dirt or some such?'

She shook her head. 'He couldn't see me. I was looking out at him through a mirrored interior wall. You saw the kind. I can see out through it, but no one can see in.'

'You didn't have any desire to find out what he wanted?'

'He wanted to come in, I knew that well enough. And when he couldn't find a door, he was willing to smash his way in. I didn't want to meet someone like that. I didn't know what he would do when he found me.'

Cray leaned back in his chair. 'Well, this is a mysterious-looking place and therefore attractive. A man passing by could easily believe that it might contain . . . anything. Silver. Gold. A beautiful maiden.' He smiled at her. 'And he would be right on that score.'

Without an answering smile, Aliza said, 'If he had broken through my walls, I would have retreated into Ice. I already knew how to open fractures for myself by then. I would have led him into one and let it close on him. And there he would have been, crushed flat in Ice forever. His reward for disturbing my privacy.'

'I'm glad you've changed your attitude toward strangers since then,' Cray murmured.

She set her goblet down and lightly fingered its stem and foot. 'Soon after he went away, I learned to bring that special sand up from deep within the earth, and to cast the spell that floats in the air above it. My grandfather had Regneniel clear the trees and undergrowth from all around the palace, and I spread the sand thick and far. No one pounded on my walls after that. No one bothered me.'

'Until I came.'

She nodded. 'Even the ice demons, when they come by, only look in for a time and then move on. Since that day, that man with the lance, you are the only one who has . . . petitioned to enter. You say you trained for a time to be a knight. Perhaps if you had become one, you would have arrived at my walls in Ice with a lance instead of a bell.'

'You mustn't judge all knights by that one. Perhaps he had heard stories of the great magical jewel growing in the middle of the forest. Perhaps he thought cold steel would break its enchantment and he would find something wonderful inside – I heard similar tales when I was training, though I always took them to be nonsense. They usually involved caves, or hollow trees, or holes under rocks, or even enchanted cottages in the depths of faraway forests, all of them entrances to netherworlds of treasure. Bold

162

men sought out those entrances and brought away as much gold as they could carry, and sometimes an enchanted princess as well, just to make the adventure complete. Mortals are full of such tales; they tell them in winter, sitting near a blazing hearth. But I never met a man who claimed to have had such an adventure. Those were always someone else, somewhere else; they had names, but no one had ever met them. And here the man came, his winters full of such stories, and he saw his opportunity to listen some cold night to a tale of himself. I'd guess the temptation to at least investigate this place was very strong.'

'He was a brave man,' Aliza remarked, 'to chance death by sorcery. I recall thinking that at the time. Brave. And very foolish.'

'I have seen men that brave and that foolish,' Cray replied. 'Sorcerers are widely scattered, and aloof. Only their nearest neighbours understand their power, and sometimes not even they. The vast majority of ordinary mortals know nothing of sorcery but what they tell each other in these winter tales. Real sorcery is as remote to them as the stars. I trained among such folk, and I know there are some of them who fear only mortal weapons, the lance, the sword, the arrow. In the stories, these weapons and a man's cleverness are always enough to overcome sorcery.'

Aliza shook her head slowly. 'Perhaps you should have enlightened them.'

'Not I. I was a simple squire, and my task was to listen and learn, not to instruct.'

Her cool dark eyes narrowed. 'You found posing as an ordinary mortal to be . . . interesting.'

'I wasn't posing, my lady. I *was* an ordinary mortal. For that winter, at least. And yes, it was very interesting. I learned things that no sorcerer ever learns. Perhaps some of them would seem pointless to you, but I've found them useful.'

163

'In your sorcery?'

'In my life.'

She cocked her head to one side, her expression uncertain. 'What sorts of things?'

'Camaraderie. Co-operation. And, I hope, some measure of understanding of other mortals.'

She shrugged. 'Things that are only important if other mortals happen to impinge upon your life.'

'Sometimes they impinge, my lady, whether we ask for them or not. Your knight, for example.'

'Or you,' she said.

He inclined his head in acknowledgement of that. 'It is always good to know how to deal with a thing effectively before being confronted with it. Who knows how many more times mortals may enter your life?'

'They won't enter if I don't want them to.'

'And if you *should* want them to?' He smiled. 'After all, here *I* am.'

She gazed at him levelly. 'I think I'm dealing with you well enough.'

'I'm remarkably easy to deal with.'

'How fortunate for me. Perhaps, then, I'll never let anyone else in.'

He looked down at his goblet. 'You may say such things now. But every life is full of possibilities. You can't predict what you'll think and how you'll feel later on, perhaps a century or two from now, when you're no longer an apprentice, no longer young.' He raised his eyes to hers. 'A day may even come when you decide to venture beyond these walls and explore the human realm, to interact with other mortals. I know that sounds repellent to you, but . . . a sorcerer's life is long.'

She was frowning, turning her half-full goblet between the thumb and middle finger of one hand, turning it back and forth, back and forth where it rested on the glowing table. At last she said, 'You are right, Cray Ormoru. I should not assume that the way I feel now will be the way I feel forever. Perhaps mortals will be of use to me someday. Perhaps. But as you said, a sorcerer's life is long, and I am young, and so there will be plenty of time for me to learn about mortals if and when I should decide to mingle with them.'

'And yet,' Cray said, 'here I am, a vast reservoir of information on the subject, totally at your disposal. When will you have a better opportunity to learn? Your demon surely cannot tell you more about mortals than I can. Nor, I would guess, can your grandfather. Why waste me?'

She looked at him hard. 'You wish to be my teacher?'

'Why not? I know myself that there is some advantage to having more than one.'

'Have you ever had an apprentice?'

He shook his head.

'And you think it might be . . . interesting.'

'Yes. For both of us.'

She played with her goblet a bit more, then drank lightly from it. 'I am too busy.'

'I don't ask for your full time, just for a supper like this now and then where we can talk. Surely you don't begrudge yourself a leisurely meal or two.'

'I usually think about my studies while I eat.'

Cray laughed softly. 'Bend a little of that dedication to understanding the human realm, and you shall be an expert in it sooner than you think.'

'Shall I?' She pursed her lips. 'Very well. For the sake of my education. For the sake of my future needs, whatever they may be, tell me about ordinary mortals.' She leaned forward, elbows on the luminous table. 'Tell me about the men you trained with. They were knights, weren't they?'

'Knights and squires,' said Cray. 'And every one of them a better swordsman than I. They made me work, I can tell you. My muscles ache just to remember it.'

* * *

Only when dawn began to drown out the glow of the table did Cray realize how long they had been talking. He had ranged far from the knights and squires of the castle yard, beating at each other's shields with their wooden swords. He had spoken of the pages, just children skittering about on their elders' errands; of the men-at-arms who walked the battlements day and night and slept there standing up, leaning against their pikes; of the stablehands with their huge and ponderous charges that wore plate mail heavy enough to crush a man; of the scullions who hung about the kitchen waiting for pots and pans to scrub and filching scraps from whatever joint was turning on the spit; of the lord and lady, elegantly clothed, gracious and generous to all, even the crudest churl; of the hagglers in the weekly market, who never let a chicken pass from one person to another without an argument. And while he spoke, he re-created that winter in his memory – the sharp cold of the blustering wind up on the walls, the sparkling whiteness of new snow that accumulated in the yard and had to be shovelled into barrows for removal out of the postern gate, and the cheerful sound of good fellowship pledged in ale about the blazing hearth. No one at that castle had known Cray was a child of the sorcerous breed; he was simply one of them, a plain person trying to muddle through life as best he could. What did the bruises of the practice-field matter to any of them? They had a roof over their heads, food in their bellies, a kind master and laughing friends. How much more, Cray wondered, could anyone hope for?

He yawned behind his hand. 'Have I really been talking all night?'

Aliza looked out to the eastern sky. 'So it seems. It was a summer night, though – much shorter than those winter ones.' She stifled a yawn with her fingers. 'Your demons will be coming back for you soon. Perhaps it would be a good idea for you to get some sleep before the long journey home.'

He yawned again. 'Not a bad idea.'

'Did you find the couch comfortable enough?'

He grinned. 'Quite comfortable, compared to my pallet that winter. But have you no guest bed for when your grandfather visits?'

'He never stays to sleep,' said Aliza.

'Ah. Then the couch will do eminently well.'

With his bundle of wool under one arm, he walked with her, back toward the heart of her palace, back toward Ice. Ahead of them, light grew in the ceilings, the floors, like sheets of cold flame, the familiar blue-white luminosity banishing the new rosiness of dawn, banishing the dark night and the strange stars. Gradually the air about them grew warmer, though even in the room with the entry to Ice, it was never as stifling as it had been when the sun was high, it was only pleasant. The heat left over from the day, Cray realized, must have nearly all been used up in holding the cold of Ice at bay for a night; now, with the rising of the sun that heat would be replenished, and by midday these rooms would be too warm for human comfort once more. He wondered how well the system worked in winter, when the sun was low and cold and the days were short. He hoped Aliza would let him come back then and find out.

The mirrored door dissolved before them, revealing the steep, tunnel-like stairway that led down to the cloudy-walled room and the part of the palace that lay in Ice. They descended.

The room seemed smaller than ever to Cray, compared to the open, unfurnished spaces he had just come from. The child-sized furniture and the bins were still there, of course, crowding close to the narrow aisle that connected the two doors. But this time Cray saw something else, something that tugged at his memory, something that made him pause while Aliza walked on. It was a boss on one of the walls, a projection not much larger than his hand. It

167

was one of a dozen such set a bit lower than the level of his shoulders at regular intervals along all six walls of the room. Apparently made of the same cloudy substance as the wall from which it protruded, the boss was a four-sided pyramid in shape, with apex toward the viewer and all sides marked by thin ribbons of copper running parallel to its base. The effect, for a person viewing one of these objects straight on, was of a lozenge with copper strands repeating the lozenge shape five times concentrically. The mind flattened the protrusion, making the four triangular sides seem like the four quadrants of some bizarre coat of arms and the subtle differences in lighting from one facet to another represent actual different shades of pale grey. This was what he had seen in the Mirror of Heart's Desire that first time, what – in that still and silent picture – he had not been able to make any other sense of. He had to smile at how completely his eyes had been fooled by the unfamiliar, by what he now perceived as just another manifestation of crystal in this so entirely crystalline place.

Realizing that he was no longer following her, Aliza had stopped just beyond the next doorway. Now she came back into the room and looked at him inquiringly. 'You've found something that interests you?'

He nodded. 'This is the room you were in the first time I saw you in the mirror.'

Her gaze swept the small room from one end to the other. 'Yes, I suppose that would be the case. I spent most of my time here as a child. This is the cradle room.'

Cray glanced at the child's bed, far too short for an adult but without any rockers that he could see. 'You threw the cradle out years ago, I suppose.'

Her lips quirked. 'No, there never was a cradle here; I was too old for such things by the time my grandfather apprenticed me. And I never throw anything out, as I think you can tell from all the rubbish that's in here. Look over in the corner and you can see the rocking horse I once rode.' She gestured toward it. 'No, I call this the cradle room because *it* was my cradle, back at the beginning, the very first room of the palace, the seed that Regneniel set in Ice, from which all the rest began to grow. It was quite cosy while I was very short. But it's been a long time since I was able to fit in that bed or that chair, and the table is just a trifle too low for comfortable eating these days.'

'Why do you keep the walls cloudy?' asked Cray.

'I don't. That is their nature, the way Regneniel made them, and they can't be changed.'

'But if this room was the seed, why is it so different from all the other rooms? How could these cloudy walls produce the perfectly transparent ones that are everywhere else?'

'Is the seed so like the plant that grows from it?' Aliza asked him.

'No, that's true enough.'

'The cloudiness means nothing, structurally. It is merely an inclusion of air bubbles in the crystal matrix. My grandfather had his demon make the walls like this because he thought the grandeur of Ice would be too disquieting for a child accustomed to the human realm. This was the shelter he thought I would need, a place from which I could venture out and experience the sensations of infinite depth and infinite dark nothingness that are the true nature of Ice even though it is solid. A place to which I could retreat and find respite from that awesome experience.' She shrugged. 'Perhaps he allowed his own fears to govern him. I know that he finds the transparency of Ice . . . disturbing. But I think he overestimated my uneasiness, for I found both Ice and this palace fascinating. And yet, I did spend most of my childhood in this room.' She sat down on the lip of one of the translucent bins and let her fingers stray over the folds of fabric that filled it. Bed linen, Cray guessed that fabric to be, fine-woven but somewhat yellowed with age. 'Even when there were rooms aplenty waiting for me,' Aliza said, 'with some of the furniture you've already seen, chairs and cabinets and so on, I spent my time here. I felt comfortable here, everything I wanted was here. Look, there's my stuffed animal.' She leaned over to the next bin and pulled it out from a jumble of small wooden cubes, rods, and pyramids. It was more bedraggled than Cray had ever seen it, and just as difficult to put a name to. It could have been a dog, a lamb, a horse, or one of the animals he had watched from Regneniel's feathered back, or it could have been none of them. Its neck was long, but not very long, its legs were short, but not extremely short, and its ears were tattered.

Aliza dropped it into her lap and rested one hand on it as she spoke. 'And this room is special in another way, of course, for you can't get to the other side of the palace, the one in the human realm, without passing through it. This is the crossroads of the building, the heart of the building.' She stroked the stuffed animal absently, without looking down at it. 'I don't come here very often. I'm not a child any more.' And then, as if suddenly realizing what her hand was doing, she stiffened and, grasping the stuffed toy firmly, thrust it back where it had come from. But even as she pulled her hand away from it, she hesitated, and her fingers brushed other objects in the bin. 'Toys,' she said, touching a perforated wooden cube here, a slender wooden rod there. 'My grandfather was always giving me toys that could be used for building. Geometrical shapes at first, and then later pillars, lintels, arches. I built many a wooden castle right here on this floor. And when I tired of that, I'd duplicate the pieces in crystal and build castles of that. I became quite a good architect. He always praised me for that, almost as much as he praised me for my studies. He said every sorcerer should know how to build.' She found a wooden archway no larger than her index finger and cradled it in the palm of her hand. 'Of course, now I can raise an entire castle from the soil of the human realm without ever touching it, without ever stacking one block

170

on top of another. Turrets, battlements, even a portcullis made entirely of crystal.' She dropped the miniature arch back among the other toys.

'It's a great skill,' said Cray. 'Most sorcerers have to command demons to build their castles, or even human masons.'

She looked up at him. 'Spinweb, your mother's castle – in which fashion was it constructed?'

'Neither. Spiders built it for the first Ormoru, back when the world was young. They quarried the stone and dragged it to the site and piled it up block upon block until it stood as it stands today.'

'Spiders?' said Aliza. 'How could such tiny creatures build a castle of stone?'

He smiled at her. 'Don't underestimate the strength of ten thousand spiders working together.'

'Ten thousand!'

'Or more. In such numbers, they move in a thick carpet, and the heaviest boulder is nothing to them. All they need is time, and they can raise whatever castle their master may require.' Dropping his bundle of wool to the floor, he sat down on the lip of the bin that held the toy building materials. 'Would you like to see the kind of castle ten thousand spiders can build? I'm sure my mother would be pleased to have you visit. It's a large and airy place, and as unlike this palace as any structure I could imagine. We don't serve Maretian wine there, but I think we have one or two you might enjoy.'

'No,' she said, shaking her head firmly. 'I have my studies. I could never go as far as Spinweb, I could never spare the time.'

'But there is so much that my mother and I could show you there,' Cray said. 'Her tower room, where she weaves spells into cloth. My workshop, where I smelt sorcerous metal, and the garden, where I blend that metal with livin* things. And more, much more.'

171

She looked at him long and hard, her cool dark eyes narrow, as if she could see into him somehow, with only her ordinary senses. Her right hand slipped from her lap to the linen fabric in the bin, and she gripped a fold of it between her fingers and worked them, up and back, up and back, against that finely-textured surface. At last she said, 'You have made me think, Cray Ormoru. You have come boldly into my life and shown me that what lies beyond these walls is not, after all, completely without interest for me. I admit that I found your tales of training for knighthood to be diverting, and I admit that perhaps it has been short-sighted of me to reject the human realm so thoroughly. Yet for now I have my studies, and a master to answer to, and I must choose carefully how to spend my time. Spinweb is far away, and if I did go there the visit would keep me long. Too long. I must return to my work. You were an apprentice – you know how short-tempered a master can be with a dawdler.'

'He can't punish you, surely; he can't even reach you, not with the spell on the sand and Ice all around you. Not now that you control the demon.'

'His anger and his disappointment in me have always been punishment enough,' said Aliza. She smiled slightly at the surprised expression on Cray's face. 'Yes, I've disappointed him before through dawdling, though not lately. I don't want to do it again. I want him to be proud of me. Surely you can understand that. You must have wanted your mother to be proud of you.'

'I was a wilful child,' Cray said. 'Her pride was less important to me than my own. But I think I understand your attitude. Still, don't reject my invitation out of hand. Thi̇̇̇ t it. I'll leave it open until you're ready to ̇d meanwhile . . .' He leaned a little toward you'll let me come here another time and

d her cool eyes. 'Yes. Another time.' A

172

moment later she rose suddenly from the rim of the bin. 'I'm very tired, Cray Ormoru. I'll lead you to your sleeping place now.'

He nodded. But before he stood and gathered up his bundle of wool, he selected a rod as long as his hand and a perforated cube the size of his fist from the bin of toys. 'Would you mind if I borrowed these for a little time?'

She cast him a puzzled glance. 'What do you want them for?'

'Just to amuse myself with till I fall asleep.'

Aliza shrugged. 'If you wish.'

In the room of the tapestry, she turned the walls to mirrors and dimmed all the lights save for a glow, equal to a brace of candles, over one end of the couch. 'You'll need this much light for your . . . amusement, won't you?' Her expression was still puzzled.

'Do you want to watch?' asked Cray.

'Watch what?'

'Watch now.' He fitted the rod tightly into one of the cube's perforations. 'I hope you don't mind if I spoil this. I didn't think you'd be using it for anything in the future.'

'Do as you will,' said Aliza, her eyes on his hands.

With his knife, he cut a deep notch in the end of the rod opposite the cube. Then he opened the bundle of wool and pulled loose a generous handful, which he slung over his shoulder like some airy pelt. Teasing a small amount of this half free of the mass, he twisted it into a string almost as long as his forearm and slipped the free end securely into the notch. Then, passing the string over one finger and letting the cube-weighted rod hang in mid-air by short tether, he gave the wooden contrivance a spin with his free hand. The rod twirled like a top, and as it did so, he began to pull more wool partly free of the mass on his shoulder; the wool twisted as he fed it out, and the rod dropped lower and lower, pulling the wool into a longer and longer thread. When the rod reached the floor, Cray

173

paused, wound the new-made thread onto it, secured the last of the twisted part to the notch, and began again.

'You're spinning yarn,' Aliza said.

'The most ancient form of spinning,' Cray replied. 'My mother taught it to me when I was a child, more as a game than for any real production of thread. But it does have one advantage over the wheel – one can walk about while doing it.' He strolled slowly around the ebony table. 'I find it relaxing. After a day of working with metal I sometimes spin.'

'Can't you do it by sorcery?'

'I could. But it wouldn't be much faster. And it wouldn't be relaxing.'

'Very well,' said Aliza. 'I'll leave you to your relaxation. You'll be able to sleep with this much light?'

'Without difficulty, my lady.'

She turned to go.

'One more thing, though,' Cray called after her.

She hesitated, looking back over her shoulder.

'Please don't lock me in this time.'

'It was for your own good,' she said. 'To keep you from wandering about the palace alone and perhaps becoming lost. I know how confusing all these rooms must be to you. Even my grandfather has trouble finding his way around without me.'

'I won't leave this room, except to visit the bathing chamber.'

'Then I'll close off all but the passage between here and there.'

'No. Please. I won't wander around.'

'Then what difference will it make to you?'

'It will make a difference,' he said. 'Here.' He tapped his chest, his heart. 'It will make me think . . . that you trust me.'

She was silent a long moment, looking at him with those cool dark eyes, without any expression at all on her face, as if he were a book open to two blank pages. Then she said, 'Very well.' And she left.

Very soon the spindle was full, the wool on his shoulder was gone, and Cray judged that he had enough yarn for his real purpose. Cutting the thread into a score of equal lengths, he dropped them to the floor and directed them to stretch out there, all neatly parallel, and begin to knot themselves in a complex pattern of linked lozenge shapes. Once they were well started, he lay down on the couch and went to sleep.

He awoke to bright light – the usual level of illumination within the palace – and the sound of Aliza's voice.

'Your demons are here.' She stood in the doorway she had left open. She wore a fresh dress, rose-coloured velvet this time, and the colour seemed to bring a flush to her cheeks that Cray had not noticed before.

'Good morning,' he said. 'I presume it *is* morning.'

'I don't know. Does it matter?'

'No, not at all.' He yawned and stretched his arms and sat up. The woollen ribbon, completed while he slept, lay on the floor at the foot of the couch, coiled like a serpent. He picked it up and examined it for flaws, expecting to find none, finding none. Its finished length exceeded that of his arm. He stood up. 'I thought I might give you something before I go.'

'I told your demons you'd be having breakfast before you left. You do want something to eat, don't you?'

'That's very kind of you, my lady.' He walked toward her, holding the ribbon out in one hand, its two ends trailing from his fingers. 'This is for you. I made it last night. From the thread you saw me spinning.'

She looked at his offering, the slightest of frowns marring her brow. 'What is it?'

'A ribbon to tie back your hair. Surely there must be times when you do tie it back.'

She looked up at his face. 'Yes, I suppose there are. When I bathe. Yes.'

'A good practical time to use a hair ribbon. You might also want it when you cook.'

'I don't cook,' she said.

'Well, you might, someday.'

She looked down at his hand again. 'But you've already given me one gift.'

'That doesn't prevent me from giving you another.' He glanced at the tapestry for just an instant. 'A wall hanging is a fine thing to have, and it does this room a great deal of good, but that was a gift from one sorcerer to another. This . . . this is a gift from me to you, from Cray to Aliza. I know you said you don't wear ornaments, but it isn't one, really. It's a very practical gift. Take it.' He stretched his hand out toward her, till the open palm and the offered ribbon were almost touching her. 'Go on, my lady. It's such a little thing. Take it.'

She closed her fingers around one dangling end and slowly pulled the ribbon from his grasp. Then she wound it loosely about her hand. 'Breakfast is waiting,' she said. And she turned on her heel and went out.

They ate quietly, fruit and bread and cheese. Regneniel, who must have laid the meal out, was nowhere in sight. Afterwards, Aliza walked with Cray toward the outer rooms of the palace, silent, her eyes downcast. But as they passed through the room where he had slept and where he picked up his bundle of wool, she stopped at the cabinet where the wine was kept. Opening its double doors, she took out a crystalline decanter filled with red Maretian wine. She held it out to him.

'Since you like this so much, take some with you,' she said. 'Perhaps your mother will like it, too.'

He accepted the container with a small bow. 'Thank you. And thank you on behalf of my mother.' He turned the decanter in his hands. It was tall, its six-sided body

176

tapering smoothly to a narrow neck, its stopper massive and gemlike with broad facets. 'You made this?'

'Of course.'

'Then it will be a beautiful permanent addition to Spinweb.'

Aliza shrugged and led him on, outwards, toward the rim of her palace.

At the outermost room, Cray saw that the demons were waiting where he had left them, pressed up against the palace wall, a hollow cylinder of ice, a sun-yellow flame, and a grey puff of cloud. At Cray's appearance, Elrelet protruded a stubby-fingered hand and waved to him. He waved back and smiled broadly. Then he turned to Aliza.

'I *will* see you again,' he said.

She inclined her head. 'Sometime.'

'Soon.'

'Have a pleasant journey.'

'Will you give me your hand in farewell?'

Her expression grew puzzled.

'Ah,' he said. 'Another of those mortal practices that you don't know.' He held out his free hand. 'Take my hand. Go on. This is a very widespread custom, my lady, believe me.'

Stiffly, she touched his fingers with her own. She offered the wrong hand, the left, for he had extended his right, but he did not tell her that. Instead, he very slowly pulled her hand toward him, bent over it, and brushed the backs of her fingers with his lips. Then he released her.

'Am I supposed to do the same to your hand?' she asked, frowning.

He smiled. 'No, my lady. This custom only goes one way, man to woman.'

She clasped her hands together, the right covering the fingers that Cray's lips had touched. 'Very well,' she said. 'Farewell.'

Cray felt a sudden cold breeze, and when he looked

around, he saw that there was an open doorway into Ice where the demons stood. 'Farewell,' he said, taking a sidelong step toward it. 'Farewell until I see you again.' He backed through the opening, one hand raised in his good-bye, and then abruptly it was closed before him, and Elrelet and Gildrum were swamping him, blurring his vision as they surrounded him, warming him, hugging him with their insubstantial bodies. Beyond the blur of light and cloud, he saw Aliza turn and leave the outermost room, and then the doorway to it closed and he could see her no more.

Elrelet and Gildrum were speaking at once, their words tumbling over one another, occasionally punctuated by a remark from Leemin, but Cray could make no sense out of any of it. 'Stop, stop, one at a time! Please!'

Gildrum withdrew from him then, leaving Elrelet to keep him warm. 'We didn't know whether to worry or not,' it said. 'We've been hanging about at the boundary of Ice and Air, trying to decide what to do if she told us to come back on yet another day.'

'And did you decide anything?' asked Cray.

'It was just talk,' said Elrelet. 'There was nothing we *could* do, and we all knew it. *I* wasn't worried, and Leemin certainly didn't care. But you know fire demons – they always expect the worst.'

'I was thinking of what I would say to your mother,' said Gildrum.

'His mother,' said Elrelet, 'is perfectly aware that Cray isn't a baby any more. *And* that you can't protect him every moment of the day.'

'Did you really think there was danger?' Cray said.

'Where sorcerers are concerned,' said Gildrum, 'anything is possible.'

'The tale! The tale!' cried Elrelet. 'You are going to tell us all about your adventures inside this strange place, aren't you?'

'I'll tell you everything,' Cray said, 'when we get back to Feldar's cave. I don't intend to go over it more than once. So let's get moving.'

'You're not going to tell us anything?' inquired Leemin.

'Not now.'

'But . . . just to satisfy my slight curiosity about why she let you in . . .'

'You're welcome to come along with us,' said Cray.

'I?' said the demon.

'Why not?'

In the end, Leemin did come along, though it rested in a dim corner, apart from the others, as Cray related his experiences. Cray himself sat on the rim of the Seer's dark pool, the lady Helaine beside him and Sepwin at his feet. Gildrum, in human form, sat cross-legged on the white sand nearby, with Elrelet like a grey wreath about his neck.

At the end of his tale, Cray produced the chunk of amethyst and handed it around for examination. 'I've never seen such concentrations of gemstones anywhere,' he said. 'The place is none I've ever even heard of before, not from sorcerer nor from ordinary mortal. The animals, the plants – it was a whole new world to me. Where can it be that the very stars in the sky are different from ours?'

The lady Helaine took the amethyst and closed her fingers about it, then thrust that fist into the dark pool. Ripples ran one way and then the other as she waved her hand beneath the surface, her eyes unblinking, and as she stared, her pale face seemed to become paler still in the wavering torchlight. She did not turn her head as she answered him. 'I see a land of strange names. Farther than a man can ride in a thousand days. Farther than a bird can fly or a ship can sail in as long a time. No one has ever come to me from there. No one has ever asked me about it before.' She sighed softly. 'And I do not know where it lies.' She lifted the amethyst into the air and shook the water from it. 'Far indeed, my child, if I cannot guess the distance.'

'And that is why Feldar couldn't find her,' Cray said.

The Seer nodded. 'Even our greatest powers have their limits.'

'What does it matter?' said Elrelet. 'We know how far away it lies through the demon worlds. No more than that is necessary.'

Cray shrugged. 'I suppose it doesn't really matter. Except for the way I felt when I was there, when I looked at those stars. I felt . . . alone and so far from anything I understood. I felt that if Aliza was of that place, then there might be a distance between us that I could never cross.'

'Yet the mortals you met in that village were just ordinary mortals, weren't they?' said Gildrum. 'They didn't have three legs apiece or an eye in the middle of the forehead.'

'No. But they lived in a land where the rivers ran with gems, and not an ornament did I see among them.'

Gildrum laughed lightly. 'A human place. My own experience among humans has convinced me that they lay no value on the common, no matter how pretty it might be. Why should they ornament themselves with mere gravel?' He clapped a hand on Cray's knee. 'What does it matter that the land is far away? The human realm is wide and contains many parts. Why should you be surprised that Aliza's part has a nature slightly different from your own? The demon realm has four sections of considerably greater diversity. What are a few stars, a few animals, a few plants, compared to the divergence of Fire and Ice? Yet one can travel from Fire to Ice, just as I'm sure one could travel from here to Aliza's neighbourhood, if only one had the proper map.' He smiled at Cray. 'If you really insist upon a map, just to know the exact distance and direction from here to there, I can piece one together, I'm sure. But it will be a tedious task, and in the end, the most important thing you'll know from it will be that the route through the demon worlds is much quicker. What is important is not where Aliza is, but can you get there. We already have the answer to that.'

'You're right, of course,' said Cray. 'She is a mortal. And I am a mortal. What do a few stars matter beside those facts?'

Gildrum's smile broadened. 'Greater distances have been bridged. After all, the land I come from has no stars at all.'

Cray smiled back at him. 'True enough.' Then he turned to the lady Helaine. 'Very well, if you cannot tell me anything more about her homeland, perhaps you can tell me something of herself.' He picked up the decanter, which, along with the bundle of wool, had been lying at his feet beside Sepwin. 'She made this.'

Wetting both her hands in the pool, the Seer took the crystal decanter between them and folded her fingers about its slender neck. She was very still for a moment, looking at the faceted stopper as if there were some message engraved deep inside it. Then, without shifting her gaze, she reached out toward Sepwin with one dripping hand. He took it, rising to his knees, and let her wrap his fingers about the decanter with her own. He closed his eyes.

'She is still an apprentice,' the lady Helaine said in a low voice, 'and her palace is an apprentice's home, or I would see nothing. Yet she and it are near their maturity, for the vision is mist-laden and indistinct. Already there is a barrier within her, hiding her heart from me, and all I can see outside that is pride and a fierce sense of independence. In the past was great sorrow, grief, and loneliness, a towering pain for a child. But I see no such pain in her now, only the barrier. She is young to have it

181

so well-developed.' She sighed. 'So much for what can be learned from a piece of crystal. Not much, I fear. Thank you, Feldar, my dear.'

Sepwin let his hands drop away from the decanter. 'I sensed a coldness to her, a coldness such as I have never seen in any other mortal.'

'She is too much in Ice,' said the lady Helaine. 'It has crept into her very being. Perhaps that is why her barrier is so effective.'

'She is cold,' said Cray. 'Yet I think that may be because she hasn't known warmth in such a long time.'

'And you intend to devote yourself to warming her,' said the lady Helaine.

'What have I to do that is more important?'

She set the decanter down and lifted both her damp hands to his face. She cradled his cheeks in her palms and looked deep into his eyes. 'You have made your choice,' she said. 'But the road will not be as easy as you hope. There is danger ahead. I can see it like a beacon in your life.'

'What sort of danger?'

'Sorcery.'

'Then I will answer it with sorcery of my own. I am not afraid.'

'I know. But perhaps you should be.'

His eyes were puzzled. 'This is only a growing friendship we are talking about, not a quest to kill some fire-breathing monster.'

'The quest has scarcely begun, Cray.'

'The quest is over, my lady. I've found her.'

'Finding her was the merest beginning. You will know when you have come to the end.' She smiled at him and let her hands drop away from his cheeks. 'This is your heart's quest, Cray, not a mere search for gold or jewels. Your heart will know when it is satisfied.'

'If such a woman *can* satisfy it,' said Sepwin. He touched

the decanter lightly with one finger. 'So cold, so very cold. Perhaps this is really a fruitless quest. Perhaps . . . if I had known this much about her at the beginning, I wouldn't have pushed you so hard to look into the mirror, to find her.' He looked up at the lady Helaine. 'It's my fault.'

'Yes,' she said. 'And if the quest is finally unsuccessful, he will blame you. You never thought of that, did you?'

Sepwin shook his head. 'I believed the mirror.'

'No. You believed in Cray. You're a true and loyal friend, my Feldar, but you can't make a woman's mind up for her.'

'So now you change your tune, do you, Feldar?' said Cray. 'Now, after all these years, after all the effort I've expended on your project.'

'The bottle is so cold, Cray,' he said. 'I never dreamed it could be so cold.'

'Then drink some of the wine, my friend; you'll find that warm enough.'

'I must meet her,' said Sepwin. 'She must be worthy. The mirror wouldn't have shown her to you if she weren't worthy.'

'Feldar, you are taking this . . . this *bottle* too much to heart. Yes, she is cold, but there is a spark of warmth within her, I know it. All it needs is nurturing. You shall meet her, if I can persuade her to visit here, and then you'll be able to judge her by her whole self and not just by a piece of crystal trash.'

Sepwin held the bottle high. 'You think this doesn't tell me the truth?' he shouted.

Cray clutched at his friend's arm. 'Feldar, Feldar, I don't doubt your abilities. But she's of the sorcerous breed. The lady Helaine admitted that her life was unclear. The bottle may tell some truth, but not the whole of it. Do you think that I could spend so long with her and not discover something with my ordinary senses? She is starved for contact with the outside and she doesn't even realize it!

183

She wants warmth, but she doesn't know how to generate it within herself yet. She won't be transformed in a single day. You're afraid for my sake – I understand that. But I'm all right. I like Aliza, and I think she likes me, and I'm happy with that. Don't you understand? I'm happy.'

Sepwin looked into Cray's face, looked deep with his Seer's eyes wide and unblinking, and then he touched Cray's shoulder with his unencumbered hand, fingers curling tight into the fabric there. 'Yes,' he whispered. 'You are happy now. But the future is cold and violent. You will be afraid.'

'Of what?' Cray whispered.

'You will be afraid of sorcery. You will be afraid, but not for yourself. For her.'

'Feldar . . .'

'The danger is yours. And the danger is hers, because of you.'

Cray gripped his friend's arm harder. 'What is the danger, Feldar? Where does it come from? Why?'

'If only I could give you those answers!' Sepwin cried. 'Why do you ask a Seer to tell you of magic? You know it's impossible. You know there's a wall between my sight and sorcery. I only know that it exists!'

'Yet you read one sorcerer well enough! You read me as if I were an open book!'

'I read Cray the man, not Cray the sorcerer.'

'Feldar, what kind of warning is this? I won't know which way to look!'

Sepwin shook his head. 'I know only one more thing about the danger – that I will share it with you.'

'What?'

'You'll need me.'

Cray looked to the lady Helaine, an unspoken question on his lips.

'Yes,' she said. 'I told you as much, if you'll recall, on the day you first saw your Aliza in the mirror.'

'When will the danger come?' Cray demanded.

'I don't know,' said the lady Helaine.

'I don't know,' said Sepwin.

'Then how can I protect her?' Cray shouted.

'I don't know,' said Sepwin.

'These mortals,' Leemin muttered, too softly for any but demons to hear. 'If I were told that another demon was going to be the cause of some danger to myself, I would avoid it forever.'

'You don't understand mortals,' Gildrum replied. 'I wouldn't expect you to, creature of Ice.'

Chapter 7

In the human realm, summer had waned and the first frosts of autumn were touching the trees. But in Ice the season was always winter, and to Cray's eyes there had been no change since his last visit. He had four companions this time. Gildrum, of course, and Elrelet, willing as always; Leemin, who professed a desire to see Cray cope with the prophesied danger; and Arvad, the first demon of Air that Cray had ever freed. Arvad had come along to serve Aliza.

'How do you know she'll be willing to come out?' Elrelet had said when the five were gathered at the boundary of Ice and Air. 'I couldn't find anyone who has ever seen her in any of the other demon worlds. She obviously doesn't have any interest in them.'

'I think you're wrong about that,' Cray replied. 'I think it isn't that she doesn't *want* to know anything about the outside; it's that her grandfather had convinced her, and with his help she had convinced herself, that there was nothing worth knowing there. Only when I spoke of my own experiences did she begin to see what possibilities lay beyond the bounds that she knew. She was interested enough in my tales of Mistwell.'

Gildrum chuckled, its light pulsing with the sound. 'You played the troubadour to the sheltered noblewoman. It's a role not unknown in the human realm. The troubadour brings tales of the world beyond the castle walls and makes the ladies sigh at the adventures of a brave knight.'

'Yes, she is sheltered,' said Cray. 'And, in spite of her denials, afraid of the outside, and of strangers. Who wouldn't be, growing up as she has? She stays in Ice because she knows that only her own familiar ice demon would approach her there.'

'No other would,' said Leemin, 'and no other could – she has a strong shield of sorcery wrapped about her.'

'Of course,' said Cray. 'Between herself and the outside, she always has a barrier.'

'Then I ask again,' said Elrelet, 'how do you know she'll come out now?'

'I don't *know*,' said Cray. 'But I think – and I hope – that she'll be willing to come with me where she would not go by herself. That's the key. She needs a guide, a buffer between herself and the unknown, an unraveller of the unfamiliar.'

'And you think if you make the offer . . .'

'It's worth the attempt. I've given her plenty of time to return to her studies. I'm sure she's worked hard these last months. She deserves a holiday.'

'I was surprised you managed to wait this long,' remarked Gildrum. 'I watched you pacing the garden this last month and more, and I could see that you were impatient to be back with her.'

'Impatient, yes,' said Cray. 'But a little afraid, I have to admit it. Afraid that she would refuse to come along with me. But my impatience has overcome my fear at this point.'

'And the danger?' said Gildrum. 'You didn't think of that?'

Cray smiled slightly. 'I thought of it, but if Feldar is to share it with me, as he and the lady Helaine insist, then I can put it off by leaving him behind, can't I?'

'Do you really think so?'

'I won't let this purported danger keep me from her, Gildrum.'

'I didn't mean to suggest that. Only that . . . you must remember to be careful.'

'Don't worry about that. Even now I find myself looking

over my shoulder constantly. But with all you demons surrounding us, what could possibly happen?'

'I wish I knew,' said Gildrum.

And the five companions had entered Ice.

At the transparent wall of Aliza's palace, Cray called her name twice. Then he began to count, slowly and silently. At twenty-five, she appeared in the far doorway of the outermost room, garbed today in green velvet. The wall melted before him as she crossed the chamber, and this time he was ready for it and remained standing in Ice as she approached.

'Cray,' she said. 'Come in.'

'For just a moment,' he told her, taking the single step that stripped him of Elrelet's protection and caused the wall to seal itself behind him.

'A moment? Were you just passing by, then, on your way somewhere else?'

'In a manner of speaking, my lady. I thought, perhaps, if you had the time and the inclination, you might wish to come with me and explore a corner or two of some other demon world than Ice. I brought a few guides to help us along.' He waved to encompass the waiting demons.

'Explore?' she said.

'Strictly as part of your education, of course. You know Ice and the human realm, in nature if not in detail. Don't you think you should know the other demon worlds as well? That strikes me as a useful sort of knowledge.'

She frowned. 'My grandfather will be arriving soon on his yearly visit. He'll have a host of questions for me to answer on my studies. I don't really have time to waste on such a journey.'

'When do you expect him?'

'Not for some time yet. Ten or twelve days.'

'Have you been studying hard?'

'Of course.'

'Then perhaps a day off would be beneficial. It would

rest your mind and leave you fresh to resume your studies with renewed enthusiasm. Like a good sleep.'

'Has that been your experience?'

'It has, indeed. When I was apprenticed to Rezhyk the demon master, I took time off to practise my swordsmanship. I found the change to be extremely relaxing.'

'And what did Rezhyk think of such activities?'

'He didn't mind. I did my work – that was all that mattered to him.'

'And you think that my grandfather, too, would not mind my taking time off from my studies?'

'Well . . .' Cray shrugged lightly. 'It's a cruel master that doesn't allow his slaves a little time to themselves. I know you must be a diligent student. I'm sure you'll be ready for his questions even if you do steal this one day.'

She pursed her lips. 'Where would you propose to take me?'

'To Air first. The demons are friendliest there. And then perhaps to Water, to see a sight that no other mortal but myself has ever seen before.'

'No other mortal?'

'So they tell me.'

She clasped her hands behind her back. 'You must know that I have no power over Air or Water.'

'Nor have I,' said Cray. 'But these demons will see that we are safe and comfortable there.'

'I must take Regneniel along.'

'Of course. I assumed you would.'

He could see the conflicting impulses warring on her face – the desire to go, the need to stay. One hand went to her mouth, the forefinger rubbing at her lower lip. 'Not an entire day,' she said.

'No, not really quite so long. But a good chunk of it.'

'I would want to be back here for supper.'

'I'm sure that could be managed.'

She let her hand drop and form a fist beside her hip. There, the fingers worked against each other for a moment. 'I've never been to Air or Water.'

'I knew that.'

'Are they really worth visiting?'

He smiled. 'Obviously I think so. Come and find out for yourself.'

She took a deep breath, exhaled it heavily. 'Very well. I'll take a look at them. Then I'll be able to judge for myself if the things you find interesting are of any real interest to me.'

'Yes, you will.'

'Wait here, then. I'll be back soon.' And, turning, she hurried away. She was almost running.

Cray glanced over his shoulder at the demons and nodded. Then, with a slow and deliberate step, he began to pace out the dimensions of the room. He had only completed three rounds of the place when Aliza returned. She had changed her velvet gown for trews and a shirt of the same material, and she had braided her long hair into a single plait. Cray thought she looked charming; he had been wondering how she could move in the weightless demon realm with such free-flowing hair and garments to tangle about her and impede her progress.

Regneniel, in his familiar angular form, followed close behind her.

'What demons have we here?' she asked Cray. 'And what are their purposes?'

Cray pointed to each in turn, mouthing their names with exaggerated care so that they would know he was speaking of them. 'Leemin of Ice to open paths through this world for me. Gildrum of Fire to light our way. Elrelet and Arvad of Air to shield us from worlds unkind to human flesh and generally to speed us on our journey. We'll especially need the last two in water. They'll surround us with their substance and keep us from drowning.' Three of the demons made signs of greeting – Gildrum briefly assuming a human form in order to bow, the two air demons expanding into puffy caricatures of men and bending almost double before Aliza. Only Leemin remained as it had been, a hollow cylinder with as much evidence of life in it as a block of ice.

'You trust them?' Aliza said.

'Completely. And they've promised to look after you as they would me.'

Her cool dark eyes studied his face. 'You visit the demon world often, don't you?'

'Now and then. Not so often as when I was younger.'

'And you've never been harmed by a demon?'

'Never. Though I have to admit that sometimes the playfulness of the demons of Air can be a bit rough. Still, here I am in one piece.'

'So I see. Very well, let us be on our way.' She raised a hand, and the wall before them dissolved, allowing the cold breath of Ice to enter the chamber. 'Lead on,' she said. 'You are my guide on this journey.'

He stepped forward. Immediately, Elrelet's greyness engulfed him and became transparent. He turned back to Aliza and found her and Regneniel almost at his elbow, the wall already sealed behind them. 'Elrelet will keep me warm while I walk through Ice,' he said. 'I believe you have your own devices for that . . . ?'

'Of course. I take the warmth of my palace wherever I walk in Ice.' She glanced at her demon. 'Shrink, Regneniel; there's no need for you to be larger than my hand in such a small space as this.' Obediently, it dwindled to a milky, dagger-sized icicle floating at her shoulder. Aliza put her hands on her hips. 'Shall we go?'

'Perhaps . . . you might greet my demon friends first . . . ?'

She looked from the ball of light to the grey cloud that was Arvad to the hollow cylinder that surrounded them. After a long moment of hesitation, she said, rather briskly, 'Good morrow to all of you. Shall we begin our adventure now?'

'Good morrow,' said Gildrum. The others were silent.

'Very well,' said Cray. 'To the boundary of Ice and Air.'

Leemin began to move.

Aliza followed the guiding demon easily, drifting along without touching the tunnel walls except to give herself an occasional push with one hand or foot. Cray tried briefly to imitate her motion, but instead of remaining smoothly on the centreline of the tunnel, he found himself constantly straying to one side or the other and rebounding from the wall. Aliza avoided his awkward, thrashing efforts by falling well behind him, keeping the fracture open by her own powers far past the point where it would have closed after Leemin's passage. She only caught up with him when he gave over his attempts at independent motion and let Elrelet carry him as usual.

'You push off much too vigorously,' she told him. 'You should touch the wall very lightly, with just the slightest strength. Under these weightless conditions, too much effort is its own undoing.'

Cray smiled wryly. 'So it would seem. I am more accustomed to the worlds of Air and Water, where there are no close-set solid barriers to expose my awkwardness, and where strength does count for something. You'll find that the small movements that serve you so well here in Ice won't be of much use in those other places. But we'll have our demon friends, so it doesn't matter. They'll carry us along whenever necessary.'

'*Our* demon friends,' she murmured.

'I think they would be willing to be your friends, my lady, if you would be willing to offer your friendship to them. I can't speak for Regneniel, of course.'

'You may have my friendship, my lady,' said Gildrum.

Aliza's eyes were startled as they swung toward the ball

of light that floated at Cray's shoulder. 'It speaks without being spoken to!'

'Of course,' said Cray. 'Just as you and I do. That's the mark of a free being. They'd all speak to you, I think, if they believed you were interested in what they had to say.'

'You must forgive the others, my lady,' said Gildrum. 'Aside from Cray, they have only known sorcerers as selfish and cruel masters. They suspect you are that sort. They suspect that if it were possible you would try to enslave every one of them. I hope you can understand how difficult it would be for them to feel true friendship for such a person. Perhaps you would reassure them on this point?'

'I have no interest in enslaving demons,' said Aliza.

'Yet you have one slave at this very moment.'

'And one is quite enough,' she replied. 'It was given to me as a gift. I have learned no demon conjurations, and I intend to learn none. Even if these demons were available to me – and I understand from Cray that they are not – I would not make any attempt to enslave them. Perhaps that will set their . . . their minds at rest.'

'They do have minds, my lady,' Gildrum said softly. 'They are thinking beings, just as you are.'

Aliza looked long at the ball of light that was Gildrum, looked long as she floated onwards through the tunnel made by an ice demon. 'I must admit,' she said at last, 'that it is a difficult thing for me to comprehend. Here you are, nothing more than light, formless, featureless. And yet you speak to me as one human being to another. And I have seen you take on human shape, a shape as real seeming as Cray Ormoru's. Yet to think of you, of any of you, as the same as human beings . . .' She shook her head.

'We are not the same,' said Gildrum. 'We are ourselves, demons, and we can never be the same as human beings, but we are . . .' It seemed to be groping for a word. Finally, it said, 'We are *people*.'

'I know that Cray Ormoru believes that.'

'Perhaps when you have come to know a few of us, you will feel the same.'

'I know a demon already.' She cast a sidelong glance at the icicle floating by her shoulder.

'You command a demon,' said Cray. 'I think there is a difference.'

'Regneniel,' she said to the icicle. 'Do you consider yourself a person?'

'Of course, my lady.'

'Regneniel,' said Cray, 'do you wish to be free?'

'What demon does not?' it replied.

'And what would you do if I set you free?' Aliza demanded. 'What mischief would you do me?'

The ice demon did not answer at once, as if it were weighing various rejoinders, selecting among them for the best. 'If you set me free,' it said finally, 'I would continue to serve you, my lady. I would come when you called and do you no mischief. I would still be your slave.'

'You would?'

'Yes.'

'But why?'

'You are my lady. I am . . . attached to you.'

'Can this be true?' said Cray. 'An ice demon that cares about a mortal?'

'I do not understand what you mean when you speak of caring, but I know that I would stay with the lady Aliza.'

'What a marvel,' murmured Gildrum. 'I would never have thought a demon of Ice capable of feeling.'

'The worlds are full of marvels,' said Elrelet. 'There are some individuals who would never have thought a demon of Fire capable of loving a mortal woman.'

Gildrum laughed softly. 'True enough, my old friend. We should not hold fast to our assumptions when confronted with evidence to the contrary. Very well, I will believe that Regneniel cares enough for the lady Aliza to continue to serve her after being freed. Therefore, she might as well free it this moment.'

'Regneniel may say anything now,' said Aliza, 'and because it cannot lie to its master, I am sure it believes what it says. But such belief would not keep it from changing its mind sometime in the future.'

'No,' said Cray. 'You are quite right about that.'

'Therefore, rather than setting it free now, as your Gildrum suggests, I think I will keep it slave for a while longer. You may trust your freed demons completely, Cray Ormoru, but I am not so sure that I could.'

'As long as you feel that you require a demon slave . . .'

'I do. I have only the one, after all, and no knowledge of how to conjure more. I'm sure my grandfather would be willing to teach me the art, but that would interfere with my true studies. Far more than this brief journey, certainly, as you must know.'

Cray nodded. 'It is not an art acquired overnight, to be sure. I had felt sorry for Regneniel, I must tell you that, as I feel sorry for all enslaved creatures. But now that it has confessed such an affection for you, I find that my pity may be misplaced. I have never known a demon before that would serve its master without compulsion.'

'But here are four of them all around us,' said Aliza.

Cray sighed. 'Don't you understand yet, my lady? My relationship to them is not as master, or even former master. They are my companions, and they've come on this journey of their own free will, for a bit of diversion and to help a friend. I would not call that service, any more than my visit to you could be called so. Must these demons all have human forms for you to see them as equal to yourself or me?'

'I feel equal to you,' said Elrelet. 'And from what I've heard, I'm a better cook than you are.'

Aliza frowned. 'I don't cook.'

'Just so,' the air demon replied. 'I can fry an egg when

195

Cray's mother lets me near the pans, and I can even spit a fowl for roasting and turn the spit so it doesn't burn.'

'Elrelet is quite fond of food,' Cray explained, 'and lately my mother has been teaching it to cook for itself rather than always badger her into doing so. The last fowl came out fairly well, but I usually find Elrelet's fried eggs a bit overdone.'

'I like them that way,' said the air demon.

'A demon that eats food,' murmured Aliza.

'An acquired taste,' said Elrelet, and chuckled softly at its own joke.

'We enjoy many things that mortals enjoy,' said Gildrum.

'Yes, *you* certainly do,' said Elrelet, and it laughed again. 'Gildrum is practically a mortal these days. *He* hardly ever wears a demon form any more. Unless the lady Delivev's candles happen to be blown out by a strong wind.'

'I wear it a little more often than that,' said Gildrum, 'but Elrelet is correct in essence. My old master Rezhyk made me a human form that my beloved finds pleasing. Why should I wear any other unless it is of some use? As now, for instance. My human form would not light our way one jot.'

'I could light our way,' said Aliza, 'at least within Ice. Look.' She waved a hand, and all about them the walls of the fracture began to glow with the pale bluish radiance of her palace.

'I prefer Gildrum's light,' said Elrelet. 'It is more pleasant.'

'You are an impudent creature!' exclaimed Aliza.

Elrelet laughed a deep, resonant laugh like distant thunder. 'Impudence is a mark of freedom, my lady. No slave can afford it.'

'I have to say that I don't much like it in . . . a travelling companion.'

'Elrelet means you no insult, my lady,' said Gildrum.

'That is just its sort of humour. Air demons tend to be a rough and rowdy lot. Elrelet is one of the more courteous of them, in its own way. Almost . . . civilized. It's a fine fellow, if you make enough allowances.' Gildrum and Elrelet laughed together at that.

Aliza turned to Cray. 'I don't understand why they're laughing. The one has insulted the other.'

Cray grinned at her. 'They're old friends, my lady, and old friends may speak to each other with mock insult. Ah, but you probably don't know about such things, do you?'

'I know that I would not so casually insult a creature with the power to do me harm. Are they so proof against one another?'

'They wouldn't harm each other, believe me. They have been friends longer than you and I have been alive. Far longer. Elrelet, tell the lady Aliza how you and Gildrum met.'

'Oh, there was an adventure indeed,' it said. 'I was a very foolish young demon at the time and I thought I could roam the demon worlds at my pleasure, without ever asking for a word of guidance from my elders. But there is a thick curtain of smoke dividing Air from Fire, and in my youthful ignorance I became lost in it on my way from the one to the other. I was there for a very long time, probably moving parallel to the curtain's face for most of it, without the sense to turn a right angle and get out. I might be there still if Gildrum hadn't chanced on me. Gildrum thought my experience quite amusing, only the sort of thing to be expected from an air demon. They haven't much respect for us in Fire, you know; they consider us the least intelligent of all demons, though of course we dispute that. Even so, Gildrum and I found we had a great deal in common – we were both young and free in those times, and we both had a strong desire to explore. So Gildrum agreed to overlook my excessive cheerfulness, and I agreed to overlook its intrusive melancholy, and we continued our explorations as a team. We were both enslaved eventually, but we've never lost our affection for each other. Friendships made early in life, I think, are the longest lasting.'

Frowning slightly, Aliza said, 'I've never thought that demons might have friends among themselves.'

'It seems there are many things you don't know about us, my lady Aliza,' said Elrelet.

'Oh, Elrelet,' said Cray, 'after all, she's only known an ice demon. You can't say *they* have many friends, either among themselves or in the other demon worlds.'

'It's a rare ice demon that has any friends at all,' said Elrelet.

'We don't need them,' said Leemin. 'We are self-sufficient.'

'We are self-sufficient, too,' said Elrelet. 'In the physical sense. Still, we are sociable.'

'Your society is not ours,' said Leemin.

'And I'm glad of it,' said the air demon. 'You are welcome to your way of life, O Leemin, but I would not choose it for myself.'

'You would, if you were of Ice.'

'Then I'm glad that I'm not – '

'Enough, Elrelet!' Gildrum said sharply. 'There's no need to insult one who freely offered us its help.'

'I am not insulted,' said Leemin. 'Elrelet has its own way of life and does not understand mine. It speaks from ignorance. If it dislikes the world of Ice and its inhabitants so, then it will not choose to return there very often, and that is good. We have no great desire for visitors in Ice.'

Elrelet's voice was deeper when it spoke again. 'I do apologize, O Leemin, even if you truly do not feel insulted. It was unseemly of me to speak so to a comrade in this adventure. I did speak from ignorance. I had hardly ever been inside Ice, and certainly not very far inside, before Cray enlisted my help. You have every right to your way of life, just as we all do to ours, and the water demons to theirs. I am what I am, and that pleases me, but perhaps if I were an ice demon, that would please me just as well. You see, my lady, we do not understand each other any better than you understand us. And so we take journeys such as this, in the name of a little understanding.'

'Don't be fooled by those lofty sentiments, my lady,' said Gildrum. 'Elrelet takes these journeys out of curiosity, pure and simple. From the very first it had an unquenchable desire to see other places and other ways of life. Why, once when I was guiding it past one of the blazing rivers of Fire, it insisted upon diving in among the demons playing there and joining their game.'

'What was it like?' said Aliza. 'In a river of Fire.'

'Exceedingly warm,' replied the air demon. 'But the game, you see, was too interesting to let pass without trying, and the fire demons were willing enough to let a newcomer try its luck, though they did laugh at my clumsiness . . .'

For the rest of the journey to the boundary between Ice and Air, Gildrum and Elrelet took turns relating their adventures exploring the demon worlds, and even Cray, who had already heard most of their stories, found himself entertained and the trip seeming shorter than ever before. He was surprised at how soon he perceived the light of Air flooding Ice, at how soon Leemin opened into a hollow cylinder to display the clear blue of Air beyond.

'Our first destination,' Cray said to Aliza, and Elrelet carried him out to the great emptiness. Gildrum and Arvad emerged behind him, but when he turned to see how Aliza was negotiating her first experience of Air, he saw that she was hesitating at the very end of the fracture, her hands and feet braced firmly against Leemin's curving hollowness. 'Come along,' said Cray.

Her dark eyes were wide and wary as she watched him approach under his own power, his arms and legs pumping as if he swam through water rather than empty air.

'Don't be afraid,' he said. 'You can't fall.'

'I am not afraid,' she replied. 'But I'd like to watch you move about a bit before I try it myself.'

'Surely.' He swam a short distance in one direction, then somersaulted smoothly to return. 'It's very much like being in water,' he explained, 'except there is less resistance to your body. If you can swim in water, you can swim in Air.'

'I've never swum in any water,' said Aliza.

'Well then, Air is a good place to learn, for you can't possibly drown in it.' He sculled to one side and back again. 'Come now – you try it. I'll be here to help you, and so will all these demons. Come.'

After another moment of hesitation, Aliza allowed herself to drift slowly out of Ice. She moved an arm in imitation of Cray's sculling, and she began to tumble slowly. She moved the other arm, then both legs, and still she tumbled, a little faster now. She began to thrash, clutching for non-existent support. She made no sound.

Cray let her struggle silently for a time before saying, 'I think you need a bit of assistance, my lady. Will you allow Arvad to touch you?'

'Yes,' she gasped.

The air demon expanded into a pallet with arms and deftly fitted itself to Aliza's back, circling her waist with its cloud appendages. Her motion stopped abruptly. She grasped the demon's arms with both hands.

'It isn't quite like being in Ice, is it?' she said, a trifle breathlessly.

'No, not quite,' said Cray.

'How long did it take you to learn to swim here?'

'Not long. But then, I already knew how to swim in water.'

'I'm sure I could master it. Tell this demon to let me go, and I'll try again.'

'Tell it yourself. It's not my slave.'

'What was its name?'

'Arvad.'

'Very well. Arvad, let me go.'

The demon withdrew, and Aliza tried again. She did not tumble so badly this time, but neither did she move from her place near Cray.

'You must use your hands as scoops,' Cray said. 'Air has substance and will resist you if you push at it properly. Keep your fingers tight together.'

She followed his directions, and with some effort she was able to paddle a short distance, though not to turn around and come back – for that, Arvad had to fetch her.

'This is very tiring,' she said to Cray. 'If you do this very much, your muscles must be stronger than they look.'

He laughed. 'Swimming is only for moving short distances. For any real travel, I ask a demon to carry me. And that is what we'll do now, I think. Arvad will carry you, unless you prefer your own demon.'

She looked around and found the icicle that was Regneniel floating very near the surface of Ice. 'No,' she said. 'This journey is your idea, so I will use the transportation you provide. That *is* what you wish, is it not?'

'I wish whatever makes you comfortable, my lady. But I must tell you that an air demon is a better-padded couch than a creature of Ice.'

'Very well, then. The air demon. Arvad. Regneniel shall only follow for now.'

At Cray's beckoning wave, Leemin joined them, assuming its star-like shape and allowing the fracture in Ice to snap shut. Their group now complete, the travellers commenced their journey through the vast and empty reaches of Air, skimming swiftly, five demons and two sorcerous mortals. The surface of Ice faded in the distance behind them, merging with the uncluttered blue of this world, and as it vanished, so did its chill. Soon, Elrelet was able to shrink to an opaque grey ring about Cray's waist and expose his skin to the balmy breath of its native land.

'How large is Air?' Aliza wondered after they had travelled for a time.

'How large is Ice?' countered Cray.

'I've never compassed it.'

'Nor have I compassed Air, or any of the demon worlds. They are all vast.'

'And one place in them is much like another,' Aliza noted, 'at least in Air.'

'Not so,' said Arvad. 'But your human eyes cannot perceive the differences.'

'Indeed,' said Elrelet. 'Why, we have passed a hundred demon homes, all solid as rocks but quite invisible to your eyes. My own was among them, and Cray knows well how solid it is.'

'Solid enough to raise a lump on my head when I bumped against one of its walls,' he said.

'He was a poor swimmer in those days,' said Elrelet.

'I would have been a better swimmer if I'd been able to see where the walls were,' Cray replied.

'If we can't see anything in Air,' said Aliza, 'why are we here?'

'Oh, you'll see something, never doubt that. The demons' houses may be invisible to us, but the demons themselves can be quite apparent when they wish. Ah, there they are now.' In the distance – though distances were hard for the human eye to judge in the emptiness of Air – a mass of grey cloud had become visible, and it was growing in size with every passing moment. 'They're expecting us, aren't they, Elrelet?'

'Very much so,' replied the demon. 'And they're eager for your arrival, too. You see, my lady, when Cray was first in Air, he taught these local demons a human game, and they're always eager to try their skill against him. It's been some time now since they've had a chance for that.'

'I fear they'll be sorely disappointed,' said Cray. 'I haven't kept up my practice.'

'What sort of game could a mortal play with demons?' Aliza wondered.

'Any game he could play with mortals, provided the demons had some interest in it.'

'They're very interested in this one,' said Elrelet. 'Excessively interested, if you ask me. But then, the demons of Air have always been the most enthusiastic game-players of all the demon realm. Ah, Cray, they have your old weapons ready and waiting for you.'

The mass of cloud had broken up into a dozen or more similar patches, and as the travellers approached, these patches assumed approximations of the forms of men, some of them more accurate than others, though none remotely mistakable for the real thing. One of the cloud men came forward to meet Cray. It had arms and legs and a head but no face, just puffy greyness where the features should have been. In its arms it carried a blank shield, a sword, and a suit of steel chain.

'No, no, my friend,' Cray said to it. 'I'm no longer skilled enough to challenge you. But I'll judge a match or two if you like.'

'No, fight me,' said the creature. 'I've been practising since last we met.'

'And I have not.' Cray shook his head. 'You'll beat me soundly, I'm sure, and I have no desire for bruises just now. However . . .' He glanced toward Aliza. 'I might name a champion to fight for me. Would that do as well?'

'No,' said the creature, 'but I'll fight your champion anyway. Who shall it be?'

'Arvad,' said Cray. 'If my lady does not mind doing

without her couch for a little time. I'm sure it will only take a little time for Arvad to beat you.'

'Arvad shall not beat me! I shall beat Arvad.'

'You shall not!' Arvad replied.

To Aliza, Cray said, 'Perhaps Regneniel could look after you while these two settle their dispute?'

'Yes. Of course. Regneniel, come here so that I may hold fast to you.' She closed one hand around the icicle. 'No need for a couch if I'm just going to be staying in one place.'

The air demon withdrew from Aliza and took on as near a human shape as any of the assembled demons. The two challengers faced off while the rest backed away to form a rough sphere around the fighters. The two sprouted long swords of grey cloud stuff from their right hands and blocky shields from their left and slowly began to circle each other.

Cray had seen many a fight, both between mortals and between demons; he watched Aliza now instead of the demon warriors. She clung fast to Regneniel, with both hands now, for as Arvad had left her she had begun to swing to one side and had only been able to right herself with the strength of both arms. As the two demons fought, as blow upon blow rang like metal, not cloud, sword against sword, sword against shield, her eyes were wide and almost unblinking, her lips parted just a trifle. She watched the battle with total concentration.

At first the demons' strengths and skills seemed evenly matched. But gradually Arvad became the more aggressive. After an initial period of sparring, it began to slash steadily, barely giving its opponent time to recover from one blow before launching another. At each slash, a fragment of the opponent's shield would break off and sail away; soon the shield was reduced to a mere nubbin, and the other demon was forced to take Arvad's blows entirely upon its sword. Then, abruptly, the sword was

204

cloven in two, and so was the stubby cloud torso of the other demon. The two parts of its body lost their form, the limbs and the head shrinking away until there were just two blobs of cloud floating beside Arvad, who raised its sword in acknowledgment of triumph.

Aliza looked at Cray, her eyes still wide. 'This is a game?'

'Just a game,' he replied, and he pointed toward the fighters.

Arvad's opponent was re-forming itself, the two halves coming together, and all the little pieces that had been hacked away from the shield rejoining the main body, which took a human-like shape once more, though weaponless now, and bowed to Arvad. 'Perhaps another time I will beat you,' it said. 'But for now, I yield to your superior skill.'

The demons all around broke into raucous cheers.

'You see,' said Cray, 'the game is gauged for demons. To a demon, being hacked in half is nothing. In fact, it is one of the few blows they count as a winning one, for a demon has no trouble fighting on without legs or a shield arm or even a head. Believe me, it's a strange experience indeed to fight a one-armed torso made of cloud.'

'You've done so?'

'Yes.'

'And you won?'

'That time, yes. Though the creature parried my blade fairly well for a while. It was long ago, of course.'

'You must have been a fearsome fighter.'

He grinned. 'No more than middling, I assure you. But most of the demons were far worse back then.'

'And how would you rank these two now?'

'Arvad was always my best student. But the other was good, I must admit. Either of them would probably put most human warriors to shame.'

'And where would you rank them in relation to yourself, when you were at your peak?'

He shook his head. 'I told you, my lady, I was only middling skilful even then. At my peak, several demons, including Arvad, were able to beat me soundly.'

'They beat you?' said Aliza. 'Then how is it you are still alive? Or can you also put yourself back together after being cut in half?'

Cray laughed lightly. 'No, my lady, though it would surely be a fine talent to have. No, I always yielded before there was any real danger. Demons never yield, but they respected it as my choice.'

'You trusted them so far?'

'I was teaching them the fine points of their new game; it would have been foolish of them to kill me as long as they enjoyed the learning. And soon enough they understood that I was just a harmless, friendly creature without any desire to be a slave master. So I've had no trouble with them at all.'

While they had been speaking, another match had begun, two cloud warriors of very nearly equal skill, and Arvad had stayed among the surrounding demons to cheer at every well-placed blow. When the match was done, it returned to the mortals, and to Cray it said, 'You and I should take each other on again sometime. It's been too long.'

'Too long indeed,' Cray replied. 'These arms have lost their affinity for sword and shield, and you would find it a poor exercise, I know. However, I will tell you that your undercut could have been faster; you might practise that.'

'I will.'

'And now, I think the lady has probably had enough of combat for one day. I had hoped to show her a few things about the world of Water before this journey's end. We can always return for another glimpse of Air at some future time.'

'You are my guide,' said Aliza. 'I'll look wherever you point.'

'Very well then – to the boundary of Air and Water, my friends.'

The audience of demons did not seem to notice their departure but remained clustered, cheering yet another set of combatants.

'Have you participated in that game, too, Elrelet?' Aliza asked as they sped away.

'Not I,' said the demon. 'My interests don't lie in bashing my fellow creatures about. I fear too much of Gildrum rubbed off on me in my youth, and I have less of a love for rough and tumble than the average air demon. I prefer to take my ease in my own house, or to visit good friends.'

'Do any of the other sorts of demons practise this kind of fighting?'

'Some few of every other sort,' said Arvad. 'Though the demons of Water and Ice have less interest in it than those of Fire.'

'Few indeed of Ice,' said Leemin. 'And those only the youngest and most foolish among us.'

'They come here occasionally to test themselves against the warriors of Air,' Arvad said. 'But it is true that this game appeals most strongly to ourselves. It suits our nature well, and we are all grateful to Cray for introducing it among us.'

'Which I did purely by accident,' said Cray. 'They saw me at my own sword practice in Elrelet's house once, and immediately they had to try their own talents at it. Little did I realize how much of a change I had wrought in Air by a bit of sword swinging.'

'We needed a new game,' said Arvad. 'We needed to develop new skills and a new way of ranking each other. And I for one am glad of it, for I am in the highest ranks of air demons now, where I was formerly lost and struggling in the middle. Of course, Cray did me the favour of teaching me personally, so perhaps that has something to do with my success.'

'Nonsense. You had considerable native skill. It would have come out even without my personal help. You only needed practice.'

'That may be as it may be, but still, whether as a result of your guidance or my own diligence, I have met nearly a thousand challenges successfully, and some of them far more formidable than this last. Far more. Why, not long ago I fought one of the champions of Fire, and the match went on so long that half the spectators tired of watching and flew away. I'd lost both of my legs by the time it was over, but I still had most of my shield, which was more than my opponent could say. You would have been proud of me, Cray.'

'I'm sure,' Cray replied, and he let Arvad chatter on about past matches until the boundary between Air and Water became visible in the distance.

The surface of Water was as vast and flat as the surface of Ice, but instead of being faintly milky with a dusting of snow, it was a clear blue deeper than sapphire. From afar, Cray and Aliza saw their reflections in it as in any pond, saw themselves approaching slowly in the arms of two demons of Air, with a miniature sun at Cray's shoulder and a sliver of white ice at Aliza's and a sparkling star behind them. They came to a halt barely an arm's length from that surface.

'Touch it,' said Cray.

Tentatively, Aliza brushed the surface with the pads of two fingers, then laid her palm flat upon it. 'It resists me. And it feels quite hard.'

'Try prodding it with just one fingertip.'

She did so, and that finger sank slowly into the surface like a spoon through jellied soup, ripples spreading from it as from a stone dropped into a still pool. When she withdrew her finger, it was wet, though her palm had not been. 'Strange water,' she said.

'It has a kind of skin,' Cray told her. 'Or else it would dissipate in Air like dew drying in the sun. Shall we enter?'

'I'm ready if you are.'

'Good. Now don't be startled as Arvad covers you completely. It will keep you from getting wet as well as from drowning.' As soon as he had said this, he saw the demon pallet expanding to envelop her in a skin-snug grey cloud which then cleared to colourless transparency.

'It seems comfortable enough,' said Aliza, looking down at herself as if searching for some spot that was still opaque. She tried to touch her thigh with one hand but could not because of the intervening cushion of demon substance. She clapped her hands together, but demon gloves kept them apart and muffled the sound as readily as woollen ones would have. She swung her arms wide, then in an arc. 'I hardly feel it at all,' she said finally.

'I'm here, though,' said Arvad.

'Its voice,' exclaimed Aliza. 'Like a breeze on my cheek.'

'Well,' said Cray, 'what is an air demon made of but breezes? Come, we'll enter Water now. I'll go first, Elrelet. Arvad can bring my lady Aliza after.'

When Elrelet had covered him completely, Cray lifted his arms above his head like a diver poised to fling himself from a high cliff. The demon tilted him toward the surface of Water and thrust him, and itself, forward, a living spear cast at an endlessly broad target. Cray pierced the surface smoothly, and as Water enclosed him, he felt it resist his motion as Air never had. Here he could truly swim, and, paddling easily with hands and feet, he turned about to watch for Aliza. Behind him the boundary was a perfect mirror, and he saw only his own reflection staring back at him, and the dimness of Water all around. The light of Air was sealed away by that mirror, and though this world was suffused with its own internal radiance, that was deep cobalt to Air's azure. But the dimness was dispelled in a moment, as Gildrum passed through the barrier, bringing yellow sunshine into Water. Aliza came next, her diver's posture somewhat awkward, but good enough to cleave the mirrored surface. Regneniel, the icicle, was at her shoulder as before. Leemin followed after her, a slender shaft that expanded itself into a star once more on this side of the boundary.

Aliza glanced about. 'So this is Water. It seems as empty as Air, just darker.'

'Don't be so quick to judge by what you see here,' said Cray. 'The demons of Water rarely spend their time so close to Air. If we want to view them and their works, we'll have to move on to more favoured haunts.'

They moved on, with Gildrum in the lead like a torch.

Presently, Cray stretched out one arm to point ahead. 'There.'

In the distance, a large cluster of yellowish lights became visible, perhaps a hundred of them, like tiers of candles.

'What is it?' asked Aliza.

'Water,' replied Cray. 'Nothing but water.'

At closer approach, the lights resolved into the multiple reflections of Gildrum's radiance upon the curved faces of a mass of transparent bubbles, the whole cluster floating in the midst of Water like a sac of fish roe in a pond. With nothing to compare it to, its size was impossible to gauge; when Cray called his party to a halt, it was only visually as large as the circle of his arms.

'This is a good vantage,' he said. 'Now, my lady, you mustn't be deceived by the apparent size of this structure – it's larger and farther off than it might seem. Each of those bubbles could easily encompass your cradle room, and so the entire mass is comparable in size to your palace.'

'And what function does this structure serve?' she asked.

He smiled at her. 'An excellent question. When I first visited, I thought it was the castle of some great Water Lord.'

'But there are no Water Lords,' said Elrelet.

'And then I thought it must be the communal dwelling of some great number of water demons.'

'But they all live elsewhere,' said Elrelet.

'Then what is it?' asked Aliza. 'A storage place for some sort of treasure?'

'They have no treasures,' said Elrelet. 'What they do have is the ritual.'

'Ritual?'

'We've come here to view it,' said Cray. 'Unless we're too late.'

'I shouldn't think so,' said Elrelet. 'They practically promised me they would wait until we arrived.'

'A water demon's promise,' murmured Arvad. 'As good as a water demon's swordsmanship.'

'There they are,' said Gildrum. 'I'll dim my glow so you can see better.' And it shrank to a single candle flame.

Without the fire demon's light, the structure of bubbles seemed to vanish in the deep blue of Water. And then, all about the place where it had been, a shimmering began to fill the blue, an iridescence that slowly solidified into a chain of glowing milky spheres. Like a living strand of pearls, they wound about the cluster of bubbles, illuminating it with a pale, opalescent light. One sphere led all the rest, swooping, now slow, now faster, and the others followed precisely. As they circled the structure, their reflections glinted from it, multiplying their presence a hundredfold. And then those reflections emerged to join the procession, leaving duplicates of themselves behind, which emerged in their turn soon enough. How many of the myriad pearls that finally danced the figure were true demons and how many mere images, no human eye could determine.

After a time, the orderly pattern began to break up, the participants finding individual movements, racing, bobbing, interweaving like gnats at sunset over a hedge. Now two would come together and bounce apart; now three or four would meet and scatter at a touch; now a handful would collide and fuse into a single larger sphere and burst, showering their fellow dancers with more pearls than had united. Soon the bubble structure was completely engulfed in a boiling mass of water demons, more each instant, until suddenly they fountained outward in all directions and vanished.

Though he had been expecting it, Cray still flinched at the fountain, as countless opalescent spheres exploded toward him. But none reached him. He and his companions were left unharmed, untouched in the blue of water that now seemed darker than ever.

Gildrum brightened and dispelled that darkness.

'I hope you weren't frightened by that last part,' Cray said to Aliza. 'I have to admit that no matter how many times I see the ritual, I'm startled by the sudden finish.'

Her face was serene. 'I assumed I was safe in the company of you and all these demons.'

'Oh, quite safe. They never come this far. And even if they had, Arvad is extremely agile.'

'Do they perform this ritual often?'

'Quite often.'

'And what does it mean?'

'Must it mean something?'

Her brows knit slightly. 'It doesn't mean anything?'

He shrugged. 'It's a physical pleasure to them, somewhat as dancing is among mortals.'

'Dancing?'

He shook his head slowly, pityingly. 'Ah, my lady, you've never danced, have you?'

'I don't know what that is.'

212

'Well, perhaps sometime when we have a little music nearby, I'll show you. You do know what music is?'

'Yes. Of course. My mother sang to me when I was a child.'

'I'm glad to hear it.' He smiled at her. 'What did you think of the ritual? Besides wondering what it meant.'

'I thought it was . . . intricate. They must have trained a good deal in order to perform it so neatly. Are they some sort of special group within the demons of Water?'

'Only in one way,' said Cray. 'They are all free. No slave demon is allowed to participate. Perhaps you noticed the two stray reflections of Gildrum's light over there just before the ritual began?' He pointed off to their left.

'No, I didn't.'

'Well, two demons were floating there, watching. They must have been slaves, visiting home while their masters had no need of them, for if they'd been free, they would surely have joined in. It's very sad, don't you think, that through no fault of their own they are barred from the ritual?'

'Why are they barred?'

'Ah, there you ask a question about the fundamental nature of demons, my lady. You ask about the difference between the slave and the free. I think a demon should answer you. Gildrum?'

'The answer is simple,' said Gildrum. 'The Free are proud and jealous of their freedom. They see it as a mark of superiority, and they look upon slaves as low and contemptible and unworthy of associating with themselves. It is thus in all the demon worlds, but the inhabitants of Water have raised it to the highest art.'

'And what of the slaves?' said Aliza. 'How do they view those who are free?'

'As foolish and self-centred. They have their own society, separate from the Free, at least in Air and Fire and

Water. In Ice, of course, no demon associates with another very often.'

'If they have their own society,' said Aliza, 'why don't the slaves of Water organize their own ritual? Why should they need to come here and watch these free demons in theirs?'

'They have tried to organize their own, occasionally, but whenever the free demons discover it, they break it up. They see the ritual as a celebration of their freedom and not a proper pastime for slaves.'

'But every free demon has the potential to be a slave. At any moment any of those performers in the ritual could have been conjured by a sorcerer.'

'That is why they celebrate their freedom,' said Gildrum. 'While they have it.'

'It must be a strange sort of existence,' said Cray, 'to know that at any moment one could become a slave.'

'I suppose it must be,' murmured Aliza.

'Would you care to meet a water demon?' Cray asked her.

She shrugged. 'I suppose I might as well. I've met every other sort.'

'Look over your shoulder, then.'

She turned and saw, not more than an arm's length behind her, a faint glow in the water, like some subdued reflection of Gildrum's sunny light, but shimmering and iridescent with all the pale colours of mother of pearl. In another moment it became fully visible as a milky globe the size of a large bear.

'Greetings, Elrelet, Cray Ormoru, and you others,' said the water demon. Its voice was deep and fuzzy, and its opalescent surface bulged here and there in rhythm to its speech, as if something inside were struggling to get out.

'Greetings, Murnai,' said Elrelet. 'We found your ritual most impressive, as always. Allow me to present the mortal Aliza, and two others you may not have met before,

Regneniel and Leemin of Ice. Murnai is the current leader of the ritual.'

'A slave,' said the water demon, 'a slave from Ice.'

Cray murmured to Aliza, 'Murnai is free, of course.'

'I am free,' said the demon. 'Will you force me to speak with a slave?'

Regneniel moved from its place at Aliza's shoulder to one nearer her hip; floating there, it seemed almost to be hiding from the water demon. Aliza put her hand on it, as if gripping a knife.

'Speak to me, then, O creature of Water,' she said. 'Tell me who will speak to you when you are a slave.'

With one curving sweep of his hand, Cray placed himself between Aliza and the water demon. The bulging milky surface was a scant hand's breadth from his face. 'Forgive my mortal friend for her bluntness, O Murnai. She is ignorant of your ways and meant no insult.'

'Is she of the sorcerous breed?' asked the demon.

'Yes.'

'They have less fear of us than other mortals. Yet she must know that I could do her some damage if I wished. Water I may be, yet I can deliver a powerful blow.'

'And you must know, O Murnai,' said Cray, 'that these my demon friends would be loath to allow any mortal in my company to be harmed. But let us let the matter pass – no one among us has any real wish to quarrel.'

'I have not,' said Murnai. 'And to show my good will, I shall answer her impertinent question, even though a slave is present to hear my words. Know, O mortal, that never again will Murnai be excluded from the society of the Free of Water. The great sorcerer set me free forever, and now I may lead the ritual in the certainty that I can never be torn away from it to answer to some greedy mortal's conjuring.'

'The great sorcerer?' said Aliza.

'The great sorcerer,' repeated Murnai. 'We demons call him so.'

'Why *great*?'

'Because he is the most important of them all to us. Because he has freed so many of us, from all four worlds.'

'How many would that be?'

'All of those you saw in the ritual, and as many more in each of the other worlds.'

'Ah,' said Aliza. 'And has this great sorcerer a name?'

'Not for you, mortal.'

She glanced at Cray, who had let himself drift to one side again. 'Is this person known to you?'

Cray shook his head. 'I know he exists, but the demons keep his identity a secret.'

'A secret?'

'To protect him, my lady. If other sorcerers knew who he was, they might try to do some hurt to the one who has so depleted the supply of potential slaves.'

'But you wouldn't hurt him,' she said. 'From what you've told me, I presume you approve of this . . . this habit of his.'

'I applaud it,' said Cray, 'but I'd rather not know his name. I wouldn't want to worry that some slip of my tongue might expose him to his enemies.'

Aliza's cool dark eyes narrowed. 'Does Gildrum know?'

'I suppose he must.'

'I do know,' said Gildrum. 'But I would not tell any mortal. Not even Cray. Not even my beloved Delivev. I wish the greatest sorcerer to continue his work until there are no slave demons at all.'

'Do many demons feel that way?' Aliza asked.

'We have a pact among us,' said Gildrum. 'No demon will reveal the great sorcerer's name to a mortal.'

'Yet a slave demon, asked by its master, would have no choice but to reveal the secret.' She looked down at the icicle in her hand. 'If I asked Regneniel for the name, it would have to tell me. It would have to.'

'Slaves do not know the secret,' said Murnai. 'How

could we trust them with it? You have given the reason yourself.'

'But why should you care if the name is known, Murnai?' asked Aliza. 'Why should any free water demon care? You despise slaves. Why did you bind yourselves to this pact of secrecy for their sake?'

'Not for *their* sake,' said the demon. 'For the sake of our unborn children.'

'Your children?'

'Yes. That they may never know slavery at all.'

'Children,' murmured Aliza.

'Does that surprise you? Do mortals care nothing for their children, would they gladly see them enslaved? Or . . . no, I see. Cray Ormoru, can this mortal truly be so ignorant that she thinks demons spring full-grown from nothingness?'

Cray looked at Aliza. 'I don't know.'

'Yes,' she said. 'I am that ignorant. I never gave the matter any thought.'

'We bear our children,' said Murnai. 'Perhaps not in quite the same way as mortals do, but still, they come from our bodies. I myself have borne two.'

'You are . . . a female demon, then.'

'That word has no meaning for demons. We pair, but any one of us can bear a child. You must instruct this person, Cray Ormoru, if she intends to move among us. Not every water demon would be so patient with her as I have been. And now I find that my patience is at an end. Another foolish question from her, and I might be tempted to do something unpleasant.'

'We thank you for your attention, O Murnai,' said Elrelet, but the water demon was already receding from them, its iridescence fading into the deep blue of Water until only a pinpoint highlight, reflected from Gildrum's glow, remained to mark its location. In a moment, even that was gone.

217

'I've never really liked water demons,' said Elrelet. 'They have no sense of humour at all.'

'Well, my lady,' said Cray, 'you'll have to admit that this journey has added considerably to your store of knowledge.'

'It has bewildered me,' said Aliza, staring after the vanished demon. 'It is too much to take in at one swallow. I need time to sort it out, to think about it. Ah, Cray Ormoru, every time you visit, you make me think so much. I wonder if you can conceive of how exhausting I find you.'

'My lady, I never meant to exhaust you, only to open your eyes to a wider experience of life than you have heretofore known.'

She tried to cover her eyes with both hands, but she could not touch her face for the layer of air demon that enveloped her. 'I would close them now. Please, will you take me home?'

'Of course, my lady. Come, my demon friends. To Ice.'

The return journey was a quiet one. Aliza hardly said anything, and as if her silence were contagious, the others spoke little, too, and only in low tones. Only when they reached the boundary of Ice itself, and Leemin opened the fracture for them, did she waken somewhat from her reverie, to take charge of her own motion. Arvad stripped itself away from her there and trailed the others as they pushed toward the palace of crystal.

At her very walls they halted, and Aliza stepped ahead of the rest and turned to place her back against the transparent face of her home. Regneniel, at her shoulder, clacked against that crystal plane.

'Thank you,' she said, surveying them with her cool dark eyes, looking from one to another, from demons of Air and Ice and Fire to Cray, at the last. 'I will not forget what I have seen and heard today. I will not forget any of you.

Now . . . go away.' Behind her, the wall melted to nothing, and she took one backward step through that space, and then it was filled with crystal once more.

Cray pushed himself to the wall and floated there, palms flat against that glassy surface. 'I'll come again,' he said, not knowing if she could hear him now as she had once heard him call her name from this same spot. 'There's more to see. So much more.' He smiled at her – encouragingly, he hoped.

Abruptly, he was smiling at his own reflection. The whole wall had become a mirror.

'That was certainly an emphatic farewell,' said Elrelet, and the group began to move away from the palace.

They had gone some way in silence before Cray sighed and said, 'Perhaps it *was* a little too much for one day.'

'Perhaps?' exclaimed Elrelet. 'For a human child who has spent most of her life locked away in Ice, I would say it was probably more than just a little too much. A journey through two new worlds, a good view of some of the best hacking and hewing to be found in Air, and the ritual as well, and then a bout of insult trading with one of the most arrogant and powerful water demons in existence – I'd say that was a bit more than an average day's entertainment.'

'I thought Murnai was particularly uncivil,' said Gildrum, 'considering that Aliza and Regneniel were in Cray's company. I wonder if it was dissatisfied with the ritual? I thought I noticed a bit of raggedness in the beginning.'

Elrelet said, 'I think it's just become a hundred times more contemptuous of slaves – and mortals – since it was freed. I thought Aliza showed commendable spirit in talking back like that. Poor Regneniel didn't deserve such a snub, even if it is an ice demon.'

'What seems strange to me,' Cray remarked, 'is that she would react so strongly to an insult to her slave. That seems to be so much at odds with the attitude she has expressed to me – that slaves are only *things*.'

'I don't think she took it as an insult to her slave,' said Gildrum. 'I think she took it as an insult to herself. Just as you might react to an insult to your taste in clothing or furnishings.'

Cray pursed his lips. 'You may be right. Still, I thought I saw a bit of the cow protecting her calf from the wolf in the way she faced up to Murnai. I don't know.' He shook his head. 'Their relationship doesn't seem to be precisely what I thought it was, what Aliza insisted it was. Even if she does see the ice demon as property . . . what do you make of its attitude toward her?'

'I don't know,' Gildrum said. 'I would never have guessed that an ice demon could feel affection for a mortal. Leemin, what do you think?'

'It is absurd,' said Leemin.

'That's certainly succinct,' said Elrelet.

'Regneniel has been with mortals too long,' said the ice demon. 'It has become contaminated with human attitudes. The very thought of that shames me.'

'Perhaps they have been together so long, just the two of them in that huge palace,' said Gildrum, 'that they've reached some middle ground between demon and mortal. Some sort of dependence upon each other. And perhaps only the demon is able to admit it, being forced to tell the truth to its master. She might not even realize how she feels toward it.'

'Are you contradicting what you said before, Gildrum?' asked Cray.

'No, I think not. I think one may become attached to property. As she once was to the stuffed animal. I wonder if the ice demon has perhaps replaced that toy in her life.'

'I hadn't thought of that,' said Cray.

'It doesn't surprise me,' said Elrelet. 'I've given up being surprised by anything that mortals may think or do. But I don't much care for Gildrum's explanation of the demon. A dozen years it has watched over her, and while that may be a great deal of time in human terms, it's precious little in the demon's life. I was with my last master three centuries, and if he had set me free voluntarily instead of dying, I would never have returned. And I am a friendly, cheerful creature of Air. I can't imagine an ice demon caring enough for anyone, demon or mortal, to stay with them out of choice. My apologies to Leemin for such bluntness, but I don't think you will contradict the sentiment.'

'I cannot,' said Leemin. 'Except for brief excursions like this, for curiosity's sake, I spend my time alone, in meditation.'

'And yet you *are* here with us, at this moment,' said Cray. 'You don't spend all of your time alone.'

'I like an entertainment now and then,' admitted the demon. 'But you must not think that I am doing this out of any supposed affection for you.'

Cray smiled. 'Of course not. I'm sure that you have not become contaminated by human attitudes. Still, that does not mean that other ice demons are proof against them. Regneniel had other masters before Aliza. Who knows how it may have been affected by them? Perhaps we have been underestimating the capacity of some ice demons for emotion. After all, not all mortals are alike. This Regneniel . . . may be an unusual case. Who is to tell us otherwise? Leemin?'

'I had never met Regneniel before.'

'Nor, I suspect, had many others of your kind.'

'We keep to ourselves. That is our nature.'

'And so you don't truly know each other.'

'We never intrude upon each other.'

'And so you could not really deny that some ice demons might be quite different from yourself.'

Leemin hesitated for a long moment. At last it said, 'That is possible.'

'I see no other explanation,' said Cray. 'Perhaps . . . because this ice demon raised Aliza, because it saw her grow and learn, perhaps, in its way, it thinks of her as its child. Even ice demons care about their children. For a while, at least.'

'I can't believe it,' said Elrelet.

'I see no other explanation,' Cray repeated.

Everand set the last of Aliza's notebooks down on her desk. He had gone through her year's accumulation of knowledge carefully, thoroughly, now and then asking for clarification from Aliza herself, now and then questioning the demon Regneniel about the quality of its teaching. Satisfied that he knew where her education stood, he leaned back in his chair and looked at her long and hard. He saw that she had changed this past year, as she always changed between his visits; she was taller and slimmer than he remembered, and the planes of her face were more angular. She had always been pretty, but now the prettiness had been refined into something more mature. She was a child no longer. Nor were her powers those of a child.

'Your studies progress well,' he said to her.

'I think so, Grandfather.' She sat on a corner of the broad desk, one foot touching the crystalline floor, one dangling. She had waited for his evaluation with patient silence, speaking only when spoken to, her eyes following his every movement, every turn of a page.

Elbows on the arms of the chair, he steepled his ring-laden fingers and gazed at her over their tips. 'Have there been any special difficulties that you wish to discuss with me?'

Her cool brown eyes met his serenely. 'No, Grandfather.'

'None?'

She shook her head.

'Distractions, then?'

'Nothing I couldn't deal with.'

His fingers slid together, interlacing and dropping to his chest. 'So you think you dealt properly with the human visitor.'

Her stiffening was barely perceptible, but he had been watching for it. 'What do you know of the human visitor, Grandfather?'

He slouched deeper into the chair and stretched out his long legs. 'I know that he has been here three times, and this latest time he took you out of the palace, and even out of Ice.' He let his eyebrows rise at the expression of astonishment on her face. 'Child, you are flesh of my flesh. How could I not know what happens to you? We have a bond, you and I, that mere distance cannot sever. Did you so doubt my power that you thought I wouldn't know about him?'

'You never mentioned this bond before, Grandfather.'

He smiled a cold smile that did not touch his eyes. 'I suppose I always assumed you knew. It seems so obvious to me. After all, you are what you are by my will. Oh, I don't know every tiny detail of your life, else I wouldn't have to come here and question you on your studies. But I know when the changes happen. I know when the outside intrudes upon you. And it has intruded, in the form of this mortal. What is his name?'

'Cray Ormoru.'

'I don't know that name. He is a sorcerer, of course.'

'Yes.'

'You find his company pleasant?'

'I find him interesting.'

Everand nodded slowly. 'And did he tell you why he came here?'

'He saw me in a magical mirror, and his curiosity drove him to seek me out.'

'Did you believe that?'

'It is what he told me. Why should I not believe it?'

Everand rose from the chair and turned his back on his granddaughter. 'Why should you believe it?' he said. 'It doesn't sound like a very likely tale to me.' He looked at her over his shoulder. 'Much more likely is the possibility that he is spying on you, trying to learn the best way to circumvent your powers. Or perhaps even to steal them. I've told you before of the jealousies of other sorcerers.'

'He doesn't seem jealous of my powers at all, Grandfather.'

'He hides it well, then. But think – how much curiosity has he shown toward them?'

'Just a small amount. He'd rather talk to me than watch me practise sorcery.'

Everand nodded sharply. 'First he ingratiates himself with you, then he discovers how to render you helpless. Such a person would make a formidable enemy.'

'I think you misjudge him, Grandfather. He's already taught me a good deal –'

'*Taught* you? What, are you his apprentice now instead of mine? Beware of the teachings of another sorcerer – he may as easily teach you false as true. And where will you be then, when you wave your hand and nothing that he *said* you learned happens?'

'Grandfather –'

'Listen to me, child,' he said, pointing a bony finger at her. 'Don't speak of *my* misjudging this Cray Ormoru. You are no judge of mortals. I know what I say, for I have had my dealings with them, and I know better than to trust any of them, sorcerous or no. Trust your grandfather and no other, and you will always take the proper path.' He let his hand drop to his side. '*But*, if by some remote chance he did not come here to make himself proof against you

224

or to do you damage, still he is not harmless to you. He is a distraction. He interferes with your studies. Yes, you have done well, I will not deny it, but you would have done better, I know, without his intrusion. Think about it, child.'

'He was only with me a short time,' she said.

'At your age every moment is precious! The young learn best. The older you are, the harder learning becomes. Would you waste the only youth you'll ever have in babble with a stranger?'

Aliza looked down at the books stacked on her desk. She reached out, and with one finger she touched the nearest, the smooth dark leather of the cover, the gilt number painted upon it. Each notebook bore such a number, and there were five or six such volumes for every year that she had lived in Ice. Stacked one on top of the other, they would make a pile taller than Aliza, taller than her grandfather, taller than the ceiling of this room. Knowledge. 'I would not wish to waste any of my time,' she said softly.

'Then if he comes to these walls again, you must send him away. You must insist that he leave you alone to pursue your studies. There will be time for mortals later, if you still have any interest in them – later, when you are mature and certain in your powers. He'll still be alive, surely, if he's one of the sorcerous breed, and you'll be able to find out what he really wanted of you then. That's perfectly reasonable, isn't it, child?'

She raised her cool eyes to his. 'Perfectly reasonable.'

'Good. Then I'll be on my way, and I'll see you next year, as always.'

'You won't stay for supper?'

'No, I have too many tasks awaiting me at home. It's best that I get back to them.'

Aliza escorted her grandfather to the other side of her palace, the side that lay in the human realm. There, in the same exterior room where she and Cray had supped, she opened the same window through which Regneniel had carried him, the window that was her only tenuous link with the ordinary world of sun and wind and seasons. Beyond it, the sky was iron grey with oncoming snow, and the coarse quartz sand that surrounded her palace was hidden by an earlier fall of heavy white flakes. In the distance, the mountains, too, were white.

'A chilly day,' said Everand, looking out over the barren landscape, 'and snow before morning unless I miss my guess.' He crossed his arms over his chest. He wore a robe of heavy velvet, but it was not proof against the breeze that entered at the window; his breath was smoke upon it. 'Still, my demons will keep me warm enough once I've reached them.'

'I'm quite willing to give permission for them to cross the sands, Grandfather,' said Aliza. She wore a woollen mantle over her gown, for the palace was cold these days, with so little sunshine available to heat it. With the onslaught of deep winter, she had caused crystalline hearths to bloom in several of the innermost rooms, and Regneniel kept her well supplied with wood from the mountains and beyond, but still the palace was not as pleasantly warm as it was in summer. 'Let them come here and take you from this window.'

Everand shook his head sharply. 'I'll have no demon of mine acquire the habit of crossing these sands. That was well enough for Regneniel, for I always knew it would belong to you one day, but the others must be kept off. I will not live forever, child, and it is best that they have no slightest power upon this area when someone else has enslaved them.'

'But the spell would be stronger than ever by then,' said Aliza, 'for I would be in the fullness of my powers.'

'Once a demon has crossed a sorcerer's barrier, it always retains some capacity to do so again. A small capacity, it is true, but I would not have your barriers weakened in the slightest degree. No, Regneniel shall take me to the other side of the mountains, where one of my fire demons waits to carry me in warm comfort. And next year, when I call to you from there, Regneniel shall fetch me just as it did this time. We shall leave it at that from now on.'

'Whatever you wish, Grandfather. Regneniel!'

On the other side of the mountains, a group of mortal men, eight in all, waited huddled about the camp-fire they had built for themselves. They talked quietly, speculating on the weather and the amount of light left to the day. All around them, the snow was hard-packed with their pacing and scattered with the bones of the small animals they had slain and cooked for their midday meal. Now they were hungry again and, having hunted in the immediate area with some success during the latter part of the afternoon, they had spitted a few more carcasses above the flames. They were just about to begin sharing these when one of the men pointed toward the nearest slope.

They stood stiff and silent as Everand approached them, trudging through the snow. In silence, they wrapped their master in a thick woollen cloak, set a stool by the fire for him, and served him their choicest meats. Only when his hunger had been satisfied did they take up his leavings and gnaw them to the bone.

Two men kicked out the fire and scattered the embers into the snow while the rest hoisted the poles of Everand's palanquin onto their shoulders. Within, sealed away from the elements by stout doors and closely shuttered windows, he relaxed amid heavy furs, his feet warmed by a charcoal brazier. As he pulled off his gloves and stripped the useless rings from his fingers, he felt the palanquin begin to move smoothly forward. There was only a little daylight left, but he had commanded his servants to use it to put as much distance between themselves and the mountains as possible. They had a long journey ahead of them.

While Regneniel crossed over to the other side of the palace, its goal the kitchen, where it would prepare Aliza's supper, she herself walked only so far as the cradle room. There, in the heart of her dwelling, the heart of her personal world, she stood for a time amid the memories of her childhood, stood and gazed upon them with her cool dark eyes. At last she reached for the rocking horse, pulled it out from behind the old, short bed, and set it in the aisle that linked the two doors. It was a small rocking horse, and much battered by a child's activities. She sat down on it, sidesaddle rather than astride, for her legs were much too long for it now. She sat and she rocked slowly, back and forth, back and forth, and in her hands she held the old, bedraggled stuffed animal, that creature of no special identity, plucked from its resting place in the translucent bin of toy building materials. She held it and she rocked, and when the demon called her to her meal, she made no answer, nor any attempt to do more than rock, staring down all the while at the remnant of her childhood that lay between her hands.

She supped very late that night.

Chapter 8

In the human realm, winter ruled the land, but even the coldest wind to rake Spinweb's battlements was a summer breeze compared with the chill of Ice. In Ice there were no seasons to mark the passage of time, and its inhabitants cared nothing for days or years or centuries save when a mortal demon master forced them to care. Yet in one way, time was measured in Ice, though the measurement was a rough one. Through time, the shape of Aliza's palace changed.

Cray noticed the change when Leemin brought him back to her walls once more. Quite near the place where he always entered the building, a blister had formed – a new room, no larger yet than a wardrobe, budding off from the rest. It was a copy, in miniature, of so many other rooms he had seen, a carbuncle with facets the span of a man's arm. He pointed to it in wonder.

'This palace grows like some sort of living thing,' he said to his three demon companions. 'Like a tree thrusting out new twigs, only much more slowly.'

'That might be because it *is* a living thing,' said Leemin.

'What do you mean? It's just a building, isn't it? A magical one, yes, but only a building.'

'You think like a mortal, for all you've spent so much time in the demon realm, Cray Ormoru. The lady told you herself, or so you said, that this palace grew from a seed planted in Ice by Regneniel. Where else would a demon find such a seed but within its own body? This palace is Regneniel's child.'

'This building is a demon?'

'It is a creature of Ice. It feeds on the forces that permeate this world, as we all do, and with the power so derived, it transforms the substance around it, as we all do. How is it, therefore, different from us?'

'Do you mean to tell me that this . . . this building can *think*?'

'Can *you* think?' asked Leemin.

'Of course I can.'

'So you say. As far as *I* know, you don't think at all, you only speak and move about. This child of Regneniel's does neither. Perhaps it chooses to do neither.'

'Have you ever tried to speak to it?' asked Cray.

'I greeted it once. It did not answer.'

'This is a building,' said Elrelet, 'nothing more. It's no more alive than the sword Arvad made out of its own substance.'

'And no less alive,' said Leemin.

'Perhaps this is why Regneniel would choose not to leave her if she freed it,' said Gildrum. 'Even ice demons care about their children for a time, and even though this child is huge in size, it is very young in years.'

'If it *is* alive,' said Elrelet, 'it is surely the ultimate creature in Ice – it goes nowhere and speaks to no one, and, except for Leemin's one small greeting, I'll wager no one speaks to it. It makes a perfect demon at that.'

'A slave born to slavery,' said Gildrum. 'It has never tasted any other life. How completely pitiful.'

'On the contrary,' said Elrelet, 'it doesn't know what it's missing and therefore cannot suffer from its lack of freedom. If it can know anything, and if it can suffer at all.'

'It can suffer,' said Leemin. 'It has a soul, and any creature with a soul can suffer.'

. 'A soul?' said Cray.

'Can't you sense it, deep within those walls? The soul, the seat of life. No, you are a mortal, and I perceive you

230

cannot sense such things at all. But these others, they are demons . . .'

'But not of Ice,' said Gildrum. 'We are not attuned to the creatures of this realm. But if you say this thing before us has a soul, I believe you.'

'Even if it looks like a building,' added Elrelet.

'My friends,' said Cray, 'once again we have found a way in which this dwelling is the strangest that any sorcerer ever had. And I thank Leemin for bringing it to my attention, and for reminding me that there are always new things to be learned, that no one can know everything. But now I think it's time to do what I came here to do.' And cupping his hands around his mouth, he called Aliza's name.

This time she did not come to answer him, but Regneniel did, hurrying awkwardly on its multijointed legs. As it approached, the wall before Cray melted, and he was able to step into the palace. Once he was sealed inside, he realized that the air of the building was cooler than he had ever known it, as if some of the chill of Ice had at last penetrated these crystalline ramparts. Winter had come to Aliza's home.

'Greetings, Regneniel,' he said. 'Thank you for allowing me to enter, but why are you here at my call instead of your mistress? I trust she is not ill.'

It dipped its snake-like neck in a kind of bow, its tiny arms fluttering with the motion like leaves in a mild breeze. 'My lady's command is that when she is not available, I am to admit you.'

'Not available? Where is she, then – out? In Ice or in the human realm?'

'No, Cray Ormoru. She is in her meditation chamber, never to be disturbed while the door is closed.'

'Do you know how long she plans to remain there?'

'No. I am to guide you to the room where the tapestry hangs, to provide you with warmth, and to serve you wine if you so desire. Will you follow me?'

'Yes,' replied Cray, and with a smile and a wave to the demons who had to be left behind outside, he moved with Regneniel into the depths of the palace.

The room with the tapestry was almost as he remembered it – the couch, the rug, the broad ebony table, the cabinet from which Regneniel took goblet and decanter to pour a generous measure of red Maretian wine for him. There was a hearth now, though, not far from the tapestry, its bright blaze sending waves of warmth through the room. And the cabinet had been moved farther from the couch to make room for a cubical crystalline bin, its lip at about the height of his knee. Through its transparent sides, he could see its contents, a mass of grey wool, fluffy with washing and carding. Atop that rested the crude spindle he had fashioned from Aliza's toy building materials. The spindle had been used by other hands than his own since he had left it in this very room. Unskilled hands. It was wound with a considerable amount of yarn, but the yarn was of varying thickness, here as fine as the thread that seamed his clothing, there almost too thick even for knitting needles. Someone had tried to imitate his spinning, had tried for a goodly length of time. He did not think that someone could be the ice demon.

'Is this your mistress's work?' he asked, pointing with one hand as he took the wine goblet from Regneniel's stubby grasp with the other.

'It is.'

'Is there some purpose to it?'

'She has not told me of any.'

Cray sipped from his goblet, then set it down on the table and took up the spindle. He pulled some wool from the bin and spun for a moment, a fine, even thread that his mother would have been proud of. It made the rest of the yarn look even worse by comparison. He tossed the spindle back where it came from and seated himself on the couch.

'Does she enter this meditation chamber often?' he asked the ice demon.

'She uses it regularly.'

'What does she do there?'

'I assume she meditates there.'

'About what?'

'I do not know.'

'Come, Regneniel – you are her only confidant. Surely you know what occupies her mind.'

'I would not presume to guess at a mortal's thoughts,' said the demon.

Cray bent over his goblet, looked down into the wine, saw his face reflected in its still surface. 'Has she spoken of me since I was last here?'

'She gave me the command to let you in.'

'No more than that?'

'No more.'

'Has she spoken of our journey to the other demon worlds?'

'No.'

Cray lifted his eyes to Regneniel, who stood beside the cabinet like some grotesque marble sculpture. 'What do the two of you talk about in these long hours you spend together?'

'Her lessons.'

'Just that? Just her lessons?'

'That is what we are here for, Cray Ormoru. That is why her grandfather gave me to her.'

Cray smiled at the demon. 'You've been with her a long time. One could even say you've been a parent to her. At least, you have been here, while he has not. *You* have raised her, Regneniel. She must depend on you very much.'

'I am her only demon slave.'

'And you care for her.'

'I am her slave.'

'You said you cared for her. Or at least you said you would not leave her even if she set you free. What did you mean by that, Regneniel? Can an ice demon truly care for a mortal?'

The demon hesitated. 'I don't believe I can explain that to you, Cray Ormoru. It is simply the way I am.'

'I am your friend, Regneniel,' he said. 'Believe me, I've known many demons in my life. Yes, ice demons among them. I want to understand you. I tell you frankly that I think if I understand you, even a little, then I'll be better able to understand her. I care for her, too, Regneniel, please believe that. But I would never tell her anything that you told me in confidence, I swear it. You may ask Gildrum if I am not one who holds his word above all else. Let us be honest with each other, you and I. I know demons who have the same capacity for feeling that mortals have. They tell me that cannot be true of ice demons, but perhaps they don't really know you. Perhaps you are more than they suspect. Tell me, Regneniel – do you love her?'

'I have heard of love,' said the demon. 'I had a master once who said he loved a woman, an ordinary mortal. He took her into his castle and would not allow her to leave. Her family came and demanded her back. He killed them all. A few years later he killed her. I did not understand his behaviour.'

Cray shook his head. 'I wasn't thinking of anything so violent. To me, love does include desiring to be with the loved person, but it also means wanting the very best for her, and doing one's utmost to make her happy. Your old master seems to have been more concerned about his own happiness than about the woman's.'

'Happiness,' said the demon.

'Surely you know what happiness is, Regneniel.'

'Happiness is the ability to move through the world of Ice at one's own whim.'

'Ah – freedom,' said Cray.

'They are the same.'

'And yet you would be willing to sacrifice that freedom to stay here with Aliza, to serve her, even if she freed you.'

The demon hesitated. 'I would not be here at *her* whim.'

'That might be love,' said Cray.

'Why are you so concerned that I love her?' asked the demon. 'Why do you wish to see this mortal . . . attitude in me?'

Cray sipped at his wine, his fingers curled tight about the stem of the goblet. He looked at the bin, at the wool, at the spindle and its crudely spun yarn. He looked at the tapestry, at the autumn colours there, the leaves, the grass, the sky. At last he said, 'Because if you can love her, then perhaps she, who was raised by you, is also capable of love. And that is a good thing in a mortal. Better still in a sorcerer. They have more need of love than ordinary mortals; they need it to leaven their power.'

The demon was silent.

'Have I asked too much of you?' said Cray. 'I apologize for my inquisitiveness, but as her friend, I would like to know that being locked up in this place for so much of her life has not completely stripped her of all feeling. She denies emotion, but perhaps the denial is only words. And perhaps though she calls you slave, you are truly more. Perhaps you are a friend, too.'

'I am a slave, Cray Ormoru. You would be foolish to think of me as more than that. Now, my lady did not command me to engage in conversation with you, so if you should desire food, tell me and I will bring it. Otherwise, I have a few tasks to perform before my lady's supper.'

Cray shrugged. 'Do as you will, Regneniel. I am not hungry. But before you rush off to these very important tasks, tell me – must I stay in this room while I wait? I prefer not to.'

235

'My lady did not instruct me to lock you in.'

'Good. I like being a guest better than being a prisoner.'

He watched the demon leave. He knew no more about the relationship between the creature of Ice and the mortal woman than he had when he arrived, and now he wondered about it more than ever. He reflected that an ice demon, with its cold pride and aloofness, might well be ashamed to admit affection for its mistress. He wondered if, questioned directly by Aliza herself once more, Regneniel would have been so evasive. A demon could not lie to its master, but some of them were very clever at manipulating the truth in such a way that it could be misinterpreted. Gildrum had practised that art when it was a slave, Cray knew, and with considerable success.

He drained his goblet and rose, stretching. Behind the couch, the door that led farther into the palace was open. He walked through it and then through a number of small rooms, all of them just as he remembered, save that now the furnished ones had hearths with well-banked fires to warm them. In Aliza's study he stopped to leaf through a few of the books on her desk. They were filled with tiny, precise handwriting, and their contents did not make much sense to him. She was long past the point at which her studies were accessible to one trained in other forms of sorcery.

In the dining hall, he took a piece of fruit from the tray on the table and munched at it as he walked on. Choosing a door at the back of the hall, he wandered through several unfamiliar – and empty – rooms. He moved in an arc, passing from chamber to chamber in a path that, he thought, would ultimately bring him back to the dining hall. He saw much of the palace, a dozen rooms and more of all sizes, and yet he saw very little, just blank walls and stairways that led to more emptiness.

He came to a room whose outside walls were perfect

mirrors, which seemed to have no exit into any of the rooms that surrounded it. Even its floor and ceiling were mirrored on the outside, proof against his sight from rooms above and rooms below. Looking down at his own reflection in its ceiling, he found himself understanding the knight who had happened on Aliza's palace when she was a child. Here was a mystery, a thing of strange beauty, a sealed box that might contain anything. Almost, he was tempted to strike its walls with his fists, to test it for hollowness. Almost. But he knew it was hollow, just as he knew that he would not be able to hear that hollowness evoked by his soft human hands. He guessed, because he had not seen her elsewhere in the palace, that this was Aliza's meditation room, that the walls were mirrored to keep out the light of the rest, to keep out the existence of the rest. It was not a very large room, not a great deal larger than the cradle room. Cray wondered if it were furnished or bare, and if Aliza meditated in light or darkness.

He waited there for a time, hoping that one of the walls would melt away and reveal Aliza, or that Regneniel would call him with the news that the meditation room lay elsewhere and that she had emerged from it. Neither of those things happened before he became restless and decided to wander on.

He came to the cradle room at last. He had tried to keep track of his turns, his climbs, his descents, and he expected to arrive there eventually. He grinned to himself as the milky walls came into view. He was on the opposite side of the room from the main living space of the palace, opposite where he had entered it last time. The outside of the milky-walled staircase should have been visible to him, leading up to the entrance to the mortal realm.

There was no staircase.

There was, instead, an open doorway on the very

spot where he thought the entry to the staircase should have been.

He peeked into the room. Directly across from him, down the narrow aisle flanked by memorabilia of Aliza's childhood, was the other door. Looking at it, studying the lie of the room, he was convinced that the other door was the one through which he had entered the cradle room before, unless Aliza had moved everything around into a mirror image of the way it had been. There was a crowded sitting room beyond that other doorway, he remembered, while behind him, behind this doorway in which he now stood, was a chamber without a stick of furniture to relieve its emptiness.

Cray found himself frowning. Did Aliza periodically rearrange her palace? She had never mentioned doing any such thing. Nor had he seen any other evidence of interior change, except for the hearths.

He stepped into the room. There was the child's bed, the rocking horse, the table and chair, the bins full of toys and linens, just as before. There was one door, and there the other, no other entrances visible. In a few short strides, he crossed the room to stand in the opposite doorway. The milky-walled stairway lay before him.

All right, he told himself, she did rearrange her palace occasionally, at least the cradle room. She probably had perfectly good reasons for it.

For a moment, he was tempted to climb those stairs, to ask Regneniel to open the mirrored door at the top for him, but then he decided he was not here to look at the sky, especially not at the grey and gloomy winter sky. Instead, he went to sit on the lip of one of the bins and rummage idly among its contents. To see a bit more of Aliza's vanished childhood.

She found him there sometime later. She found him building a toy castle on the floor, with wooden blocks piled to knee height.

He did not hear her soft footfalls, did not realize she was near until her velvet skirt brushed his arm. At that, he looked up and smiled at her. 'I think I'm trying to prove myself as fine an architect as yourself. What do you think of my creation, my lady?'

She knelt beside him, and he saw that she had tied her hair back with the ribbon he had made for her. She pointed to one corner turret of his toy castle. 'That will fall in a moment or two. You've placed it off-centre.'

He peered at the indicated section, then brushed it gently with the tip of one finger. It collapsed, bringing down much of the adjacent wall, which had pressed against it. He laughed softly. 'I haven't much skill with dead wood, I'm afraid. Now, if these blocks were a few potted plants instead, I could grow you a fine castle, and its crenellations would bloom, too, if you wished.'

'Is that how you played as a child?'

'No, my lady. That was how I played as an adult. I have a full-sized castle of two-score rooms grown from a grove of trees. Making one small enough to fit inside this room would be a simple enough task after that.'

'A castle of wood? What a strange notion.'

'No stranger than a castle of ice, I think.'

'But my ice is as strong as stone. It *is* stone, save for its transparency.'

'My ensorcelled wood is just as strong. No wind can break my trees, no fire char them, no axe or saw cut them as long as I live. And should I ever wish more room than my castle now contains, they will grow into whatever shapes I command; I need not wait upon their own random whim.'

She sat back on her heels and crossed her arms over her breast. 'So you think your castle of wood is superior to this palace, do you?'

He smiled at her. 'I think that my power over it is

superior to your power over this place. Aside from that the two are very much alike.'

'Alike? Wood and ice?'

'Surely. After all, both of them are alive.'

'Alive?' Her expression was one of incredulity.

'Yes. My trees live and bloom and drop their leaves in the autumn and put forth new ones in the spring. Did you think they could grow into new rooms without being alive?'

She shook her head, and then she rapped on the floor with one fist, and the sound was hard and sharp. 'Ice is not alive.'

'Ah,' he said. 'You didn't know.'

'Know what?'

'That your palace is a living thing.'

'What do you mean? What are you talking about?'

'Your grandfather never told you? Regneniel never told you?'

'What nonsense are you spouting, Cray Ormoru?'

'I don't think it's nonsense,' Cray said. 'Leemin told me, and I know of no reason why it should lie to me. This palace is Regneniel's offspring. That is why it grows.'

'Regneniel's offspring? Absurd. This palace is a crystal, and crystals can grow without being alive.'

'I know very little about crystals, my lady. I know only that Leemin insists that this building is a living creature of Ice, with a living creature's soul and source. I would think that a demon of this world would be an adequate judge of what lives here and what does not.'

'Nonsense! Leemin is foolish and ignorant. Come along with me, and I'll show you how alive this palace is.' She climbed to her feet and, turning sharply, strode toward the doorway that gave on the stairs.

In his hurry to follow her, Cray knocked in a wall of his toy castle and then stumbled over the spilled blocks; he clutched at the nearest bin to keep from falling. By the time he regained his balance, she was no longer in the cradle room. She was no longer in sight. He loped the few paces to the stairway and up three steps before he stopped.

She was not on the stairway.

'Aliza?' he said. He climbed the rest of the way up the milky tunnel. At its top, the mirrored panel sealed it. He knocked on the panel, a blunted sound that betrayed no hollowness beyond. 'Aliza?'

Her voice came from below him. 'Cray Ormoru.'

He turned. He saw her standing at the foot of the stairs.

'You came in the other door,' she said.

He descended to stand beside her on the bottom step. 'My lady, that was as neat a piece of sorcery as I've ever seen. Did you use invisibility, or did you open a second passage from the upper part of the staircase to down here?'

She smiled slightly. 'You think I climbed these stairs?'

'I saw you walk through this doorway.'

Her lips quirked, as if she were almost about to laugh. Instead, though, she said, 'You saw me walk through the doorway that leads to the small sitting room. The same doorway I used to enter the cradle room, the one I ordinarily enter by. But you didn't enter that way, did you? You came in from the other side, from the unfurnished rooms on the other side.'

'Yes. I did.' He frowned, looking back to the cradle room with its bins and child-sized furniture, and the ruins of a toy castle marking its centre. 'But how could you come in from the sitting room? That's where this stairway is now.'

'So it is, from your point of view. And so, in order to leave the cradle room without climbing these stairs, you will have to go back into it, cross it, and go out the other door. Then you'll have to make a half circle about it

241

through the surrounding rooms to come to the sitting room. Go on. I'll use the other door and meet you.'

'What other door?' said Cray.

'The door to the sitting room.'

'You mean you'll open a new one?'

'No. It's there. But you can't use it right now. Ah, I see you're confused. I suppose I must have been confused about it myself at the beginning. But it's quite ·simple, really. The cradle room has two doors to other rooms in Ice and a stairway to the human realm. Whichever door you enter by, you must exit by the same if you wish to stay in Ice, and by the other if you wish to go to the human realm. Since you and I have entered the cradle room by two different doors, we must leave it by two different doors.'

'What a peculiar arrangement,' said Cray.

'Is it?'

He laughed. 'Truth to tell, this whole place is peculiar. There isn't another like it anywhere, or so the demons tell me.'

'I wouldn't want there to be one,' said Aliza. 'Now, I had something to show you, remember? Go on. I'll meet you in the sitting room.'

'Wait. You're on this stairway – does that mean you went out the door that I didn't go out?'

'Yes.'

'Then what do you see in that room? Do you see the rocking horse over there to the left of the other doorway and the bin with the old linens closest to where we stand?'

She shook her head. 'I see the room from the other side, of course. The rocking horse is close to me and the bin of linens is at the other end.'

'Then what would happen if we linked arms and walked down this last step and through the doorway together?'

The faint smile faded from her face. 'This is a strong

spell, Cray Ormoru. After all, it was laid by my grandfather. I think it would be a mistake to tempt his sorcery.'

Cray leaned against the wall, looking out into the cradle room. Through the opposite doorway, he could see part of the empty chamber, and try as he might, he could not imagine how Aliza was seeing some fragment of the furnished sitting room in that same place. 'Strong the spell may be,' he said, 'but it seems unnecessarily complicated to me. Surely it would have been simpler to set the stairway at one end of the room and the exit to Ice at the other and be done with it.'

'I'm sure he had good reasons for arranging things this way,' said Aliza. 'He always has good reasons for everything.'

Cray turned his head and looked into her eyes. 'Does he?' he said softly.

She nodded. 'Even on those few occasions when I've disagreed with him, I've always known that his reasons were good.'

'You've disagreed with him?'

'Does that surprise you so?'

'I thought you were . . . an obedient grandchild.'

'I am. But I do have a mind of my own. Perhaps you didn't think I did.'

'I don't know what I thought,' said Cray. 'But I'm glad to hear that you don't consider yourself completely his slave.'

'Even a slave may *think* what it likes.'

He smiled at her. 'There was a time when you would have denied that slaves could think at all. For how can a *thing* think?'

Her lips curved for just a moment. 'I've learned something since then. I'm still an apprentice, remember – still learning.' She gestured toward the room. 'Shall we go?'

'You first. I'm curious to see what happens.'

She shrugged. 'What happens is sorcery. Surely you've seen plenty of that.'

'There is sorcery and sorcery, my lady. Go on. I'll meet you in the sitting room.' When she hesitated, he added, 'I won't lose my way, don't worry.'

'I don't know how you could,' she said. 'The cloudy walls would guide you. But . . . I'll meet you in the empty room beyond the door, just to be sure.'

'As you wish, my lady.'

'In a few moments, then.' And she plunged down the last step and through the doorway.

And vanished, like a soap bubble popping in air.

And reappeared at the same instant on the opposite side of the room, striding purposefully toward Cray, as if she had just stepped through that other doorway to cross the room. Six swift paces brought her almost to him, and, involuntarily, he retreated a step to avoid the collision. But she vanished again at the instant she should have crossed the threshold before him.

Cray clutched at the milky walls to his left and right. Though he had expected something of the sort, he found the actual event to be a trifle unnerving, and he had to sit down heavily on the step behind him. He had seen sorcery, true enough – all kinds of sorcery. He had seen mortals call lightning down from the sky and lava up from the depths. He had seen demons change their shapes from glorious to grotesque, and he had seen them vanish or reappear in the blink of an eye as they dived through their portals between one realm and the other. But this jumping about of mortal flesh, this frenetic winking in and out of existence of a being of his own sort, was another thing entirely. It was only apparent, he realized, only a trick of viewpoint. From Aliza's viewpoint, *he* had been the one to vanish, or he would have if she had been looking back at him. As she had walked through the room itself, she had not seen him, even though she appeared to be looking straight at him; instead, she had seen the doorway to the sitting room which, in some fashion he could not fathom, was in front of her. The notion made his head spin. Doorways that were or were not there, depending on one's point of view – it was nothing to Aliza, just old, familiar sorcery. But to Cray it was proof again that there was a great deal he did not know, that he had never dreamed there was to know. And was it also proof, he wondered, that sorcery had no limits save the human imagination?

Aliza stepped through the doorway opposite him, the one that led, for him, to the empty room. 'You're still there,' she said.

He sprang to his feet and, in the same motion, through his own doorway. She did not vanish – he did not expect her to, for she had obviously traversed the rooms that surrounded this one in order to enter at the same door he had. Now they both saw the room from the same point of view, and both could use the same door to reach a single goal. They halted in the middle of the room's aisle, each on his own side of the fallen toy castle.

'I was contemplating the marvel of this chamber,' he said. 'Please accept my apologies for dawdling over-much.'

'Not overmuch,' she replied. 'I ran.'

He smiled at her. 'Were you afraid I'd become lost without a guide?'

'No, but I do have something to show you.'

'Another marvel?'

'Not to me. But you might think so. Come to the kitchen with me.'

'The kitchen?'

'Oh, you haven't been in the kitchen, have you? That's where Regneniel prepares my meals.'

'I know what a kitchen is, my lady.'

'Very well, then, come along.' She turned toward the door, but she had hardly taken a step when she looked

245

back at him. 'And don't call me *my lady* any more. You're not my slave, after all. Call me Aliza.'

'Only if you call me Cray. All my friends do.'

She gazed at him levelly, over her shoulder, and her cool eyes were unreadable. 'So we are friends now?'

'I hope so.'

She pursed her lips. 'Very well. We are friends, Cray.'

'Will you give me your hand on our friendship?' He held out his own.

After a long moment, she extended her hand toward his but did not touch it.

'The other hand,' said Cray, and when she offered it, he grasped it firmly. 'This is a handclasp, Aliza. It is a symbol of trust. I have been your friend from the moment I first saw you. I would never willingly do you harm. Rather, I would always try to help you in whatever way I could. I hope that you will come to feel the same way toward me.'

She looked down at their clasped hands. 'I have no desire to harm you,' she said. 'As for the rest – you ask a great deal.'

'I ask nothing. I only hope. In the meantime, I find you a pleasant companion, and I suspect that you have not been totally bored by me.'

'Not at all.'

'And I look forward to whatever it is that you wish to show me in the kitchen.'

'Yes, the kitchen,' said Aliza, and she pulled her hand from his and strode briskly through the doorway.

The kitchen was half a dozen steps up from the dining hall, through a door that Cray had not previously used. It was a long, narrow room, with a hearth on the nearest wall and only one piece of furniture – a small cupboard whose doors stood open to reveal a few metal pots and utensils and some small, transparent jars of salt and dried herbs. Regneniel leaned close to the hearth, and with a crystal rod clenched in its beak, it stirred the simmering contents of the pot that rested amid the flames. A human cook would not have pushed the pot so deep into the fire, but the ice demon, of course, had no fear of being burned.

Aliza went to the cupboard and, kneeling, reached to the back of its lowest shelf. She brought out a metal pot no larger than her two cupped hands, a footed crystal vase narrow enough for a single rose, a transparent rod slimmer than the one Regneniel was using, and a purple-tinted jar tightly closed by a cork.

'I haven't touched these things in a long time,' she said, motioning for Cray to join her at the cupboard. When he had seated himself cross-legged on the floor beside her, she uncorked the jar. Inside was a white powder. She shook some of it into the pot. 'Regneniel, fetch me a goblet of water.' While the demon was out of the room on this errand, Aliza inspected the rod and the vase, wiping them thoroughly with a cloth that hung from the handle of one of the cupboard doors. 'Regneniel used these for some of my earliest lessons, to help me understand the nature of crystals.'

Cray picked up the purple jar and peered inside. 'What is this stuff?'

'A salt. But don't taste it. It isn't the kind of salt you'd want to put on your food. Regneniel prepared it from the incrustation at the edge of a salt lake in the human realm. It hasn't any name, nor, as far as Regneniel knows, any use beyond this one of teaching me. And now you.'

'What will it teach me?'

'Wait and watch and you'll see for yourself.'

When the demon returned with a brimming goblet, she poured a small amount of water into the pot. With the crystal rod she stirred powder and water until most of the former had dissolved, leaving just a thin layer of residue to settle to the bottom. Then she held the pot out to Regneniel, saying, 'Set this on the fire to boil.'

Two of the demon's stubby arms lengthened to grasp the pot and to place it beside the larger one in the midst of the flames.

'It won't take long for so little liquid,' said Aliza. 'And while we wait, perhaps you would like to sample supper. I know I would. You will be staying for supper, won't you?'

Cray grinned. 'I am a bit hungry. But I was going to invite you to Spinweb for supper. After hearing so much about you from me and from Gildrum, my mother would like to meet you.'

'Spinweb?' Aliza sat back on her haunches, almost as if recoiling from him.

'Yes, and you could even stay overnight if you wished. We have plenty of guest room.'

'Overnight?'

'You could bring Regneniel along. My mother said she wouldn't mind.'

Aliza was frowning. 'Your mother would let another sorcerer inside her home?'

'She would let a friend of mine inside. Yes.'

'And a demon as well?'

'A demon lives with her. And others have visited from time to time. She is accustomed to them.'

Aliza shook her head. 'No. No. I couldn't.'

Cray reached out and, very lightly, touched her hand. 'You've had your yearly examination already, haven't you?'

'Yes.'

'And you did well, I'd wager.'

'Yes, I did well.'

'And there won't be another for the better part of a year. Plenty of time to make up a lost day, one single lost day.'

Hesitantly, she nodded.

He squeezed her fingers gently. 'Then come along with

me. Let me be your host for an evening. Let me serve you *my* favourite wine. And we can look at the stars above Spinweb. I promise you, they're different stars.'

Her lips compressed into a thin line as she looked away from him, down at the floor. 'I can't.'

'Would you disappoint my mother? After she made you that beautiful tapestry?'

'I've repaid that several times over, I think.'

'Not to *her*.'

'And you yourself said no repayment was necessary.'

Cray leaned toward her. 'You're not afraid to meet my mother, are you?'

She raised her dark eyes to his face. 'I am not afraid of anything.'

He smiled. 'I'm glad to hear that. Then you'll come.'

She pulled her hand away from his, pulled it back to shelter behind her other arm. 'No.'

'Why not? Give me one good reason why you won't come to Spinweb with me for supper.'

'I don't have time.'

'A better reason than that, Aliza.'

She looked into his eyes for a long moment, and then she said, 'Very well. My grandfather wouldn't like it.'

'Your grandfather?'

'He has already expressed his displeasure at the amount of time I have spent with you, away from my studies.'

'You told him?'

'No, but he has his ways of knowing.'

'His ways of spying, you mean.'

'I am his apprentice. It is right that he should be concerned with the way I use my time.'

'He was displeased . . . yet you commanded Regneniel to admit me, and here we are once more, together.'

'That was by my choice.'

'Then choose to come with me to Spinweb. You've travelled with me to Air; Spinweb is only a little farther.'

She shook her head.

Very softly, Cray said, 'Is it the human realm that you fear, or is it your grandfather, who wants you to spend your whole youth inside these walls?'

Her gaze was defiant. 'I told you I don't fear anything or anyone. Don't accuse me of your own weaknesses.'

'Then come with me to Spinweb.'

'I don't wish to displease him more than I already have. I owe him too much.'

'Must your every act please him, Aliza? Why not please yourself? Why not please me? You'll give him his due – you always have. Now take some small fragment for yourself.'

'But all of this *is* for myself!' She turned her whole body sharply, toward the hearth. 'Regneniel, is that pot boiling yet?'

'Very nearly, my lady.'

'Then bring it here.' She directed the demon to fill the vase with the steaming liquid. 'Observe, Cray Ormoru, that the powder is now completely dissolved. Next we must chill the container. When I was a child and first practised this, I let it cool naturally, but I don't care to spend the time for that now, so Regneniel must breathe cold, very gently, upon it. Very gently.'

The demon bent close to the vase and opened its beak. Cray, sitting opposite, could see no entry to its gullet, just seamless whiteness at the inside base of its beak, as smooth and blank as alabaster. But he could feel the cold coming from it, not as a breeze but as a slow seeping, as if chilled metal lay close to his flesh, drawing the heat from him. He shivered and moved back.

'It is enough,' Regneniel said after some moments. It closed its beak, and with that closure, the cold vanished, abruptly replaced by the soothing warmth of the hearth-fire.

Aliza glanced at Cray. 'Now watch closely.' She crouched

over the vase, crystal rod in hand. Then she gestured to him peremptorily. 'Closer.'

He eased forward till their heads were almost touching.

'Now,' she whispered, and she tapped the side of the vase with the rod.

Crystallization began at the point of disturbance and moved outward, spiky shards like ice forming one after the other almost too fast for the eye to follow. Within two heartbeats the liquid in the vase had become a solid. Aliza picked up the vase and turned it upside down to show that no fluid remained to spill out.

Cray took the vase from her hand and turned it, staring down into its crystalline contents.

'I didn't have to tap it,' she told him. 'I could have dropped in a speck of salt or even a speck of dirt. That would have been enough of a disturbance to start the crystals growing. You see, the liquid had all the proper raw materials to form these crystals; all it needed was an impetus to begin – the vibrating wall of the vase or some bit of foreign matter. Just so, Ice has all the proper raw materials to form this palace; and the cradle room was its impetus. But the palace is no more alive than the liquid was or than these crystals are.'

Cray set the vase down on the floor. 'You used no sorcery for this?'

'Any ordinary mortal could have taken these materials and achieved the same result.'

'Even . . . me?'

'Of course.'

He clasped both hands around the vase. 'There is a pattern here,' he said. 'I can feel it. There was none in the liquid, but the solid is . . . interlocked. Interlaced. One could almost call it . . . woven.'

'Of course the solid is interlocked. How would it hold together otherwise?'

'Indeed, how?' He chuckled softly and laid one hand

251

flat on the floor in front of him. 'And how did I not realize that before now? I've been surrounded by such a solid, yet I had to see one born before I could comprehend its nature. Aliza, you've given me a whole new world to study.'

'What – crystals?'

He nodded. 'Shall I learn to build myself a palace out of quartz sand, Aliza?'

She shrugged. 'Do as you will. It doesn't matter to me.'

'Nor to me, I assure you. Nor do I care whether this palace is alive or dead.' He reached out to her, touched her shoulder with one gentle hand. 'All that matters to me is that you come to Spinweb for supper with me this evening. An evening, Aliza, no more unless you wish it. You needn't stay overnight. But my mother is an excellent cook. And I have a special gift waiting for you there.'

'Another gift? Why do you persist in giving me things, Cray Ormoru?'

'Cray. Just Cray.'

'Very well – Cray.'

'I give you things because I derive pleasure from the giving. Would you deny a friend such a small pleasure?'

'If you wanted to give me something, why didn't you bring it along with you, then?'

'No, no. Part of the gift will be your seeing how the gift is made. And that must be in Spinweb.'

'You think to lure me with mystery.'

'I must lure you with something.' He climbed to his feet. 'Come with me, Aliza. I promise you good food, good wine, and good company. Make your decision now, for I told my mother I'd return quickly, and I've been gone too long already; I don't want her to think something terrible has happened to me.'

Aliza scrambled up. 'You're leaving?'

'I must.'

'But you haven't been here very long.'

'Long enough. Waiting while you were in your meditation chamber used up most of the time I'd allowed myself. And my demon friends are outside, surely wondering about me.'

'We can tell them you're safe. They can tell your mother.'

He shook his head. 'I must go home.' He bowed to her. 'Forgive me, but . . . farewell.' He turned toward the stairway that led to the dining hall.

'I thought we could talk over supper,' she said to his back.

'Forgive me.'

She hurried to catch up with him. 'You know, you can't leave unless I allow it.'

He paused on the steps and, without looking back at her, said, 'Am I a prisoner?'

'Yes!'

The doorway at the top of the stairs suddenly filled with mist that solidified into a mirror.

'Aliza,' he said quietly, 'this is foolish. You won't keep my friendship by locking me up.'

Her fingers touched his elbow lightly, tentatively. 'Stay.'

He shook his head. 'If you want my company, come along. I'm more than willing to talk over supper at Spinweb.' He turned to her at last and caught her hand with his own, pressing it firmly against his arm. 'Prove to me that you are not afraid of the human realm. Or of your grandfather. Spend an evening in a strange, exotic place.'

She looked up into his eyes. 'Is it evening in the human realm?'

'It is, at Spinweb. And the moon has probably just risen.'

'And your mother really wants to meet me.'

'Very much.'

'I'm not . . . accustomed to meeting people.'

'You'll find that she is a very kind and tolerant lady.'

253

'The human realm.' She shook her head. 'I'm only doing this because you and I are friends.'

'We are friends,' said Cray, and when he looked to the doorway once more, it was open.

Because neither Leemin nor Regneniel had ever visited Spinweb and, therefore, did not know where it lay, Cray and Aliza had no means of reaching it directly from Ice. Instead, they had to journey to Air, to use Elrelet's portal there. Elrelet easily carried both of them, one cradled in each of two arms extruded from its cloudy mass, while Gildrum sped to Fire and its own route home. Leemin stayed behind, having no interest in supper. And Regneniel stayed, too, until such time as Aliza should call to it from the human realm, her presence there a beacon to guide it to Spinweb.

Elrelet's portal opened high above Spinweb's walls. From that vantage, the sun was still visible, riding the horizon like a huge cabochon ruby. The sky opposite was already a deep, pure ultramarine, and a few stars were visible there. Below, the garden at the heart of Spinweb was lit by a host of torches.

'Call your demon now, if you like,' Cray said as they sank slowly toward that beckoning glow.

'No,' said Aliza. 'I would not insult another sorcerer by bringing a strange demon into her home. I respect her boundaries, just as I would expect her to respect mine. Unless, of course, you foresee some need for it . . .'

'No. Not at Spinweb.'

'Then let it stay in Ice until I am ready to return.' She looked down, toward the torches.

Though the season was deep winter and snow lay heavy among the trees that surrounded the castle, there was no snow on Spinweb's parapets, and none in the garden. There, a perpetual sorcerous summer reigned. Illuminated by flaring torchlight, a thousand fragrant blossoms lay open to the night sky, blossoms that did not ordinarily spread their petals after dark but which, in obedience to Delivev's will, displayed themselves for this evening's meal. A table was set in the midst of all this colour and perfume, a table laid with an embroidered cloth and slim tapers in silver candelabra, with dishes of fine porcelain and goblets of crystal to rival Aliza's own. At one end of the table sat Delivev, an embroidery frame in her lap, her head bent over the work. Before her, the candles were burnt halfway down.

The gust of wind that marked Elrelet's descent into the garden made the candles flicker wildly. Delivev looked up and, seeing the travellers, set her embroidery aside and rose to greet them with a smile. Cray embraced her quickly and then turned to present Aliza.

'My dear,' said Delivev, holding her hands out toward the young woman. 'I have heard so much about you. Welcome to my home.'

Aliza stared a moment at Delivev's outstretched hands, then hesitantly raised one of her own to grip one of them.

Delivev immediately grasped Aliza's hand with both of hers and urged the young woman toward a seat at one side of the table. 'It's so very late. You must be famished.'

'I know *I* am,' said Cray, pulling the chair out for their visitor and then taking the one beside her for himself.

'I'm sure Gildrum won't mind if we sup without him. Elrelet, you'll stay, won't you?'

'For your cooking, I will always stay,' said the demon and, moulding its cloudy substance into a vaguely human form, it took the seat opposite hers.

'Wine?' inquired Cray's mother, and without waiting for an answer from Aliza, she filled the young woman's goblet with a pale amber fluid. 'Cray tells me you like a tart wine, so this may be too bland for you. Still, I find it goes quite well with fowl.'

Aliza sampled it as the others poured their own shares. 'Very nice,' she said.

'I hope you're not saying that just to please me.'

Aliza frowned. 'Why should I do that?'

Delivev laughed softly. 'Why indeed? I must remember what Cray said about your straightforwardness.'

Aliza shot a sidelong glance at Cray. 'What did he say?'

'That there was no guile in your soul.'

Aliza folded her hands about her goblet. 'And is there any in his?'

Delivev laughed again. 'Some, but he doesn't choose to employ it very often.'

'I am always honest with my friends,' said Cray. 'And since I am with friends here, I propose a toast to friendship.' He raised his goblet.

Elrelet and Delivev drank with him and, after a moment of watching the others, so did Aliza.

As they were lowering their goblets, a line of cloth servants came marching through one of the doorways that led to Spinweb's interior. Single file they paraded, six of them, each bearing in its fabric arms a covered silver tray. They formed a ring about the table and, stepping close to the diners, swept the covers from their burdens to reveal steaming vegetables, roasted meats, crisp greens. Following Delivev's example, Cray, Elrelet and Aliza served themselves with deep-bowled silver spoons and sharp-tined forks.

'Ah, you are the finest cook I have ever known,' said Elrelet, sampling the vegetables. 'The smell of these dishes alone would be enough to hold me for days.'

Cray chuckled. 'Then why bother to eat them?'

'The eating will support me for months. Or until I am invited again.'

Delivev smiled. 'Somehow I can't quite envision you searching the human realm for fine cooks, Elrelet. Peeking in at kitchen windows as a small grey cloud and asking the goodwives for a taste from their pots.'

'Oh, I've managed it more often than you might think. One of the forms my old master gave me was that of a cat, a fine and fluffy grey cat, quite clean and an excellent mouser. Goodwives appreciated me, as well as some cooks in a castle or three I could name. I did my mousing, and I rubbed up against a few well selected legs, and I had my taste of the pot often enough. I grew quite fond of onions cooked in butter, which I see my lady Delivev has generously provided here, along with this excellent beef.'

'Why did your master give you the form of a cat?' inquired Aliza.

'To spy. Cats can go anywhere, after all. And unlike dogs, they don't have to waste their time by squabbling over scraps under the dinner table. Noisy creatures, dogs. And as a cat, no one expected me to fetch sticks or go deer hunting or anything like that. A perfect existence, actually. Next to being a demon.'

'Whom were you spying on?'

'Quite a few people, ordinary mortals all – my old master found them amusing. Three things he loved above all else in his youth – sorcery, travel, and gossip. He gave me a horse's form, and we travelled the human realm together for many years. He knew all the castles within fifty days' ride of his own, and he was well known in them, and always shown the greatest hospitality. They would give him wine and fine food and answer all his inquiries, even the most intimate, for he was a powerful sorcerer, and they feared his anger. And later, when he was no longer young, and travel itself no longer lured him, still he wished to hear the gossip; so he sent me to bring it back. I spent more years as a cat than I did as a horse.'

'What an odd way to use a demon,' said Aliza.

'Eventually he tired of gossip, too, and in his last few decades he hardly used me at all. But I employed the cat form on my own from time to time. I never had to give up onions in butter. My one bit of profit from all those years of slavery.' Elrelet laughed, a very human-sounding laugh. 'I'd say I was one of the few demons to make any sort of profit from slavery. I, and Gildrum, of course. Gildrum found love through slavery. Gildrum always says love is superior to onions.'

'I'm not sure that one can fairly compare the two,' said Delivev.

'I wouldn't know, myself, but here's the one who does.' Elrelet lifted a cloud hand toward the sky.

High above their heads, a brilliant star was visible, and as they watched it, it waxed brighter and brighter, surpassing the other stars, the moon, even rivalling the vanished sun with its warm yellow luminosity. The flame that was Gildrum descended into the garden, drowning all the torches in a flood of radiance, banishing the night and dazzling the watching human eyes for a moment before it coalesced into the semblance of human flesh. When their vision cleared, the diners saw that Gildrum's arms were laden with fruits of yellow, red, and green, with sweet citrus and melons. He spilled his bounty onto one end of the table.

'I thought these might make dessert,' he said.

'Gildrum,' said Delivev, rising from her chair, and he went to her and embraced her and kissed her with passion.

'At times like these,' murmured Elrelet, 'I do believe that Gildrum's profit from slavery was greater than mine.'

The man who was Gildrum first transferred his kiss to Delivev's forehead and then loosed her slowly, smiling into her eyes, until he held her only in the open circle of one arm. At that, he turned his smile on the others at the table. 'Forgive me,' he said, 'if my glare hurt your eyes, but I couldn't help my happiness at the sight of all of you here. And especially my own dear lady.' He pressed his lips to her forehead once again. 'Being away from her, for any time, is a source of great pain to me.'

'On the other hand,' said Elrelet, 'I never miss onions quite that much. I'm afraid I shall never understand my old friend Gildrum's feelings toward your mother, Cray. I suspect that only another demon of Fire could.'

Cray smiled. 'Most mortals wouldn't have any trouble understanding it.' He glanced sidelong at Aliza before reaching out to the fruit that Gildrum had set on the table. 'What have you brought us here, Gildrum?'

'Fruit from lands where the sun still heats the earth instead of hiding behind clouds of snow. Lands where the heat is so great that the people walk about naked and the sweat cloaks their bodies like garments.'

'That sounds like the perfect place for you,' said Elrelet. 'A most wintry place, compared to Fire.'

'I would much rather be here in Spinweb. I see you've eaten most of your meal already. Well, no matter, I'm no glutton like Elrelet here. But do try this melon, my lady Aliza,' he said, indicating a yellow oblong larger than a man's head. 'I think you'll find it reminiscent of your Maretian wine.'

She cut a thin slice and tasted it. 'You're right. It's quite good.'

'I'll show Regneniel where to find it, if you wish. It's a wild plant and grows quite thickly, so I'm sure the natives won't miss the number you'd be eating.'

She nodded at him. 'That's very . . . obliging of you, Gildrum.'

Loosing Delivev to return to her own chair, he took the seat opposite Aliza and poured himself a goblet of wine. 'What do you think of Spinweb, my lady?'

'I've only seen this much, so far.'

'Then Cray must take you on a tour. We have some beautiful rooms here, with beautiful hangings on the walls.'

Delivev laughed softly and laid her hand upon his arm. 'Time enough for her to look at my handiwork later on. We've scarcely finished with supper, and I for one prefer to sit here in the open air and talk a bit while my food settles. Tell us about yourself, my dear. Or tell me, for I know the least about you of all who sit at this table.'

'There is little to tell,' said Aliza. 'Your son has convinced me that I have led a very uninteresting life.'

'What interests him and what interests me are not necessarily the same. Tell me what it's like to be a mortal living in Ice. I've never been there.'

Aliza shrugged. 'For one who has never been there, it is difficult to describe. It is so different from this. Ice is strong and solid and resists change, unlike this human realm. One cannot use a spade to dig a hole in Ice as one could in common soil. Ice is a world without stars, without sky, without up and down.' She shook her head. 'You would really have to visit it to comprehend it.'

'May I visit it, with you?' asked Delivev.

Aliza stared at her. 'What? With me?'

'What better guide could I find?'

'Why, an ice demon, of course.'

'They hardly know what a mortal would find interesting. I would so like to see Ice for myself, and this wonderful palace of yours as well. Cray has told me of it, but I cannot truly imagine living in such a place. What was it like, growing up yourself and knowing that the palace was growing, too? What was it like to find new rooms branching off from the old ones where there had been nothing before?'

'It seemed strange at first,' Aliza admitted. 'Exciting and disturbing all at once. But I soon grew accustomed to it. In fact, I looked forward to the new room buds. I would crawl into them when they were barely large enough to hold me, and I would look out into Ice and try to see the demons there.' She went on to describe the slow transformation of the palace into the maze it now was. Under Delivev's skilful prompting, she spoke of her life there, and of her sallies into Ice. She spoke of her rejection of the human realm and of the creation of the mountains and the sandfield. She spoke of the growth of her powers and, at last, of her grandfather's expectations. 'He wants me to be one of the greatest sorcerers who ever lived. *The* greatest, I think, though he's never actually admitted that.'

'How unusual,' Delivev murmured, 'that he would want you to be greater than himself. How selfless of him.'

'Study is everything to him,' said Aliza. 'He never stops. Perhaps I shall never actually catch up with him. Perhaps I shall only surpass him after he is dead.'

'He certainly wouldn't care then,' said Cray. 'And until then, of course, he is himself proof against your sorceries. On that count he will always be more powerful than you.'

'I accept that,' said Aliza.

Delivev sighed. 'It isn't a life I would have chosen for myself, or for my son, but you seem to have weathered it well enough. And I don't doubt, from what Cray has told me, that you will accomplish whatever goal you set yourself.'

'My grandfather is reasonably satisfied with my accomplishments. Though they seem like little enough to me, measured against his powers. They seem, to me, like a child's game.' She picked up her empty goblet, turned it in one hand. 'This goblet, for example. This is the stuff I know well. It's a pretty thing as it is, but I would have made it taller and slimmer.' And in her hand, the goblet shifted, changed, elongated, became a thing of greater grace and fragility. 'Such a simple power, isn't it?'

'You are young,' said Delivev. 'There is time for such simple powers to grow vastly. Still, you've done something here that I cannot. And that goblet shall be yours alone

261

from now on, waiting for you here whenever you come to visit.'

Aliza set it down before her. 'It doesn't match the others any more.'

'That doesn't matter.'

She looked at Delivev. 'You are so certain that I'll come back again.'

'Why not? You have friends here. And it's a pleasant place, or at least I've made it as pleasant as I could.' She rose from her chair. 'Come, I think it's time we showed you a little more of it than the garden. Gildrum?'

The demon took his lady's arm, and the two of them led the others indoors.

Spinweb had been an ancient castle when Delivev inherited it, its pale stone walls yellowed with age, its thresholds worn into shallow grooves by the footsteps of generations, its hearths darkened with the soot of countless fires. But Delivev kept her castle bright with the power of her sorcery – almost every wall was hung with a tapestry, every floor softened by a carpet, every surface accented by embroidery, needlepoint, or weaving. Only Cray's workshop was not so embellished but was rather stark and bare and totally utilitarian, for sparks and molten metal splashed there.

Aliza lingered there for a time, looking at the sacks of ore and the bars of pure copper, tin, silver, and gold, at the brazier that always held glowing coals and the smelting furnace that was now dark and cool. On one wall, protected by metal-sheathed cabinets, were Cray's notebooks; he opened a door to show them to her, but she made no attempt to touch them.

The last room she saw was the web room, and Delivev demonstrated the power of the webs, conjuring up a scene in a distant palace for her. After she had watched for a moment, she said, 'Elrelet's old master would have been pleased with something like this.'

262

'It has many uses,' Cray said. 'I speak to my human friends this way, and they can call to me whenever they like. Perhaps . . . you would wish to take one of my spiders home with you to Ice, so that you can call to me whenever *you* like. Then I can visit you at your convenience rather than at my own whim.'

Aliza's lips curved slightly. 'And you could look in on me whenever you wished, without my knowing it.'

'If you fear for your privacy, Aliza, you have only to set the spider in some room you never use or, even simpler, place a screen in front of its web. As you can see, an opaque wall shields the web from whatever lies beyond.'

Aliza rubbed her lower lip with one forefinger. 'It might be a convenience at that. To eliminate your unpredictability. But I'm not accustomed to having animals about the palace.'

'A spider requires very little care. Just a morsel of food once in a while no bigger than a crumb that might slip off your table. And spiders are very clean.'

'Not quite like a dog or cat, hmm? More like . . . a stuffed toy?'

'Very much like.'

'Well, I'll think about it.'

They went up to the parapet finally and, after Elrelet had snuffed the torches in the garden, Cray pointed out the stars that were familiar to him and unknown to Aliza. And he tried to speak of the feelings he had experienced upon realizing how far her part of the human realm seemed to be from his own. The stars were bright and crisp in the winter sky, but they shed little light, and she was just the faintest of shadows standing beside him. Some distance away, he knew, Elrelet and Gildrum and his mother looked up at those same stars, but they were invisible in the darkness; he and Aliza seemed to be alone with the night. Gildrum, he thought, surely had his arm about Delivev's shoulders, his cheek bent against the top of her head. Almost, Cray

263

wanted to put his arm around Aliza, to make some sort of tangible bond between them there in the darkness. But he did not.

'What does it matter what stars are up there?' she said. 'The stars are only lights in the sky, with no more effect upon us down here than a breath of air a hundred days' journey away. Do you worry that the stars of early morning are different from those of early evening? How foolish that would be. I do not truly understand how you can feel lonely and isolated in any part of the human realm, for everywhere above it there are stars, and everywhere upon its surface there are human beings. The demon realm has no stars and no humans. It is so much farther from here than any place in the human realm could be – don't you feel *that* distance when you visit Air or Water?'

'I have friends in the demon realm. I can never feel far from home where I have friends.'

She touched his arm lightly. 'You have a friend where my palace is, remember?'

He found her hand in the dark. 'I have one now. I wasn't so certain of that then.' He raised her fingers to his lips and kissed them. 'Will you come down into the garden now? I have something for you. Something special.'

'What, a gift?'

'Yes.'

'You've given me enough gifts already.'

'This one is very special.'

'Oh, if you wish.'

He did not loose her hand as they descended an open stairway to the garden, which seemed a pool of blackness with the torches extinguished.

'It's so dark,' Aliza said, lagging behind him on the steps.

'Gildrum?' said Cray.

Gildrum did not answer, but a flame emerged from a doorway on the opposite side of the garden, and when it had rekindled the nearest torch, Cray saw that it was a burning brand held aloft by Elrelet. The air demon moved about the perimeter of the garden, methodically relighting the torches that had illuminated their supper. 'Gildrum and the lady Delivev have retired for the night,' it said, 'and I think that if you have no need of me I will do the same.'

'I'll need you to take the lady Aliza home,' said Cray.

'No,' said Aliza. 'I'll call Regneniel when I wish to leave.'

'Very well, then. Good night, Elrelet.' The grey cloud sprang out of the garden and vanished in the starry sky.

'Here,' said Cray, pulling Aliza along by the hand. 'Come over here.'

In the corner of the garden stood the tree with the gold-shot trunk. It was still a stunted thing, its topmost twigs standing well below the parapet. But, like all the other plants of the garden, it was fully leafed in spite of the season. And it glittered in the flickering torchlight.

Cray caught one of the lower branches in his free hand, pulled it toward him. 'Watch.'

Upon the twig nearest his hand, a swelling appeared, a knot that seemed to gather all the glitter from the surrounding twigs and concentrate it in a single spot of metallic sheen. As they watched, it grew, a nodule of gold, like a soap bubble fattening at the end of a child's pipe, but opaque. When it was the size of a man's fist, it opened suddenly into a golden blossom, its petals as thin as beaten foil, petal upon petal swaddling its shimmering heart. Though it grew on a tree whose other blooms were most like daffodils, this flower was a rose. And like the other roses of the garden, it gave off a sweet, delicate scent.

With gentle fingers, Cray plucked the blossom from its branch and, cradling it in his palm, offered it to Aliza.

She took it with her free hand and stared down at it. 'What shall I do with this?' she whispered. As she spoke, she tilted it one way and then another, catching the torchlight on its gleaming petals.

'Keep it,' Cray said, his voice as low as hers. There was something about the night, about the silence and the darkness, that kept him from speaking in a normal tone. 'It's for you. It will never wither, never need water. It will always be as beautiful as it is this moment. Which is . . . much less beautiful than you are.' And when she did not raise her eyes from the flower, he leaned close to her and softly kissed her cheek.

She recoiled slightly from the touch of his lips, and she would have dropped his hand except that he held hers so firmly. She looked into his eyes. 'Why did you do that?'

'To show my affection for you.'

'Your mother and the demon Gildrum – they did that.'

'They did considerably more. Because they love each other very much.'

Aliza looked back down at the flower. 'Love,' she said. 'The dependence of one person on another. I don't understand why an adult should wish to experience it.'

Cray sighed, then brought her hand to his lips and kissed it lightly. 'My poor Aliza,' he whispered. 'What do you really know of love? Locked up all alone in Ice, without mother or father, with only the cold companionship of an ice demon.'

'Grandfather has told me of it. He said my parents loved each other, and they were very young and foolish.'

'And you believed him. Of course. You believed a man whose heart is probably a black and withered husk. Ah, Aliza, I find myself hating him for what he has done to you.'

He felt her hand stiffen in his grasp. 'You take too much upon yourself, Cray Ormoru,' she said. 'My grandfather has done very well by me. I have no complaints.'

'Oh, you do, Aliza. You do. But you don't know it.'

She raised her cool dark eyes to his. 'What – that he

hasn't taught me more about love? It doesn't matter. It's unimportant.'

'It *is* important,' said Cray. 'Ask my mother. Ask Gildrum.'

'And you?' she asked. 'What of you? Do you love?'

He nodded. 'I love *them* very much.'

'Then, as an expert, tell me what you think love is like.'

He smiled. 'It's like friendship, only a thousand times stronger.'

'A thousand times? That seems . . . excessive.'

'Not to the people who feel it.'

'You feel this toward a demon?'

'Why not? Gildrum has been a father to me. Ah, but you don't know what that means, do you? Poor Aliza, what I'm talking about lies so far outside your own experience.' Once more he kissed her hand. 'Forgive me, my lady. It's enough that you understand friendship for now.'

'You think I do?'

He smiled again. 'You're wearing the ribbon I wove for your hair.'

'I thought it would . . . please you.'

'Then you do understand friendship, for why would you bother trying to please someone who was not your friend?'

'I try to please my grandfather,' she said.

Cray laughed softly. 'I hope I am nothing like him.'

'No. You are nothing like him.'

'And you will keep that flower, to remember how different from him I am?'

'I'll keep the flower.'

'And whenever I grow another golden flower on this tree, I shall think of you.'

She shook her head. 'How can you compare a mortal with a flower? It is absurd.'

'Not at all. Troubadours do it all the time. Ah, but

you've never heard a troubadour, have you?' Without waiting for her answer, he continued, 'Well, it happens that I know where several of that breed are spending their time just now, and I'm sure that one of them, at least, must be singing in some great hall at this very moment. Will you come to the web chamber and listen with me?'

She shrugged. 'Would you go there and listen if I were not here?'

'I do so often.'

'Then I will.'

After a brief search, Cray located Lorien, greatest of the singers that he and his mother followed with their spiders. Of all of them, only Lorien was aware of the enchanted mites that lived among his belongings, for he and Delivev had met once. When, occasionally, he seemed to be smiling directly at a watcher in the web chamber, it was because he saw the spider whose web transmitted his image to Spinweb, and he was sending his regards to Delivev.

Lorien was singing in a small room this evening, singing for a group of ladies whose heads were bent over needle-craft, some sitting on cushions on the floor, some on low stools, the eldest of the lot on a sumptuous couch. Few of them ever looked up at him as he sang of love and pain, of heroic death for love's sake, and of pining death for its loss. Perhaps, Cray thought, they had heard it all before. He had.

Aliza sat on a corner of the velvet-draped bed that occupied the centre of the room. She sat with her knees drawn up and encircled by her arms, and she watched Lorien steadily. After some dozen songs, she said, 'It seems to be a very powerful force, this love that you consider so important.'

'It can be,' said Cray. He sat near her, but not so near that she might feel crowded. He would have taken her hand once more, but it was locked with the other one in front of her knees. 'Some people, it seems, are willing to risk anything for love's sake. They are the ones that troubadours make songs about. Listening to him, one might presume that there were no other forces at all, no duty, no loyalty, no blood ties. No selfish desire for power. When I was a child, I might have thought that all the truth of the human realm was encompassed by these songs if I had not also used these webs to watch real people act out their lives. Without moving from this room, I could see hate and treachery as well as love, and all those other forces that buffet mortals back and forth. I led a very simple life here in Spinweb, with no one but my mother and our plants and animals for company, but through these webs I saw all the complexities of life beyond these walls. That was valuable knowledge for a boy who left home to try to become a knight. That would have been valuable knowledge for anyone.'

'For any sorcerer?' murmured Aliza.

'Especially for sorcerers, for they almost always grow in some isolation.'

'As I did.'

'You are an extreme case. You would have profited, I think, from these webs.'

She glanced at him. 'What? Spend my precious time watching other people live?'

'It's simpler than actually going out among them. It's less dangerous, certainly. And if you tire of watching, you can always walk out of the room. That's far easier than terminating a conversation with a real mortal. Of course, here in the web chamber, you don't participate, but I don't think you really want to do that just now.'

'What are you saying, Cray?'

'That you could stay here as long as you wish, and watch the webs as much as you wish. I know my mother would be glad if you stayed.'

She shook her head firmly. 'You know I can't do that.'

He laid a hand on her shoulder. 'For your education,' he said. 'So that you will understand what love and duty and loyalty and all those other things mean.'

'I understand duty. And I think I understand loyalty, too. As for love, from what I've heard this night, I am not convinced that I should know more. It doesn't seem to be always the best of experiences.'

'Love is a leavening,' said Cray. 'A little of it would not harm you. Don't think that these few songs have told you everything you need to know about it.'

'I think these songs have told me only what I already suspected – that love is strange and inexplicable. I mean no insult to your mother and Gildrum, nor to you, but . . . it seems something that should have been put away with toys and childhood. It has nothing to do with me. My childhood lies behind me.'

'So you've told me. And yet you still visit the cradle room, the site of your childhood.'

'I must pass through it now and then, to visit the other side of my palace.'

Cray slid his fingers lightly down her arm, to her hand. 'You do more than pass through it. I looked into those bins. I saw that their contents had been disturbed since my last visit. And the rocking horse had been moved. You go there to sift through the remnants of your childhood, don't you? What do you think about when you do that?'

'I think of how far I've come since then.'

'And nothing more? Not even when you pick up that poor, ragged, stuffed creature you loved so much?'

'I didn't love it. It was just a stuffed toy.'

'I think you did. I think that while you were growing up it was the only thing you loved. Unfortunately, a toy couldn't return that love.'

She turned her face away from him. 'You confuse me, Cray Ormoru. Sometimes I think we are speaking different languages.'

270

'Perhaps we are. But perhaps someday you will understand mine.'

'Or you mine.'

'No. I can't pretend that I grew up as you have. I can't lose my knowledge. But you can gain it. Let me help you.'

'You've helped me quite a bit already.'

'It may seem quite a bit to you, but it seems just a grain of sand to me. There's a whole beach waiting for you. Look!' He waved a hand, and the image of Lorien singing among the ladies dissolved into a grey blur and resolved into a great hall, seen from one end, a blazing hearthfire at the opposite extremity and tables and benches nearer, with men drinking at them. 'This is the hall of a king, where intrigues flow like ale. See the dark-haired man in the green surcoat – the king's new wife used to be his mistress, and the king no longer quite trusts him, though he was once one of his closest advisers. I've been following these people's lives for years, and the complexity of their existence would defy any songmaker. Yet they have taught me much about how to deal with jealousy, ambition, betrayal, and revenge. Sorcerers meet such things, too, in their lives – would you be ignorant when the time comes for you to face them?'

'These things will not touch me behind my barriers.'

'You're foolish to think so, Aliza. You have a long life ahead of you; how can you know now what will touch you a century hence?'

'Enough!' she said, and she loosed her locked hands and stood up, turning away from the web where men drank and laughed and whispered together, turning away from Cray, too, toward the window, where torchlight from the garden spilled into the room. She went to that window and sat down on the low sill, looking outward. 'You are too stern a teacher, Cray Ormoru. I am not ready for such lessons yet.'

'I don't mean to be stern. There is so much you have missed – I find myself thinking of you as a parched plant, needing all the water I can give just to bring you back to life.' He went to her, to stand behind her and gaze down at the top of her dark head. 'Forgive me. I don't mean to drown you.'

She heaved a deep sigh. 'I am drowning. Must I know all these things, or are you wrong in thinking they will benefit me?'

Hesitantly, he touched her hair, stroking it back from her temples. 'If you could be sure of staying alone in Ice forever, of never meeting another creature, either demon or mortal, then I would say stay as you are, don't listen to me. But who could promise such a life? There is your grandfather, and there is Regneniel. You are not alone even now.'

'No,' she said. 'Not even now. But you would surround me with people. Yourself, your mother, all those demons. You would throw me in among them, throw me into the water and force me to swim whether I will or no, whether I *can* or no. What kind of teaching is this?'

'The only kind I know. At least these people are all friendly to you. Better this than falling in among enemies.'

She folded her hands over one knee. 'My grandfather thinks that I should not have any dealings with other mortals until my powers are mature. He doesn't trust you. He thinks you want to spy on me or steal power from me or make yourself proof against me.'

'Your grandfather!' exclaimed Cray. He dropped his hands to his sides and curled them into fists. 'He knows nothing of me or my motives. He is a fool, and he is trying to make you into a creature just like Regneniel, without feelings, without the slightest fragment of humanity in your spirit.'

She looked up at him sidelong. 'And you, Cray? What are you trying to make of me?'

He shook his head. 'I am only trying to open your eyes to the greater universe that exists outside of pure sorcery.'

'You would make me like yourself.'

He hesitated a long moment, then lifted one hand to touch her hair again. 'Does it seem such a bad way to be?'

'I don't understand you.'

'I hope one day you will.'

'One day,' she murmured. 'Right now that day seems like it must be a lifetime away. Oh, if you could see through my eyes, Cray, you would understand how foreign you seem to me.'

'Not completely foreign, I hope,' he said, shifting his hand to the curve of her cheek. Her skin was cool under his fingers.

'No, not completely.'

He bent to press his lips against her temple and then the corner of her jaw, and he would have tried to brush her lips except that she slid away from him, across the window sill, and stood up, just out of reach.

'I'm very tired,' she said, gazing at him with a faint frown creasing her brow. 'This has been a very long day for me. Much longer than I expected.'

'Ah,' he said softly. 'I had hoped that we could talk the night away again. Even if it is a long winter's night.'

She shook her head. 'I'm really very tired.' She lifted one hand to the white sapphire that hung at her throat.

'Don't go,' he said. 'We have a lovely room prepared for you, and I guarantee the bed is comfortable. Stay, and spend tomorrow with me. With us.'

She cradled the sapphire in her hand and looked down at it, saying nothing.

'I have a couple of mortal friends who very much want to meet you. One of them is the keeper of the mirror, my best friend, Feldar Sepwin. I've told him a great deal about you, and he would be terribly disappointed if I brought you to Spinweb and not to his home as well.'

Still, she said nothing.

'He and the lady Helaine live in a cave far from other mortals, quite alone. I could make sure that no one else would disturb us, not mortal or demon. Just the four of us; we could take the midday meal together. Gildrum could transport us there, or, if you wish, your own Regneniel. It isn't far from here, as demons fly. You could still be home early in the day.'

At last she raised her eyes to his. 'I would like to see this mirror you've spoken of.'

Cray felt himself relax, and only then did he realize how taut all his muscles had become as he had urged her to stay. He smiled at her. 'I'm sure you'll find it most interesting.'

He lay awake for a long time that night, knowing that she was just a few rooms away, knowing that her head rested upon a pillow he had formerly used himself, that her body was covered by a quilt he had helped his mother fashion. He lay awake, staring into the darkness, seeing her in his mind's eye, seeing her move gracefully in the halls of her palace and just as gracefully in the weightless corridors of Ice. He saw her as in a mirror of his imagination, but now she moved and breathed and, upon rare occasions, even smiled. He could almost hear the sound of her voice and feel the touch of her hand in his own, of her hair and her cheek beneath his caressing fingers.

Toward dawn, he slept at last.

In the morning, the four of them broke fast together – Cray, Aliza, Delivev, and Gildrum.

'I'm so glad you chose to stay, my dear,' said Delivev, passing Aliza a bowl of fruit. 'You can have that room any time you like.'

'You never have other visitors?' Aliza inquired.

'Oh, if Feldar happens to be staying there, we'll just

move him down to the stable,' said Cray. 'He won't mind. He's slept in worse places than that.'

Delivev chuckled softly. 'Putting up an extra bed is a simple matter in this household. Cray just grows the frame from the plants in the garden, and I always have plenty of coverlets.'

Gildrum was lounging in his chair beside Delivev's, lazily peeling a melon with a small knife. 'Shall I take you to the lady Helaine's?' he inquired. 'Or shall we call Elrelet?' He carved out a chunk of the melon and, spearing it with the point of the knife, offered it to Delivev, who accepted it with a smile.

'You could drop us there if you don't mind,' said Cray. 'And I'll call to you when we want to come back.'

'When are they expecting you?'

'Any time this morning. I spoke to Feldar just after I woke up. He's very eager to meet Aliza.'

'I can imagine it,' said Gildrum. 'Well, we don't want to keep poor Feldar waiting, do we? Especially after you've so easily condemned him to sleep in the stable. For that he deserves some sort of reward.'

They finished eating quickly.

When they rose from the table, Gildrum kissed Delivev soundly. 'I won't be long, my dear,' he said, and then his human form burst into heatless flame and bobbed in midair before the three true human beings. 'You might be most comfortable if you put one arm about his waist, Aliza, and you put one arm across her shoulders, Cray. Otherwise, I fear you'll find yourselves bumping together somewhat unpleasantly. I'm not accustomed to carrying two mortals at once, and I don't bifurcate as neatly as Elrelet does.'

Aliza hesitated only an instant before slipping her arm about Cray's waist.

Gildrum enveloped them, and Cray could no longer see Aliza, though she was warm and solid in the circle of his arm. Before his eyes was a sheet of pale yellow, blotting out everything else. He felt himself lifted from the ground, and the next moment the pale yellow brightened, dazzling him, forcing him to close his eyes against it, and he knew they were in Fire. Their passage there was brief, though, a mere skip between two places not far separated in the human realm. The brightness vanished as they emerged from the demon world, and a few heartbeats later Gildrum deposited them on the snow-covered path that led to the lady Helaine's cave.

She and Feldar Sepwin were waiting for them there.

Sepwin stepped forward as Aliza disengaged herself from Cray's arm. He bowed stiffly. 'Feldar Sepwin at your service, my lady. I have wanted to meet you for a very long time.'

'Good morrow,' she said. 'I've been told that you were the keeper of the mirror in which Cray Ormoru first saw me.'

'I am. And this is the lady Helaine, my teacher and a Seer of the first order.'

Aliza nodded to her, but when she spoke, it was again to Sepwin. 'I have some desire to see this mirror, Feldar Sepwin. Is it here?'

'It is indeed, my lady. If you'll follow me, you may see it to your heart's content.'

With gentle pressure on his arm, the lady Helaine held Cray back several paces behind Sepwin and Aliza as they entered the cave. 'Are you sure you want this?' she murmured.

He looked at her warily. 'Have you seen something amiss about it?'

'No, nothing. But I feel that you ask too much of the mirror. You have no guarantee that it will show her your face.'

'I don't know what it will show her. But she asked to see it. I never urged her to it.'

'You spoke of the mirror to her.'

276

'Yes, of course.'

'Then you can blame no one but yourself for what happens here.'

'Blame? Will there have to be blame?'

The lady Helaine halted as they were about to step into the chamber of the pool. Already, Sepwin and Aliza had almost crossed it on their way to the mirror beyond. 'There is something about her that is very wrong,' she said softly. 'I can feel it in her nearness. I can feel it without even touching her. There is an aura of danger about her. You are caught up in it, Cray. The quest is not over, I promise you that.'

'I thought it wasn't. But I'm doing the best I can upon it.'

'Do you know yet if you love her?'

Cray's eyes followed Aliza as she moved farther and farther into the depths of the cave. He found himself wanting to run after her. 'What is love?' he said. 'I tried to explain it to her. And to her demon. I think I failed both times. It came out sounding so flat. I love my mother, and I love Feldar and Gildrum. What I feel toward Aliza is not the same. Not at all.' He turned to the lady Helaine. 'I don't know what I want her to see in the mirror. But what I want doesn't matter, does it? The mirror will give her what *it* will, not what I will. And I want to be there when it does.' He started walking toward the mirror room once more, then broke into a run to catch up with Sepwin and Aliza.

Sepwin was taking a torch from its bracket by the chamber's entrance, and he gestured for Cray to kindle another torch from it so that they could place the lights on either side of the mirror. Having done that, they stayed in the alcove behind the black velvet curtain, each on his side of the mirror, its surface glinting silver between them as Sepwin directed Aliza to look through the eyeholes. Cray saw her dark eyes there, saw the torches reflected in them like stars in the night sky. Then he looked at Sepwin and found that Sepwin was looking at him. Cray tried to smile, but his lips would not obey. He knew what Sepwin was thinking, knew that he and the lady Helaine had surely discussed this moment between them. But it was out of his hands; he had no control over Aliza's desire to look, no control over what the mirror would show. He couldn't even guess if she would tell them, once she had seen.

'Just gaze steadily into the surface,' Sepwin told her.

'The surface glitters,' she said. 'But I don't see any image.'

'Sometimes it takes a moment or two.'

And then Cray realized that something was happening to the mirror itself, that ripples were forming about its centre and moving outward from there, as if the mirror were a pool of water and a pebble had been dropped into it. The first ring of ripples reached the outermost edge of the mirror and bounced back toward the centre, meeting a second ring that was freshly formed. Where they collided, they broke into multiple eddies, meeting and colliding with each other and with the new ripples that kept expanding from the centre. The mirror began to shiver with the force of these collisions, to shiver and to shimmer and, very faintly, to rattle like distant chain mail. Cray had never seen anything like this before. He glanced at Sepwin's face and saw the look of puzzlement there.

It changed abruptly to one of shock.

The polished surface of the mirror was beginning to sift away from its wooden support in a glittering, powdery shower.

Chapter 9

The Mirror of Heart's Desire was no more. On the wall, between the two torches, its wooden backing still hung, but all the surface of the mirror now lay on the floor, a mound of sparkling dust. Sepwin fell to his knees beside it. He reached out tentatively to touch it, to feel of it, and the metal powder clung to his fingers, glittering there like a spray of stars.

Aliza pulled the curtain aside, and the draught of that moving fabric blew some of the mirror dust back against the wall. 'What's this?' she said.

'I don't know,' said Sepwin. He buried both hands in the sparkling powder. 'I've never seen anything like it before.' He looked up at her. 'What did you do, my lady?'

'What you told me, no more.'

'Then, what are you, my lady?'

Aliza frowned. 'I don't know what you mean.'

The lady Helaine had joined them in looking at the destroyed mirror, and now she set her pale hand on Sepwin's shoulder. 'She doesn't know. I'm sure of that. But there is some terrible secret within her; I felt it the moment I saw her. Perhaps the mirror could not tolerate it.'

'I never meant to damage your mirror,' said Aliza.

Sepwin got to his feet, dusting his hands on his shirt. 'Cray and I can make another; that is not a problem. But I would know why this happened. I would know what terrible secret could do this.'

'I have no terrible secret,' said Aliza.

'It is hidden even from yourself,' said the lady Helaine.

'What nonsense!'

'The lady Helaine never speaks nonsense,' said Sepwin. 'She is one of the greatest living Seers, and when she says a thing is so, all mortals know she speaks the truth.'

'Then what is this secret?'

'To tell that, I must read you by the pool,' said the lady Helaine. 'Do you wish it?'

'What do you mean – *read* me?'

The Seer smiled softly. 'A human life is like a book to me. I can turn the pages and see what has been and, with somewhat greater difficulty, what will be. I can read the joys, and the crimes, of the people who come here. And though you are of the sorcerous breed, folk who are usually nearly closed to me, still you are a young and unformed apprentice, and you have spent most of your life in a place that, Cray tells me, is not completely formed itself. I make no promises, but from what I feel as I stand here beside you, I think you will not be totally opaque to me.'

Aliza withdrew one pace, as if that extra space could be a barrier between them. 'If you read my life, you'll read all about my powers. I don't know if I should allow that.'

'I have no interest in your powers. But the decision must be yours.'

Aliza looked to Cray. 'If you were in my place, what would you do?'

'Let the Seer read me. Indeed, she has done so several times.'

'My grandfather would forbid it. And yet . . . she is not another sorcerer, is she?'

'Not at all,' said Cray.

'But sorcerers might come to her and buy information from her, might they not?'

'Aliza, if some sorcerer wanted to learn of your powers, he could ask an ice demon to tell him all about them. You think they don't know what you do there in Ice? You think they don't watch and learn about you?'

She pursed her lips. 'I have no experience of Seers. You trust her completely, do you?'

'Yes. She has always been my good friend.'

Aliza clasped her hands behind her back. 'Will she . . . will I feel anything while she is reading me?'

'She'll hold your hand.' He glanced at the Seer, who nodded.

'Very well,' said Aliza. 'I do wish to know this terrible secret. I can't imagine what it might be.'

Aliza and the lady Helaine sat down on the rim of the dark pool while Cray and Sepwin knelt on the white sand a few paces away. The Seer took Aliza's left hand in her right and slipped her own left hand into the cool water. Then, rather than gazing at Aliza herself, she stared down into the darkness of the pool, as if there were something to see in those depths, though no other eyes could see it. She stared thus for a long time, unblinking, unmoving, like a statue of pale marble.

After a time, Cray glanced at Sepwin, but his friend just shrugged and shook his head.

At last, the Seer spoke, her lips barely moving, the words so soft that only in the silence of her cave could she have been heard; the slightest birdcall would have drowned her out.

'You are one alone. There has never been another like you. Half mortal and half Ice you are, and empty. That is the terrible secret – that deep within you, where the seat of all emotion should be, where the heart, the soul, should be, you have only a void. You cannot know any emotion, not love or hate, not joy or sorrow. Not even fear. The Mirror of Heart's Desire died seeking that which does not exist in you.' She blinked slowly. 'Yet it was there once, long ago; I see the traces of its removal. Why would you do such a thing to yourself?'

'I?' said Aliza. 'I don't know what you're talking about.'

'Then someone else did it to you. Someone stole your soul.'

'Who?' said Cray, rising to his feet. 'Who, and why?'

'Sorcery,' said the Seer. 'Beyond that, I cannot say.' She looked up at him. 'She cannot love, Cray. Not without her soul.'

'She cannot *feel*,' said Cray.

'No.'

'When was this terrible thing done?'

'That I cannot see precisely. Quite some time ago.' She looked at Aliza. 'Do you remember it happening?'

Aliza frowned, her eyes shifting from Cray to the Seer and back. 'I don't know what you're talking about.'

The lady Helaine raised her free hand from the pool to Aliza's forehead; water droplets wet the young woman's hair and ran down her cheek like tears, but the grip of the Seer's other hand would not let her pull away from that cold contact. The lady Helaine closed her eyes. 'There was a time when there was no sorcery in you at all, not of your making or of anyone else's. There was a time when you played among the trees of the forest and also in a small wooden building barely larger than this chamber. You had a stuffed toy that never left your sight.' She fell silent, and her wet hand made small stroking motions upon Aliza's dark hair. Behind her tightly closed lids, her eyes were moving, seeing. Suddenly she cried out in a high, plaintive voice, a voice filled with loss and sorrow: 'Mother!'

Her eyes opened slowly, and now they had a look of pity in them. 'Poor child,' she said, dropping her hand away from Aliza's face. 'You grieved for her so, and then someone stole that grief away. Some people would be grateful to have their grief taken from them, but in this case the price was high indeed. So very high.' To Cray she said, 'The soul was taken soon after her parents died. I suspect that's why she remembers so little about them. All the love she felt for them, and the sorrow at their death, just vanished as far as she was concerned. Like a dream. She has grown up accustomed to being without any emotions.'

'Who would have done such a thing?' said Cray. 'Grief fades of its own accord; she needed no such drastic surgery.'

'I can think of another reason for it,' said Sepwin.

'Yes?'

'To guarantee a quiet life. To guarantee a total lack of distraction while she devoted herself to study.'

'Her grandfather,' said Cray.

'It's of a piece with locking her up in Ice, wouldn't you say?'

'Yes. Of course. The villain!' His lips made a firm line as he looked at Sepwin. 'This is the quest,' he said. 'We must get Aliza's soul back.'

Sepwin stood up. 'Yes. This is the quest. The lady Helaine said you would know its end, and now I know, too. The soul lies there, and you and I shall find it.'

'Wait, what's happening here?' said Aliza, springing to her feet and pulling her hand from the Seer's grasp. 'What are you planning?'

'We can manage it,' said Sepwin. 'Cray will provide the sorcery and I'll locate the soul itself. He's probably got the thing in a bottle in his bedroom.'

'Good,' said Cray.

'Just a moment,' said Aliza.

Cray gripped her arm. 'Trust us, Aliza. We'll find it for you.'

'Find *what*? I'm not missing anything. I don't care what your Seer may say. You seem to be planning some kind of assault on my grandfather's bedroom to retrieve this piece of nonsense that you think has some value to me. But have you asked me once if I wanted it?'

'You need it,' said Cray.

'I need nothing. Whatever it is, if it *is* something, I don't feel its lack. I won't have you disturbing my grandfather with this foolishness.'

'You don't understand,' said Cray. 'But when you have your soul back again, you will.'

'And what do you think this soul will do for me?'

'You'll be able to feel all those emotions the lady Helaine spoke of. Joy and love and the others. The emotions that the rest of us live with every moment of our lives. The emotions that give flavour to life.'

'And fear, too. She did mention fear.'

Cray nodded.

Aliza turned away from him. 'My grandfather has told me of fear. How it makes one weak and foolish. How it takes over the mind and twists it away from rational thought. If having a soul means knowing fear, I don't want one.'

'You can learn to deal with fear, Aliza.' He stepped up behind her and laid his hands on both her shoulders. 'It need not be so incapacitating. It is unpleasant – I wouldn't lie to you about that. But it's a small sacrifice to make in return for the other emotions.'

'To you, perhaps,' she said. 'You have no choice. But I do. I am content the way I am. And if my grandfather did take this soul, whatever it is, I'm sure he did so for my own good. To make me a better sorcerer.'

'Perhaps he removed his own soul as well,' suggested Sepwin, 'and so, having no feelings himself, thinks that's best for everyone. The perfect sorcerer – fearless, loveless, joyless. Clearly he has no desire for great-grandchildren.'

Gently, Cray turned Aliza to face him. 'How well do you really know your grandfather? What do you know of his motives, his desires?'

'I know that I am his apprentice, and he could have selected another in my place, or none at all. After my parents died, he could have given me to some peasant family in the human realm and been free of me, but he chose not to. He is very powerful and wishes me to be so also. What more need I know?'

'Considerably more than that, if you are to judge him.'

'I? Judge him?'

'He has made your life what it is. By judging him, you judge it. Gildrum can help us. Your grandfather is a demon master, and so demons will be able to tell us of him. And their tales will not be coloured by any of his own lies.'

'You think he has lied to me?'

'I don't know. But it would be the least of his crimes against you.'

The afternoon was waning by the time Gildrum joined them. Aliza had become restive after the midday meal, suggesting that she ought to be returning to her studies, but Cray managed to distract her with a stroll through the snow-laden forest. There, he called a few sleeping plants into leaf and even grew a chair for her from some woody vines at the edge of a frozen pond. Then he showed her how to build a snowman. They had scarcely finished it when the clear sky began to cloud over and the first soft flakes began to dust their hair. They dashed back to the cave and found Gildrum waiting for them.

In his human form, he was sitting with Sepwin and the lady Helaine at the rim of the pool. 'Ah,' he said, 'now I won't have to tell the tale twice.'

'What tale?' asked Cray.

'The tale of the fraudulent sorcerer. And a most enlightening one it is, my dears.'

'Fraudulent?' said Cray.

'Yes, and perhaps the lady Aliza would like to sit down before she hears it?' He stood to make room for her by the pool. 'It seems that this very powerful grandfather of hers is nothing of the kind. A sorcerer he is, but one of extremely limited and trivial skills. The other sorcerers who know of him scorn him, he has never commanded

285

more than one demon slave, and his needs are served by a pack of mortals who live inside his castle.'

'Mortals?' said Cray.

'Well, he hasn't any demons now, and apparently no power over animals or inanimate objects either. He seems to be nearly a complete failure at sorcery.'

'No,' said Aliza, rising to her feet to look into Gildrum's face. 'No. He has human servants, true enough, but they are in addition to his demon slaves.'

Gildrum's expression was sceptical. 'Why would he need mortal servants if, as you say, he has demons?'

'They amuse him. He has a special relationship with one particular village. He takes all the cripples, the deformed ones, the ugly ones. Their fellow villagers are glad to be rid of them, and they are glad to find a home and work. And he finds them amusing.'

'This is what he's told you,' said Cray.

'Yes.'

Gildrum shook his head. 'He has no demon since Regneniel left him. None.'

'You lie,' said Aliza.

'No,' said Cray. '*He* lied. He lied about everything he was. Knowing that, can you believe anything he ever told you?'

'My lessons . . .' Aliza faltered.

'You could prove their truth. But as long as you never visited his home, you could never know about the rest. And he made sure you never visited. You believed him. Why not? Who was there to tell you otherwise?'

'But he visited me,' said Aliza. 'His demons brought him.'

'Did you ever see them?'

'Regneniel.'

'I mean any others.'

She shook her head. 'But he visited me after he gave me Regneniel. He had to have demons for that.'

286

'You saw them?'

'No, he came to the mountains, and Regneniel fetched him from there. He said it wouldn't be good for his demons to learn to cross the sand barrier, that someday they might use that power against me, after he was dead.'

'There are other ways of travelling besides with demons,' said Sepwin. 'There are horses, after all. And one's own two feet.'

'But his castle is far away. It would take so much time to make the journey in the way of ordinary mortals.'

'He wanted to maintain the illusion,' said Cray. 'He wanted you to keep thinking that he was the powerful sorcerer.'

She looked at him, and her eyes were defiant. 'You're so sure it was an illusion.'

'I have no reason to doubt Gildrum's word.'

'And I have no reason to accept it. Gildrum's word against my grandfather's.'

'Why don't you ask Regneniel?' said Gildrum. 'Regneniel will surely know.'

Aliza clutched the white sapphire that hung at her throat. For a moment she held it, her eyes raised to Gildrum's, steady, challenging, and then she let it go. 'You are too sure of Regneniel's answer. I see no point in summoning it.' She dropped her eyes at last. 'Very well. He lied.'

'And now we must ask ourselves why,' said Gildrum.

Aliza took a deep breath and let it out as a heavy sigh. 'I know the answer to that. Isn't it obvious?'

'I'm not sure it is,' said Cray.

'I am his apprentice. The apprentice must respect the master. Yet how could I respect a sorcerer without power? He had to seem greater than myself, to give me something to strive for, something to match myself against. It was for my own good that he lied, to make me what he thought I could be. And I would say that he has been quite successful at it.'

Cray folded his arms across his chest and regarded her thoughtfully. 'You think that's a reasonable explanation?'

'Yes, I do.'

'All those lies – for your own good.'

She frowned at him. 'What would you say?'

He rocked back on his heels. 'I say that it's a peculiar sorcerer indeed who wants his apprentice to surpass him. I've known quite a few sorcerers in my time, and I've never heard of such a sentiment. Even my own mother, who taught me a good part of what I know, is proud that in her own range of sorcery, with spiders and snakes and twining things, she is more adept than I. And . . . such selfless generosity seems somewhat at odds with the physical and emotional distance that has always been a mark of your relations with your grandfather. Quite simply, I can't believe he loves you so much. There must be profit in the situation for him somewhere. There must be.'

Gildrum said, 'I wonder why, if he has no other demon slaves, he gave her Regneniel.'

'To maintain the illusion,' said Cray. 'The master of a hundred demons can afford to give one away. It must be very important to him, this illusion which is supposed to keep Aliza working diligently for as long as she needs in order to become one of the greatest sorcerers who ever lived. She could become that, couldn't she, Gildrum, under Regneniel's tutelage?'

Gildrum shrugged. 'Regneniel is a demon of some knowledge. But Aliza's most significant advantage is her intimate connection with the world she seeks to manipulate. Through that alone, she could be a very great sorcerer, in time.'

'Why?' said Cray. 'Why must she be great? If we can only answer that question, I think we will begin to understand this matter of the soul.'

'Obviously you have some notion of an answer.'

'Perhaps.' He turned to Sepwin. 'What can be done with a soul, Feldar? How can it be used?'

Sepwin spread his hands in perplexity. 'I've never known a soul to be removed from its body before. I have no idea.'

'O Seer, what do you say?'

The lady Helaine shrugged. 'The soul is Aliza. Even though they have been separated, there is a connection between them that cannot be severed.'

'So her grandfather actually possesses a living part of her.'

The Seer nodded.

'And this part of her that *is* her,' continued Cray, 'could it be used somehow to transfer power from her to the one who possesses it? Could he absorb her knowledge of Ice from her soul?'

'Nonsense,' said Aliza. 'Only one who was as much of Ice as I am could possess my knowledge. It is something that must be lived as well as learned.'

'Well, if that is such nonsense, my lady Aliza, then I see only one other possible explanation. Your grandfather has your soul, which is still connected to you. What should happen if he destroys it?'

'He can destroy it, for all I care,' said Aliza. 'I don't want it back.'

'What would happen?' Cray asked the Seer.

'She would die,' said the lady Helaine.

Aliza frowned at the Seer, tight-lipped. 'Then he's probably keeping it quite safe.'

'Your soul is his hostage, Aliza,' said Cray. 'You are in his power.'

'Of course I'm in his power. I'm his apprentice.'

'And you will always be in his power. Always.' He gripped both of her arms tightly. 'He hasn't needed to tell you yet. You've been an obedient apprentice. You've done exactly as he's told you. But someday your skills will be mature. And then you'll serve him. He won't need any demon slaves. He'll have one of the greatest sorcerers who ever lived as his slave.'

She peeled his hands away. 'This is too wild a tale for me, Cray Ormoru. You don't know my grandfather. You haven't the faintest notion of what he wants. And I have had enough of all this airy speculation. It's very late, and I wish to go home. If you and your demon friends will take me there, well and good. Otherwise I shall call Regneniel.'

'You can't be angry with me,' said Cray. 'Anger is an emotion, and you have none.'

'I am not angry. I am merely weary of your suppositions, your inferences, and your unwarranted conclusions. You have judged a stranger. I don't think you are in a better position than I am to do so. I trust my grandfather. I have never known any reason that would prevent me from trusting him. If you must believe the worst of him, perhaps that reflects more of yourself than of him.'

'But Aliza, he has your soul.'

'And I say, if he has it, let him keep it. I see no value in such a thing. Now there's an end to the matter.' She bowed stiffly to Sepwin and the lady Helaine. 'I thank you for the fine meal and your attentions to me. I hope you will accept this small gift as some repayment for your mirror.' She gestured to the sand at her feet, and a patch of it began to swirl like a tiny dust devil, coalescing into a faceted crystalline bowl large enough to hold several pieces of fruit. When it was fully formed, she picked it up in both hands and gave it to the Seer. 'And now,' she said, 'I must leave.' She glanced questioningly at Cray.

'I suggest you call Regneniel so that it will know where this place is and be able to return whenever you wish.'

She nodded and raised her hand to the jewel.

'But first – I think it might be best if you did not mention the soul and our conversation about it to your grandfather. If you are correct, and he has it for his own good reasons, then you should not insult him with our speculations.'

'And if he has it for his own evil reasons,' added Sepwin, 'then you wouldn't want to make him suspicious.'

'You're not going to try to get it back, are you?' she asked, looking from Cray's face to Sepwin's. 'You would have to find some way to violate the spell around his castle to do that, and that would be a terrible insult to him. There is a spell around his castle . . . ?'

'Yes,' said Gildrum. 'He knows that much sorcery.'

'Then I ask you not to take on this quest of yours. I don't want the soul. You would be gaining his enmity for no purpose.'

'The enmity of such a man amounts to very little,' said Gildrum.

'He dislikes you enough, Cray,' said Aliza. 'Don't give him another reason.'

'I care nothing for his likes or dislikes,' Cray told her. 'But for your sake, I would not incur his anger. He is capable of anger, is he not?'

'Oh, yes. How else do you think I know what it is?'

'Very well, then. I respect your wishes.'

'Then I shall respect yours.' Touching the jewel, she spoke Regneniel's name softly.

'I have a farewell gift for you,' Cray said.

'Not another gift – you've given me too many already.'

'One can never give too many gifts.' He held his hand out, palm up. It was empty, but only for a moment. From his sleeve crawled a spider no larger than a lentil, a short-legged brown mite marked by transverse white stripes.

Aliza smiled slightly. 'Ah, one of your tiny spies.'

'You'll be able to call to me by touching any strand of its web with a finger and speaking my name. Just remember that it takes me a little time to reach the web chamber from my workshop. But I promise that if you call, I'll answer.'

'There are no insects in my palace for it to eat.'

'I'm sure Regneniel would have no trouble catching one or two flies in the human realm every few days.'

'Yes, I'm sure that could be managed. But how shall I carry this creature? Or have you a tiny cage all ready for me?'

Cray grinned. 'No need for any cage. It will ride, without moving, wherever I place it. Your shoulder, your sleeve, even your finger. The choice is yours. And to settle it in its new home, you have only to brush it very gently against some hard surface, and it will cling there and begin to spin.'

'Very well,' said Aliza. 'My sleeve will do. Right there.' She pointed to a spot just below her elbow, and once Cray had set the spider there it was frozen, like a single dark bead upon the fabric.

Abruptly, as if it were stepping through a doorway in the solid rock of the cave wall, Regneniel materialized half a dozen paces behind Aliza. 'My lady,' it said.

'Oh,' said Aliza, her hand flying to her mouth, 'I shouldn't have summoned it inside. I meant no insult by calling my demon into your home, believe me, lady. It won't happen again.'

'Demons have been here before,' said the Seer. 'But it is a bit startling when they don't use the entrance like everyone else.'

'We shall always use the entrance in future, I promise.'

'I'm glad to hear that you intend to return.'

Aliza gazed at her questioningly. 'Why glad?'

'Because, child, I like you. I like people. I couldn't be a Seer if I didn't. But most people come to me once in their lives and never again. It's good to know that a familiar, and charming, face will be back sometime. And thank you for the beautiful gift. We have gold and jewels aplenty here, but it is rare that someone thinks to give me something made with his own skills. I doubt I could buy as fine a bowl anywhere.'

'It's nothing,' said Aliza.

'Nothing to you, perhaps. But I shall treasure it.'

Aliza's lips parted, as if she were about to say something further, then she lifted a hand in farewell instead, to the Seer, to Sepwin, to Gildrum, to Cray. Then she gestured sharply to her demon, and it followed her to the tunnel that led to the mouth of the cave and the snow-covered path beyond.

Cray followed her into the daylight, but he said nothing, just waved as the ice demon encircled its mistress's waist with one elongated arm. The two of them vanished.

Inside once more, he found the others still by the pool.

'I never thought the quest would end so abruptly,' said Sepwin. 'That's a strange young woman the mirror found you, my friend, who doesn't want to have anything to do with love. And yet she seems to like you well enough.'

Cray asked the lady Helaine, 'What did you see in her future, O Seer?'

'Great danger.'

'And?'

'And you. Did you really think otherwise?'

He shook his head. 'The quest is far from ended, Feldar.'

'How not?' said his friend. 'You told her you would respect her wishes, and she doesn't wish you to go on the quest.'

'And I shall not. I shall not go to her grandfather's castle in search of her soul. But you shall. O Feldar Sepwin with the two mismated eyes, you shall enter her grandfather's service with the rest of the crippled, the deformed, and the ugly. Oh, he'll love you, Feldar, I'm sure of it.'

Sepwin smiled.

Chapter 10

Standing outside Everand's castle, Feldar Sepwin was not impressed with the place. He had seen castles just as large and sprawling, but none in such a poor state of repair that were still inhabited. The walls were jagged with missing stonework, and where the gaps bit deepest into them, wooden beams bridged the open spaces. Atop the battlements were only a few stubby towers, irregularly placed, tall enough to hide a man from outside eyes, but only just; Sepwin could see places where there had been more of them, once. The roof of the inner keep, which should have been visible over the top of the wall from any reasonable distance, was not. The gate, which sealed the castle from the world of ordinary mortals, was of thick logs bound together by rope, with tapered points uppermost, like a row of fangs; above them, the arch that had formerly roofed that entry was mostly gone, only its lowest stones still flanking the opening, standing above the crenellations like twin sentries.

The only aspect of those walls that was truly intact, Sepwin knew, was the spell that encased them, like a jacket of steel. He could feel it there, pervading stone and wood, rigid and unyielding. No demon could pass that barrier unless Everand willed it, no sorcerer, no ordinary mortal. Weak and ineffectual Aliza's grandfather might be, but he knew how to cast one spell at least, and to cast it properly.

Sepwin went to the gate, which was closed, and, cupping his hands around his mouth, shouted, 'Ho the castle of my lord Everand!' He had to call three more times before someone appeared at the top of the wall, leaning out between the crenellations to look down at him.

'Who would you be?' asked the man, a stocky, dark-haired fellow with a large puckered scar twisting one side of his face into a permanent sneer.

'A wanderer in search of employment,' replied Sepwin. To bolster that impression, he was wearing a travel-stained tunic and a threadbare cloak, and his boots had holes in them. 'I was told at the village that there was some to be had here for one like myself.'

'And what would you be like that that might be true?' inquired the disfigured man.

'Folk say my eyes are the ugliest in the world. That is a condition of employment here, is it not – ugliness?'

'One of them. But I see nothing ugly about your eyes.'

'If you were a bit closer to me, you'd see well enough.'

The man peered down at him for another moment, then said, 'Wait there.'

Shortly, the heavy gate eased open just the width of a man's body, and the scarred fellow stepped into the gap. From there, both his hands clutching one of the ropes that bound the upright logs, he eyed Sepwin suspiciously. 'We've never had anyone *ask* to serve here before.'

'It's difficult for me to find work,' said Sepwin. 'Or even hospitality, as I'm sure you can understand.'

The man squinted into Sepwin's face. 'There are worse things in the world than eyes of two different colours, stranger. Far worse.'

'Some would disagree with you. I've been hounded out of villages, beaten, and stoned. I've been accused of the vilest sorcery, of making cows sicken and crops fail. All because of these eyes.'

'Sorcery?' The man laughed dryly. 'If you were a sorcerer, you'd never have been beaten. Sorcerers don't have to fear ordinary folk.'

'You're not afraid of me, then?'

'Why should I be? I have a sorcerer for a master, and he'll protect me from the evil eye. Whichever eye it is.' He laughed again.

'At first they were afraid at the village,' said Sepwin.

'Yes,' said the man, bobbing his head. 'They are afraid of everything there.'

'But after I talked with some of them awhile, they thought it would be a good thing if I came here. They told me that I could take the place of one of the men who serves here and send him home. His name is Demas.'

'Ah, you must have spoken to his mother.'

'It was an old woman who first made the suggestion.'

'Yes, she never wanted to send him here at all, but my lord needed another man. Yes, you might take his place; you look strong. Those eyes don't tax your strength, do they?'

Sepwin shook his head.

'Well, you must wait here for now. I can't let you in without my lord's approval. But he might approve. You look strong, and Demas, poor Demas is not.' He disappeared inside, swinging the gate shut behind him.

Sepwin strolled a few leisurely paces away. Beneath his well-worn boots, the bare ground all about the castle was soft and yielding, though not quite mud. The back of winter had been broken, and now only scattered patches of snow remained to be melted by the warming sun. It was decent weather for travelling, believable weather for travelling the ten days from the village to Everand's castle, and Sepwin looked dirty enough to have made that journey, though actually Gildrum had carried him almost the whole distance.

He sat down on a boulder that lay near the path to the gate. It was a broad, deep-buried boulder, one of several that were the only blemishes on the earth around the castle. Such boulders were common enough in the forest, but here, uncloaked by trees or grass, they seemed like strange sentinels, keeping watch on Everand's walls. Sepwin had passed several of them in his circuit of the place, and at each he had let a few spiders fall from his sleeve. The very boulder on which he rested harboured two or three of the mites, and though he did not try to look for them, he knew they were busy spinning their webs so that Cray could watch those walls as if he were sitting before them.

The gate opened once more, and Sepwin sprang to his feet and trotted to it. The man who greeted him this time was tall and gaunt and pale-bearded, and though he wore a robe of plain brown homespun like any village elder, Sepwin knew from his imperious gaze that this was Everand the sorcerer. Sepwin bowed deeply.

'So you wish work,' said the sorcerer. 'We have work here for mortal hands. And in return for that work, a roof over your head, a bed of straw, food and clothing. Does that attract you?'

'My lord is most generous,' said Sepwin. 'I have not had such an excellent offer in many years.'

'I have never seen anyone with eyes like yours,' said Everand.

'We seem to be very rare, my lord. I have never met another.'

'I wonder why you were not killed at birth.'

Sepwin bowed again. 'My lord, that is a question I cannot answer.'

Everand studied him for a long moment. 'You must know,' he said at last, 'that once these walls embrace you, you will be totally within my power. You will not be able to leave unless I will it. And if you give me cause, I can strike you dead at any time without the aid of sword or spear.'

'I have no wish to give you any such cause, my lord. I am a simple man, with a great desire to fill my empty belly, nothing more. It is not easy for one like me to find a place where he is accepted, and once I have found it, I would not willingly leave.'

'Come in then,' said Everand, and he stepped back through the gate.

Sepwin smiled and entered. He felt the magical barrier as he stepped through it, like some invisible fog that penetrated his clothing and even his flesh with a damp chill. Like all such spells, it enveloped the castle in a secrecy impenetrable to any Seer outside the walls. But now Sepwin was inside, and for the length of his stay that barrier would allow him to use his power within its circumference while it sealed the rest of the human realm away from him.

'Yltra will show you where to sleep,' said the sorcerer, indicating the man with the scarred face. 'Demas will show you his duties, and when you have learned them, he may go back to the village.'

Yltra bowed low before the sorcerer, and Sepwin imitated him, saying, 'Thank you again, my lord,' and Everand walked away from them.

Save for a few simple wooden huts built against one of the walls and the small, squat keep itself, the interior of the castle was quite open, a broad expanse of hard-packed earth. Near the huts, a low fence and some scanty remains of beans and lettuce showed that part of it had been cultivated as a kitchen garden. The rest was as flat and empty as if it had been trampled by thousands of feet. As Yltra guided him toward one of the huts, Sepwin saw that Everand was entering the keep.

'This is Demas,' Yltra said. 'Today it is his turn to cook.'

The hut was a kitchen, very warm, with a broad hearth built hard against the stone wall – built, it seemed, of fragments of the same stone that formed the walls themselves. In the hearth, a side of venison was spitted over the flames, and three large pots rested on trivets set among them. Moving from pot to pot, stirring with a long-handled wooden spoon, was a boy of twelve or thirteen years. He turned his sooty, sweaty face to Sepwin and Yltra as they entered.

'Not ready yet,' he said. 'You'll have to wait.' Then, as his eyes lit upon Sepwin for the first time, he let the spoon go and wiped at his forehead with the back of one arm. His other arm, exposed by his sleeveless smock, was too short, shrivelled and curled tight against his chest. 'Who are you?' he said.

Sepwin inclined his head. 'Your replacement. Feldar Sepwin at your service.'

'Replacement?'

'Yes, your mother wants you to come home, and I have offered to stay here in your stead.'

The boy looked to Yltra. 'Is he mad?'

The scarred man shrugged. 'Be thankful that he's come. You have only to teach him your duties and then go. The master has said it, and if I were you I would hurry before he changes his mind.'

The boy's eyes were wide and wary. 'Shouldn't someone else go? I haven't been here very long. Surely one of the others, or you, Yltra, it ought to be your turn.'

'Your mother asked for you,' said the scarred man. 'No one asked for any of us.' He glanced at Sepwin. 'Did they?'

Sepwin shook his head. 'Just the old woman.'

'There, you see. No one wants any of us. You're a lucky boy, Demas. Your mother still remembers rocking you to sleep in her arms.'

'Do you know anything of cooking?' asked the boy.

'I've cooked for myself for many years, and I'm not dead yet,' said Sepwin.

'I cook every third day. The other two I work at the laundry and I scrub floors. But perhaps, since you are big and strong and have two good arms and two good legs, Yltra would prefer to give you some other tasks?'

Yltra said, 'The master directed him to take over yours.

But if we find that he's a poor cook, we'll give him something else. You'll watch him for a few days, boy, and let me know how he does here in the kitchen. That takes some skill; the rest any fool can do.' To Sepwin he added, 'I'll make you a pallet next to the boy's this evening. Now I must get back to my own work.' He went out.

Demas gave the side of venison a quarter turn and then returned to stirring the pots, one after the other.

'That's quite a lot of food you have there,' said Sepwin. 'How many do you feed?'

'Everyone in the castle. Eighteen, counting you.'

'The master, too?'

The boy nodded. 'So be certain you take care not to burn anything. His punishment is hard.'

'How hard?'

The boy glanced at him over one shoulder. 'Oh, he might shackle you to the wall without food or water for a few days. Or, if he's very displeased, he might kill you.'

Sepwin's eyebrows rose. 'Does he often kill his servants for trivial things?'

'Not very often,' the boy replied, returning his attention to the pots. 'Only once since I've been here.'

'And what was that one's crime?'

'As I recall . . . not taking the slops out early enough. He had given the man a chance or two already, I believe. They didn't tell you about my lord at the village?'

'They told me that he is very powerful, and that he holds all their lives in his hands.'

'And so he does,' said Demas. 'But he has promised that as long as we serve him faithfully here, he will spare the village.'

'But he doesn't spare those inside the walls.'

The boy shrugged. 'He is a man of temper. You are mad to come here without compulsion. But if your madness means I can go home, I have no objection to it.'

'Your mother said you'd been here almost three years. A long time in a young life.'

'There are many who've been here longer. Truly, I didn't ever expect to leave. The village has run out of cripples for him. I was the last. And I suppose even so I'll be back eventually, when one of the others dies.'

Very softly, Sepwin said, 'Do you hate him?'

The boy turned to him with an expression of surprise on his face. 'Hate? What good would my hate do? It wouldn't help me live and serve here. It wouldn't help me return when the time comes.'

'Would you have to return?'

'I have no choice.'

'You could run away. The world is wide. Your village is the smallest part of it.'

'Leave my mother and family to face his anger?'

'They could tell him that you died.'

The boy lowered his eyes. 'You are a fool, stranger, if you think a sorcerer can be lied to. He has every one of us in his power, and his arm is long. A man did run away once – ran away instead of hunting as my lord commanded. It was many years ago. Yltra told me – he was found sixteen days after, hanging by the neck in one of the towers. He hadn't been there before that day. My lord's arm is long.' He licked his lips, which were dry and cracked from bending over the fire. 'And now he has touched you with it. You won't leave here unless he wills it, stranger. Perhaps they didn't tell you that in the village.'

'He told me himself,' said Sepwin. 'But I have nowhere else to go, no other roof above my head. I will be content here, if the food is always as good as those pots smell now, and if your master, temperamental though he is, appreciates devoted service.'

'The food is good unless you spoil it,' said Demas. 'My work has never given my lord cause for displeasure.'

'Then I will endeavour to do as well.'

301

He helped Demas with further preparations for the evening meal, though the boy did not really need his help, for he was marvellously dexterous in spite of his useless arm. Later, sitting down to that meal in the refectory, he met the rest of the household, ten men and five women besides Demas and Yltra. Each of them had some deformity that Sepwin would have called pitiful; Yltra's facial scar, ugly though it was, was the least of them. There were twisted spines and crippled legs, missing fingers and lost eyes, darkly mottled skin eruptions and harelips – all the sad disfigurements that most villages hid from outsiders. In age the people ranged from the youth of Demas to the ancient decrepitude of a withered crone who scarcely looked strong enough to hold herself upright, let alone serve a master. She had a club foot.

They were kind to Sepwin, joking mildly among themselves that he did not belong with them, that he was too plain looking in spite of his eyes. They were glad, all of them, that they would have a chance to go home. But several of them sighed because it was not their chance, because they thought there would never be a chance for them. And Sepwin wondered what they had left behind in the village when they had come here – parents, spouses, children? But he thought it would be unseemly to ask.

Yltra served their master and did not come to the table till the others were all finished. Most of them, however, stayed to keep him company while he ate, and as Demas was one of these, Sepwin found himself there also. In the course of the conversation, he discovered that, like so many other duties in the castle, serving the sorcerer directly rotated among them.

'He enjoys viewing our deformities,' said Yltra. 'Be certain you never drop anything in his presence, though.'

'I am not a clumsy person.'

'He'll pay quite a lot of attention to you at first. He

always does with a newcomer. And he hasn't had one since Demas came to us.'

'I hope you will advise me on the proper behaviour.'

Yltra shrugged. 'Bow frequently. Don't drop anything. And do as he says immediately. I don't know that there is anything else.'

'Don't speak unless spoken to,' said Demas. 'Unless you have something very important to tell him. And when you give him bad news, apologize for it.'

'I've never known that to help much,' said Yltra.

'It depends on the news,' said Demas. 'I always apologize when there are no carrots with dinner. He likes carrots. I try to put them in everything I cook.'

'Yes,' said Yltra. 'You must remember to do things exactly as you're shown – those are the ways he likes them done. With a master like him, that's always safest.'

'I'll remember,' said Sepwin.

During the next few days he learned the routine of the castle – which tasks belonged to whom, when they were to be done, and how. He learned that only four of the servants regularly went outside the walls, to hunt and to gather wild herbs, that almost everyone took a turn at working the kitchen garden, and that Everand was likely to make a surprise inspection of any part of the castle at any time and therefore nothing could be put off for another day when it was supposed to be done on that one. He learned that the master liked to be served hot, damp cloths before his meal, to swab his face and hands, but that he was not so fastidious about the rest of his person. And he learned that he was not to open certain doors unless the sorcerer himself had given permission.

'He'll know if you do,' said Demas. 'He always does.'

For several days Sepwin accompanied the boy everywhere, sharing his work, imitating his methods. Together, they even served Everand a day's meals, Sepwin carrying the tray each time while Demas conveyed the dishes one by one to his master's table. Sepwin watched closely, noting the order in which the dishes were offered, how they were placed, where their lids were stacked, what further service the sorcerer required, whether slicing or mixing or addition of condiments. A dozen days later, when he and the boy were called to serve again, they exchanged places, and Sepwin duplicated his instructor's actions so perfectly that the boy chose the following morning to pack up his belongings and leave.

'You make a good servant,' he told Sepwin. 'The master should be pleased with you.'

'I hope so,' Sepwin said as he walked the boy to the gate. Everand had given his permission for the departure, and now Demas had only to open the gate and pass through. 'Are you going to make the whole journey home alone?'

'I know the way.'

The gate was barred. Demas shoved the bar aside by himself, but he needed Sepwin's help to pull the log barrier open enough to let him pass. 'I haven't been outside since I came here,' he said, gripping the rough surface of one of the logs with his good hand. 'It was summer then.' He swung the bag containing his few possessions over his shoulder and took one step out and then another. He turned to Sepwin. 'Farewell, madman. With any luck, I won't see you again for years.' And he faced away once more and began to walk toward the forest with a swift, resolute stride.

Sepwin took a single step toward the boy's retreating figure, or rather, he tried to take a step, but he was halted in the middle of that motion by the invisible barrier of the spell. It was like a wall before him, hard and cold as winter-chilled metal. It was a far more effective gate than any logs could be. Sepwin pushed the visible barrier shut and rebarred it and could not help wondering why it was barred at all.

When he asked Yltra, the man said, 'Why, to keep out the wolves, of course.'

'Wolves?' exclaimed Sepwin.

'Yes. My lord can't be bothered to kill them every time they try to sneak in.'

'But won't his sorcerous barrier keep them out?'

Yltra shrugged. 'He is concerned with demons and people, not with animals. A good stout gate is all that's needed for wolves.'

'Do they try to get in often?'

'Oh, they smell the meat cooking and they want a share. We have a great many wolves hereabouts. Didn't you see any on your journey from the village?'

'No. No, I didn't. I guess I was fortunate. But if there are so many, why did you let young Demas start home all alone? Aren't you afraid they might attack him?'

'Oh, they're just thieves. They won't attack a man. Not with easier game so plentiful in the woods. Demas has a knife, and I'm sure he's cut himself a stout staff by this time. He'll be all right. Anyway, the master didn't give his permission for any of us to accompany the boy. So there's an end to it.' Then, as an afterthought, he added, 'But I don't think the master would let the boy come to harm. He'll surely need him again someday.'

'But how will your master help him against wolves on the journey?'

'Oh, his arm is long. There's no need to worry about *that*.'

Sepwin marvelled at Yltra's image of his master the sorcerer. Here was a man feared by an entire village, a village that was willing to give him its own flesh and blood in return for a promise of safety, and yet the same man was scorned as a weakling by his fellow sorcerers. What was weakness to the strong seemed strength to the weak. Yltra did not wonder that the barrier that kept him inside the castle could not keep wolves out; he did not see that as a sign of weakness. Instead, he saw Everand's ability to kill at a distance by sorcery as a sign of strength. Sorcerers did not judge a person's strength, Sepwin knew, by his ability to kill; they considered that the most trivial power of all.

Sepwin himself, in the short time he had been in the castle, could not judge the level of Everand's power. At night, when the servants' quarters were lit by beeswax candles, an eerie blue-white glow, like continuous silent lightning, showed in the upper windows of the keep. That was the master, Yltra told him, conjuring, but what he conjured, no one knew. By day his workshop bore some resemblance to Cray's. Sepwin had brought him two meals there and had seen the furnace and the bellows, the charcoal and the greenish copper ore, the bars of pure metal and the wire that had been drawn from them. Everand's power was obviously bound up in copper, for he wore it all about his person, as necklets and bracelets and even a band about his forehead that left a greenish mark from his sweat. But what particular powers that copper gave him, beyond the power to encircle his castle with a sorcerous barrier, and to kill, no one could say. He did not practise his sorcery in front of his servants. They did not even know if he had ever commanded a demon. Only one, the old crone, said she had seen him summoning a storm once . . . or perhaps he had merely been standing atop the wall when the storm arose of its own accord.

None of them wanted to see their master's sorcery. One and all, they feared it could as easily mean their deaths as not. The barrier was more than enough for them, and those who had to pass through its chill to hunt or gather herbs in the forest shuddered every time they did so.

The only way Sepwin could make any sort of estimate of Everand's power was by judging his wealth. And he had very little of that.

Gildrum had often said that, in general, those of the sorcerous breed tended to surround themselves with comforts and with objects that pleased the eye. If they could not acquire such things directly through sorcery, they would barter for them or steal them. Precious metals, fine fabrics and needlework, sumptuous furnishings, tireless demon or unliving servants – these were the things one found in a sorcerer's castle. Everand had none of them. His clothing was as plain as a peasant's, his furniture no better than his servants', and the only pretty things in the keep were crystalline and obviously gifts from Aliza.

Sepwin had noticed this lack of wealth while prowling the castle. Though he had been in residence only a short time, he had already visited every room in the place. Some, their doors open, he had merely wandered into, with a newcomer's excuse of being confused about the location of something in case he was noticed. Some, their doors otherwise closed to him, he entered in the company of someone else, having offered his help for some task. His help was almost never refused. And so he discovered that there were no forbidden places in the castle, no caches of mysterious implements or substances, only the master's desire for privacy keeping them out of his workshop while he was busy and out of his bedchamber while he was sleeping.

A sorcerer with so few secrets, Sepwin thought, must be a feeble sorcerer indeed.

He had been searching for Aliza's soul. He had been certain he could find it. He, the keeper of the Mirror of Heart's Desire, he who read men's souls in the dark pool, he who had felt Aliza's lack in the crystal vase but had not known a name for it until the lady Helaine gave him one – he was precisely the right person to find it. He had known that once inside the sorcerous barrier, he would hear it calling to him, as the mirror web had called to him that day in the forest. He was attuned to souls – that was the Seer's whole existence.

But inside the barrier, he neither heard nor felt it. He

opened himself to its voice, and he perceived the souls of all the other people around him, all the servants, like a crowd of cackling geese. One by one, he determined the owner of each soul and shut it away from himself. He even perceived Everand's soul, though faintly because of the years of sorcery that muffled it. But once all of them were accounted for, there was nothing left but himself, no thin voice crying out, no faint vibration of being, nothing.

Then he thought that it must be hidden behind a barrier like the one that enveloped the castle, a barrier within a barrier, a place that would give back only the blankness of sorcery to his searching mind.

But he could not find such a place.

As he was scrubbing the flagstones of the ground floor of the keep, casting his mind in search of the soul for the dozenth time – or perhaps the two dozenth – he tried to decide what to do next. He could report to Cray, but he hated the thought of reporting such utter failure. Had they both been wrong? Was the soul not here at all but hidden in some better hidey-hole? It was not in the forest, he knew, not languishing in some hollow tree or under some stone; he would have felt it there while he was still outside. Yet where else could it be, he wondered, where Everand would still have control over it?

As he mused so, and as he scrubbed, the sorcerer himself strolled into the room. His head was down, he was not watching where he was going, and only at the last moment, when he was scarcely two paces from the bucket of soapy water, did he notice Sepwin. He veered sharply, but his foot slid on the wet floor and he lost his balance. He would have fallen, save that Sepwin bounded up and caught him under the arm.

'My lord, forgive me for being in your way!' exclaimed Sepwin. 'Are you all right?'

Everand glared at him and thrust him away. 'Who told you to wash this floor?'

Sepwin bowed. 'My lord, Yltra said this was the usual day for washing it, and it was my turn.'

Everand grunted deep in his throat. 'Yltra says he is pleased with your work. He says you are a better worker than Demas ever was.'

Sepwin bowed again.

'But next time you wash this floor, or any floor in the keep, see that you sing while you do it.'

'My lord, I don't sing very well.'

'I don't ask you to sing well. I only ask you to make a little noise so I know you're there!' He showed his teeth in something that was not quite a smile. 'You react quickly. That's a good quality in a servant. If you hadn't caught my arm, you'd probably be dead this very moment. Think about that the next time you wash a floor.' He walked away, carefully giving the wet part of the floor a wide berth.

Sepwin looked after him till he had entered the next room and closed the door between them. He was not thinking of his narrow brush with death, nor of the fact that none of the other servants ever sang while they worked, not even while they scrubbed floors. He was thinking instead of that split second in which he had caught Everand under the arm, that instant in which he had supported the man's whole weight. Their faces had been at the same level, Everand's cheek to him, his pale stringy hair falling to his shoulder. In that moment, as his body jerked to Sepwin's sudden grip, his hair had swung back, revealing his ear.

Or, rather, revealing that he had no ear. Where once that fleshy shell must have been was now a thin, ridged scar curving three-quarters of the way around the earhole.

Sepwin had felt a sudden shock go through him at the sight – a shock not of revulsion but of perception. His Seer's senses had been, at that moment, sharpened to their limit in his effort to perceive the slightest murmur from Aliza's soul; his hands had been wet, and though the water was not from the lady Helaine's pool, still it was water and it joined his flesh to Everand's through the sorcerer's sleeve. In that moment Sepwin saw, not into the sorcerer himself, but to the surface of that scar, to the place where that ear had once been, and he knew that its removal represented some event so important in the sorcerer's life that his whole existence turned upon it. And Aliza was involved. Even as he had asked Everand's forgiveness, his mind had been spinning with that awareness.

The rest of the day seemed to pass as if it were being paced out by an ox turning a millstone. Sepwin was busy the whole time, but each task seemed to require an eternity of effort. Even after supper, there were new candles to be dipped, and every servant took part in the procedure so that they would have light for another score of evenings. The sun had been gone quite some time and the gibbous moon was high when he was left to sleep at last in the room that he shared with six others. They all settled down on their pallets, the straw rustling as they wrapped themselves in their blankets, and soon faint snores told Sepwin that the others were asleep. Silently then, he threw off his own cover and slipped from the chamber.

Moonlight flooded the yard, revealing its emptiness. He walked softly but without stealth, making no attempt to hide in the shadows. He seemed like a man too restless to sleep but mindful of his fellows' need for quiet. He seemed like a man who just needed a little time alone with the night and the moon and the stars.

At equal intervals along the inside of the wall were stone staircases leading up to the battlements. The nearest to the servants' quarters was crumbled above the fourth step, but the next was whole enough to climb, with care, and Sepwin did so. At the top, the banquette – that broad walkway that circled the castle just inside the crenellations – was brightly lit by moonlight, the rough planking that covered its many gaps easy to see. Sepwin had been up there several times by day, and now he could stroll without paying much attention to where he placed his feet. He moved in a leisurely fashion, as befitted a man without a goal, gazing down at the yard or up into the sky, occasionally leaning for some moments into an embrasure to look out at the forest. He heard no footsteps but his own, and all around him the shadows were motionless. Even the keep was silent and dark, Everand having finished with his conjuring for one night.

The last embrasure he chose to halt at was quite a distance from the servants' quarters, well out of earshot of anyone who might be awake there. Far from any tower or bend in the wall, it was completely exposed to the moonlight, and standing beside it, so was he. But no one could creep up on him unnoticed there. He rested his forearms on the cold stone floor of the embrasure. In an ordinary castle, this might have been the post of a man-at-arms guarding the place, waiting for some enemy to emerge from the forest. In this sorcerous castle, no such sentries were necessary, for the barrier that enclosed it sealed out those enemies and their power. Sepwin stretched a hand out to the other end of the embrasure and felt the damp chill of that barrier – it was a solid thing to him, pressing back upon his questing fingers, an invisible cage that sealed preternatural powers out and also, except for Everand's own, in.

But there was nothing sorcerous about Sepwin's voice, only about those to whom he spoke, those who waited among the boulders in the clearing that surrounded the castle. With teeth and tongue he made the soft chirruping sound that would attract the attention of those magical spiders. They would signal to Cray, far off in Spinweb, and he would run to the web room to listen.

Sepwin whispered so softly that a mortal standing more than an arm's length away would not have been able to make out the words, but he knew Cray would hear: 'I haven't found it yet. I'd say it wasn't here at all, but there's a possibility that it's disguised somehow, so I'll keep searching. Meanwhile, I've discovered that Everand is missing his left ear. If you can find it, I know it has an important story to tell, perhaps even the location of the soul. The lady Helaine can help you. Good luck.'

He expected no answer, no sign that he had been heard. The clearing around the castle was as silent as the forest, as silent as the yard behind him. He turned away from the embrasure and sauntered down the banquette to the stairway. He yawned. There was cooking to be done in the morning, and another surreptitious examination of certain areas of the castle. He wondered if the soul could be concealed inside a turnip, perhaps, and buried in the root cellar beneath the servants' quarters. It was a possibility worth looking into.

'How are we going to find this ear?' Cray said to the lady Helaine. Gildrum had flown him to her cave as soon as they heard Sepwin's message. 'Surely it's long decayed by now, or eaten by some wild animal or maggots or some such.'

The lady Helaine smiled at him. 'We must presume that such is not the case. We must consider how a man might lose an ear, and what might happen to it afterwards.'

'It was lost in a fight, I suppose. Cut off by some enemy's sword or knife.'

'Sorcerers rarely take part in hand-to-hand combat, Cray.'

'Rarely, but not never. Perhaps it was when he was an apprentice.'

The lady Helaine shrugged. 'Perhaps. And perhaps . . . his enemy still has it. As a memento.'

'A grisly memento!'

'No more so than the horns of a deer, I think.' She turned

312

to Gildrum. 'This is a sorcerer's ear, my friend. Surely your fellow demons will know where it is, if it does still exist.'

Gildrum laughed. 'I'll ask among them. I'll wager that none of them has ever been asked about an ear before.'

'One can never be sure of such things,' she said.

Cray looked long at her after Gildrum was gone. She sat by the pool, her fingers trailing in the water; she seemed to be gazing at her own reflection in the dark water, but Cray knew better. 'What do you see?'

'Sorcery. For you and Feldar and this quest, always sorcery.'

'You have some suspicion about the ear, haven't you?'

'Feldar knows a significant thing when he sees it.'

'More than that.'

She did not raise her eyes from the pool. 'I have lived long, Cray, and seen many things in that time. Where sorcery is concerned, I never assume I know all there is to be known. I'll keep my suspicions to myself for now.'

'My lady, that's hardly fair. Here we are trying to help Aliza and you are keeping secrets . . .'

She laughed softly. 'Oh, Cray, you are so young. If you had been a sorcerer half as long as I have been a Seer, you would have your own suspicions and no need at all for mine.' She stood, drying her hand on the skirt of her gown. 'Come, let's have a cup of wine to help us sleep, and perhaps in the morning Gildrum will have returned with news. And if not, the pool tells me that a petitioner will arrive shortly after dawn, a king's second son come to ask what fate lies before him – he will help to pass the time.'

Cray nodded. 'I could use a cup of wine.' He followed her to the kitchen, where she poured goblets of pale white wine for both of them. Cray drained half of his at a draught. 'Poor Feldar,' he said, looking down into the remainder. 'As a servant he probably doesn't drink much wine in Everand's castle.'

'He'll survive that privation,' said the lady Helaine, sipping delicately at her own cup. 'I'm sure he still remembers the days before he ever tasted wine.'

Cray sighed. 'It seems like he's been there so long. And still he hasn't found it.'

'Who knows what magical hiding places a clever sorcerer might devise? You must be patient, Cray.'

He folded both his hands about his cup. 'Sometimes I think my days of patience are long gone.'

'A sign of youth,' said the Seer. 'The blood flows fast, and you think everything else must match it. But you have lives and lives ahead of you, Cray. Time enough for anything, for everything. We who are old should be the impatient ones, for we know how little is left, and how much must be squeezed into that time. But we are too tired for impatience; our blood runs too slow for it.'

He looked at her face, at the fine network of crepey wrinkles that patterned it, at the brows and lashes so pale and sparse that they were almost invisible, at the eyes that seemed slowly to have lost their colour over the years he had known her. She would never tell her age, and so he did not know if she were merely old as ordinary mortals were or if her span had been increased by sorcery and she were living in the final years, decades, centuries of some greater time. He had offered to lengthen her life himself, and she had – gently – rejected the offer. Sometimes he wondered if she had done so because sorcery had already worked to its limits upon her or because she simply did not wish to live beyond her natural term. Or . . . had she seen her own death in the pool and chosen not to struggle against that fate? How much time, he wondered, did she really have left?

'Do you miss Feldar very much?' he asked.

'Yes.'

'I'm sorry. Somehow he seemed so confident, I didn't think it would take this long.'

314

'It was his choice.'

'Can you tell – does the pool tell you yet if he'll return safely?'

'The quest is far from over, Cray. Very far.'

He slept that night in Sepwin's bed, but he dreamed of Aliza in her palace of crystal.

It was afternoon when Gildrum returned. The king's son had long since departed, and Cray and the lady Helaine had eaten their midday meal from the gold plates he had brought in payment for his future.

'Every time I think I understand your kind, I discover some fresh marvel to amaze me,' the demon said, taking its human form behind Cray's chair.

Cray turned to face him, one arm over the back of the chair. 'Did you find some trace of the ear?'

'I did. I found a demon who saw it no longer ago than yesterday.'

'Where?'

Gildrum chuckled softly. 'It's a piece of jewellery, of sorts, hanging on a golden chain about the neck of a sorcerer.'

'Jewellery?'

'By sorcery, he has preserved it as soft and flexible, and even as warm, as the day it was cut off Everand's head. My informant, an ice demon, particularly commented on its warmth.'

'The demon is this sorcerer's slave?'

'Yes, though it spends most of its time in Ice. From it I learned that although the sorcerer, one Taranol, has a great many demons of Fire, Air, and Water, none of *them* has enough leisure to spend time in the demon realm. Apparently, he has very little use for ice demons. Which, I would guess, is why he sold Regneniel to Everand.'

'Sold? I've never heard of a sorcerer selling a demon.'

'Nor had I, before this. But sell he did, and the price of that sale was Everand's ear.'

Cray shook his head. 'Why would this Taranol want Everand's ear?'

'That, the demon could not tell me.'

'The ear is the man,' said the lady Helaine. 'As long as it lives, it is a part of him, and obviously Taranol has maintained its life with his sorcery. Thus he holds it hostage, to prevent the one who bought the demon from ever raising a hand against him. As Everand can harm Aliza through her living soul, so can Taranol harm Everand through his living ear.'

'A careful man, this Taranol,' said Gildrum. 'He must have known how weak Everand was – it seems to be common knowledge among those who have heard of the man – yet wished to protect himself just in case that weakness gave way to something more formidable.'

'I would never give another person such power over myself,' said Cray.

'I suppose he thought he had a good reason for it.'

'An ice demon? I can't even imagine why he would do it for a fire demon!'

'Perhaps the ear will tell us,' said the Seer. 'It will certainly speak to me of the time before his apprenticeship, and if he is as weak as you have said, it may tell more than that. Feldar seems to think it will.'

'But how can we get it?' asked Gildrum. 'Taranol wears it constantly. And he never goes out of his castle without a retinue of demons. I don't see any way we could steal it except to overwhelm them all with sheer numbers, and that would mean a full-scale battle. Do you want a war with this Taranol over an ear?'

'No battle. No war,' said Cray. 'I don't want to steal it at all. I just want to borrow it.'

They met in a forest clearing, some days' travel, by

ordinary means, from Taranol's residence. Cray stood on one side of the clearing, Gildrum and Elrelet with him in their demon forms. Taranol entered from the opposite side, an entourage so numerous accompanying him, of fire and air and water demons, that had they been courtiers Cray would have guessed the man a king. He was very short, this Taranol, and very fat, and he did not walk but was carried on a couch of cloud. He was smooth-shaven, his garments immaculately clean and richly ornamented with golden thread and the plumes of rare birds, and his short fingers were heavily laden with rings and flashing stones. The ear seemed a grotesque and incongruous bauble against his silk-draped torso.

Cray stepped forward and bowed deeply. 'Lord Taranol, I thank you for so graciously accepting my invitation.'

Taranol spoke softly to the demon nearest his shoulder, was silent during an equally soft reply, and then laughed, the thick folds of flesh beneath his chin quivering with that laughter. 'Well, young Master Cray, I was intrigued by your request, and by your little gift as well. I am willing to listen if you can continue to be so persuasive.'

By Gildrum, Cray had sent the sorcerer a miniature tree made of gold. It was as tall as a man's knee and would not grow taller, being a dead thing, fashioned in his workshop rather than sown in the garden, but when the slightest breeze stirred its burnished leaves, they rang against each other like the sweetest bells.

Cray said, 'Lord Taranol, I see by your garments that you are one who appreciates fine needlecraft.'

The man inclined his head in agreement.

'Now, I happen to be acquainted with one of the greatest practitioners of needlecraft alive today, and to demonstrate just a fraction of her skill to you, I have this modest footstool, which I made and which she decorated expressly for you.' He stretched a hand out to Gildrum, and from the depths of its flame, the demon produced the stool that Cray had grown from the darkest ebony and that his mother had cushioned with her finest embroidery. The cushion was black velvet, its perimeter studded with gold, a proud, spreadwinged bird worked in crimson silk upon its centre. Cray took the stool from Gildrum and held it out to Taranol with both hands.

The sorcerer gestured to one of his demons, who floated forward to receive the gift and to display it to its master. 'A pretty piece of work,' said Taranol. 'I will be pleased to have it in my home.'

'In addition to these trifles,' said Cray, 'I offer a bed coverlet of cloth of gold backed by plush, which I guarantee is as warm as any five woollen blankets.' Elrelet brought this item out of its cloudiness and, with Gildrum's and Cray's help, spread it out to catch the sunlight. Cray and Gildrum had made it, drawing the gold into thread as fine as silk and weaving it with sheerest linen under Delivev's direction. The rich amethyst of the plush showed through the glittering surface as through a fine mist.

Taranol's eyes glittered almost as brightly as the cloth. 'You tempt me strongly, Master Cray,' he said, one plump hand moving to cover the ear, to press it against his chest. 'All of this for the half day's loan of a piece of rubbish.'

'Do you consider it rubbish, Lord Taranol, and yet wear it at your throat every day of your life?'

Taranol laughed a low, sardonic laugh. 'I wear it because one can never tell when one might need the smallest piece of rubbish. Everand is a fool, and fools can be dangerous. Now tell me – why do you want it?'

'A Seer has told me it has information I need, about his life and motives.'

'His life is wretched and his motives are obvious. The man wants to be what he cannot be. What more do you need to know?'

'Among other things, why he chose to buy an ice demon.'

'I can tell you that, Master Cray. He bought because he could not conjure, and he bought an ice demon because I would not sell him any other kind. *I* am not a fool. As it was, I gave him more power than he deserved.'

'He gave you considerable power in exchange.'

Taranol held the ear out toward Cray. 'This? This is nothing. Oh, power over him – yes, I have that. But power over nothing is still nothing. The exchange was all to his advantage. I had no use for the ice demon.'

'So I see from your hands,' said Cray. 'Even a fool must know that you are a powerful sorcerer indeed. I would think, therefore, that you had no need for the ear. Surely you could defend yourself against him, whatever he might become, with all your other power.'

Taranol shrugged. 'Probably true. But I dislike fighting. This keeps Everand from even thinking of attacking me. He doesn't like me, you know. Some years ago, when he was looking for a master to take his granddaughter as apprentice, he asked me, and I refused. A child of his line apprenticed to me – how absurd. So I take no chances on any unpleasantness from him. With this ear in my hands, I could control his entire existence. I could make him so dizzy that he would fall down and vomit his innards out. He'd have a very difficult time doing anything at all under those circumstances. He knows this, of course, and he fears me. But he also knows that I won't use the ear if he does not give me cause.' He smiled broadly. 'You know, if I do loan you the ear, you won't be able to use it against him.'

'I had not intended to.'

'But you are looking for some kind of hold over him. You think the ear can tell you how best to find one.'

Cray hesitated. 'I cannot deny that such a thing might have its uses.'

'Perhaps you and his granddaughter are plotting something against the old man?'

'I and his granddaughter?'

Taranol laughed that low, sardonic laugh again. 'You needn't pretend that you don't know her, Master Cray. I assure you, I'm aware of your journey through Ice. And I know a great deal more about you than that. These demons don't spend all of their time carrying me about.'

Cray inclined his head. 'I can appreciate your wish to know as much as possible about me before trafficking with me. But believe me, Everand's granddaughter and I are not plotting against him in any way. I merely wish to understand the man better, for my own personal reasons.'

Taranol interlocked his fingers over the ear. 'Well, I would never want to pry into your personal reasons, Master Cray. Still, you want this thing from me, and I am loath to part with it even for an afternoon, in spite of all these lovely persuasions you have given me. On the other hand, I know from my demons that you are no weakling where sorcery is concerned, and that although you wear no rings, you do command the services of a number of powerful demons. I understand that you are not a man to cross.'

'I have a few friends among the demon races,' Cray admitted. 'I don't command them, but they do me favours now and then. I know they wouldn't wish any harm to come to me.'

'Of course not. So perhaps we can reach a compromise of sorts – I will loan you the ear for an afternoon, but I really cannot allow it out of my sight. Therefore, either you will do whatever it is you want to do with it here in this clearing, or I and my demons will accompany you to do it where you wish.'

'It can't be done here,' said Cray. 'And your demons would crowd the place where it must be done until we humans could not breathe.'

'Oh, they are quite skilled at making themselves small and unobtrusive. I think we can manage without suffocating.'

Cray folded his arms across his chest. 'Very well. If that is your only condition, I will not dispute it. Which way do you choose to go – through Air or Fire?'

Taranol's lips twisted slightly in an expression of distaste. 'Must we go through the demon realm?'

'I know no other route.'

'Oh, Air, then. It's the least unpleasant of the lot.'

With one hand, Cray indicated Elrelet. 'This demon will show you the way. I shall meet you there.'

'You won't travel with us?'

'No, I have preparations to make. I won't be long.' He bowed a farewell, and Gildrum took him up and lifted him into the sky.

Once they were in his own world, the fire demon said, 'He may look fat and slothful, but you'd be wise not to underestimate his intellect.'

His eyes tight shut, Cray said, 'I wouldn't want to underestimate anything about a sorcerer with so many demons. He knows we are dependent upon his good graces in this matter, and he knows that our purpose is most likely not to Everand's advantage. I think we should stop in the south for some of those exotic fruits that my mother likes so well, and then we might pick up a cask or two of the finest vintage that the cellars at Oldun can offer.'

'Yes, he's obviously a man who enjoys food and drink. Perhaps it would not hurt to serve something more substantial in the way of refreshments, in addition. It can't hurt to leave him with good memories of your hospitality.'

'No,' said Cray. 'It can't.'

In the end, Gildrum, with the help of Delivev's cloth servants, provided an eight-course meal for Taranol, Cray, and the lady Helaine. Afterwards, Taranol leaned back in his well-padded chair, belched softly, and praised his hosts for the excellence of their table. Then he drew the golden chain over his head, the chain that carried the ear, and held it out to Cray, saying, 'I think you've waited long and patiently enough for this.'

Cray took it gravely, with both hands, bowing deeply before he passed it to the lady Helaine. She carried it into the chamber of the pool, with the others following like some strange pilgrimage – Cray and Gildrum and Elrelet in the forefront, and Taranol trailing behind, surrounded by his miniaturized demons, like bees guarding their hive. While the Seer seated herself by the water, Cray and Gildrum set a comfortable chair on the white sand for Taranol. Then they all waited.

The lady Helaine cupped the ear in her hands, half submerging it in the chill water. She stared downwards at the magically preserved fragment of flesh, stared at the slow ripples that glided outwards from her caging fingers, stared into the unplumbable depths of the dark pool. After a very long time, she began to relate the story that she read in the ear.

Everand had been born an ordinary child. His parents were lord and lady, but not of the sorcerous breed; no, they ruled by the power of sword and lance over warriors who bore their colours and peasants who tilled their soil. The boy was the youngest of five brothers, his mother's favourite, uncommonly pretty, and spoiled by petting and sweetmeats. When he was old enough, he came to serve his father as a page, but his duties were light, and he spent most of his time in play. He was barely eight years old when the sorcerer visited their house.

Verdrinar was the sorcerer's name, and he was greatly feared in that country. When he entered the great hall, everyone bowed low before him, even Everand's parents.

He had come to demand a certain handsome goblet, of gold intricately chased with silver, a recent gift from an ally. When the goblet had been handed over, he also asked – almost as an afterthought – for the boy.

Everand's mother wept, and his father pleaded, but in the end a demon carried the child away. Everand was frightened by the demon, and by the strange man who had so cowed his parents, but he was too proud to let that fear show.

Ten years he lived behind Verdrinar's spellbound walls, not stepping beyond them once in all that time, so that there was a gap in his life, a space that the lady Helaine could not fathom. But when those years were done, Verdrinar died, and the spell that had cloaked his castle crumbled along with its walls.

The youth Everand barely escaped with his life. Bruised and bleeding, his garments half torn from his body, he stumbled away from the ruins and sat down heavily on a nearby boulder, to catch his breath and to watch the dust settle on his master's tomb. He had brought nothing out of the castle with him but the clothes on his back and the knife at his belt. Every other material thing that he had acquired in ten years with the sorcerer lay buried inside the wreckage. He didn't care. He was glad to be free.

He found a spring and bathed his cuts and then drank deep before setting out on the long journey home. He had only the vaguest notion of where home lay. To the south, he thought, remembering the sunset on his left as Verdrinar's demon carried him through the sky. The rolling hills, forest, and meadows looked very different from ground level, and he could not guess how far off his father's house might be, but he was confident that he would find it at last. That evening he killed the first of the animals he would eat along the way, a rabbit that did not tumble into its burrow quickly enough. He stunned it from a distance, with an invisible magical blow, then hurried to wring its neck before it could recover. By magic, too, he kindled a fire, sparks raining from his fingertips to ignite the punk he had scooped from a dead tree. He was hungry and ate the rabbit rare and bloody. It was very tough.

Ten days' walk brought him to a village, where he convinced the inhabitants to give him their best horse by threatening to call lightning down from the sky and burn their village to the ground. He did not actually know how to call down lightning, but the sparks that showered from his hands frightened them sufficiently. They also provided him with food and fresh clothing. After that the days passed more agreeably.

Three months of wandering, of asking directions at small houses and great, brought him back to his father's gate. He was not surprised that none of the guards recognized him; he scarcely knew any of them. But he was surprised when he approached his parents in the great hall and they did not rush to embrace him. Instead they stood aloof, even backed off as he would have laid hands on them. His mother hid behind his father, and his father stared at him stiffly, as at a stranger.

'How do we know you are who you say?' his father said in a strained voice, and when the youth had given a hundred proofs from his memory, his wary expression did not change. 'You could be a demon sent to deceive us. Verdrinar is a wily man.'

'Verdrinar is dead,' said Everand, 'and his demons have flown away. I am your son, come home.'

'Ten years,' said his father, shaking his head slowly. His hair was grey, and there were many new lines in his face, and age in his eyes. 'Ten years ago I lost my youngest son to sorcery. Why would a sorcerer want to live among ordinary folk?'

'I am not a sorcerer,' said the youth.

'After ten years?'

'Even so. I was never his apprentice, just his . . . plaything.'

Nervously, his father looked at his mother. 'Are we to believe that after ten years of . . . close association with one like Verdrinar you have no powers greater than ordinary folk?'

Everand fell to his knees. 'My lord and father, I am simply your child, nothing more, and I have travelled a very long way to come to you. Won't you at least offer me your hospitality – some bread and water and a place to lay my head?'

'Oh yes, of course. Immediately.'

A sumptuous meal was laid out for Everand, and his parents sat with him as he ate, but they said nothing. Silent men-at-arms stood about the table, too, eyeing the newcomer as if they had never seen a man in a travel-stained cloak before. Afterwards, he was led to a well-cushioned pallet in a secluded part of the house, a small room all to himself, with three candelabra to light it and a carafe of wine to quench his thirst. He paced out its confines many times, unable to sleep, though he had ridden hard and long that day, to cover the final distance to his home.

In the quietest part of the night, his mother came to the room. One hand shielding her candle, she leaned in the half-open door and, seeing him still awake and dressed, she entered.

Taking the candle from her hand, Everand embraced her. She accepted his embrace but did not return it, and she stepped back from him as soon as he loosed her. She looked up into his face, obviously seeking some trace of her little boy in the young man who towered over her. Seeing the uncertainty in her eyes, he asked her to sit down with him on the edge of the pallet and, there, he took one of her hands within his own.

'Mother,' he said, 'this is a cold welcome for your favourite child. Have I truly changed so much that I seem like a stranger to you?'

Slowly, she nodded.

'I know we've lost all those years,' he said, 'but I never left off thinking of you and father and the boys, not for a moment. If I could have escaped and come back to you, I would have, believe me. But as long as Verdrinar wished it, I was his slave.'

She pulled her hand away from his and, looking down at it, clasped it tightly with her other one. 'My son,' she said in a very low voice, 'I am afraid of you.'

He hardly knew what to say to that. He sputtered, 'Mother, how can you fear your own son?'

'I don't know you,' she said. 'I don't know anything about you. Ten years with a sorcerer! How can you say that you are nothing more than my son? How can I believe that?'

'Oh, I know a trick or two,' he said. 'Nothing of any moment. Look, I'll show you –' He raised a hand and pointed toward the nearest wall, but before he could shower yellow sparks upon it, she gripped his arm with fingers like claws.

'No, don't show me, please!' Her eyes looked up into his like a wounded dog's. 'Don't you understand? Whatever you learned from the sorcerer, however trivial it may seem to you – it frightens us. *You* frighten us. We never expected to have you back. We resigned ourselves to that. Now your brothers are all married and have given us grandchildren, and that is all we want, just the ordinary things of life. *You* are not ordinary, not after ten years with Verdrinar!'

'Mother, I swear to you –'

'No, swear nothing. How can you even understand an ordinary life by now? You were taken so young. Please, Everand – I am the mother who bore you. No one could understand you better than I. You are changed. Not just by the years. There is a look in your eye; it makes me quail inside. You don't know how you seem to us.'

Hesitantly, he touched her shoulder. 'Mother, you'll

grow used to me, surely. It's just that I left a child and I return a man. That's all it is.'

She slid away from his hand and stood up abruptly. Her clasped hands were wringing each other now, as if she were cold, though the night was pleasant enough. 'Please go,' she said. 'Everyone in the house is afraid of you, and there will be no peace until you've gone.'

He stared at her open-mouthed. 'But this is *my* house. I belong here.'

She shook her head. 'You will destroy us. The peasants will run away and the men-at-arms desert their posts. The house will be empty. If you're truly my son, if you truly love your father and me, don't do that to us. Find some new sorcerer to serve. You'll be happier there, I know it.'

'You don't know anything about sorcerers, Mother.'

'Perhaps not. But I know about ordinary folk. Please, my son.'

'You ask . . . a great deal, Mother.' He could feel the tears starting in his eyes, and he clenched his teeth against them.

'This is Verdrinar's evil,' she said. 'Blame him.'

'That does me little good.' He leaned forward, elbows on his knees, and a single teardrop escaped his lids, falling to make a tiny spot of moisture on the smooth stone beneath his feet. 'I dreamed of this homecoming, all the long way here, walking, riding. I dreamed of your faces. And what have I got for my pains – turned out by my own mother.'

'Perhaps you can find some place where they don't know who you are,' she said. 'Perhaps you can still lead an ordinary life, if you really want one.'

He rose to his feet. 'You don't care what happens to me, do you? As long as it never brings me back to this house.'

'I care,' said his mother, still wringing her hands. 'I do love you, my son. But I fear you more.'

He gathered up his cloak. 'Bring me food for my journey, the best horse in the stable, and a few pieces of silver. I ask no more.'

'Thank you,' whispered his mother, and she turned and hurried off.

At first he wandered aimlessly, the distance between himself and his father's house ever increasing, till at last he reached lands where no one knew his father's name. He stayed in one place or another, chopping wood for peasants or helping them harvest their grain, serving in the kitchens of a few great houses as butcher or scullery servant, once even enlisting in the ranks of a prince's men-at-arms. But these things never held him long; always he wandered on, restless, unhappy. And no one ever seemed sorry to see him go.

At last he came back to the ruined castle.

Looking at the place, at those crumbled walls and fallen towers, he felt he had come home. He led his horse inside the shattered archway that had once been a gate and tethered it to a small bush growing amid the rubble. Then, using a bough trimmed of its twigs and leaves, he began to lever the fallen stones aside to make room for his shelter. He cleared a space five paces wide that day and, using the bough as a tent pole, put up his roof of canvas and slept where once sorcery had held sway, but no more.

The next day he began to dig in the keep. One man, with only the tools he could shape with his knife, he laboured for two months and more before he uncovered Verdrinar's study, where the sorcerer had kept his books, and where he had died.

The body, which had been so freshly out of breath, so warm and ruddy when last he saw it, was a pile of dust now, the common fate of sorcerers. The books were intact, though much scattered by the collapse of shelves and cabinets under the weight of the roof and upper floors. He took them to his tent, and he began his studies.

He was diligent, but diligence was not enough. Sometimes he was not even sure of what the books were telling him, though he practised the passes and the words anyway. He lost patience a thousand times and swore to leave the ruin, never to return, but the few times he actually tried it, he could scarcely bear to lose sight of the place before turning back and resuming his labours. He did learn some small skills, how to make the clouds whip about to cause a storm, how – at last – to call the lightning to him, unless the sky was very clear. His small skills eventually attracted the attention of another sorcerer, one who had thought the ruins deserted and who sent a demon to investigate the activity he sensed there. Everand asked the demon to petition its master for him; he wished to become an apprentice. But the demon conveyed only its master's laughter – what mad fool would take an ordinary human as apprentice? he asked. Out of some whim, the sorcerer relayed Everand's request to others of his kind, but the answer was always the same, reported by the same demon – no, no, a dozen times no. Generations before, the first sorcerers had been ordinary humans, folk of small power, but those days were gone, and now the breed was well established and scorned anyone unlucky enough to be born of ordinary parents. If Everand was to become a sorcerer in truth, he had to do so without their help.

The years passed, and Everand was fortunate enough – he thought – to discover the spell of longevity, and so he gave himself extra lifetimes for his studies. Yet even so, even a hundred years after his original span should have ended, he had to admit to himself that time alone was not enough. To become truly powerful, he needed the guidance of someone powerful. Without it, he had learned as much as he could from Verdrinar's books, and still he was constantly disappointed in himself. Comparing himself to Verdrinar made him want to cry out against the unfairness of the universe; he knew how contemptible his few powers were. And he envied other sorcerers. He envied their power, their wealth, their lives of ease, demon-served. And envy brought with it, eventually, resentment and hate. But what could his hate mean to a sorcerer, his petty, powerless hate? Knowing that, he hated more strongly still.

A brief liaison with a peasant woman from the village ten days' walk away left him with a daughter, and her he tried to raise as a real sorcerer would. She was scarcely more than a baby when he began to teach her sorcery, and she became proficient at everything he knew so quickly that he was astonished. He began to hope. He began to think that perhaps through his daughter, if not through his own efforts, he could come at last to have at least the material trappings of power, the wealth and slaves, the appearance of great sorcery. He began to hope that he could even have the ruin rebuilt someday. He guided her through Verdrinar's books, and he saw that she understood all of them more readily than he, more thoroughly, and with greater strength. By the time she was fourteen summers old, she knew everything that he knew, and more. He again petitioned the sorcerers that had refused him, this time on behalf of his daughter, to whom sorcery seemed as natural as air.

The sorcerous breed were kinder to the daughter than they had ever been to the father. Several had their minions bring her to them for interviews. Finally one, who already had a young man as apprentice, agreed to take her for a trial period. Everand suspected that her person appealed to the sorcerer as much as her intelligence, but he thought that she would profit from the association anyway. He had not counted on the other apprentice, a rather plain young man, slow, only apprenticed because he was a child of the house. He had not counted on the two young people finding each other more interesting than sorcery. Within a few short months, their master was angry enough at their negligence to throw them both out, and Everand's daughter came home with her lover. Everand railed at her for tossing away the greatest opportunity of her life, but she paid little attention to his anger. She and her young man were too happy with each other. They let their sorcerous studies lapse completely and spent most of their time in the woods, together.

They had a child, Aliza.

His daughter was a failure – Everand resigned himself to that. But with her child he could start afresh, try again. But when he voiced his desire to begin teaching the baby, he was astonished to discover that her parents did not wish it. They had, in fact, decided to give up sorcery entirely and to live as ordinary mortals. They would not listen to his protests, to his anger, to his pleading. Aliza was scarcely old enough to walk when they left the ruined castle, taking with them only her and a few tools with which to start their new life.

Everand followed them stealthily. For five days he lurked behind them, hiding himself when they looked back. For five days they travelled through the rolling forested landscape, and on the sixth, the young people halted and began taking turns felling trees with their single axe. Everand watched them lay the first logs of a small cabin in a clearing just below the crest of a hill, in a place where there was water and game in plenty, a place where no human being would bother them. As they worked, they laughed frequently, and the child laughed, too, playing about them in the sunshine, like any ordinary mortal.

Everand went home and brooded over Verdrinar's books, his only legacy from the man who had made him unfit for the society of ordinary mortals, who had shown him what might be, but never helped him toward that goal. Once more he immersed himself in those volumes, hoping to glean some scraps of knowledge that he had somehow overlooked before. And every night he cursed his own incapacity, cursed his parents, cursed the sorcerers who had not been willing to take him as apprentice. Two years he spent so, though they seemed more like two centuries to him.

One morning, red-eyed from late and fruitless study, suffused with frustration and anger, Everand donned his worn woollen cloak, packed a few days' provisions in an old sack, and set off through the woods. Though he had gone that way only once, the route was engraved in his mind like silver chasing on a golden goblet. He scarcely slept along the way, and when he did, he woke soon, his limbs shaking with anger from dreams of formless impotence. It was night when he came to the cabin, but the full moon and all the stars shone down to illuminate the place. A few clouds scudded across the moon, a thin veil to its mellow light. The season was full summer, the night pleasantly warm.

Everand looked up toward the moon, toward the wispy clouds, and he raised his hands to them, his fingers clawed, and he called in a harsh whisper for the clouds to obey him. Slowly, very slowly, they thickened, as cloudlets from beyond the horizon came to join them. Slowly, very slowly, they blotted out the pale moonlight until only the cool stars shone down in the warm night.

Silently, Everand worked his way close to the cabin. It was very small, no larger than the first shelter he had built himself in the ruined castle. Its walls were made from the boles of young trees, each log no heavier than two people alone could lift and sealed to its neighbour by mud and turf. Its peaked roof was shingled with bark. There was a stone chimney on one wall, but not a trace of smoke escaped it. The cabin had no windows and only one door; testing the door gently, Everand found it barred from the inside.

He retreated a dozen paces, and with a convulsive gesture he called down lightning from the clouds. It struck where he pointed, squarely in the middle of that stout, barred door, and with a deafening crash split the wood asunder. Everand leaped through the gap, one shoulder striking the charred and smoking edge of the doorway, flinging blackened fragments of wood ahead of him. Behind him, lightning struck again – the ground this time – and illuminated the interior of the cabin well enough for him to get his bearings. His daughter and her lover were on a pallet to his left, she sitting bolt upright, transfixed in the ghastly light. The child lay in a small bed beside them, a stuffed toy clutched in her arms. Everand scooped her up and leaped back through the doorway. He had barely cleared it when he nodded sharply for lightning to strike it again. And again. He ran, and he did not look back until he reached the bottom of the hill.

No one was following him. The cabin was well lit now, but not by lightning. It was afire.

From the shelter of the trees, he watched it burn, and he saw no one emerge, heard no one cry out. By morning it was a charred ruin, and without the support of the walls, the chimney at last collapsed. The child, who had cried for a time, was asleep by then, and Everand slung her over his shoulder like a sack of meal as he began the long walk home.

She was quicker than her mother had been, or perhaps Everand had learned something about teaching since then. Or perhaps he was simply more desperate to impart information these days. Whichever was true, he found himself greatly pleased by her prospects. But this time he began casting about for a sorcerous master much earlier; he thought that by apprenticing her while she was very young he would avoid the human entanglements that had so swayed his daughter from her proper path. And this time, too, he would not clutch at the first sorcerer to say yes if that one already had another apprentice. He reasoned that sorcerers so rarely took apprentices, surely that would not be a problem again.

On the contrary, the problem this time was that no one would take the child. Word of Everand's daughter's laxness had spread through the sorcerous community, and no one to whom Everand appealed would take his granddaughter and chance the same. Apprenticeship, they told him, was not to be wasted on the idle.

If he had cursed them before, those curses now seemed as nothing to him. He raged, he railed, there in the ruins where he had built a meagre sorcerous existence for himself; his fury would have been terrible if he had had the power to express it. Instead, he could only fell a few trees with lightning, crack a few rocks, terrorize a few animals. Even the child Aliza was not frightened, for she had quickly become accustomed to his skills, and she, too, could call down lightning from a cloudy sky, though it was still only strong enough to make a bucket of water steam.

Everand stood by the parapet of the ruined wall, stood by the part of it that was least damaged, so that if he looked outwards from there he could almost entertain the illusion that behind him the castle was whole and sound. How many times had he yearned to make that structure so? How many times had he wished to move these stones by the power of sorcery, by the wave of a hand and the intonation of a few words? How many times had he tried to imagine the sight of his own fingers ornamented by rings whose creatures would obey his slightest whim? He pounded his fists on the sun-warmed stones, and they felt cool compared to the hot rage that bubbled inside him. He needed help, and the world denied him.

It was then, at that very moment, that he decided to beg. He spent almost a year in finding someone who would answer his plea. And then, when he found charity, or as close to charity as any sorcerer would come, the price was his ear.

The Seer lifted her cupped hands from the pool and carefully dried the ear and its chain on her skirt. Then she handed them back to Taranol.

He slipped the chain over his head. 'He told me he wanted the demon as a tutor for himself and his grand-daughter. I saw no reason to doubt that. And I knew that Regneniel would be no great servant in any case – it seemed something of a joke to me, to give him such an untalented creature in exchange for power over him. Perhaps if I had understood how much he hated us all, I wouldn't have agreed to the trade. I laughed at him, though not to his face. Actually, I pitied him. He pleaded so humbly. I never realized what a mask it was. I'm almost tempted now to give him a taste of real enmity.' He fingered the ear for a moment. 'Almost.'

'He murdered her parents,' said Cray.

Taranol shrugged. 'That's nothing to me. They stood in his way.'

'His own daughter.'

'I don't care much for my own children, to be honest. But I was one of those, one of the many, who refused his granddaughter an apprenticeship. He was cursing me.' He closed both hands about the ear. 'I've teased him over the years, not in malice, but just for amusement. He's had to close up the gaps in his walls and put bars on his gate against certain wild animals that keep trying to get inside. He doesn't know that I sent them. His spell is too weak to keep them out, you see; it's only good for humans and demons. But that's just a petty annoyance to him, just my little joke. I could do far worse if I wished.' Then he smiled slightly. 'But I suppose I must realize that ordinary humans always hate the powerful, be they sorcerous or no. And he's truly just an ordinary human still, and a pitiful

335

one. He has tried so hard to be one of us, and failed so dismally. What a shame he gave himself such a long life in which to be so unhappy.'

Cray clasped his hands behind his back and turned away from the others, away from the pool and the Seer, from Gildrum and Taranol and his flock of tiny demons. 'Thank you for the loan of the ear, my lord Taranol. It has been extremely helpful.'

'Has it?' said Taranol. 'And what will you do with all it has told you, Master Cray?'

'I don't know yet. You must excuse me now. I have to think.'

'Let me show you out, my lord,' said the lady Helaine, rising from the rim of the pool. 'I know you understand that we must consider this information in private.'

'Oh, of course, of course. But you'll give me a hint, won't you, when you decide? I really must know, to be sure that I get full value from the ear.'

'Full value?' said the lady Helaine.

'Well, of course – if you decide to kill him, I want to be ready to conjure my demon back. A dead man's ear won't be any use to me.'

'You presume too much, my lord. We seek to understand, not to destroy.'

'I'll know when he dies,' said Taranol. 'You won't be able to keep it a secret from *me*.' He let himself be guided toward the tunnel that led to daylight, but at the last moment he turned back toward Cray. 'Don't expect any help from me, though. I won't battle another sorcerer, not for someone else's sake. I won't allow you to use this ear against him.'

'We would not expect you to,' said the lady Helaine, and with a light touch on his elbow, she eased him and his demons out into the sunshine.

Gildrum came up beside Cray and laid an arm across his shoulders. 'Will you tell her?'

Cray looked down at the white sand beneath his feet. 'I must. I only wonder if it will matter to her.'

'Of course it will matter. Her own grandfather . . . '

'I don't know, Gildrum. She has no soul, no capacity for love or hate or grief. Her parents are like a dream to her; they have no reality in her mind. Perhaps she'll merely say that her grandfather did this, too, for her own benefit.'

Gildrum's arm tightened. 'Then you must convince her otherwise.'

Cray sighed. 'Help me, Gildrum.'

'Of course,' said the demon.

Chapter 11

Aliza was yawning and knuckling sleep from her eyes when she admitted Cray to her palace.

'Forgive me,' he said. 'I didn't think you'd still be asleep so late in the morning.'

'The sun doesn't rule in Ice, so why should I let it command me? Come, break fast with me. Regneniel should have some food ready by the time we reach the dining hall.'

'It's midday meal for me,' he said with a smile, 'but I'll join you gladly.' He waved to his three demon friends, who waited in their usual place just beyond the transparent wall, and then he fell in step beside Aliza to move deeper into the palace. 'I tried to call you through the web. I thought surely it would work even here in Ice, but nothing happened. Have you tried it from your side yet?'

'No, I never had the chance. The spider died soon after I brought it home, and the web fell apart quickly after that.'

'Died? It was a healthy spider, and young. Did Regneniel forget to feed it?'

'No, but Regneniel is not accustomed to having other living creatures here, certainly not any so small. I had the spider make its web in my bedchamber, and while removing the bedclothes for laundering, Regneniel accidentally stepped on it. I was very annoyed, and Regneniel was very apologetic, but of course that did no good. I was thinking . . . of asking you for another one. I'll put it in a safer place this time, I promise you.'

'Stepped on it,' murmured Cray. 'I had no idea that ice demons were so clumsy.'

'It assured me it would take greater care if you gave me another one.'

'I would hope so,' said Cray. 'Well, I happen to have a few about my person just now, so that shouldn't pose any problem.'

In the dining hall the long table was set with fruit and cheese, bread and cold meat, and two cups of a steaming herbal infusion. Cray seated himself opposite Aliza and took up a slice of meat.

'Where is Regneniel?' he asked, after a moment of silent eating.

'Is there something you want?'

'Yes. I was thinking of that fine Maretian wine.'

Aliza yawned again, behind her hand. 'It's a little early for wine, isn't it? Even if it is midday for you.'

'I wasn't thinking of drinking any now. But . . . truth to tell, my mother thought it some of the best wine she had ever tasted. She'd very much like to have a cask of it for Spinweb.'

'I haven't that much here at the moment, but Regneniel can easily get it.'

'I was thinking,' said Cray, 'that Regneniel could show a couple of my demon friends where it comes from, and then she could have more whenever she wished.'

'Surely,' said Aliza. 'Are they out there waiting for you still?'

He nodded.

'Regneniel,' she said, and the demon came to her from the doorway that led to the kitchen. 'Show Cray's demon companions where Maretian wine comes from. And bring a fresh cask for me as well.'

'As you wish, my lady,' said the ice demon, and it marched out of the room.

Cray rose from his chair and went to the doorway to watch Regneniel go and, keeping well back, followed the demon through the furnished rooms and even the unfurnished ones, till he saw it step through a new-made gap in the outer wall and join his friends. Only then did he return to Aliza. Running.

He found her staring at the doorway through which he and the demon had gone, a piece of bread forgotten in her upraised hand. 'What are you doing?'

Instead of returning to his own chair, he leaned over hers. 'They'll keep Regneniel away as long as they can. I must talk to you alone.'

'Alone?'

'I don't think you can trust your demon, Aliza. I don't think it really belongs to you.'

Her free hand went to the sapphire pendant. 'What are you talking about?'

'I know a great deal more now about your grandfather than I did the last time we spoke. And I know now that he isn't the sort of man who would give up something as valuable to him as a demon slave. I think that your jewel is a fake and that your grandfather still controls Regneniel.'

'What? Nonsense. I command Regneniel.'

'I doubt it. Your grandfather gave you the demon to make you believe in his power, his good will, and your own independence. All three were illusions. Besides being weak, he is an evil, self-centred man, and I can't imagine that you mean more to him than a dead leaf. All he cares about is the sorcery you can use on his behalf.'

Aliza looked up at him, the corners of her mouth turned down by her frown. 'Must we go into these foolish suppositions of yours again?'

'Yes, we must. He doesn't have your best interests at heart, Aliza, believe me. He never did.' He sank to one knee beside her. 'I'll tell you what I know, and then you can tell me if I'm not right.' Quickly he related the story that the lady Helaine had read in Everand's ear, and through it all Aliza's expression did not change, seemed rather to be

340

frozen upon her face, as if she were in some sort of trance. Even the part about her parents' fiery death did not move her. 'Don't you see,' Cray finished, 'that all he cared about was power, if not directly for himself, then through your mother or through you? He tried to enslave her. He has succeeded in enslaving you.'

In a remote voice, she said, 'I remember that night. I remember the flames.' Her eyes seemed unfocused, as if she were seeing the scene again in her mind, but as if it were something innocuous, an empty landscape, a cloudless sky. 'I dreamed of it for a long time afterwards, I remember – the burning cabin.' She shook her head and blinked and looked at Cray once more. 'No, it was an accident of sorcery. He told me so.'

'He lied. He's lied to you about a great many things.'

'Or you lie.' She leaned back in her chair, away from him, and folded her arms across her bosom. 'Who am I to believe – my own grandfather, or you, whoever you are?'

'I am your friend. You know that.'

'Do I? No, all I really know is that you want to turn me against him, for reasons that I don't understand.'

Cray stood abruptly. 'He killed your parents, and he intends to use you as a slave. Aren't those enough reasons?'

'If he did kill my parents . . .' Her mouth made a thin line.

'Don't tell me you think that's excusable. Your future as a sorcerer could not have been worth their lives. If you think it was, then their deaths are on *your* head as well as his.'

'No,' she said. 'It wasn't excusable. They had just as much right to live as I do. It was wrong for him to kill them. If he did.'

'You can ask Taranol,' said Cray. 'He heard the tale, too.'

'He heard what the Seer told him.'

341

He backed off a pace. 'You would rather believe that the Seer and I are lying, wouldn't you?'

Aliza's cool dark eyes narrowed. 'In my place, wouldn't you?'

Cray said, 'I would want to know the truth.'

'As do I.'

He turned away from her, clasping his hands behind his back. 'If I show you that you do not truly command the demon, will that convince you I'm not totally wrong?'

'And how will you show that?'

'Your grandfather doesn't like me, does he?'

'That's something of an understatement, I'd say.'

'He thinks I distract you from your studies. He doesn't like me to visit you. And he knew of those visits even though you didn't tell him about them.'

'Does that seem so strange to you? After all, we have a bond of blood, he and I.'

He turned back to her. 'Now I say nonsense, Aliza. If he were a great sorcerer, I might say yes, a bond of blood, and power, might enable him to spy on you himself. But he has no power, not by any standards I know. Regneniel does his spying for him. And I don't think Regneniel would allow me to stay here for any length of time unobserved. I think that nearly all the hours you and I have spent together have been watched, whether we knew it or not, whether here or in the Seer's cave. Only my mother's castle would have been beyond your icy spy, and she would have been willing to let it in if you had asked. But you didn't ask. Oh, how he must have gnashed his teeth over *those* hours!'

Aliza stroked her lower lip with one forefinger. 'He told me himself about this bond between us. He told me just the last time I saw him.'

'He lied, Aliza. One lie among many.'

She touched the sapphire. 'Very well, if you can prove to me that I don't command the demon, I'll give some thought to believing some of the other things you've said. I'll have to.'

Cray nodded. 'Then you must do two things when it returns with the wine – send it back to its home in Ice for a long vacation, and let Gildrum into your palace.'

Her frown was deep. 'No demon but Regneniel has ever been inside this building.'

He gripped her shoulder. 'Aliza, I'm trying to prove that Regneniel is the slave of your greatest enemy. Won't you let a friend help me do that?'

Her cool dark eyes looked up into his. 'Grandfather has always said that any demon who entered here while I am still an apprentice would have an easier time doing it later, even against my will.'

'That's true,' Cray said softly. 'And Regneniel is such a demon. Your grandfather can use it against you, Aliza, and you can't bar it from these walls. But Gildrum would never harm you, and he can't be enslaved and forced to it, either.'

'He would do it for your sake, though, wouldn't he?'

His fingers tightened on her shoulder. 'Do you think that I would ever wish to harm you? Do you think that I could allow you to visit my home, to share a meal with my own mother, if I wished you any harm?'

'I don't understand you, Cray Ormoru,' she whispered.

'I have not cultivated your friendship just to destroy you, Aliza. I could have done *that* during our visit to Air or Water. Please trust me now. What I do is for your sake.'

'I don't understand you,' she repeated, and then she just stared into his face, as if somehow she could read his motives there, until the demon Regneniel returned, a cask of Maretian wine clutched by its snake-like neck as by an arm.

'I apologize for the delay, my lady,' it said, 'but the other demons were somewhat confused by the route. They

343

have your wine, Cray Ormoru, waiting for you where you entered the palace.'

'Thank you,' said Cray, walking around the table to his own chair. There he made a show of resuming his interrupted meal.

'Regneniel,' said Aliza, 'pour us two fresh, hot cups of the herbal infusion.' When the demon had done so, she added, 'And invite Cray's friend Gildrum to join us here for dessert.'

Regneniel hesitated. 'Gildrum is a demon,' it said.

'I know that very well.'

'As your tutor, I must remind you that allowing demons that do not belong to you inside your palace is a dangerous practice.'

'You have reminded me. Now do as I command.'

'As you wish, my lady.'

Gildrum wore his man shape as he entered the room. At the doorway, he bowed to Aliza and then he took the chair that she indicated, a crystalline chair that she had just raised from the floor beside Cray's wooden one.

'Fruit?' she said.

With a smile, he took a pear and began to eat it.

She turned to Regneniel again. 'I have been thinking about all I have learned about demons these past months, Regneniel. I have been thinking that you have served me faithfully, and my grandfather before me, for a very long time, without any opportunity to live as you did when you were free. I believe I understand, a little at least, what sadness slavery must be to you, taking you away from the peace and quiet of your home in Ice, making demands of you when you really only want to be left alone. So I have decided to give you a vacation. I want you to go home and enjoy yourself for two months.'

The demon stood very still for a long moment, its tapering beak pointed at her, as if there were an eye on the end that could see her. 'My lady,' it said at last, 'your studies.'

'My studies go well, and I know what I have to do for almost the next year. I don't need your tutoring for now.'

'If not my tutoring, then my services. How will you live if I go away for two months?'

'Cray has promised me that his demon friends will bring me food, and he himself will teach me to cook.'

'But the laundry, the cleaning, the water . . .'

'They will be taken care of.'

'But I have always taken care of them, and I know best how they should be done.'

Aliza's expression became stern. 'Are you arguing with me, slave?'

Regneniel sank to the floor at her feet. 'My lady, your grandfather charged me to look after you, and when he finally gave me to you, that was still my purpose. I don't trust these other demons you speak of. *They* are not your slaves. Why should they serve you?'

'If they don't serve me, Regneniel, I'll call you soon enough, be assured of that. But I think everything will work out well. Now, I command you, go home and do whatever it is that free demons do for the next two months unless I call you sooner.'

The demon climbed to its feet. 'As you wish, my lady.' And, like a javelin thrown by some doughty warrior, it flew from the room.

Aliza watched Cray and Gildrum as they sat in silence at the table. Neither of them looked after the departing Regneniel. Cray quartered a pear and ate each slice with slow relish. Gildrum slouched in his chair, as if its crystalline surfaces were cushioned comfort. At last Aliza said, 'I thought you'd follow it, to make sure it really went away.'

'No need for that,' said Gildrum. 'I know it's no longer within these walls.'

Aliza looked to Cray with raised eyebrows. 'So you were wrong.'

Cray finished the last slice of pear. 'Wait,' he said. 'It's just gone to report your command to your grandfather, and to receive his instructions. It will return. In the meantime, why don't we show Gildrum about your palace, Aliza? I've told him of it, but words never could match the reality of something so marvellous.'

They spent an agreeable time wandering through both sides of the building, and Gildrum appeared to have no difficulty comprehending the mechanism of the connection between them, though he could not explain it to Cray's satisfaction. 'Perhaps only a demon could truly understand such a thing,' he said. 'Humans simply are not accustomed to living in more than one plane.' The other side of the palace was pleasantly warm now, not stifling as it had been in summer; beyond its walls, snowcaps were still visible on the surrounding mountains, snowcaps as sparkling with sunlight as the bare crystals that showed there in summertime, but covering a greater area. Between palace and mountains, the coarse quartz sand was clear of snow; for Gildrum's benefit, Aliza caused a patch of it to fountain upwards and form a slender column.

They returned to the Ice side of the palace at last, but when Aliza would have halted in the dining hall, Gildrum moved on, as if curious to see the kitchen, though he had already done so. Just inside the kitchen doorway, he halted. 'Come here, my lady,' he said.

Aliza and Cray joined him.

He pointed up at the ceiling, which was well above the reach of human arms. 'Regneniel.'

Cray and Aliza looked up. They saw the ceiling, its broad horizontal facet glowing, half concealing the room above.

'Where?' said Aliza.

'There's a thin sheet of transparent crystal overlying

the real material of that section,' replied Gildrum. 'That's Regneniel.'

'But Regneniel isn't transparent.'

'Why not?' said Cray.

'It's never been transparent.'

'You didn't know it could be a bird or a mouse, either.'

Aliza pursed her lips. Then she raised one hand to the sapphire. 'Regneniel, if that is you, come down here and assume your usual form.' When nothing happened, she turned to Cray. 'Well?'

He shrugged. 'If you're not its master, then it doesn't have to obey you, does it?'

Aliza looked to Gildrum. 'You're *sure*?'

He smiled. 'A demon knows a demon, my lady. Regneniel is as obvious to me as a man would be standing out on your plain of sand. But if you doubt, just invite Elrelet or Leemin in, and they'll point to the same place, I promise you.'

'Coached by you.'

'You aim your suspicions in the wrong direction, my lady,' said the fire demon.

'Regneniel must find itself in something of a dilemma here,' said Cray. 'Its true master has ordered it to keep watch on you. It knew, of course, that Gildrum could see through its disguise; it probably even warned your grandfather of that. But he couldn't let the two of us be here unobserved and probably doing twice the damage to your studies that I did alone. So here it is, recognized yet not daring to reveal itself because it is still masquerading as your slave, and if it is your slave it has just disobeyed you. A dilemma indeed. How can it obey your grandfather and you at the same time? It can't. The masquerade is over, Regneniel. We know you for what you are.' After a pause, during which no Regneniel revealed itself, he added, 'It must be hoping that you won't believe us.'

'We'll prove this one way or another,' said Aliza. 'Regneniel! Come here! Immediately!' She pointed peremptorily to a spot two paces in front of her feet.

For a moment yet, nothing happened, and then the ceiling facet that Gildrum had indicated peeled away from the rest of the ceiling and floated lightly to the floor, changing its shape and opacity along the way so that in a few heartbeats the familiar form of the demon stood before them. It sank to the floor before Aliza, laying its beak at her feet.

'Forgive me, my lady,' it said. 'You told me to go to my home in Ice, but this is my home in Ice, my only one. I have no other place but at your side.'

Aliza's pale face was hard as she looked down at the demon. 'And why did you not obey me when I commanded you to come down the first time?'

'My lady, I feared your displeasure.'

'But *how* did you disobey me, slave?'

The beak tipped up toward her. 'You neglected to say *when* I was to come down, and so I took the liberty of interpreting the command . . . liberally.'

Gildrum chuckled softly at that, and Aliza turned on him sharply. 'Why is that amusing?'

He bowed to her. 'I did the same, my lady, when I was a slave. A demon master must always be very careful of how he phrases his commands, especially those that the demon does not wish to carry out.'

'Then you're acknowledging that Regneniel *is* my slave.'

Gildrum shook his head. 'Only that it is *someone's* slave.'

To the ice demon, sternly, she said, 'Regneniel, I command you to go out of this palace, to go out of sight of this palace, and to stay that far off until I call you back. I command you to go now.'

'Please, my lady,' it said, 'don't send me away. My life is nothing away from you. My only contentment is by your side.'

She recoiled a pace. 'Do you beg to disobey me, slave?'

'My lady, have pity on me and let me stay.'

'She has no pity, Regneniel,' said Cray. 'You should know that.'

'Please don't make me go,' it whispered.

Aliza crossed her arms over her bosom. 'Are you disobeying me?'

'My lady, I am only asking you to reconsider.'

With a sidelong glance at Cray, she said, 'Regneniel, are you truly my slave?'

'Yours alone, my lady, yours faithful as long as you wear the stone.'

'Did you expect any other answer?' said Cray. 'It has been most carefully instructed.'

'Set it a task,' said Gildrum. 'Not just to leave, which I perceive it will postpone one way or another forever at this rate, but a concrete task. Test your control by giving it a command that Everand would never allow.'

'For example?' asked Aliza.

'For example, it can come and go as it will in Everand's castle; therefore, command it to bring you back his head, without his body attached.'

Aliza's dark eyes widened. 'That's a fine test but somewhat . . . final, don't you think?'

'Quite final. But you care nothing for your grandfather, he's seen to that. This is only just recompense for his crimes.'

'An excellent idea,' said Cray. 'And Gildrum, Elrelet, and Leemin shall go along, as far as they can, to see that Regneniel does not dawdle on the way.'

Aliza looked from Cray's face to Gildrum's and back again. Then she closed one hand about the sapphire and said, 'Yes, Regneniel, I command you to go to my grandfather, to kill him, and to bring back his head as proof. I command that this be done immediately.'

The creature seemed to be looking up at her with its eyeless head. Its beak opened and closed once before it finally spoke. 'My lady, I cannot penetrate the spell that surrounds his walls. No demon can.'

'Nonsense,' said Cray. 'You did it a thousand times when you were his slave. I don't doubt that you have a portal directly into his quarters.'

'That portal closed when he gave me to the lady Aliza!'

'And it can be reopened whenever you wish. Don't think you can lie to me about demon powers, Regneniel. I may not wear rings on my hands, but I know demons. Your portal into Taranol's castle is still there as well, but if you used it, there would be demons in plenty waiting to bat you aside. Fortunately, that is not a consideration in Everand's case. He has no other slaves to turn you away, nor any other powers that would keep you from doing your duty.'

'My lady,' said Regneniel, 'will you believe this mad human or me?'

Gildrum said, 'Cray knows demons.'

'His accomplice, my lady, not to be trusted any further than himself!'

'Enough of this!' cried Aliza. She pointed a finger at Regneniel. 'Not another word from you. Go to the demon world of Air this moment, and do not return until I call you. This moment!'

'And don't try to come back and hide in the palace,' said Cray, 'because Gildrum and I will be staying for a long, long visit, and we'll find you.'

'Go!'

The demon crawled backwards a short distance, its polished belly sliding upon the crystalline floor, its tiny arms flapping like stunted wings. It fetched up against the hearth, one narrow foot slipping in among the embers, raising a spray of grey ash to dust its pale marble flesh.

Then, slowly, it raised its beak and neck like a proud man facing insult, and it came erect stiffly on its spindly legs. 'As you wish, my lady.' In a sudden burst of motion, it leaped into the hearth, shot up the chimney, and was gone.

Aliza turned to Cray. 'Regneniel has never given me this kind of trouble before, but it is gone. You seem to have been . . . incorrect.'

Cray looked at Gildrum. 'Well?'

The fire demon leaned over the embers and peered up the flue. 'These chimneys all connect with each other and lead out to the human realm by way of the cradle room. Regneniel would seem to have taken that route. It certainly isn't in the palace any longer.'

'So you have to admit that you were wrong,' said Aliza.

Cray shook his head. 'I admit only that Regneniel is a very clever creature. Obviously, your grandfather forbade it to reveal that you are not its true master, and yet he also commanded it to stay here and spy on you even if you dismissed it. It tried very hard to do both, but that just wasn't possible as long as Gildrum and I were here. Now, I wager it's gone back to him for fresh instructions.'

'Or it's obeyed me,' said Aliza.

'Do you really believe that?'

Her cool dark eyes bored into his. 'I don't know what to believe.'

He touched her arm softly with just the tips of his fingers. 'You do care for your grandfather. You must or you wouldn't hope so hard that I'm wrong.'

She frowned. 'I don't want to believe without proof. I don't want to believe just because *you* say I must. Who are you, after all? Just a stranger. He is my blood.'

'He is,' said Cray, 'and that makes his actions all the more shameful.' His fingers slid gently up her arm to her shoulder and rested there with the least possible pressure.

'A little while ago you were willing to command his death because a stranger suggested it.'

'If Regneniel had gone then, I would have called it back immediately. Just beginning the journey would have been proof enough.'

'Perhaps. But the journey wasn't begun. And now you must ask yourself why. You must consider who lied to you – two strangers or the demon that has tended you most of your life. I know this is a hard choice for you. I wish it could be easier.'

She twisted away from him and covered her face with her hands. 'You have disrupted my life, Cray Ormoru. You have deluged me with sights and sounds and notions I never asked for and never needed. You have made me doubt everything that was certain in my life, even myself. And all in the name of a mirror that broke when it saw me. Oh, that mirror is well broken, may it never be remade! Friendship you call it, but I call it devastation. How little I suspected what would happen when I allowed you inside these walls!'

Cray went up behind her and, taking her shoulders between his two hands, laid his cheek against her smooth, dark hair. 'My dear Aliza, I only wanted what was best for you.'

Again, she pulled away, and now when she spun about to face him, her hands dropped down to her sides and her eyes blazed defiantly. 'Do you presume to know what is best for me? You and your demons and your Seers? Do you think that just because you have power over the things of the human realm, you know what *I* need? You, who presume to know so much about my grandfather, whom you've never even seen!'

Her vehemence took him aback. Where was the line, he wondered, between indignation and anger? She might not be able to cross it, but he had never seen her so close to it before. Her voice was like a tangible force, beating at him, and when he answered her, his own voice sounded strangely thin and uncertain in his ears. 'Yes, I did think I knew what you needed.' He hesitated. There was a thickness in his throat as he looked at her, as he tried, with his eyes, to bridge the gap that lay between them, a gap of mere air that now seemed to him like a bottomless chasm. He wanted to reach out to her, but he knew she would only back away. So well, he knew her, but beyond that? They had touched, but that had only been flesh to flesh, a brief meeting of exteriors. What she was, inside, behind those eyes, seemed still as distant from him as at that first moment he had seen her in the mirror. Were they friends? Or had they just passed near each other a few times? He did reach out, with a truncated gesture. Now he understood the mirror's message only too well, and pity rose in him for every person who had ever looked into that glittering surface. For himself. The words came hard to his lips. 'But . . . perhaps . . . I only really knew what *I* needed.'

She shook her head. 'I don't understand.'

His hand fell limp against his thigh, as if it were made of stone. His whole body felt heavy, strengthless, and Ice seemed to press close upon him, chilling him to the marrow. 'No, of course you don't. You can't.' He looked down at the crystalline floor. 'I didn't understand myself. I didn't want to understand. I must have denied it a thousand times. But now I see it clearly.'

'What?'

Very softly, he said, 'That I love you. That I love you more than I have ever loved anyone or anything in my whole life.'

'Love?' she said sharply.

He nodded. 'Everything I have done for you, to you, because of love. Oh, not at the beginning. I don't think so, anyway. At the beginning it was pity. I felt so sorry for you, shut away here without any human leavening for

353

your life. Who else was there to help you but myself? I thought of it as help, truly I did. I don't precisely know when pity turned to love. Perhaps it was over a goblet of wine. Or under the stars. Or perhaps it was only just a moment ago, when I realized how deeply I have distressed you. Forgive me, my lady. Forgive me.' He took a deep breath and felt a shudder pass through him. 'Perhaps . . . we would both have been better served if you had never let me into your palace at all.' With an effort, he straightened his back and raised his head. He met her eyes and saw their fire replaced by . . . puzzlement. He tried to smile, but his lips could only make a crooked grimace, and his own eyes were bleak as the winter he felt sweeping through him. 'It might be best if Gildrum and I left now. I'm sure you can explain to your grandfather that you've broken off your friendship with me; that will please him. You can return to your studies and be just as you were before.' His throat had so thickened that those final words were a mere whisper that would have been lost if the barest breeze had stirred the room. He wanted to turn away from her at that, to punctuate his statement, but he could not force himself to do so. He could only stand and look into her face with that farce of a smile on his lips.

'Wait,' she said, even though he had not moved a step. 'I didn't mean for you to go.'

'No?' he whispered.

She frowned and clasped her hands together tightly. 'It isn't that you haven't been interesting. Or educational.'

He made a stiff, awkward little bow. 'Thank you.'

'But you pushed me so hard, you demanded so much.' She shook her head sharply. 'But we can't undo the past. It's foolish to speak of what might have been or what should have been. No matter what happens now, I'll never be what I was before you came here. We have our friendship, for good or ill. I don't want to abandon it. Truly I don't, even if I can't ever completely understand you. And

I don't want to give up learning about the worlds beyond Ice. I just want there to be some compromise between us. Is that impossible?'

He tried to shrug, but the motion was nearly invisible. 'What would you suggest?'

'For now, for the near future, just simple talk, not of my grandfather, not of my soul, not of love. Just simple talk. Perhaps near the tapestry. Perhaps . . . over a goblet of wine?' Her eyes were wide, almost pleading as she looked into his face.

'Your grandfather won't like it,' he said.

'We won't speak of my grandfather.'

He felt his terrible smile begin to relax. 'Are you sure, Aliza? Are you absolutely sure?'

She pursed her lips for a moment, then said, 'You've made a place for yourself in my life, Cray Ormoru. I want you to continue to occupy it.'

He felt the stiffness drain out of him like a windy breath, and suddenly he became aware of a thousand aches, in his back, his legs, his neck, overstrained muscles making their protest known at last. 'Very well,' he said. 'I think I could relish a goblet of wine just now.'

He had scarcely passed through the doorway with Aliza when he remembered Gildrum and glanced back. He saw the fire demon still standing by the hearth, watching the embers as if they held some fascinating secret. 'Will you come along, Gildrum?'

The demon shook his head. 'I think I'll stay here and look for Regneniel to come back. I'll call you when it happens.'

Cray hesitated, looked sidelong at Aliza, then said, 'No, don't call. We'll discuss the matter later, at home.'

Gildrum shrugged. 'Then I'll prepare dinner. Regneniel left plenty of food.'

'If you like,' said Cray, and he followed Aliza from the room.

In the chamber where the tapestry hung, they spoke very little at first, both lavishing most of their attention on the wine, admiring its colour, inhaling its bouquet, sipping, but actually consuming very little of it. They sat at opposite ends of the couch, and when words did pass between them, they were mostly reminiscences of their experiences in the other demon worlds. Compromise was a barrier between them, and neither wished to be the first to test it.

As they talked of nothing much, Cray watched Aliza and thought of love. Now that he had admitted it, to her and to himself, he felt the terrible irony of it. He had denied that he loved her, but only he had been fooled by that denial. His mother, Sepwin, the Seer – all of them had known. He had thought to interpret the mirror in his own way, but the mirror was its own master, and gave only the simplest truth. What a perfect song this would make for some troubadour, he thought – the man in love, the woman incapable of returning that feeling, incapable even of understanding what it was. And how perfect was the pain that he felt in his chest as he wished to reach out and pull her into his arms, and dared not. Just simple talk, she said, and no mention of love.

Perhaps, he thought, she was better off this way, better off without a soul. Sepwin hadn't found it anyway; it was hidden more cleverly than he or Cray had hoped. Perhaps they would never find it, never be able to offer it to her. Perhaps she wouldn't accept it, even if they did. Who was to say that she was really not better off without love, without anger, without grief? Without pain. Cray looked long and long at her, and in the unnatural light of the palace, her flawless skin seemed to glisten, as if she, too, were made of some kind of crystal.

'Why do you stare at me so?' she said at last, shifting her posture on the couch as if her muscles were cramped.

He smiled. 'Haven't I always stared at you?'

'Not like this.'

'You are very beautiful,' he said. 'I've never realized quite how beautiful. Such beauty warrants staring.'

'I find the tapestry beautiful,' she said, gesturing toward it.

'It is, but I would rather spend my time here looking at you. I would like to stay here and be able to stare at you always.'

'I'm sure you would find it rather boring after a while.'

'I assure you, I have nothing better to do with my life.'

She shook her head. 'I can't imagine how it must feel to have no compulsion to study, to learn.'

'Someday you may understand it. Someday you may discover that sorcery is not the whole of life.'

She looked down into her goblet. 'Are you going to speak of love now?'

'There are other things besides love. The worlds are wide.'

She rolled her goblet between her palms. 'I am very young, Cray.'

'Yes.'

'I haven't your perspective.'

'I'm not old, Aliza, not by our standards. I'm really not much older than you are.'

'But you have experience with other people, with things beyond me.'

'That's not a difficult thing to have.'

'Grandfather always said I was . . . special.'

'And so you are,' Cray said.

'He always said I was the brightest, the cleverest, the best. That no other sorcerer would ever match me once I reached my full potential. He said I must work hard to achieve that potential.'

'An admirable goal,' said Cray.

She looked up at him. 'But if I am the best and the cleverest, why does my head spin at the thought of all the things you've shown me? Why do I want to go to the cradle room and clutch my stuffed toy instead of going back out to see more?'

He gazed at her sadly. 'I don't know what lies inside you, Aliza. I only know how it seems from here, at the other end of the couch, behind another pair of eyes. To these eyes, it seems that this palace and Ice are your refuge and your prison. I saw a leopard once, kept in a cage by a sorceress, well fed, with a golden collar. The sorceress died, and one of her demons took pity on the beast, and rather than leave it to starve in that cage, opened the cage door. Forest lay beyond that door, where deer and smaller game were plentiful. But the leopard would not go out. It knew nothing of hunting; it only knew how to lick the hand that gave it food. It died of hunger at last, and its bones are still there, in the rusted cage, for any passerby to see. The golden collar, of course, was stolen by one of them some years since.'

Aliza touched the sapphire with one finger. 'Is this my golden collar?'

'If you see it so.'

She held the glittering gem up for a moment, and then she loosed it, sighing. 'But I am still young. There is time yet.'

'Time enough for everything, if you wish, my lady.'

'Time enough to travel again someday. Not soon, but . . . someday?'

'If you wish it.'

'And you'll show me more of the human realm, when I'm ready?'

He smiled at her. 'You have only to ask, and I am completely at your service.'

She tilted her head to one side, as if to see him better from that fresh angle. 'And you won't . . . kill yourself or put out your eyes or go on some long, pointless quest after you leave here today?'

358

His smile broadened, and then he laughed softly. 'I don't think I was planning on any of those things.'

'In the songs, rejected lovers did one or another of them. They jumped off cliffs and suchlike.'

He shook his head slowly. 'Perhaps I shouldn't have let you listen to so many of those songs. You are too innocent to consider the possibility that a troubadour may embellish reality for the sake of drama. And for the sake of his purse. A tale of unrequited love and suicide earns a prettier payment than one of unrequited love and a return to ordinary existence. Such is the nature of the audience.'

She leaned farther back on the couch. 'Good. I wouldn't want your mother thinking I was responsible for your death.'

He laughed again. 'Dear Aliza, by asking me to remain your friend, you have given me life. If I had left, thinking that I would never see you again, then truly some part of me would have died. But here we are, and I'll ask no more than to spend whatever time you will with you.'

She fingered the rim of her goblet as she gazed down into the translucent red of the Maretian wine. 'Is it that you think, someday, I may come to love you?'

'We weren't going to speak of love, Aliza.'

'No, but . . . the sound of your voice when you said . . . you loved me. I will never forget that. What is it like, to love?'

'I don't think it's something you can understand with your mind, Aliza. You understand it with your soul.'

She raised her eyes to his. 'Then I'll never know, will I? Unless he gives it back.'

The silence that followed, a silence in which they drank more wine and avoided each other's eyes, was broken by a voice calling Aliza's name. It was a resonant voice, echoing, as if it were reaching them through a long tunnel.

Aliza sprang to her feet, her goblet falling from her fingers, spilling its contents across the couch. 'Grandfather!'

'I await you, Aliza,' cried the voice.

A moment later Gildrum appeared in the doorway that led to the inner rooms. 'There's a human outside, in Ice.'

'Come to me, Aliza!' said the voice.

Lifting her velvet skirt above her knees, she ran. Cray and Gildrum followed her through the unfurnished portions of the palace, to one of the outer chambers, not the one Cray knew well, but the newest one, which was still scarcely larger than the cradle room. Beyond its transparent wall, in a fracture held open by an ice demon, floated a tall, pale-bearded man. He was heavily swathed against the chill of Ice, in hooded cloak and boots; one gloved hand showed, clutching the cloak together at his throat.

'Come in, Grandfather,' said Aliza, and the wall that separated her from him melted away like frost touched by a breath of flame.

The chill of Ice entered the room like a fist, and though Aliza did not seem to notice it, Cray shivered, gooseflesh rising all over his body. Gildrum stepped close to him then, radiating warmth even though he wore a human guise.

Everand eased back against the body of the demon, a blunt cylinder like a plug in the fracture. 'No,' he said. 'We will talk like this. I am too displeased to enter your home.'

Aliza lowered her eyes. 'I regret that you are displeased, Grandfather.'

'Do you? Yet I see this fellow here, this Cray Ormoru, even though I asked you not to associate with him again. And a fire demon, too, inside the very walls of your palace. Did you think these things wouldn't displease me? You waste your time travelling about with them when you should be studying. You listen to their attempts to turn you against me – me, your teacher, your master, your own flesh and blood, to whom you owe everything. Did you think I knew nothing of these matters? Foolish child, you have precious few secrets from me.'

360

Slowly, Aliza lifted her gaze to his. 'What do you wish of me, Grandfather?' she said quietly.

'Obedience, child,' he replied. 'Nothing more or less. You have paid too much attention to this *friend* of yours. You have forced me to reveal that which I would have preferred not to – that Regneniel is mine. Yes, it's true. You are far too young and inexperienced to have total control over such a powerful creature. I allowed you to think it belonged to you because I believed that a tangible reward would spur you to study harder than ever. But now I see that your studies have become unimportant to you, and you no longer deserve that illusion. Now, I think, it will be better that you know my eye is at your shoulder every moment Regneniel is with you. And it shall always be with you. Always.'

'You misjudge me, Grandfather,' said Aliza. 'My studies have not become unimportant.'

'Disobedient child, I judge you precisely. I set you a course of study to make you the equal of any sorcerer living, and now this man has become more important to you than my teaching.' He pointed at Cray with his free hand. 'He is your enemy. He wants you to be weak. You must send him away, never to return.'

Aliza's lips tightened to a thin, pale line. 'I have never given over studying, Grandfather, and I shall not in future. You may test me if you wish, and you will not be disappointed. But I shall not give up my friendship with this man. Do not ask it of me.'

'I do not ask it,' Everand said in a strained voice. 'I command it.'

Aliza shook her head. 'I cannot obey that command.'

'His influence is injurious to your development as a sorceress, child. For your own sake, you must obey me.'

Firmly, she said, 'For my own sake, Grandfather, I must not. I believe that he has a great deal to offer me in knowledge and experience. But I promise you that I won't neglect the studies you set me. I have the capacity for both, in proper proportion. I know it.'

'You know it?' Everand shouted, and his whole body shook with the force of his voice, so that he would have begun to tumble if the fracture had not been so small. He stopped his motion by thrusting out both arms, and he stood there, braced within the fracture, his cloak billowing about him as if it had some life of its own. 'What do you know?' he shouted. 'How to disobey me? How to betray me! I took your soul so that you'd never betray me, but you've done it anyway. Now listen to me, Aliza my apprentice – I have your soul. Yes, I know this *friend* of yours has been looking for it most diligently, but it's hidden where he and his minions will never find it. And while I have it, I have *you*. I hoped this day would never come, believe me. I hoped that you and I could reach some satisfactory arrangement, when you were mature. I'm not greedy, Aliza. I won't need you to serve me every moment of every day. But you *will* serve me, now and always, and you will serve me with sorcery as excellent as any that exists. They laugh at me now, child, but they won't laugh when you are mature. Now get rid of this interloper, permanently, and get back to your studies, or I will use your own soul against you.'

Aliza stared at him with her cool dark eyes. 'Grandfather, are you threatening me?'

'My child,' he said in a hoarse whisper, 'you don't dream of the extent to which I am threatening you.'

'I am not afraid of your threats,' she replied. 'You yourself have seen to that.'

He showed his teeth in a grimace that was half smile, half snarl. 'Then let us move a bit beyond mere threat.' His right hand made a twisting gesture, sharp as a blow.

Aliza gasped, her eyes widening, one hand clutching at her belly.

'More?' said Everand.

She doubled up and fell to one knee. Her breath came hoarsely, ragged. Her free hand formed a fist, opened, closed spasmodically, on empty air.

Cray dropped to her side and put his arms around her. To Everand he said, 'Stop! Stop this!'

'Very well,' said Everand.

Aliza went limp in Cray's arms, her head lolling against his chest. She panted as if she had just sprinted to safety ahead of ravening wolves. Then she pushed Cray away firmly and staggered to her feet. She stood, swaying a little, her back straight and her head high. 'You would do that to me?' she said, her voice shaking. 'Your own flesh and blood, Grandfather?'

'I will do it again if I must,' he replied. 'If you do not obey me.'

'I am your apprentice, Grandfather, and I do owe you a great debt. But repayment does not mean that I must be your slave for ever.'

'Ah, but it does, child. That is exactly what it means.'

The expression on her face was stark, and she was paler than Cray had ever seen her. 'I am not afraid of pain, Grandfather. You may strike me down as often as you wish, but you will not win my obedience.'

'No? Taste this, then!' His hand moved again, and Aliza clutched her belly with clawed fingers and pressed her other fist against her mouth. She did not fall this time, and she made no sound. She seemed, in fact, to be holding her breath.

'Gildrum!' cried Cray, and the demon turned to flame and flashed toward Everand. At the open end of the fracture, where the wall of the palace had formerly been, there was a crackle as from a blazing log, and a flash of blinding blue-white light, and the ball of fire that was Gildrum rebounded from an invisible barrier. A sharp, sour smell pervaded the small chamber.

'Don't think you can touch me, any of you,' said

Everand. 'They laugh at me, but I have my defences.' He looked to Aliza. 'Have you had enough, my child? Or must the pain go on and on?'

Through clenched teeth Aliza said, 'You took my soul, but you gave me will, Grandfather. Your mistake.'

His cheeks grew red with his anger. 'You are too like your mother. I killed her, and I can kill you! Think on that, ungrateful wretch!'

'Kill me, then,' she gasped. 'I have no fear of death.'

He screamed incoherently, like an animal howling in anguish. He raised his two gloved fists. 'Not death then!' he shouted. 'Not death, but pain! Till you grovel before me and beg for release!'

Aliza closed her eyes. 'You'll get nothing from me while the pain goes on,' she whispered, swaying like a young tree in a strong breeze. Beads of sweat had broken out on her forehead and cheeks. 'And nothing when the pain is gone. Nothing.'

Cray gripped her arm and found it rigid, every muscle tensed. 'Aliza,' he said, 'give in. Even slavery is better than this.'

She shook her head sharply. 'I would have given him a thousand gifts, freely, out of gratitude. I would have built him a castle. I would have brought him anything he wanted. But of my own free will. Not this way. Not for ever. No!'

'It won't be for ever,' said Cray. 'Nothing is for ever.'

'Not for another moment,' replied Aliza. 'He is wrong to demand slavery of me. I have as much right to freedom as he has, and I will not be coerced!'

Cray looked to Everand. 'You must stop! She can't think clearly through the pain. Give her a chance to be rational!'

Everand glared at Cray, his mouth twisted, his brow creased with hate. 'If I could have killed you, I would have done it long since. This is your doing. You have turned her away from me.' He made a slashing motion with one hand. 'Very well – think!'

Cray felt the muscles of Aliza's arm relax and begin to quiver. He stepped between her and Everand, gripping both her elbows. 'Listen to me,' he said. 'There's no need to suffer this any further. Do as he says for now. Surely you have years of study left before you're ready to serve him properly. When the time comes, you may not find it so odious.'

She opened her eyes, and they were glazed and staring. 'I thought he wanted the best for me, for my own sake,' she murmured. 'And now I find that it was all for him. For him.' She closed her eyes again. 'You don't understand me any better than I do you, Cray Ormoru.'

'You once thought apprenticeship was very much like slavery.'

'And you once said they were different because slavery lasted so much longer. I haven't forgotten that. Have you?'

'He won't live for ever, Aliza. No one does.'

'Would you say that to a demon friend enslaved?'

'Of course.'

She opened her eyes slowly and gazed over his shoulder at Everand. 'But then, a demon has no choice. The ring compels. My soul can only punish. I prefer punishment to slavery.'

'Trust me,' Cray whispered.

'I will not be his slave. Not for one heartbeat.'

'You think to find her soul,' said Everand. 'You think to give it back to her and set her free of me. Fool!'

Cray half turned to him. 'Any feeling human being would try it, Everand. And only a monster would do this to his own flesh and blood.'

Everand shook a fist at Cray. 'If I am a monster, you and your kind made me into one. I was born a duke's son, but a sorcerer stole that from me and gave me nothing in

365

return. Nothing! I became a sorcerer because I had the will to do it. No one helped me. They laughed instead. But they shall pay for that laughter. She will be my arm, and through her I shall be greater than any of them. She shall rule Ice, and every ice demon shall do her bidding, rings or no rings. They shall all be her slaves! And through her, *my* slaves!'

'No,' said Aliza. 'I want no slaves.' She tore the sapphire from her throat, the gold chain breaking against the nape of her neck, and threw it at her grandfather's feet. 'There shall be no slaves. Not human, not demon. Never again shall I command a thinking creature to do my bidding. You are wrong to desire it.'

Everand pointed at Cray. 'This, too, is your doing.'

'No,' said Aliza. 'It is *your* doing. This day you have taught me everything I know of slavery. It is as ugly as you are, Grandfather. As ugly as your vengeful soul. I should thank you now for taking mine away, for I don't wish to understand your need for vengeance. Nor to share it.'

'Don't think of vengeance, child,' said Everand. 'Think only of pain.'

'Do your worst. You will not be pleased by the results.'

'Aliza, listen to me,' said Cray.

'Yes, Aliza, listen to him,' said Everand. 'He is sure his friend Feldar Sepwin will find the soul and free you. His friend Feldar Sepwin, who will never find the soul and also never leave my castle. Convince her, Cray Ormoru. Compensate for your evil influence upon my granddaughter. Convince her, and perhaps I will allow your friend to live.'

'I have no friend in your castle,' said Cray.

'Oh, no need to lie to me. Regneniel told me long ago. An inquisitive fellow, this Sepwin. I may chain him somewhere damp and unpleasant, just to keep him from bothering me. Yes. I may even feed him occasionally, while the rats gnaw his toes. Convince her, Cray Ormoru.'

'Everand . . .'

'He hasn't her will, I'm sure. He is just an ordinary human. He will beg to be my slave. But I don't need him as a slave, unless a prisoner can be considered so. A tortured prisoner.'

Cray looked into her eyes. 'Aliza.'

She would have stepped back from him then, but he held her tight between his hands. She seemed to have lost all her strength. The pain, he thought; it had drained her.

'Don't ask this of me, Cray,' she said.

'He is my friend, Aliza.'

'He should never have gone to the castle.'

'He did it for you, Aliza.'

'I told you not to search for the soul. I told you I didn't want it.'

'He did it so this could never happen. He did it to spare you pain.'

'Well, he failed dismally at that, didn't he?'

Cray looked at Everand over his shoulder. 'I'll go away. I'll never see Aliza again, I promise you. But let Sepwin go.'

Everand shook his head. 'Only she can save him.'

'Aliza,' Cray whispered, 'Feldar is a thinking creature. Would you give him over to this terrible form of slavery? Aliza, I ask you for the sake of our friendship, to give in to your grandfather.'

Her face was pale and bleak as she stared at him. 'For the sake of our friendship?'

'And for your own sake as well. Why fight so hard and suffer such torment? Slavery need not be so agonizing. Ask Gildrum. He knows.'

She bowed her head. 'You would rather I be a slave than your friend Feldar, is that it?'

'I would rather see neither of you suffer.'

She was silent for a time, and when she looked up again she looked past Cray, not at her grandfather but outwards, to the vastness of Ice beyond her walls. 'Very well, Grandfather,' she said, and her voice sounded tired, beaten. 'What are your terms?'

Loudly, he replied, 'Send this Cray Ormoru and his minions away, never to return. Take up your studies as before you met him. Regneniel shall serve you as always. And Sepwin shall not be harmed.'

Cray said, 'He shall be freed.'

'No, you won't find me that foolish, Cray Ormoru. Sepwin shall remain in my service, just to make certain my granddaughter does not change her mind.'

'I accept your terms,' Aliza said tonelessly. 'Now go away and leave me alone. All of you.'

'I will see that this man and this fire demon leave before I go,' said Everand.

'Farewell, Cray,' she said, still not looking at him. 'You'll find a door open for you in the usual place.'

'Aliza,' he said, his grip softening on her arms. He tilted his head to intercept her gaze, but her eyes would not focus on him. 'Aliza.' He could not resist kissing her pale cheek, and to his lips the skin was cold as the breeze that drifted in from Ice. She did not push him away now. She did not move. He felt as though she had already excised him from her existence. 'This is all my fault,' he whispered to her. 'Can you ever forgive me, Aliza?'

'We can't undo the past,' she said. 'We can only go on from here. I will remember you. Always.'

He let her go then, and turned from her. 'Come, Gildrum. We have a long journey home.' Without glancing back, he left the small chamber and entered the one where a doorway waited. Gildrum followed, and together they joined Leemin and Elrelet to move out into Ice. There, Cray was silent. And not once as they pressed through the dark transparency of the demon world did he look back, not when they were still near enough to Aliza's palace for him to see it, not when it had fallen so far behind that even

368

its glow had vanished. Sometime in that journey Leemin said, 'He's gone through a portal now, out of Ice,' and Cray only nodded and forged ahead.

He had entered Air before he spoke. They were gathered about him, floating without weight in the vast empty blue, the many-spiculed snowflake, the living flame, the cloud. Ice lay behind them, its snow-dusted surface glittering like a vast frozen lake on a midwinter morning.

'It doesn't end here, friends,' he said to them. 'On the contrary, it has barely begun.'

The low rumble of thunder caught Sepwin's attention. There had been rain several times since he had come to Everand's castle, rain that made the servants scurry for shelter and confine themselves to indoor tasks, rain that made a place by the kitchen hearth seem cosy, welcome. Yet when it rained, Sepwin always went to a door to watch the dark clouds blow and the lightning shiver. He went now, as the first droplets began to fall, threw aside his rag and bucket, and leaned against the doorjamb to watch the sky.

This time he saw what he had always looked for – the special cloud, not obvious among the others unless one expected it. A shape like a bear, compact and rotund, paws extended as if to bat at an enemy. Its outlines wavered in the rising wind, as if it had fur shaggy as a horse's mane, that could ripple and flutter. Sepwin stepped out into the rain, heedless of the drops that spattered upon him, his face uptilted. One of the bear's paws waved at him. He did not wait another heartbeat.

Up to the banquette he ran, the storm wind ripping at his clothing. Even as he went, the sky darkened more than ever, till the wan light of the day was banished and the false night of the storm brooded over the castle. He had a hammer with him. He used it upon the crenellated wall closest to the stairway, battering the stonework to knock some

369

fragments loose. By touch alone, he gathered them up in the darkness. He wore a sash about his waist, a double-layered length of thick canvas, open at one end and sewn shut at the other, like a long, narrow sack. On previous nights he had acquired bits and pieces from the other walls of the castle, a handful of stone shards and crumbled mortar from every span, and he had stuffed them into the sash. Now he added these final fragments and knotted the open end securely. The lumpy belt was tight about his middle, and a large chunk near the front prodded his ribs at every move. He climbed into the nearest embrasure, bracing himself there against the torrential wind. The sky was pitch black. Behind and below him, even the kitchen fire had blown out; the only light in the immediate world of the castle was the blue-white glow from Everand's keep and an occasional flare of sheet lightning that showed the clouds crowding close above the ramparts. Sepwin knew that one cloud crowded closer than all the rest. Into the wailing wind he shouted, 'Elrelet!' and he leaped into the darkness beyond the wall.

To any of Everand's other human servants, that leap would have seemed impossible. They knew they were sealed inside the castle by its encompassing spell, a wall more solid than stone and as transparent as air. They knew that they passed through that invisible wall only at Everand's pleasure.

And so it was with Sepwin. He did not pass through the spell at all. He took it with him. He leaped, still surrounded by Everand's magically reinforced castle walls, still completely surrounded by the fragments of stone inside the sash about his waist. He leaped, and a small piece of the spell broke away from the parent body with him, like a snowflake blown from a field of fallen snow by some high wind.

He leaped, and the descent through the stormy blackness seemed to last an eternity.

He landed feet first on a bed of yielding softness – wool, smelling only slightly damp, as if it had only been out in the rain a few moments. He thrashed, sinking deeper into it, until it suddenly pulled apart beneath him and he tumbled another arm's length or two to the muddy ground.

'Are you all right?' someone asked him. The voice was close to his ear but still muffled by the howling wind. Cray's voice. In the dark, Sepwin could see no one, and then sheet lightning illuminated his world for an instant, illuminated the castle wall that loomed on one side, the forest in the distance on the other, and Cray standing before him, beckoning sharply. There was no wool anywhere.

'I'm not hurt,' Sepwin said.

'Come then, let's get away from here.'

Sepwin lost Cray to the darkness once more but crept in the direction he had indicated, his hands low, waving, in search of boulders. He found one, skirted it, and finally ran into a tree.

'Here, Feldar,' came Cray's voice, and a faint light showed ahead, like a firefly. Sepwin moved toward it, toward Cray's voice, into the shelter of the trees. After a time the firefly brightened, and he knew it was Gildrum, guiding him to safety. The rain faded away behind him, and the sound of the wind softened with distance.

'At last,' said Cray, as wan daylight began to filter through the leaves. 'Feldar, you're limping.'

'One of the trees forgot to move aside,' he said. He smiled hesitantly. 'I'm out. I'm really out.'

'What, you doubted me? Oh Feldar!'

'I thought Elrelet was going to catch me when I leaped.'

Cray shook his head. 'Elrelet decided that was impossible because of the spell, so we borrowed a storehouse of wool for just a few moments.'

'It surprised me, I have to admit that.' Sepwin touched the sash at his waist with both hands, running his palms along it. 'The spell . . . It feels very strange, Cray. Much stronger than when I was in the castle itself. I feel . . . as if I'm sealed up in a very small room. A very close room.' His smile faded. 'I feel as though I'm not a Seer any more. All my perceptions seem to bounce back at me. This would be a terrible way to spend the rest of my life. You're sure . . . ?'

'Quite sure,' Cray said, and he took out his knife, an ordinary knife made by an ordinary blacksmith. Holding it delicately with two fingers, he slipped it between Sepwin's sash and his jerkin. He did not touch either piece of clothing with his own flesh; he could not, for they were within the spell, and he was outside. 'A small piece of a spell is weak, as a small piece of a great wall is weak. Both can be smashed by a strong man, even though the structures they came from would be proof against him. I have power over this woven sash, and as I tear it, so will the piece of the spell that lies inside it be torn.' He wrenched the knife suddenly, and the sash was cut through. It fell away from Sepwin's body, dribbling crumbled stone and mortar.

Sepwin staggered, as if the spell had been holding him up, and Cray caught him, and they both laughed suddenly as they realized what that contact meant. Then they embraced, and Gildrum, as a living flame, surrounded and embraced them both with its cool brilliance.

'Now I suggest we seek some safer place to discuss our future plans,' said the demon. 'Everand will know who freed Feldar, and he will be angry.'

'Spinweb?' said Sepwin.

'No,' said Cray. 'Regneniel surely knows where Spinweb lies. This is my quarrel; there's no need to involve my mother. We'll go to my castle.'

Gildrum swept them away.

The storm had dissipated quickly, leaving the bare earth of the courtyard a sodden mire. Everand ignored the mud that sucked at his heels as he paced back and forth, unconsciously tracing the dimensions of his workroom within that larger space. He raged, with waving arms and reddened face and veins standing out upon his forehead, and his servants – the crippled, the deformed, the terribly scarred – cowered before him in the muck.

'How could you not notice when he left?' he shouted. 'How could you not notice where he went? *How* he went? He broke my spell and *you* saw *nothing*!' He kicked mud at them savagely, then kicked the nearest man in the shoulder and slammed the back of his fist into the nearest woman's face. She fell sideways, sobbing, and a frightened babble burst out among the others, mixed of pleas for mercy and denials of guilt. 'You serve me ill, every one of you!' Everand screamed. 'I should kill the lot of you!' And they drew together, clutching at each other and shaking their heads.

Everand raised his fists to the sky and called for his demon.

The human servants of the castle had never seen a demon before, and when Regneniel arrived, floating downwards as a great snowflake, they fell silent, staring open-mouthed, staring still as it took on its two-legged bird-like form and bowed to their master.

'Carry me to my workroom, demon,' said Everand, and Regneniel wound its long, flexible neck about his waist and launched itself and him upwards, toward the highest window of the keep. Behind them, the human servants gaped.

'Sepwin is gone,' Everand said as soon as his feet touched the stone floor of the workroom, 'and I know where the blame lies. I command you to kill him!'

'Sepwin, my lord?' murmured Regneniel.

'No. Cray Ormoru!'

The demon bowed very low. 'My lord . . . that may not be an easy task. He has several demon companions, and I am only one, poor and weak.'

'I want no arguments from you, creature. Poor and weak you may be, but you are clever. Find a way!'

'My lord, you do ask too much . . .'

'I said find a way! Immediately!'

With a final bow, Regneniel leaped out the window into the sky.

Cray's wooden chair fitted him as if it had been moulded to his body. He sat in the great hall of his living castle, a broad, vaulting chamber that would have pleased any lord of the ordinary realm. Sepwin was beside him, and Gildrum in human form, Elrelet, and Leemin completed the circle.

'I'm not surprised you couldn't find the soul,' Cray was saying. 'Now that I've met the man, I'm convinced that it's better hidden than that. He'd never chance a stronger sorcerer stealing it from him. Taranol, for example.'

'Then where does that leave us?' asked Sepwin.

'With an enemy. He hates me, that's certain, and he probably doesn't feel much different toward you. We can't assume he won't try to harm one or the other of us. Especially you, Feldar, for you've no sorcery to protect you. And however weak his personal powers may be, he does command a demon. I think it would be best if we didn't leave these walls without bodyguards.'

'That's easy enough,' said Elrelet. 'I know any number of demons willing to protect you and any friend of yours, Cray.'

'But the soul,' said Sepwin.

Cray sighed. 'We'll have to force him to tell us where it is, somehow.'

'But how?'

'I'm not the only person capable of thought in this room. Don't any of you have suggestions?'

'I have a suggestion,' said Gildrum. 'The only possible suggestion.'

Cray frowned.

'You'll have to kill him, Cray. If you try to force him, somehow, to tell you where the soul is, he only has to torture her a bit to make you leave him alone. I'm sure he knows that. I'm sure he understands quite well why you want her soul. And how worthless that soul would be to you if she were dead.'

Cray pushed himself out of his chair and turned his back on the others. 'You're speaking of a battle royal, Gildrum. He is a sorcerer, and he has his defences. The spell about his walls, the demon, and his personal powers, whatever they may be. It would not be a simple matter. And he has human servants with him inside those walls – they would be endangered.'

'I can't deny that,' said Gildrum. 'But perhaps protecting them would sap his strength. That would be to your advantage.'

'Hah,' muttered Sepwin. 'He wouldn't protect them any more than you'd protect a stone. He'd line them up in front of him to catch the first blows.'

'Then they'd quickly be out of your way,' said Gildrum.

Cray looked at the demon over his shoulder. 'Sometimes I have to remind myself that you were born in Fire and not of any human mother, Gildrum. Just at this moment, it's hard for me to reconcile the man who loves my mother with the demon who would so blithely kill a dozen innocent people.'

Gildrum shrugged. 'I love your mother, and I love you, and I want what she and you want. I am willing to kill for that, yes. I think you'd find a goodly number of human men who would do the same for those they love.'

'I love Aliza,' said Cray. 'And I would kill *him* for her sake, if I had to. But how many innocent lives is my love worth? How can I sweep them aside as if they were fallen leaves? They are people.' He looked down at the rough-grained wooden floor. 'No, I can't do it. We'll have to wait until he leaves his castle. Feldar, have you any notion of when that might be?'

Sepwin shook his head. 'I wasn't precisely his confidant. I understood from the others, though, that he does not leave very often.'

'So – there will have to be a watch on the castle at all times, and we must be ready to strike at a moment's notice.' Cray passed a hand across his forehead. 'We'll need an army of demons for all of this. A standing army.'

'It can be arranged,' said Elrelet, 'though some will grumble a bit.'

'If I were Everand,' said Gildrum, 'I wouldn't come out at all until my sorceress slave was ready to shield me from all possible attack. He knows he's made an enemy in you, Cray; he'd be a fool to think you'd given up. Waiting may be a terrible mistake.'

'You'd attack now.'

'I would throw everything I could muster at that castle. Trees. Rocks. Wild animals. Bewilder him. Attack in so many different ways at once that he can't guess what to do first.'

'And his servants?'

'Hope that they know where to hide until the battle is over. It's a big castle.'

'Ah, Gildrum, you tear my heart!'

'You've never even seen these people.'

'Does that make them less real?' Cray turned to face him. 'If my mother were among them, you wouldn't speak this way.'

Gildrum rose from his chair and crossed the small space that separated him from Cray. He put his hands on Cray's shoulders and looked into his eyes. 'The decision is yours, Cray. I will abide by it.'

Cray's face was bleak. 'I feel helpless. Help me.'

'You know,' said Sepwin, 'he does let them out some-times. Some of them. To hunt. We could carry them off one by one as they leave.'

Cray's expression brightened. 'Yes, we could.'

'Of course, he'd probably become suspicious after a while.'

'And he'd set Regneniel to fetch game instead,' said Gildrum. Suddenly, he cocked his head to one side and frowned, as if he had heard some unusual sound, or as if someone had called to him from far away. He let go of Cray's shoulders and turned slowly away from him. He raised one arm and pointed across the room, toward a wall that was blank save for a few barren twiglets. 'There's a demon outside. It's calling your name.'

'A demon?' said Cray. 'Who?'

Gildrum seemed to listen for a moment, and then he said, 'Regneniel.'

With Gildrum in the lead, the whole group ascended to the ramparts. There, only a few paces beyond the parapet, floated the ice demon, a spiculed white mass that seemed to Cray now more like a morning star than a snowflake. Boldly, Cray stepped forward and leaned into an embrasure that in summer would have been arched over by leaves. Now the sheltering branches were barren and showed their interlacing structure clearly, like some gnarly bramble.

'Have you some message from your master?' Cray asked the demon.

'My master has commanded me to kill you,' replied the creature.

Cray stared at it for a moment, then broke into a harsh laugh. 'I hope you don't expect me to come out there and allow you to do it.'

'I am not a fool. I understand full well how difficult it is to kill a sorcerer. Unfortunately, my master understands it less well. And I have not been able to convince him.'

377

'What do you want of me, then? Do you want me to tell him? I don't think he looks forward with relish to any future conversations with me.'

'It is hard being the sole demon slave of a sorcerer,' said Regneniel. 'One must do everything. One must report everything, even those things which will surely displease one's master. One must, for example, report that eleven spiders are now living in a certain palace in Ice, and that though the lady Aliza has discovered three of them, she has as yet made no effort to kill them.'

Cray folded his arms across his chest. 'Perhaps a certain ice demon should go through the palace and kill them, as it did once before.'

'Perhaps. But the disobedience cannot be erased.'

'She has not made any attempt to reach me.'

'She has not made any attempt to do anything,' said Regneniel. 'She sits in the cradle room and says nothing to her tutor when it happens by.'

'Perhaps she needs a little more time to accustom herself to slavery.'

'Ah, yes, we all need time.' And the demon laughed, a sound like a human laugh, but with the brittle overtones of crackling ice. 'Do you know how long I have been a slave, Cray Ormoru?'

'No.'

'With one master and another, more than three centuries. Nearly all my life.'

'You are young, then.'

'And I've known very little freedom. My first master was quite old, and I thought myself lucky in him, for he seemed likely to die soon and thus free me. He did, but I was conjured again almost immediately by Taranol, and then after two centuries sold to Everand. Slavery stretches out before me farther than I can see. Must I say that I would not have it so?'

'I've never met a slave yet who delighted in slavery,' said Cray.

'Exactly,' replied the demon. 'And so perhaps you and I can strike a bargain.'

Cray leaned his shoulder against one side of the embrasure. 'A bargain?'

The icy morning star floated closer, as close as it could come to the barrier about the castle. 'I am not a fool, Cray Ormoru. I didn't bother to ask in the demon worlds where this castle lay. I knew no one would tell me. They protect you there. I followed Leemin instead. I haven't told my master where you are, but I will be forced to do so eventually. Just as I will be forced to tell him that you are the sorcerer who sets demons eternally free. He won't like that. He knows how to conjure, but he also knows that there are no demons available for conjuring. What do you think he will do when he finds out you are responsible for that?'

'You're wrong, Regneniel.'

'Am I? I think not. You were the fool, Cray Ormoru, to take my lady Aliza into the other demon worlds, where the demons wait upon you as if you were master of them all. I was there. I saw.'

'You misinterpreted what you saw, Regneniel. Through Gildrum I have many friends in the demon worlds, nothing more.'

'You lie, Cray Ormoru, and I am not misled by your lie. Long ago, my master commanded me to report the slightest hint I might encounter of that sorcerer's identity. I have that hint now . . . *if* I care to recognize it. If I exposed you to him, I do not doubt that he would tell as many other sorcerers as possible. Surely most of them resent your depletion of the available demon population. Surely, as a group, they would want to do something about it. And then, after you were dead, my lord would be able to conjure demons, eventually, and he would have no further use for the lady Aliza. He might set her free then. Or he might kill her. He takes a certain pleasure in killing, occasionally.'

Cray set a hand flat upon the side of the embrasure. He could feel the sweat on his palm there, cold and clammy against the wintry wood. 'You are making a terrible mistake, Regneniel.'

Again the laugh, and within it the sound of icicles cracking away from high branches. 'We can strike a bargain, we two. I want my freedom, and you want the lady Aliza's. We can both gain our ends if you will kill Everand.'

'Kill him?' said Cray, as if the very thought amazed him. 'But I haven't the power for that.'

'Gather yourself a demon army and smash him!' cried Regneniel. 'I know you can do it. Call them all! They owe you their freedom; surely they can do this small favour for you!'

Cray shook his head. 'Please, Regneniel, this is absurd –'

'Then you force me to report my discovery to him right now.'

'No, you mustn't!'

Gildrum leaped from the parapet, transforming to flame in midair and enveloping Regneniel. Elrelet followed, and ice and fire and cloud tumbled wildly a spear's length from the wall.

'This will not stop me!' shouted Regneniel. 'They can't follow me to Ice!'

Leemin floated to Cray's shoulder, a snowflake, too, but small as a pear. 'Shall I?' it said.

'Stop! Wait!' shouted Cray.

The midair fight slowed, but the demons did not separate.

'How much can you help me, Regneniel?' Cray asked.

'I can ignore the hint of your identity, unless he questions me about it directly; after all, I *might* have misinterpreted what I saw. And . . . once I am free of his will, I can tell you the location of a certain object in which you seem quite interested.'

'You know where Aliza's soul is?'

'Of course. I put it there.'

Cray nodded slowly. 'Indeed, being the sole slave of a sorcerer means many things.' He clasped his hands behind his back. 'Perhaps we can make a bargain after all. You are the only one besides Everand who can enter or leave the castle at will.'

'True.'

'You must promise me that you will do everything in your power to safeguard the lives of his human servants.'

'But how? I can't bring them out of the castle with me unless he wills it. And there will be no safe place inside the walls once the attack begins.'

'You can bring them out,' said Cray, and he swiftly explained the method by which Sepwin had left the castle. 'Scarves, bags, anything that will hold the fragments will do, as long as it makes a continuous loop about the body. Do this immediately, and we will attack as soon as they have gone.'

'They are very much afraid of me,' Regneniel said doubtfully.

'Then frighten them into doing it.'

'And in return for all that I can do for you, what is your side of the bargain?'

'I will free you for ever.'

'I trust you, Cray Ormoru. And if you enslave me instead, I will not keep your secret, not though every demon in our realm tries to stop me.'

'Trust me,' said Cray, 'and I will trust you.'

'Very well,' said the demon. 'Gather your army.'

Chapter 12

Everand sat silent in his workroom. There were slender bars of copper lying on the table beside him, waiting to be drawn into wire, but he did not touch them. Anger was too thick in him for such demanding work. He wanted to destroy, not to create, and he knew he would ruin anything he set his hand to this day.

He got up at last and went to the window. Below him, the yard was deserted. That was something of a pity, he thought, for in his present mood he felt as though he could derive some benefit from sending a lightning bolt after someone. Anyone. Yes, he felt very much like burning someone to a crisp and leaving only a charred skeleton and a steaming spot on the barren earth. He wished he had Cray Ormoru for a target.

The sound of a footstep made him turn around. It was Yltra, with the supper tray. The scarred man set it down on the workbench.

'Is there anything else I can get you, my lord?' he asked.

Everand glared at him, tempted, then decided he didn't want the smell of burnt flesh in his workroom. 'No, nothing else.' He came back to the table and looked at the tray. Venison stew – someone had been lucky at his hunting. Everand pulled the knife from his belt and skewered a piece, his sour mood faintly pierced by the expectation of the meal. The cooks always prepared venison well.

Almost, he was taken unawares. He saw the movement only from the corner of his eye. Yet that was enough to make him turn as Yltra struck, and so the thrust that was aimed at his back glanced off his arm, slicing fabric and laying open the skin. Then the man was upon him, bearing him to the hard floor with the full weight of his body. Everand's breath was knocked away by the fall, and for a moment his only thought was to struggle, to hold that knife at bay. Then, as air filled his lungs, fury filled his heart. Sparks fountained from his hands, and Yltra, whose arms he gripped, stiffened, his mouth agape in a silent scream, his eyes too wide. The smell of searing flesh filled the room.

Thrusting the dead man aside, Everand staggered to his feet, his anger unassuaged. Savagely, he kicked the body, and then he grasped it by both legs and dragged it to the window. There, he tipped it over the sill and pushed it out, leaning out himself to watch it tumble to the courtyard below.

'This fool tried to harm me!' he shouted. 'Come out and get him, you monsters, and learn a lesson from his death!'

There was no one in the courtyard, and no one appeared at the sound of his voice.

'Come out, you scum!' he screamed.

No one.

He turned from the window and, heedless of the blood that welled from his arm, raced down the keep stairs to the yard, to the servants' quarters.

The doors were all open. No one was there. The cooking fire was still lit, and a large pot hung over it, with venison stew bubbling gently inside. A long-handled spoon protruded from the pot, but there was no one to lift it out and taste. No one.

Everand went out to the yard once more, scanned the walls, saw no movement, heard no sound but those he made himself. 'Show yourselves to me, you monsters!' he shouted.

His voice echoed back at him, as if he were alone

in the bottom of a canyon. And then he realized that though winter had been waning for some time, the air was very cold. His breath, which had been invisible only moments before, was now a frosty cloud, and his woollen garments seemed thin and draughty. He looked up at the late afternoon sky. It was clear, almost cloudless, and the sun shone brightly. But it seemed to give no warmth.

He hesitated only another moment, and then he returned to the keep for his cloak.

'Go to her, Feldar,' Cray said. 'Leemin and Gildrum will take you. Tell her what we're doing here. Tell her I'll be with her as soon as it's over. And if he starts to hurt her . . . tell her it won't last long.'

'I hope you're right.'

'He is weak, Feldar. And ignorant. For all the years he has spent studying those books, he still knows precious little of sorcery, or he would never have tried to kill me. He thinks he is proof against all attack behind those spell-encased walls. He doesn't dream that no sorcerer is ever entirely safe from a determined enemy.'

Sepwin embraced Cray. 'Good luck, my dear friend.' And he was wafted away by the two demons.

With Elrelet at his elbow, Cray inspected the work of his spiders. He and they were in the forest that surrounded Everand's castle, some distance behind the trees that edged the barren area, hidden by their boles and shadows from any eyes that might look out from the ramparts. The servants had all run away as soon as Cray freed them from their pieces of the spell; now there were no human beings here but Cray and Everand. And soon they would both be isolated from the rest of the world by the gossamer netting that the spiders wove from tree to tree to tree, all around the castle.

As they wove, Cray laid his spell, encompassing silken

threads and bare but living branches in a barrier proof against demons and sorcery unless he willed otherwise. And like the barriers that all sorcerers spun about their castles, it extended upwards into the sky, an invisible dome through which there was no passage.

Elrelet, Gildrum, and Leemin had spread the word quickly – the nameless sorcerer was calling for help from Water, Air, and Ice, and all who felt the least sliver of gratitude could reckon this day's work as payment for the boon he had unselfishly given them. Some stayed away, secure in their freedom and aloof. But many others gave over their pastimes and flocked to the rendezvous. Elrelet left Cray periodically, to see to their organization. A few fire demons had come, just to watch, and Elrelet directed them to stay well back. Its fellow air demons it asked to stand aside till they should be called. The water demons, who came in a group led by Murnai, it sent for water. The ice demons it bade stay ready.

The magical barrier was finished.

At Cray's signal, the water demons floated past the barrier, a stream of gigantic bubbles, each one bloated to a dozen times its usual size by its cargo of water. Close behind them came the ice demons, glittering like stars come down from the distant sky. The whole group swooped low upon the barren earth just outside the castle walls, and when the water demons spewed out their liquid burden, the ice demons breathed a bitter wind upon it, freezing it into great sheets. Like impossibly rigid draperies, the ice stood in a ring about Everand's residence, and spiders scurried to spin on both sides of that ring, to reinforce the wall of ice with sorcerous webwork stronger than steel. The demons returned again and again, building the draperies higher and higher, and gradually tilting them inwards. But well before they had finished their icy dome, Cray, floating above the trees on the couch that was Elrelet's body, saw that Everand had climbed to the roof of his keep and raised his arms to the sky.

High above the castle, clouds were gathering.

'Come to me! Come to me!' Everand shouted, and from beyond the horizon in every direction, clouds raced to obey his will. They were small, but they piled up quickly, darkening against the blue of the sky, blotting out the low sun with their bulk, dulling the gleam of the icy wall with their shade, till it looked less like ice than like some sleekly polished metal. The clouds were still arriving when he bade them give birth to lightning.

The first bolt cracked a section of the wall, but the demons simply poured more water on that place, to reinforce it. Further strokes did other damage – chipping at the upper edge of the ice, even blasting a hole through it just in front of the gate. But then the cold wind that had made Everand wrap himself in furs and woollens intensified, began to howl as it became a gale that shredded his thunderclouds and blew them in every direction. He made a violent gesture, intended to sweep them back together, but he could not overcome that wind. Air demons, he realized. He could see their pale, compact forms moving among the real clouds, circling, circling, but never moving very far from the sky above the castle. Very soon, the only clouds he could see were demons, a dome of demons keeping his own lightning-bearing servants away.

Ice, water, and air demons.

'Who are you?' he shouted, scanning the wall of ice for some human architect, for he could see none in the sky. 'Who are you? What do you want?'

There was no answer, and amid all the demon activity around him, he could not make out any human form.

'Regneniel!' he said, for the third or fourth time since he had seen the icy wall a-building. The demon had not answered his summons. 'Leave off what you're doing and

386

come to me this instant!' he screamed, and he raised the fist that bore the ring and shook it, as if that could compel its obedience.

The wall rose, and it gleamed again with the clearing of the sky. Only now the sun was hidden behind its translucent bulk, dimmed by the many-flawed ice into a smear of pale light sinking toward the horizon. Below it, the forest was a grey blur.

'Regneniel!' Everand shouted.

And this time the demon appeared, a star of ice blinking into existence in midair, just above the keep.

'What took you so long?' screamed the sorcerer.

Regneniel alighted beside him and assumed its usual form. 'My lord, it was not easy evading these other demons. They are everywhere.'

'Who is this attacking?' demanded Everand.

'My lord,' said the demon, bowing, 'you don't need me to tell you that, I'm sure.'

'Then it is Cray Ormoru?'

'Yes, my lord.'

Everand's mouth tightened, and he struck one fist into the other palm. 'I told you to kill him!'

'He is too well guarded, my lord.'

Everand shot one glance past his slave, to the wall of ice, then glared at the demon once more. 'So I see. He seems to have a great many demons working on his behalf for one who commands none. You told me he had no rings; how could you be so wrong, Regneniel?'

'He has none, my lord.'

'Then where did all these demons come from?'

'My lord . . . they came at his request.'

'His request?'

'Yes, my lord.'

Everand stared at his slave, his upraised hands working stiffly, clenching and unclenching spasmodically. The rage within him was a force that threatened to burst his brain, and yet beneath that rage a new sensation was beginning to grow – fear. He clamped down on it with all his strength. 'Regneniel,' he said, and in his voice there was now just the slightest tremor. 'Regneniel, he is the one. No sorcerer has this many demons. They serve him now in return for their freedom. Regneniel, you must kill him!'

The ice demon sank to the stones at Everand's feet. 'My lord, you do not know how impossible that is.'

'Then you must tell the other sorcerers. They will band together. They will kill him for me! Go, Regneniel. Tell Taranol first – he'll spread the word. Go quickly!'

'Forgive me, my lord, but I cannot.'

'Cannot?' shouted Everand. 'What's this you say?' He raised a hand high, as if to strike his slave, but then his eye was caught by the wall once more, and he only remained standing there, with one upraised arm and his face very pale.

'Forgive me, my lord,' said the demon, 'but I cannot even leave your castle now. The spell that lies beyond that wall of ice will permit neither human nor demon through it without Cray Ormoru's permission.'

'Then go through Ice, of course!'

The demon shook its blind, beaked head in an eerily human fashion. 'A dozen creatures of Ice crowd about my portal, preventing me from passing through it. My lord, I am imprisoned here with you.'

'I am not imprisoned!' cried Everand. 'I am in my own home, safe behind my own walls. No one can pass through my barrier, not human or demon. I am safe!'

'You are imprisoned, my lord. Unless Cray Ormoru chooses to let you out.'

The wall stood above the castle ramparts now and arched well inward. Everand took a deep breath. 'I may not be able to get out,' he said, 'but neither can Cray Ormoru get in.'

'My lord,' said Regneniel, 'that is quite true.'

Everand braced his hands against the low stone parapet of the keep roof and, at the top of his voice, shouted, 'Cray Ormoru, hear me!' He waited a few heartbeats, and when there was no answer, he turned to Regneniel. 'Go up there and tell them I want to speak to him. But don't pass beyond my barrier; I don't want them to take you from me.'

'Yes, my lord,' said the demon, and transforming to its star shape, it floated up almost to the rim of the ice wall. Shortly, a puff of cloud bearing a human being sailed into view and hovered in midair higher than the ice.

'You called me,' shouted Cray, his voice thin with distance.

'I want to talk to you!' replied Everand. 'Come closer so we needn't shout.'

'My apologies for the inconvenience to your throat, but this is as close as I'll come. What do you want?'

'Why are you doing this?' asked Everand.

'I am protecting myself from an enemy.'

'I am not your enemy.'

'No? Well, you can prove that.'

'How?'

'By giving Aliza back her soul.'

Everand stared up at him till the muscles of his neck ached with the effort of holding his head at that angle. 'So that's it,' he said at last. 'You have not given over coming between my granddaughter and me.'

'That's it,' said Cray.

No longer could he keep the rage bottled up inside him. The icy wall, the loss of his human servants, the figure of Cray Ormoru floating contemptuously above his head – they all conspired to break him open. He flung both hands up, and ten spheres of blue fire and a shower of sparks erupted from his fingertips and cascaded upwards like a topsy-turvy waterfall. Each sphere bore death in its heart, a crisping, charring death that would leave nothing but ash behind if it struck man or beast. The cascade reached the level of the dome and then, as if it had struck some barrier, though none was visible in that place, it rebounded and sprayed back toward Everand. None of it reached him.

'I see what you mean by my not being your enemy,' shouted Cray.

Everand sent a second wave of blue fire toward him, but this one was no more successful than the first.

'Did you think that I would expose myself to your power, Everand?' shouted Cray. 'I'm not such a fool!'

'There is another who *is* exposed to my power!' screamed Everand. 'Shall I send her pain, Cray Ormoru? Shall I send her death? You know I can do it! Take your minions and your spells and go, or I will, I swear it!'

'Too late, Everand. Already you are completely sealed in by sorcery, if not quite by ice, and the barrier is proof against all your powers. As long as it stands, you can't harm her. Tell me where her soul is and surrender your demon to me, and I will dissolve the spell. Otherwise you will stay inside your walls for ever, without food or water, and without any use from your demon slave.'

'Is this true, Regneniel?' demanded Everand. 'Is his barrier proof against my mastery of her soul?'

Regneniel hesitated, floating just beneath the icy dome that continued to grow while Cray and Everand spoke. Now there was just a circular gap left at the zenith, perhaps a dozen paces across, with a patch of sky showing beyond, and Cray.

'Is this true, Regneniel?' repeated Everand, his voice pitched higher than before, almost shrill.

'No, my lord,' replied the demon. 'It is not true. This barrier will not stop you if you wish to command the soul, for such commands go directly through Ice, not through the human realm at all.'

'You see!' shouted Everand. 'I can hurt her. And I will, if you don't stop immediately!'

The gap had been closing swiftly, but at a signal from

Cray that closure came to a halt, leaving a space as wide as the span of a man's arms, a round frame for Cray's floating form. He looked down at Everand. 'Very well. I have stopped.'

'Now take it all away,' Everand shouted, waving peremptorily. 'Ice, spell, and all. *And* all those demons.'

'And if I do . . . ?'

'I'll leave her be. But if you don't . . . she'll survive this day, perhaps, but she'll wish to die every moment of it!'

'I'll consider your offer,' said Cray.

'Don't consider very long, Cray Ormoru. I have very little patience just now!'

'I'll let you know my decision shortly.'

'*Very* shortly!'

Cray disappeared from the gap, and through the translucent ice, Everand could see his form as a dark blur, moving into the sky, dwindling till it was gone.

Then the wind began.

There had been a stiff breeze since the wall had begun to rise, a stiff, cold breeze that turned his breath to frost and pulled shivers from his body in spite of fur and woollen wrappings. But it had been nothing compared to this. This was the gale that his clouds had felt when the air demons scattered them. Beyond the gap in the dome, and dimly through the dome itself, he could see demons churning together in a vast, dark cyclonic storm.

'You'll consider it, will you?' Everand shouted. 'Liar! You'd free me, wouldn't you? You'd turn me to a statue of ice with your demons! No, no. You're wrong about that!' He abandoned the roof of the keep and raced down the stone stairway to the empty courtyard. There, in the midst of that broad open space, with the icy dome all around, he invoked his most powerful defence.

Copper. Copper bracelets on his arms, copper necklaces at his throat, copper anklets, a copper band about his brow. He spoke to the copper that ornamented his body,

391

and through it he spoke to the copper in his walls. Copper wire, all of it drawn laboriously by his hands, obedient to his will, lined his castle. Now he called to it with all the strength of his being, and it drew power from him and began to grow warm. All around the perimeter of the castle, where copper strands reinforced the mortar that human servants had laid upon the stone, where copper outlined jagged crenellations, window slits, and gate, the metal grew hot. Upon the ramparts, frost on the stones melted and turned to vapour with that heat, and mortar long set began to dry excessively, to crack, to crumble. Everand called and called again, and the copper obeyed, until it began to glow dully, lines of fire upon the battlements. Then the dull glow brightened to orange, to yellow. To white.

The ice began to melt.

Everand could not see the first daylight break through the dome from where he stood. But he did hear the crackle of flames as the wooden gate of his castle caught fire from its copper-clad hinges. And when the gate had burned away, the charred fragments falling inward, there was a hole in the ice beyond, large enough for a man to pass through.

'You'll rue this day, Cray Ormoru!' he cried exultantly. 'And she will pay for your deed!' In his pride and fury, he sent a bolt of pure hate toward Aliza's soul, commanding it to kill her. Slowly.

'He is too much for us,' reported Berith, the young ice demon that had helped with the making of the Mirror of Heart's Desire. 'We can't keep the dome frozen against all that heat. It's patchy already, and I can't guarantee that it will hold together much longer.'

'Keep working at it,' said Cray.

'We need more ice demons,' said Elrelet.

'This was all that would come,' said Berith. 'Of the many that were asked.'

'Ask again,' said Cray. 'They owe me their freedom, and this must be the repayment of that debt.'

'I'll try, but we'll need more than a few. Is there time?'

'There has to be time,' said Cray.

In the depths of Ice, Sepwin, Gildrum, and Leemin beat upon Aliza's crystalline walls and called her name over and over again. Gildrum even rang the bell that had so shivered through the whole body of Ice, and Leemin did not complain but merely redoubled its pounding with a hammer made of its own substance.

Aliza did not answer.

Inside, in the heart of her castle, the cradle room, Aliza sat on the crystalline floor, her knees drawn up to her chin, the old stuffed animal clutched under one arm. She had heard the pounding and the calling. She had tried to answer, tried to open a doorway for her visitors, but she could not. Both exits from the cradle room now led to milky-walled stairways, and both stairways were sealed at the top with mirrored panels. She could not open them. She could not make the smallest hole in any of the cradle room's walls. She was locked in.

There was a spider locked in with her, a tiny mite, brown with white stripes. It had woven its web between the legs of her rocking horse. Aliza knew it was Cray's spider. Touching the web, she called to him, called for eyes and ears outside the room, knowing that he must have something important to tell her or his friends would not be pounding so heavily on her walls. She touched the web, but it remained simply a web, with a spider sitting at its edge, waiting. Just as Aliza herself was waiting, locked in the cradle room, waiting for she knew not what.

'I hear you! Gildrum! Feldar Sepwin!' she shouted. And she knew that they could not hear her.

*   *   *

'You must journey to Ice,' said Berith. 'Only you can convince it. It won't listen to me.'

'Who?' asked Cray.

'The Old One. The eldest of all ice demons. Its master died recently, and it has the power to help you, but it won't listen to a child like me.'

'Very well,' said Cray. 'Quickly.'

Berith changed places at the dome with the ice demon whose portal lay closest to the Old One's residence, and in a short time Cray and it were there, with a fire demon for light and Arvad for warmth. To Cray's eyes the place was no residence at all, just a crack in the body of Ice, without furnishings or ornamentation, without distinction from any other fracture. Its whole extent was taken up by the body of the Old One, the largest ice demon Cray had ever seen, five times the height of a man and bigger around than the bole of an ancient oak.

'My lord demon,' said Cray, bowing awkwardly as he braced himself with both arms and legs in the narrow fracture opened by his ice demon escort. 'I am Cray Ormoru, he who sets demons eternally free, and word has come to me that you are between masters at the moment and, therefore, eligible for my services. If you would allow me, I offer them to you.'

The Old One's voice was as deep as distant thunder, and its words were not easy to make out. 'I have often heard of your existence,' it said. 'But I have never believed. These young demons are selfish, lying creatures, seeking new slaves for their masters, betraying their own kind.'

'My lord demon,' said Cray. 'I wear no rings, nor will I ever wear them. I have freed a thousand and more demons in my life, and I will not stop till there are no more who desire freedom. You are free now, but you could be enslaved at any moment. I can prevent that.'

'You could enslave me now,' rumbled the demon.

'My lord,' Cray's icy escort said in a small and timid

voice, though it was not a very young creature, as demons counted age. 'The human speaks the truth. He freed me twelve years ago, and I have never had to answer a summons since.'

The other two demons murmured their agreement.

'I could crush you, sorcerer, where you stand,' said the Old One. 'Nothing of your power could stop me. I am the Old One of Ice, and it bends to my will.'

'You could crush me,' said Cray. 'I am at your mercy. Yet my offer remains, and if you doubt me, I can show you a vast number of demons beyond these three who will swear that what I say is true.'

'Where are these demons?'

'If you will come with me to the human realm, you will find them all gathered together in one place, giving me aid for a brief afternoon.'

'Giving you aid? And yet you say you command no demons.'

'They give me aid in gratitude for their freedom,' said Cray. 'But they are equally free to refuse it.'

'Payment,' said the Old One.

'A small payment.'

'And what would be the price of *my* freedom, assuming you would actually give it to a creature as powerful as I?'

'Your help in the same endeavour, my lord. A few moments of your time in exchange for a lifetime of independence.'

'It is true, my lord,' said Cray's icy escort. 'I have been helping, but we younger ice demons are not adequate to the task. Your power would make all the difference.'

The Old One shifted its huge body slightly within the confines of its home, and Cray felt the substance of Ice shiver all around him. 'I do not like human beings,' the Old One rumbled. 'I have been enslaved too many times for that. And lately you creatures have been moving through our Ice, making terrible noises and disturbing the brief

395

freedom I know now. I would not deal with one of you by choice. Yet I have not much life left to me, and I would not spend it as a slave. Bring a few more demons to me, and let them assure me of your good faith, and I shall consider the matter.'

'My lord,' said Cray, 'they are engaged in a matter of the highest importance to me, and I cannot ask them to leave it to come here. If you will accompany me, you can question any or all of them to your satisfaction. But, my lord, please hurry, for I need your help this very moment, and if you delay much longer, I will have to withdraw my offer of freedom. And believe me, I have no wish to do so.'

'So I must decide now, must I?'

'My lord, I am pressed. You must decide now.'

The Old One moved again, and this time the shifting of its huge body was an earthquake in Ice. Cray was tossed about his small space like a rag in a high wind, in spite of his bracing arms and legs. His icy escort groaned.

'Do I receive my freedom first?' asked the Old One.

'There is no time, my lord,' said Cray. 'You must help me first.'

'As I thought,' said the demon. 'Very well, I will speak to these other demons. Lead me.'

Water and ice demons circled the dome, over and over again, pouring, freezing, yet they could barely keep pace with the heat of the copper. No sooner would they repair one gap in the dome than another would melt through, and the whole structure was showing signs of weakness, threatening to collapse in spite of the reinforcing spiderwebs.

'You see how much we need you, my lord,' Cray said to the Old One as they floated well out of the way of the hurrying demons. The Old One had assumed a starry shape, but larger than any other demon, a bristling hill in the sky. The sun, which was beginning to set, glittered redly from its spicules, and these in turn were reflected in the curve of the dome. 'The heat of the copper is too strong for these demons,' said Cray, 'even though some of them are powerful indeed.'

'The only heat too great for me is the heat of Fire itself,' said the Old One. 'He has no fire demons, this Everand?'

'None.'

'Then let the water demons pour, and the dome shall not give way before mere copper. And mark you, Cray Ormoru.' It breathed softly at him, and he felt his face go numb with that chill. 'Mark you, I believe these demons, but if you withhold my freedom later, for whatever reason, you will not sleep easy for the rest of your life. I have power in Ice, and the demons you have already set free will become your enemies because of my wrath.'

'My lord, you will be free, I swear it.'

'Come, demons!' rumbled the Old One. 'We kill a mortal this day!'

Everand had never known such cold. He could not bundle himself sufficiently against it; only the coils of copper wire he wore about his person kept him from freezing, and even so, the air that sang in his nostrils was sharp and bitter as ice water. The dome was all but repaired, and though his copper glowed white-hot, it could not melt the freshly made ice. White-hot the copper was, and then, under his continued urging, hotter still, till it softened and began to run, dripping down the castle walls like porridge and pooling on the ground, useless except to make the soil sizzle and the tortured stone crack and pop.

And the wind had intensified, buffeting him like a mailed fist, frigid and shrieking. He could scarcely walk against it. Above the hole at the top of the dome, he could have seen the demons still circling in a wild vortex, had he looked up. He did not, though, for lifting his chin from his chest let a freezing draught inside his cloak. The cold stung his eyes and his throat, but he knew he could stand it. And in a few moments, when he had reached the keep and his workshop, he would wind more wire about himself, a mask for his face, mittens for his hands that were now stuffed into his sleeves, good copper wire that would keep him warm and comfortable against all that Cray could muster. He could survive the cold; Cray was mistaken if he thought Everand the sorcerer could be frozen into submission. Or frozen to death. But right now it took all the strength he had just to keep moving, just to stand upright against that terrible, ripping wind.

He staggered toward the keep, and his whole body seemed to agonize at that effort. Above him, the sky was darkening, and not simply because the dome was thicker now; the sun was sinking. He felt that this had been an exceedingly long day, a sapping day, and as the keep drew erratically nearer, he found himself thinking that all he really wanted to do was lie down and go to sleep. It wasn't the cold, he knew. Aside from his nose and cheeks, he was warm enough, without any numbness of the extremities. He was just very tired. And a little dizzy. Fortunately, the wind had begun to abate. Yes, it was definitely dying away, and he moved more easily, though his route to the door of the keep seemed just as erratic as before. The dizziness. He needed rest. But more, he realized, against the background of his spinning head, he needed to go back to old Verdrinar's books and find some proper way of striking back at his enemy. Killing Aliza was well and good, but it wasn't true revenge. True revenge was a direct blow at the enemy. Verdrinar had been very powerful. Everand had barely penetrated the surface of his powers. The books, yes. Revenge for the cold, the terrible windborne cold.

He gained the door of the keep, though not without some groping for the handle. He entered and, beside the stairway that led up to his workshop, he fell to his knees, his hands scrabbling at the stones of the floor. He managed to lift one, exposing a pair of iron rings linked together by a massive lock; the stone had been hollowed to fit over them without rocking. He closed his fingers over the lock, and their flesh froze fast to the bitter metal. Looking down at them, in anger, in wonder, he suddenly realized that his chest was drenched in steaming redness.

Then he pitched forward into unconsciousness.

Regneniel called to the demons that whirled above the gap in the dome, the air demons that by their cyclonic motion had drawn all the air out of that sealed space, leaving nothing to sustain Everand's life. 'You can stop now. He's dead.'

They did not stop, but three of their number left the demon storm and dived through the gap to test Everand's barrier. They found it vanished and, diving deeper still, led by Regneniel, they found his lifeless body.

Cray opened the dome to the sky and air and descended with Elrelet to see for himself. What he saw was a gaunt old man, blood still leaking from his nose and ears, frozen into his pale beard, frozen upon the cold stone and the cold metal beneath him.

Cray pushed the body aside with his foot, but it would not roll far, for the hands were frozen in place. 'What's this?' he asked Regneniel, pointing to the iron rings.

'His secret place. The lock opened only to his hand, and no one else was ever allowed inside, not even his demon. I saw him enter once, though. The room is small and full of books.'

'A secret place,' repeated Cray. He bent to examine the lock. He was wearing gloves, and so the bitter metal could not trap him. 'We'll ask a fire demon to melt this off.'

'You needn't bother,' said Regneniel. 'A spell seals the vault now. No demon can open it.'

'But Everand is dead,' said Cray. 'His spells have died with him.'

'He was very jealous of his books, Cray Ormoru. He would not even let Aliza read them unless he was standing by her side. Would such a person let other sorcerers take them from the ruins left by his death? No, it was his very death that set the spell. It is a powerful one, I grant you. But I tried to teach him many powerful spells in our years together, and this one, at least, he seems to have learned thoroughly.'

'If you taught it, then you can breach it,' said Cray.

'No more than you could uncook an egg.'

'Regneniel is right, Cray,' said Elrelet. 'I can feel the strength of this spell. It's proof against us. Do you really need those books?'

'I wasn't thinking of the books,' said Cray.

'Her soul is not there,' said Regneniel. 'It never was.'

'Then it is in her own palace, isn't it?'

'You've guessed.'

'It was the only other reasonable place.'

'It lies in the cradle room,' said Regneniel. 'Come, I'll show you right now, and then you can complete your side of the bargain.'

Regneniel's portal in Ice opened a short distance outside Aliza's walls. As soon as they emerged, the demon's body spreading a fracture wide to accommodate the human, Cray heard the racket that Sepwin and his companions were making – shouting and hammering and ringing that piercing bell over and over again. He could not see them.

'Stop!' shouted Regneniel, moving swiftly in a jagged path to join them, nudging Cray along as if he were a dust ball before a broom. Cray was glad enough for the speed, though, for he had left Elrelet behind to thank the other demons, and without its protection

400

he began to shiver almost immediately in the terrible chill of Ice.

Sepwin turned as they approached, recognized Cray through the intervening Ice, and waved; his voice was muffled till Regneniel's opening merged with that of Leemin, but it was audible. 'She won't answer, Cray. We've done everything we could think of to catch her attention, but she just won't answer.'

As the spaces prised open by Leemin and Regneniel became one, Cray felt a flood of warmth, Gildrum's radiant heat, and as if he had approached a hearth, he put his hands out to it and rubbed them vigorously. He was about to suggest that he call out himself, but Regneniel cut him short.

'She can't answer you. I sealed her into the cradle room before you started building your dome. I knew your barrier would never stop his commands to her soul – they travelled directly through Ice, invisibly, and no demon could grapple with them to keep them from their goal.'

'But how can you be sure that your seal was adequate?' said Cray.

'The palace obeys me,' said Regneniel. 'Its soul may be Aliza's, but its flesh is my own, my offspring. The seal was more than adequate. And now it is gone.'

'Then she is all right?'

'Yes. He would have killed her, you know. He did give the order. I knew he might, and I couldn't allow it, just in case losing her might cause you to change your mind about our bargain.'

'I wouldn't have changed my mind,' said Cray. 'But . . . I didn't want to think about what might be happening to her while he lived. The dome took so long, so very long.' He was leaning against the transparent wall now, as if that pressure could help push it in, and he gripped Sepwin's arm tightly. 'It's time to resolve this matter of the soul now, my friend. Regneniel?'

401

The wall dissolved abruptly, and Cray half fell, half stumbled through the gap, pulling Sepwin along behind him. They were halfway across the big, empty chamber when he realized that something was strange about it. Something had happened.

He halted, still clutching his friend's arm. He had expected the demons to be close behind him. But they weren't. Nor could he see them waiting at the opening Regneniel had made, for it was gone, and in its place was opaque crystal, as white and gleaming as marble. And all around, every visible exterior facet of the palace had also been replaced, in a matter of heartbeats, by the same opaque whiteness.

'Regneniel?' he shouted.

There was no answer.

He looked at Sepwin. 'Something is wrong. These walls should be transparent.' He strode back to the place where they had entered. 'Regneniel?' He rapped on the panel with his knuckles, then pounded with both fists. 'Regneniel! What trick is this? Open!'

Beside him, Sepwin touched the blank whiteness with both hands, sweeping his palms across it, feeling of its smoothness. 'There's a spell on these walls, Cray, to keep people out.'

'Of course there is, but I've never seen it make the walls turn white before.'

'Well, it's Aliza's palace – she'll be able to make an exit for us.'

Cray gave over his pounding. 'Yes, of course. Let's go to her. She must be wondering why she's been locked into one small room.' Then he ran, and Sepwin could scarcely keep up with him as they passed through room after strange and wonderful faceted room.

They saw Aliza in the dining hall, and Cray ran to her and seized her in his arms and whirled her once around, laughing. 'I was so afraid for you, my dearest!'

She let him hold her as she said, 'I was locked into the cradle room. I heard them calling, but I couldn't go to them, nothing would obey me!'

'It was Regneniel's doing, just to protect you, but it's all right now. He'll never harm you again.'

'Who?'

Cray set her down gently but kept her in the circle of his arms as he said, 'Your grandfather. He's dead. I killed him.'

She leaned back to look into his face. Her eyes were very grave, very dark and cool. 'Thank you,' she said.

'And now Regneniel will show us where your soul is hidden, and you can have it back. If you wish.'

'Regneniel?' said Aliza, and she glanced past Cray's shoulder, to the left and to the right. 'Where is Regneniel?'

'Outside in Ice. Come, you'll have to let it in.' He took her hand and led her back to the room where he and Sepwin had entered. But long before they reached it, the whiteness of the outer walls became apparent through intervening facets, above, below, and before them, and he could feel a change in her hand, a stiffness, a dragging backwards as she took in the sight.

In front of the final wall, she said, 'What is this?'

'You've never seen it this way before?' asked Cray.

'Never.' She touched the gleaming surface gingerly, as if afraid it would be burning hot or bitter cold. It was neither, Cray knew, no more than any wall of the palace was.

'Regneniel, Gildrum, and Leemin are waiting outside,' said Cray.

'Regneniel?'

'Yes.'

'But it can always enter, whenever it wishes.'

'Not now, apparently.'

Aliza frowned, then she gestured sharply at the wall, and again. Then she cried, 'Open!' She flung both arms

403

wide. 'I command you to open!' But the wall remained smooth and flawless.

Sepwin touched Cray's shoulder. 'If it won't obey her will, it cannot be her spell.'

'Is this Regneniel's work again?' Aliza asked.

'It must be,' said Sepwin.

Cray said, 'No. We had a bargain. This is Everand's work.'

'But Everand is dead,' said Sepwin.

'He had a spell on his library that outlasted his death, so that no one would ever be able to use his secrets. I should have thought – Aliza is his secret, too.'

'But we came in,' said Sepwin. 'There was no white spell then.'

Cray looked upwards. Above his head was another chamber very much like this one, its exterior walls as white as milk as well. And he knew that all around the palace the whiteness stretched unbroken, or else Regneniel would have entered long since. 'Everand's commands to the soul travelled directly to it through Ice, Regneniel said. But the soul was in the cradle room, sealed away when the command sent by his death must have arrived. Therefore, the soul *did not know* that he was dead. But I saw him dead, Feldar. I touched his lifeless body. When I passed through the wall, the soul knew what message I carried, what message I reeked of, and it acted. That I was inside by the time its barrier went up made no difference to it. That anyone was inside made no difference. It obeyed its master, as always.'

Sepwin's eyes had become wider and wider as Cray spoke. 'Does that mean we are trapped inside this palace?'

'It means,' said Cray, looking at Aliza's face, 'that we must give the soul back to its rightful master.'

'But you said you needed Regneniel to show you where it was,' she said.

'I know the room. Beyond that, I have great faith in my friend Feldar. Eh, my lord Seer?'

'Surely,' said Feldar, 'if we know the room.'

Cray took Aliza's hand again and headed for the cradle room.

There, the chamber seemed smaller and more cluttered than ever, and the cloudy walls were an uncomfortable reminder of the barrier that locked them inside. There, Aliza gently slipped her hand from his and stooped to pick up her old stuffed animal, which lay in a forlorn heap in the middle of the aisle.

'It was strange,' she said, looking around at each of the walls in turn, 'being unable to get out. It was as if I were a child again, and this was all there was to the palace, nothing but Ice beyond these walls.'

'You weren't frightened,' Cray said.

'I was . . . bewildered. And even more so when I heard my name called. I didn't know what to think.' She hugged the toy to her. 'I tried to call to you.' She pointed to the rocking horse, where the web was, its maker barely visible upon the dark wood of the horse's leg. 'But it wouldn't work.'

'No. Not through the barrier, I'd guess. Regneniel seems to be a powerful creature indeed. Certainly much more powerful than Taranol ever realized.'

'And now free, at least until another sorcerer conjures it.'

'Yes.'

She looked into his eyes. 'Will you do something for me, Cray? For the sake of our friendship?'

'If I can.'

'Set Regneniel free for ever as you did Gildrum.'

Cray cocked his head to one side and regarded her. 'I thought you might want it for your own. Truly, this time.'

'No, I don't want any slaves. I haven't changed my mind about that.'

'Without a slave, how will you live? Where will you get food? Clothing?'

A trace of uncertainty showed in her cool dark eyes. 'You'll help me, won't you? You'll teach me to look after myself? For the sake of our friendship?'

He smiled at her. 'Yes. Of course. A true friend can always be depended upon.'

While they had been speaking, Sepwin had prowled the room, poking into bins, looking under the child's bed, even rapping on the rocking horse. 'It is here, I know it,' he said at last. 'I can feel it calling to me. But where?' He turned in a slow circle. 'Aliza, which objects in this room have been here from the very beginning?'

'None of them. When I first set foot in this room, it was empty. Grandfather brought me all these things later that day.'

Cray touched the stuffed animal. 'What about this?'

'I had it before.'

Sepwin laid his hands upon the toy, then shook his head. He set his fists on his hips and looked from one wall to the other, to the floor, to the ceiling. 'Empty,' he muttered.

'Could it be spread out somehow, through all the walls?' Cray asked.

'Hush,' said Sepwin, and slowly he walked to the nearest wall, to the cloudy crystalline boss set at shoulder level there, one of the dozen identical bosses placed at regular intervals around the room. Sepwin closed both of his hands over it, covering its four copper-banded sides completely. Then he shook his head and moved on to the next one.

The seventh boss he tried, the one he had to climb over the child's chair, table, and bed to reach, made him sigh with satisfaction. 'Here it is!' He prised at it, trying to wedge his fingernails between it and the wall proper, but there was no space, not even a hairline crack. Boss and wall seemed to be one piece.

Aliza and Cray pulled the furniture into the aisle to make room for themselves beside Sepwin.

'You're sure?' asked Aliza.

'Absolutely,' replied Sepwin. 'I can hear it crying out to you to take it back into yourself.'

'I hear nothing.'

'Of course not. You are not a Seer. But if you will place your hands as mine are and call to it, it will come to you.'

Aliza took a deep breath. 'Very well.' She raised her hands to the crystal, and as Sepwin slid his own away, she set her flesh against the cloudy facets. 'Soul of Aliza!' she said in a low, firm voice. 'Aliza herself calls – oh!' Sparks suddenly shot out from beneath her fingers, and she recoiled from the crystal as if thrust back by a powerful blow. She would have fallen but for Cray. 'It pushed me away!' she gasped.

'What, the soul?' said Sepwin.

'Is it still in the crystal?' Cray asked him.

With a touch of one finger Sepwin confirmed that.

'Then this is more of Everand's sorcery,' Cray said. 'A last little bit of selfishness to rob Aliza of what belongs to her.'

'The copper,' said Sepwin. 'A last barrier.'

'Well, we'll get rid of that now,' said Cray, and he took the knife from his belt and prised and cut the copper wire from the cloudy surface of the crystal until it lay all shredded at his feet. Then he gathered it up and squeezed it into a ball in his fist and tossed it out the nearest door. 'Try again,' he said.

Aliza touched the crystal, and this time she had no chance to speak; it threw her back in a shower of sparks at that first contact. 'No!' she said. 'He is dead, and I will not be ruled by him any longer.' And she touched the crystal again and again and again, and each time she was thrown back, each time she could not force her flesh to remain in contact with the faceted surface. At last she gave it over and clenched her hands tightly together, though that could not hide their tremor. 'You told me he was weak,' she whispered, 'but he was strong. Strong.'

Cray took her hands between his own. They were very cold. 'Are you all right, Aliza? You tremble.'

'The sparks. They are . . . somewhat painful. But it ebbs. Yes, I'm all right.' She slipped her fingers from his grasp. 'But it seems that I'm to stay soulless after all, in spite of all your efforts.'

'I can think of worse ways to spend the rest of my life than locked in here with you, my dearest Aliza,' said Cray, 'but I don't much care for the notion of starving along the way. We must find a way to give you back your soul.'

Aliza gripped his arms suddenly. 'You are a sorcerer of some skill, Cray Ormoru. Or so you've told me. Use that skill to breach these walls and set us free!'

Cray shook his head. 'I have no power over Ice, Aliza. If you had been one to keep green things, I might manage something with their growth, but . . .' He shook his head again.

'Just a leaf, a slip, a seed,' said Sepwin. 'Surely one of us has some tiny seed caught in the hem of a garment, even a bit of dandelion fluff down in a boot, somewhere . . .' He turned the hem of one sleeve and began to pick at the stitching, but Cray laid a hand on his arm to stop him.

'We have a seed,' he said.

'A handy thing to carry around with you,' said Aliza, 'when you can do magic through it.'

'You misunderstand,' said Cray. 'I haven't carried it at all. The seed has been here in Ice for years. You told me yourself that Regneniel set it here, and *this palace* grew from it.'

She frowned. 'What? This room?'

'Not the room, Aliza. Do you remember when I told you that this palace was a living creature, and you insisted that crystals could grow without being alive? But the palace *is* alive. When Regneniel established it here, he gave it demon flesh from his own body, and he gave it a soul – *your* soul. Your soul is the seat of its life. Its seed!'

Aliza looked at him blankly. 'But it is not a plant.'

'No.' He touched the crystal boss with one hand, and it was cool to his skin. There was no repellent force in it for him. 'But it is a seed. And it lies inside this crystal. A seed holds the pattern of the plant that will be, and I can bring forth that plant. A crystal holds a pattern, too. You showed me that. I thought someday to investigate that patterning further, perhaps with your help. Now I must do what I can. I have no power over the world of Ice, but perhaps over this tiny fragment of ice . . .' He looked into the crystal, but there was nothing to see but a cloudy surface and the reflection of his own face, so he closed his eyes and concentrated on the feeling under his hand. On the perception of pattern in that surface and beneath. He willed himself to open the crystal, to lay back the surface and dive into the hard, glittering depths.

He found it to be a lattice, as surely as the cloth he wove on his mother's loom was a lattice, as surely as the trellis in her garden was a lattice, as surely as the stuff of his own body, of all life, was a lattice-work of interlocking strands. He probed at it, coaxed it, commanded it. With all the will that had grown his castle of living wood, he required it to grow.

He felt the crystal splitting open under his hand, felt the first delicate shoots thrusting at his palm, brittle and prickly as the thinnest sugar candy. Slowly, he removed his hand.

It was a flower. A pale, crystalline flower. Its narrow, ribbon-like petals pushed outwards from the boss, lengthening as he watched, drawing their substance from that jewel until it was no more than a fragile husk, a dried-out seed coat. Delicately, the petals curled as they grew, like the tendrils of true plants or – Cray found himself thinking – like wood shavings. When the blossom was complete, it was like none other Cray had ever seen. It was more like a spray of curly plumes, more like a fountain of water frozen for eternity, than any sun-loving blossom.

But one attribute it did share with real flowers – it exuded a faint perfume that was sweet and compelling.

'You must breathe in your soul from the flower,' Cray said to Aliza.

She nodded her understanding and bent close to it, but she had not even sniffed, had certainly not touched the blossom when a blue spark leaped the gap between the nearest petal and her nose and threw her back, just as she had been thrown back by the crystal itself.

Aliza covered her nose with one hand. Tears were brimming in her eyes and she tried to blink them back and could not. She dashed them away with the back of her wrist, saying, 'Perhaps that was the last of it,' and she leaned close to the flower once more. This time sparks leaped from several petals to her nose, her cheeks, her lips, and she fell back against Cray as if a door had slammed in her face. As she wiped her face with one sleeve, she said, 'It's remarkably painful. I remember once I fell and hit my nose on a chair and it was just like this. Grandfather appears to have known a great deal about pain.' She glanced over her shoulder at Cray. 'We don't seem to have achieved our objective, do we?'

'Nothing has changed,' said Sepwin, 'except the shape of the soul's container. Can't you break the spell, Cray?'

'I thought I had. But no, I'll have to do something more extreme. I'll have to breathe the soul in myself and break the spell inside my body.'

Sepwin caught his arm. 'Cray, no! Two souls in one body? They'll battle for possession. They'll burn you up with their war!'

'I'm young,' said Cray. 'And strong. And I see no

other way. I know the spell could not survive inside me.'

'If only we could ask Gildrum about it. He'd know if you're right.'

'I'd think Regneniel would be a better choice. It took the soul; it could probably tell us how to put it back. But neither of them is here, so . . .'

'No,' said Aliza. 'I wouldn't have you harmed on my account.'

'My dear lady, I see no other way.' He smiled at her. 'Listen carefully, for I think I won't be able to give any instructions after I've taken in your soul. You must allow me a moment to crush the spell, and then, when I signal, you must press your open mouth to mine and breathe in my breath. Understood?'

She nodded. 'What is the signal?'

'I'll make a fist with my right hand, open it, and close it again.'

'Understood.'

To Sepwin he said, 'Don't let me fall and break my head on anything.'

'I'll catch you.'

'Very well.' He leaned over the flower, and its sweet perfume enveloped him. He cupped the fragile crystalline petals between his hands, as if they were the open petals of a rose, he emptied his lungs with a great slow exhalation, and then he breathed in the fragrance, the blossom, the soul. Between his hands, the crystal flower collapsed into dust.

His head reeled as the soul entered him, and he staggered and threw both arms out to the wall, which seemed to be tilting crazily before him. A whirlwind possessed his body, spinning his muscles, his bones, his innards. He grappled with it, tried to tie it down with ropes that existed only in his mind, but the ropes turned about to tie him down instead. He thrust them aside. He realized

411

nothing could hold the intruder. He realized that his only choice lay in embracing it, not just with his body, but with his own soul. It was Aliza. In a burst of effort, his soul embraced hers.

Sensations rushed over him – giddy happiness, black despair, love, hate, anger, grief. They were a torrent he could not fight; he could only roll with them, tumbling, drowning, breathing them in as a doomed swimmer breathes water. Memories surged through him: a woman, a man, not strangers even though he had never seen them before, lifting him up, tossing him high in the air and catching him in strong, sure hands, laughing as he laughed, and the sunlight was bright upon them. Mother, father, centre of the universe. And then the smell of burning things, the crackle of flames, and the dark night all around as cruel arms carried him away, away, into black, black grief and loneliness. Loneliness, like a weight on his face, smothering him, pressing him into a dark box, where only the memories remained, and the feelings beat upon the walls, begging for escape.

And the box, which had formerly been crystal, was now Cray Ormoru.

Somehow, he raised his hand, though he could not see it for the whirlwind that roared behind his eyes. Somehow, his right hand made a fist, opened it, closed it again.

When he came back to himself, he was on his knees, huddled against one wall of the cradle room, and Aliza lay limp in his arms. He stared down at her for a moment, the last wisps of dizziness ebbing from his brain, and then he looked up to find Sepwin hovering near. 'What happened?' he whispered.

'She kissed you and fainted,' Sepwin told him. He was chafing one of her hands. 'But it worked.'

A distant crackling, not unlike the sound of flames, came to Cray's ears. At first he confused it with Aliza's memories, then he realized it was real. 'That noise.'

Sepwin glanced up. 'I don't know.'

It became louder, as if the flames were approaching them.

'The furniture,' said Sepwin. 'A few stray sparks from a hearth . . .'

Louder.

'We'd better take a look,' said Cray, and he set Aliza gently on the floor and climbed over her and over the furniture to the door by which they had entered the room. He looked into the next chamber, the sitting room.

The sound was louder than ever.

'I don't smell any smoke,' said Sepwin.

'And I don't see any flames. But what's that?'

Motion among the farthest facets they could see. Dark shapes moving.

And then a ball of flame flashed through the sitting room's opposite door. 'You must get out!' Gildrum's voice. 'The palace is collapsing!'

The dark shapes were furniture being pushed inexorably inwards as Ice closed about the building.

'Where is Regneniel?' Cray shouted, backing into the cradle room. The crackling was so loud now that it sounded like wood being snapped beside his ear.

'Here!' said a small star shape, skidding into the room behind Gildrum. 'I can't open a large enough fracture! There's too much debris piling up – it will crush you. Take the stairway!'

'If it's open,' said Cray, scooping Aliza up into his arms.

'It's open,' said the ice demon, and it darted up the cloudy-walled tunnel. 'Come along!' Its voice echoed in the enclosed space. 'You have to survive long enough to free me!'

With Aliza in his arms and Sepwin and Gildrum close behind him, Cray pounded up the stairs.

The panel at the top of the steps was open, but beyond

413

it lay darkness. The light from the tunnel spilled into that darkness and was swallowed, illuminating neither wall nor floor nor ceiling, but only the glittering ice demon floating two paces away.

'It's gone, collapsed,' said Regneniel. 'And the tunnel will go, too, in a moment.'

'Come,' said Gildrum, and the ball of flame engulfed the three humans and lifted them away from the tunnel mouth. In a few heartbeats they had descended to ground level, to the coarse quartz sand that had surrounded the palace and that sparkled in Gildrum's light like a field of diamonds.

Cray set Aliza down on the sand, and he and Sepwin knelt beside her. Far above them, the mouth of the tunnel was a blue-white oval, like some eerie, gibbous moon, and as they watched, its light faded, faded, and was gone.

'And so my child dies,' said Regneniel.

Cray looked up at the demon. 'I'm sorry about that. But we really had no choice.'

'It doesn't matter. It was a strange hybrid, not a proper creature of Ice at all.'

'You didn't . . . care for it? Flesh of your flesh, after all.'

'I created it at my master's whim. I did everything at my master's whim.'

'Including telling Aliza that you would never leave her.'

'It was a lie,' said the ice demon. 'The lie that made you think I loved her. Love a human? No, I hate them all. All but you, Cray Ormoru, if you keep your word.'

'I'll keep it, don't worry. And it doesn't matter that you don't love her. I'll love her enough to make up for that.' Gently, very gently, he shook her. 'Aliza. Aliza, you must wake up. Hear me, Aliza. Wake up.'

At last she moaned and raised a hand, groping; Cray caught it in his own. 'Oh, Mother,' she whispered, 'I had such a terrible dream.' Her eyelids fluttered, and then her dark eyes opened, unfocused and searching. They took in Sepwin, the demons, and the dark vault of the sky. They found Cray's face and stared at it for a long moment. Then she said, 'It wasn't a dream.'

'No.'

With a deep, quavering sigh, her tears began – not reflex tears this time but true weeping, great racking sobs that threatened to choke her till Cray helped her sit up. Then she leaned against him and wept and wept, and all the time she did not let go of his hand. And without realizing it, he started to rock with her, as a mother rocks her frightened child, back and forth, back and forth, his arms around her, sheltering, comforting.

'It's all right,' he whispered into her hair. 'Everything is all right now.'

After a time she quieted, but still she clung to him, as if he were a spar in a wildly tossing sea. 'Don't leave me,' she whispered. 'I couldn't bear this without you. This . . . this tempest you call a soul. It frightens me, Cray. It's a stranger that has broken into my home and keeps shouting words I can't understand. Don't leave me!'

He cupped her cheek with one hand and tilted her face up. By Gildrum's light, her skin was still pale, but her dark eyes no longer seemed cool and aloof. Instead, they seemed to draw him toward them, to tug at his own soul. Softly, he kissed her lips. 'I won't leave you. I promise.'

'You're all I have left,' she whispered. 'Everyone else who ever cared about me is gone. And the palace – it's destroyed, isn't it? All the memories in the cradle room, all my childhood, even my poor stuffed animal, all gone.'

'Yes,' said Cray, 'but you can always build another palace, one completely your own this time, with every pillar, every wall, just exactly as you wish it. And you can fill it up with new memories, with all the future that lies before you.' He smiled down at her. 'But there are other people who care about you, Aliza. My mother. Gildrum. Feldar. The lady Helaine. I'm merely the one who cares the most.'

A fresh tear welled up in each of her dark eyes as she slipped her hands up behind his neck. 'I trust you,' she whispered, and she pulled his head down for another kiss.

Sepwin stood and walked a little way from them, beyond the range of Gildrum's glow, to be by himself and to look up at the stars. The unknown stars. He smiled at them and thought of the Mirror of Heart's Desire. They had not got round to remaking it yet. Perhaps now they never would.